About the au

Thor F. Jensen, born Copenhagen 1981, is a Danish adventurer, filmmaker and illustrator. He has produced two award-winning adventure documentaries and written articles about traveling and filmmaking. Thor is a member of the Adventurers' Club of Denmark.

Photograph: Annette Petersen.

SALT WATER AND SPEAR TIPS

Thor F. Jensen

SALT WATER AND SPEAR TIPS

Vanguard Press

VANGUARD PAPERBACK

A CIP catalogue record for this title is
available from the British Library.

ISBN 9781784656 85-0

Vanguard Press is an imprint of
Pegasus Elliot MacKenzie Publishers Ltd.
www.pegasuspublishers.com

First Published in 2020

Vanguard Press
Sheraton House Castle Park
Cambridge England

Printed & Bound in Great Britain

For my parents

Lars Jensen and Marie Frederiksen

Salt Water and Spear Tips

The World's First Circumnavigation of the Island of New Guinea in a Traditional Sailing Canoe

by

Thor F. Jensen

"Sailing a traditional outrigger canoe around the vast island of New Guinea is a journey through time, across myriad cultures upon the far-flung seas of Arafura, Seram, Bismarck, and the Pacific Ocean. Thor's voyage shows that, in the 21st Century, there are still great adventures!"

Peter Hillary
www.peterhillary.com

"The very first circumnavigation of New Guinea in a traditional sailing canoe again illustrates, as my father auspiciously once said, "To travel, to experience and learn… that is to live."

Norbu Tenzing Norgay
www.himalayan-foundation.org

"Thor's adventure is an encouragement to anyone who — dares to do."

Sarah Outen
www.sarahouten.com

Contents

Foreword

Since my first expedition in 1947, I have had the privilege of befriending the Bushmen of the Kalahari, the last Aboriginal nomads of Central Australia and the remote tribes of New Guinea. With my books, films and public lectures, I aimed to introduce the world to the wisdom and customs of these extraordinary people, honour their millennia-old traditions, and document the impact of the modern world on their societies.

A reviewer of my book *The Last Cannibals: Primitive Beliefs and Customs in New Guinea* (originally published in 1956) wrote, "This remarkable book is the first ever written by the young Danish explorer, Jens Bjerre. Mr Bjerre writes with such fresh vigour that it is easy to lose sight of the fact that *The Last Cannibals* is both an original anthropological study and the best kind of travel book — accurate, provocative, highly readable, and magnificently illustrated."

Some 60 years later the same words could also be written of my young Danish countryman, Thor F. Jensen, and his remarkable circumnavigation of the Island of New Guinea in a traditional Milne Bay sailing canoe.

In the best tradition of adventurous Danes crossing barriers of time and civilisations to tell important stories about a changing world, I warmly commend to you *Salt Water and Spear Tips.*

Jens Bjerre

Honorary Member of the Adventurers' Club of Denmark
Fellow of the Royal Geographical Society
(RGS Cherry Kearton Medal and Award 2014)

Copenhagen, February 2019
https://adventurersclub.dk

Acknowledgements

Our historic voyage was not only fuelled by wind, *saksak* and *dirty watar*, it was also supported by *The Fellowship of the Tawali Pasana* — comprising a host of welcoming villagers across Papua New Guinea and West Papua, enthusiastic social media followers from around the world, family and friends in Denmark and Australia, as well as business sponsors and institutional supporters.

Accordingly, the expedition is indebted first and foremost to the people of the island of New Guinea. It was thanks to their hospitality, generosity and traditional knowledge that we were able to complete this voyage. This is especially true of my Melanesian crewmates — the great circumnavigators, Milne Bay master sailors Sanakoli and Justin John and Job Siyae. As you will soon discover in the pages of *Salt Water and Spear Tips*, there are far too many people, villages and places to mention here, nonetheless I thank you all.

Special thanks go to Chris Patterson, my adventure mentor and the expedition's first supporter, expedition photographer Paul Kerrison for his generous donations, captivating image making and friendship, and to sea kayaker extraordinaire Sandy Robson for her invaluable advice, connections and reports. Gratitude also extends to Wendy Stein OAM for sharing the Kula Spirit, to Kevin Alo and his family for looking after me in Port Moresby, and to Dr Rob Goodfellow and Peter O'Neill OAM from Cultural Consulting for editorial assistance. Appreciation is also expressed to Andrew Hughes for sharing his expedition notes, to Kate Goodfellow for sharing our story on Boogaloo Radio (London), and to Frederic J. Goodfellow and Paul Newby for their insightful comments on early drafts. To renowned adventurers' Peter Hillary, Norbu Tenzing and Sarah Outen I say a heartfelt thank you for their insightful backpage recommendations. Finally, I acknowledge the legendary Jens Bjerre for his wonderful foreword.

I also wish to warmly acknowledge the professional publishing support of Elaine Wadsworth (Pegasus Editorial Department),

Suzanne Mulvery (Commissioning Editor Vanguard Press) and Jenna Evans and Vicky Gorry (Production Coordinators Pegasus Elliot, Mackenzie Publishers Ltd.).

To the Babon-Whyte family (including Ava and Teddy) I say thank you for hosting me in Melbourne during the writing of this book. To Ruth and Tony Ford for welcoming me into their home in Bellingen, and Jo Ford and Alley Pascoe. Finally, to my partner Sophie Pascoe, I say, "I couldn't have done it without you" for her support during both the expedition and the writing of this book.

In Denmark I would like to thank Per Brammer, my grandparents Hanne and Jørgen Frederiksen, my parents Lars Jensen and Marie Frederiksen and my brother Bjørn Fred Jensen who have always supported my adventures.

Finally, below is a list of the names of people and organisations who embody the spirit of the voyage of the *Tawali Pasana* and for whom I will be forever grateful.

External support team

Emergency coordinator: Charlotte Quizau; Organiser: Kristian Krantz; Endorsers: Mathilde Norholt, Professor Christian Nielsen, Associate Professor Morten Lund; Copywriter: Luke Cooper; Television consultant: Katrine Seidelin; Film Consultant: Michael Haslund; Media consultants: Ania Poullain-Majchrzak, Lars Jellestad and Eliza Winkler; Papua New Guinea advisor: Jonas Bernburg; West Papua advisor: Janus Birk, Medical expert: Dr. Casper Roed; Weather expert: Karell Vissel (kayakweather.com); Editor: Bjørn Fred Jensen; Cameramen: Morten Spuhr, Robert Weber; Film logger: Ivan Elmer; Drone: João Craveiro; Sound design: Søren Elbæk; Graphics: Sam Moore; Therapist: Titt Lyngsøe.

Expedition sponsors

BNG Trading Company — bngtrading.com.pg
Cape Arkona Guest House — facebook.com/leoa.kolopen
Consort Shipping — consort.com.pg
Croctyres — croctyres.com.au
Jakera Tours — jakera.com
Kayak Wondama — facebook.com/kayakwondama
Lietzen Møbelgalleri
Madang Resort — madangresort.com
Marie Frederiksen
On the Wallaby (Paul Harris and Laura Van Der Waarde) — onthewallaby.com
Pacific Maritime and Training College — pacificmaritimetrainingcollege.com
Tawali Resort — tawali.com
The Stanley Hotel and Suites — thestanleypng.com
Total Fluid Solutions (Rob Toombs) — tfsolutions.com.au
Tupira Surf Club (Hon. Nicolas Kirriwomn) — tupira.com
M & K Talents
Sarah Barsøe-Nichlasen

Private donors

Adrian Alkjær
Anders Jørgensen
Alison Goodfellow
Ann Goodfellow
Anne have Lietzen
'AVJ'
Bjarne Karstad
Bjørn Fred Jensen
Biancha Van Dijk Jensby
Brendan Topp
Carsten Ramsdahl Rohde
Casper Haarløv
Claus Busk Jørgensen
Chris Patterson
Charlotte Snedig Rhode
Charlotte Vilhelm
Daniel Frost
Dietlev Lodberg Strand
Esben Plenge
Felix K. Jensen

Frank B. Th. Schmidt
Fleming Grøfte
Fred Goodfellow
Frederik Hesseldahl
Frede Jensen
Gorm Steen Johansen
Hanna Kruse Reiband
Henrik Jensen
Henrik Klingberg
Ingela Wendell
Ivan Elmer
Jacob Christian Ipland
Jacob Urth
Janus Birch Jazventures
Jens Jensen
Jens Maigaard Berg
Kate Goodfellow
Jens Skovgaard
Jesper Lynge
Janus Birch Jazventures
Jens Jensen
Jens Maigaard Berg
Kate Goodfellow
Jens Skovgaard
Jesper Lynge
Jesper Yngvesson
Katrine Seidelin
Karoline Elmer
Karsten Egedesø
Kenneth Jensen
Lars Have Lietzen
Lars Jensen
Lars Oxfeldt Mortensen
Lene Simonsen
Lasse Toftbæk Helledi
Leo Enrico Jensen
Lina Jensen
Louan Wang
Louise Kanne
Louise Rasborg
Luca Capelletti
Lui Ivan Lezzi Madriz
Mads Rahbek
Marie Tancula Lund
Martin Gammelgaard
Martin Lund Christensen
Martin Lærkesen
Martin Winkler
Mette Møller
Michael Sørensen
Morten Blohm
Morten Lund
Niels Kristiansen
Nis K. Sørensen
Oliver Vonsil
Oskar Fanta
Peggy S. Koopman
Peter Kristensen
Peter O'Neill
Poul Møller
Preben Gullev Søndergaard
Rasmus Brejnrod
Richard Lozell
Rob Goodfellow
Sidsel Rudolph
Thorleif Stenaa Ørvad

Simon Goodfellow
Simon Tarp Mortensen
Steven Biccard
Søren Christensen
Søren David Skou Finsen
Søren Kjeldman Hansen
Thomas Spang Thomsen
Thomas Sørensen
Tim Poulain Patterson
Vibe Rudolph
Victor Nelleman
Vincent Achon Karker
Moos and Company
Morten Spuhr Poniwozik

Lodges that generously hosted us during the expedition

Madang Resort — madangresort.com
Paradise New Wewak Hotel —
acebook.com/ParadiseNewWewakHtl/
Tufi Resort — tufidive.com
Triton Bay Divers — tritonbaydivers.com
Vanimo Surf Lodge — vanimosurflodge.com

Institutions who assisted the expedition

Kenu and Kundu Festival
Milne Bay Tourism Bureau
Papua New Guinea Consulate Jayapura
Papua New Guinea Immigration and Citizen Service
Papua New Guinea National Maritime Safety Authority
The Government and people of Sandaun Province
Navy of the Republic of Indonesia

Editorial assistance by www.culturalconsulting.com.au

Chapter One

A near disaster

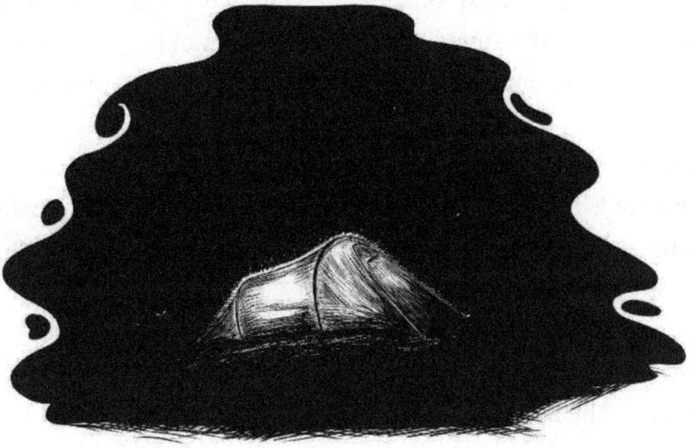

Expedition Log 30 August 2016

11:13 hrs. The plastic storm sail ripped as it was being hoisted.

12:30 hrs. Canoe flooded, we almost sank.

The first logbook entries of the expedition should have been joyous ones. We were full of optimism, under way with all the hard work needed just to get started behind us. But that night, sitting in wet clothes, with squadrons of insects bouncing off the wall of my tent, I almost felt like going back to the comfortable 'safe harbour' days of planning and preparation. Still, at least we had covered the first 41 nautical miles of the route, from the beautiful jungle bay of the Tawali Resort to a remote coastal village.

I had suspended my head torch from the tent ceiling as a precaution so that the villagers wouldn't see the glaring blue light from my laptop. I was trying to recall the name of the village but I was too exhausted to remember. The damp navigational charts were littering the floor. The 'waterproof' map case wasn't as waterproof as it should have been and, to make matters worse, the printed topographical maps had started to dissolve. Inside the tent, my video files were being slowly uploaded, whilst outside loomed the Papua New Guinean (PNG) darkness, the sounds of crickets, the crackling of the fire, low mumbling voices and the sounds of breaking waves on a moonless beach.

My sailors were talking with the locals and the mood seemed more relaxed. The crew had been very nervous — especially when we first landed. They were accustomed to sailing the islands and atolls of Milne Bay and were now far from their villages, in fact, further up the coast than any other Milne Bay canoe would dare to venture. I had thought that sailing in a traditional canoe, or *sailau*, would make us less likely to be attacked by pirates but the crew had warned me that, "If people see white man on the canoe, they rob us." I had come to PNG with the intention of debunking myths associated with violent stereotypes but now the experience of arriving unannounced, at night, into a pitch-black village was making everyone apprehensive. I didn't know my sailors very well or even if they could be trusted but, so far, they seemed well intentioned and even concerned for my safety. I traced my finger over the map; the village was called Dobura.

Although my clothes were wet, and a fair amount of black sand had found its way into the tent, this little space was my 'cocoon of comfort' — the last reminiscence of the safe world I had left behind, and not least a break from peering, curious eyes. Most importantly, it was a welcome opportunity to gather my thoughts and consider the events of the first day of the expedition.

Launching an expedition

Our day began at the Tawali Resort, which is built on an outcrop of jungle-clad rock overlooking a pristine coral reef. (*Tawali* means 'reef' in the local Tawala language). The Padi Dive centre is situated in Milne Bay Province, PNG, on the easternmost tip of the island of New Guinea. It was from here, on 30 August 2016, that our great adventure began.

The voyage was supposed to have been launched a day earlier but strong winds forced us to postpone. My friend Paul Kerrison and I had already outstayed the hospitality of the resort by four days and I was frustrated that everything in PNG took longer than anticipated. But now the canoe was berthed and the rough-hewn planks of the pier were echoing with bare feet as the last of the equipment was loaded by the three Milne Bay master sailors. The flags on the canoe were whipping and the sea looked dark and choppy as grey clouds formed from the mountains behind us. It was already late in the season.

I looked down at the canoe, the vessel that was to take us 6,300 kilometres around New Guinea, the second largest island in the world after Greenland (a nice fit for a Dane). And what a vessel! It was basically a nine-metre-long dug out tree trunk with a 30-centimetre strake (wooden plank) on each side. For each half metre of deck, round beams or *kialo* were lashed connecting the outrigger pontoon that ran diagonally to the canoe, one and a half metres out. Between the outrigger and the canoe was a platform where our main sail and spare paddle rested, together with our stove and two open plastic boxes — one for kitchen gear and the other for fishing equipment and a canoe repair kit.

In the middle of the canoe was a wooden mast standing four metres in height. This was fastened with five lengths of nylon rope and old wire tied off to the outrigger. To counter the pull from the rigging, there was a *sowa sowa* — a sturdy arched branch with the top end tied to the mast with the forked bottom end resting on the outrigger. This very simple system allowed the mast to be angled and tilted according to sailing conditions. To my inexperienced eyes, it seemed crude and inefficient. A hand-operated bilge pump was fastened next to the mast. This was certainly not a common sight on a traditional sailing canoe but I had thought it wise to bring it with me from home — and it turned out that we would need it much sooner than I imagined.

Our supplies were packed in the hull and covered with two sections of movable boards on each side of the mast. Underneath, were food supplies and goods, such as rice and a few conserves, together with our clothes and personal belongings. All our equipment was obtained from PNG general stores, except for some essentials that I had brought with me, such as two waterproof barrels, a tent, a solar charger kit, batteries, emergency devices and navigational aids. All my outdoor gear and waterproof kayaking clothes were left in Denmark. My philosophy was that I wanted the people of New Guinea to see that they had everything at hand to make a world record and that no outside special equipment was needed to achieve this.

One of my last chores before casting off was to set up waterproof cameras on the canoe. I climbed down on to the railing and the deck boards inside the canoe. Then I stepped over the outrigger platform and on to the outrigger itself to fasten the camera grip to one of the elongated sticks, called a *patoto,* connecting the platform to the outrigger pontoon. The outrigger was also just a carved tree trunk made from a more buoyant type of wood, but, as I rested my foot on this outrigger, the whole thing began sinking.

At first, I thought the tilting was natural, but, to my great fright, I soon realised that it wasn't stopping. The canoe began to sink in a continuous motion as I mistakenly saw what I thought to be a counterbalance — the main canoe hull, rising steadily out of the water. The three crew all yelled in unison from the pier, "Get back in the canoe!" I made a fast step up towards the platform and next to the outer railing of the canoe to counter the sinking motion. At the same time, one of my sailors, Job Siyae, jumped down from the pier onto the hull and the outrigger slowly rose from the engulfing sea. The entire pier, which had come to an anxious standstill, audibly sighed with relief.

I looked at Job and then to my other two crew members — brothers Justin and Sanakoli John — with an expression of relief and gratitude. I thought, what a start it would have been to tip the canoe, fully provisioned, on the first day of the expedition. The last month in PNG had already taken its toll on my nerves, but this, so to speak, nearly tipped *me* over. Job's dark, sun-leathered shaved head was one big grin as he said, "The outrigger is full of water." Sanakoli looked at me and added, with a serious tone in his voice, "The outrigger is old and very heavy… you cannot walk on it."

Justin, who was standing next to him with his white plastic bucket in hand, just puffed on his newspaper-rolled cigarette — or '*bruce*', as it is known in PNG — and looked towards the sea that was now forming white tops.

"But we can sail like this?" I asked.

"Yes, but we need to dry it out soon," Job instantly replied with a tone of confidence. Job Siyae was my first contact in PNG and the man who introduced me to the two brothers. In turn, the brothers had an uncle who was willing to sell us his canoe. So far, Job had been honest and helpful. If Job said we could sail, I was going to take his word for it — I was, after all, the novice and they were the masters.

Heavy footsteps sounded as Paul Kerrison strode down the pier with his camera in hand, accompanied by the Tawali Resort manager. Originally from Brisbane, Australia, Paul had been working around the world as a professional photographer for over 20 years. Tall and slim, Paul always seemed to be dressed in a 'uniform' consisting of a khaki outdoor shirt with rolled-up sleeves and a brown cap with a short brim covering his long blonde hair tied up in a bun.

Paul was an old friend from the travel industry with broad expedition experience. During the planning and preparation for this trip, he had been a great mentor and adviser, and even sponsored our satellite transmitter — an Iridium Go — and solar kit. Now he was in Milne Bay to help me set things up and photograph our launch (in the hope of a major commission with *Australian Geographic*, which I was counting on as a way of funding part of the voyage). The manager had granted Paul and I a three-day stay free of charge but now we had been there for a week and he was probably happy to see us off. The manager looked at the canoe and then at the sea and said, "Well, the sea could be looking worse. You all set up mate?"

To say I was keen to get going is a huge understatement. I had planned to be sailing some eight to ten days after arriving in the country but now it was day 31 and we were only just pushing off. Unfortunately, the additional four complimentary nights at the Tawali Resort had come at a great cost, not in terms of money — but more in terms of a principle I had to compromise.

As the arrival of the crew and canoe had been delayed, Paul and I had to ask the manager to extend our stay — in a luxury suite overlooking the reef. In return, he asked us to name the canoe 'Tawali' after the resort. I was, of course, grateful for the manager's support but I was also flat out of cash (not the best way to start a world-record breaking expedition). Ever since the early preparations of this, my greatest adventure, I decided on a strong ideal of not accepting commercial advertisements on the canoe. Instead, I was planning to get the side planks of the canoe decorated with traditional motifs carved by the tribes we encountered during the voyage.

In fact, I had promised the sailors that we would come up with a name together, not least to make them feel more invested in the voyage. But on the other hand, we also depended on Tawali Resort's facilities — and I had many more pressing tasks at hand. I ended up agreeing that 'Tawali' would be part of the canoe's name. It tormented me a great deal that I had to sacrifice something like this before the expedition had even begun but, as Paul argued, "It's quite a big ask but it is a local name after all." And so, the crew and I named the canoe *Tawali Pasana* — which translates as 'Reef Flower' or 'Beauty of the Reef', depending on the local dialect. I comforted myself with the fact that at least our proud vessel wasn't named after a soft drink or a mobile phone company.

Five years had passed since the idea of circumnavigating the island of New Guinea was first conceived and I hadn't succeeded in any of my attempts to raise sponsorship money. The idea of making a documentary series hadn't gained any traction either — instead, I dismissed the television people as too blinkered and decided to do my own recordings and produce a series myself. My shoe-string budget consisted of contributions from family and a few friends. This up-front money had already been spent on airline tickets, the canoe, basic provisions, wages for the crew and support for their families. However, fundraising was not my main concern at that time. Soon the Southeast Trade Winds, which should blow us all the way up the north coast of the island, would turn against us.

Until this stage in my long preparations I felt like Sisyphus of Greek mythology, burdened by the never-ending, laborious and futile toil of pushing a boulder up a mountain — but now that the canoe was packed, the crew were ready and the wind was blowing, I started feeling more like Indiana Jones being chased by a giant rolling rock through an ancient jungle temple. This was the point of no return. Everything I had worked for had led up to this very moment.

Before leaving Denmark, I had said goodbye to my nearest and dearest and signed my digital Last Will and Testament. But as organised as I was, at that moment it was hard to gather my thoughts. I tried to record myself, but strong emotions got the better of me. I wanted to tell the story of what had motivated me, but I couldn't find the words; instead, I just looked into the camera and said that I was… "happy." I turned to the pier; the sun was high, and the tide had turned. The manager and staff of the Tawali Resort, together with some tourists, were there to wave us goodbye. Paul was positioning himself here and there with his camera, shooting photos as our security escort arrived in their dinghy.

I had long-since prepared a set of stirring words for this occasion, something about the significance of a world record but as I was about to speak, I could feel my throat tighten and my eyes moisten. The farewell party were all looking at me, 164 centimetres in height, in swim shorts and a dirty T-shirt. Suddenly, I felt like a little boy who had taken a bite of something bigger than he could chew. This was my great moment. The dream was finally about to come true, and I wasn't even able to give it the go-ahead.

It was all very confusing; my feelings were a mixture of fear and excitement. Instead of addressing my audience, I looked at the three sailors in the canoe and simply asked, "Are you ready?" I nodded to the skipper of our security dinghy and he complied. Then I looked back at the crowd on the pier and announced, "The time is 11 a.m. and the expedition has begun — *woo hoo*." And with that I jumped into the canoe, grabbed my paddle and we pushed off.

We paddled the heavily-laden canoe away from the pier and out into the bay, and then into open water where we could catch a steady wind. I was trying to pull my weight as a paddler, but I was also eager to document this great event. I asked the crew, How do you feel?" Job answered laughing, "Now we make a world record!" Sanakoli added in his typically low, shy tone, "Woo hoo… I am very excited to go on this great journey." Justin just gave a thumbs up. Then he yelled something to Sanakoli in their native language, *Bwana Bwana*, as he prepared the sail. (Between them, the sailors spoke three different languages.)

It was only my second time sailing the canoe since we had bought it on Basilaki Island almost 20 days prior. I noticed the sailors were hoisting the smaller storm sail, sewn in black plastic and tied to both a wooden yard (the diagonal spar holding the sail) and a boom cut from a stem of bamboo. Justin tugged on the crude nylon rope and set the sail. However, as soon as Sanakoli pulled the sheet, the sail expanded in the fierce gusting winds. In the same instant, we heard a loud flapping sound; the wind had torn a rip through the side of the sail. There was no time to dwell on this because the canoe instantly set off at a rapid pace; the outrigger rose out of the water, skating along the waves as the bow ploughed through the rising swells.

It was like a magical burst of nautical energy — this was our 'Apollo 11 launch.' The *Tawali Pasana* was flying. Everyone was hooting, and even the perpetually stern Justin had a big grin on his face. I barely knew my companions and I had very little in common with these island men who had lived their lives in thatched bush huts, fishing and hunting and gardening to sustain themselves. Despite our differences, in this very moment, we shared the same feeling. This was a primal sensation that must have pounded in the hearts of Neil Armstrong, Buzz Aldrin and Michael Collins as they shot into the stratosphere — the same lure and thrill of adventure that was inspiring the four of us, who later became known in the PNG press as, 'The Fellowship of the *Tawali Pasana*.'

The winds were strong and, though I had little experience of sailing a traditional canoe, it was obvious that we were running on the edge of what was sensible, surfing along the ocean swells, sometimes so fast that we would catch up with the wave cresting in front of us as we ploughed right through it.

I yelled to Job, "What about the hole in the sail? Is this a problem?"

Job answered, "No it's all right, we just have to go out to sea, away from the mountain winds. The wind out here is also big but it is only coming from one direction."

The canoe felt very dynamic, not least because the rattan-covered platform between the outrigger and canoe flexed beautifully with the waves. This was thanks to its wooden beam construction. However, where the *kialos* connected to the hull, there were cracks and holes in the side plank — this caused water to constantly spray into a hull that was slowly filling with water, with the rest of the water in the canoe coming in from bow waves. The only solution to this was to regularly empty the canoe by working the battered white construction helmet which was our bailer. Job was on bailing duty frequently scooping the hull, while Justin stood aft, his muscular frame steering with the great carved wooden paddle that acted as a rudder. Sanakoli was controlling the sail, slackening the sheet as the outrigger rose out of the water and heaving to when the craft dove. It was a wet, bumpy ride. The *Tawali Pasana* was gallantly resisting our efforts to tame her — in fact, she was taming us.

Soon we had outrun the gusting mountain winds and it was time to *yaya-towa* (to tack). Since a *sailau* can only sail with the outrigger windward, both ends of the canoe are identical and can act as both bow and stern. To change course, Job untied the front of the sail from the bow and walked along the ridge of the strake while pushing the front end of the thrusting boom past the mast. Then he tied the front of the boom on to the once stern, now bow. Meanwhile Justin had run to the other end of the canoe together with Sanakoli who was now using all his strength to pull the sail with the sheet and we instantly started shooting up the coast with the wind at our backs.

Paul was following us in the security boat together with armed guards — one of them sporting a pump-action shotgun. He was guiding the driver, while photographing us from different angles. The boat only had enough fuel to escort us for an hour and a half, and after that Paul and the guards would return and we would be on our own. There had been genuine concern amongst my crew about '*raskols*' (rascals) or bands of violent, criminal thugs. The crew had instructed me to be quiet about our plans as they feared that, if local *raskols* heard that a white man was venturing out in a canoe, they would pursue us and attack. I had already heard several accounts of passenger dinghies being set upon by pirates, with the unfortunates chopped with bush knives or shot. So, to calm the crew, I hired two armed guards to follow us out. But looking back, one would have to be a dedicated buccaneer indeed to venture out in such bad weather.

This was everything I had dreamt of, the pinnacle of my adventuring career, the expedition that would challenge me to the utmost and put all my previously accrued skills to the ultimate test; a great exploit, far from the social safety net of Scandinavian society. Here the consequences of negligence were real, prompt and dire. I was 35 years old and I had no attachments, except a small apartment in Copenhagen and an obligation to my family to come back alive. But I had also made a promise to myself not to return home before I had circumnavigated the island of New Guinea. I was, after all, walking in the footsteps of my heroes, from Odysseus to Huckleberry Finn, to less fictional giants such as Thor Heyerdahl, Knud Rasmussen and Jens Bjerre.

When I first contemplated the idea of a circumnavigation, my plan was to undertake it by sea kayak. In the run up to the expedition, I organised two extraordinary tours in Danish waters with my German kayaking friend Kay Polaniok, first to a remote island in the Baltic Sea and then 1,200 kilometres around Denmark. I filmed our exploits and produced two award-winning documentary films, but, as I did more and more research into my New Guinea trip, I realised that it had to be undertaken in a sailing canoe.

First, it almost goes without saying that I would learn much more about the island if I were travelling in a traditional vessel and, second, it would probably, well possibly, be safer. Finally, I would feel like a complete *wally* rocking up to a remote community in a space-age fibreglass kayak wearing all sorts of technical kayaking clothing, trying to pretend that I was down with the locals. My personal goal was to learn to live and sail like a 'real' New Guinean sailor and my plan was to acquire this knowledge within a month or two. This would make me independent of the sailors should they wish to go home, and then I could change the crew along the way and enlist many different people from around the island to join the journey.

I wanted to do more than make a 'first-of-something record'. I needed to present a balance account of modern-day New Guinea and challenge the sensational stories of tribal war and cannibalism that continue to dominate the popular press. Surely this was a dangerous place, but I was certain that there was more to to New Guinea than mere negative stereotypes. With this world record, I would document a people-to-people story of daily life in New Guinea in all its richness and complexity. For me, this was the only honest and respectful way to approach the circumnavigation.

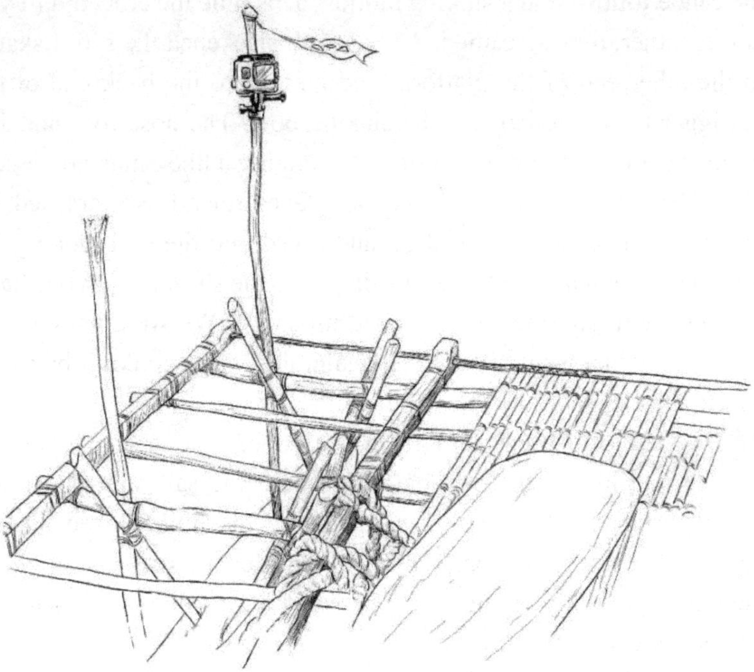

And what a glorious vessel I had chosen for this quest, a sweeter expedition boat the world had yet to see — except perhaps the double-hulled Polynesian canoes that first navigated the South Pacific. The canoe was surfing along with the wind at our backs. Who would have thought that a dug-out tree trunk packed with four men would set such a pace? I looked at my GPS. We were running at between seven and nine knots — impressive. If we could hold that pace, we'd be around this island faster than the six months I had calculated.

I remembered my GoPro camera that was attached to the front end of the outrigger and noticed that the bouncing motion of the canoe digging in to the heaving seas had made it tip downwards.

I asked Job if I could walk out on the outrigger and adjust it.

He thought for a second and replied, "Yes, but you must be quick." I waited for a steady set of waves and then clambered out on to the outrigger. As I reached the end of the canoe, the outrigger plunged into a wave and water ploughed over the deck as the bow of the canoe followed in a sinking motion. This time the crew didn't yell at me, rather, they screamed. As Sanakoli slackened the sail, I skated to the other end of the platform and jumped to the back end of the outrigger to counterbalance the sinking bow. The nose rose and Job jumped to the bilge pump and started operating it like a man possessed.

The canoe filled with water as waves relentlessly crashed in. Sanakoli handed Justin the sheet and dived into the hull looking for the construction helmet bailer. Justin pulled the sheet in with one hand and his teeth, and the canoe picked up speed. We were back in the game. Now that we were running again, the waves couldn't break on us and the canoe seemed to stabilize.

I yelled to Justin, "Can I get in the canoe?"

He had his hands full controlling both the sail and rudder but quickly replied, "You go." I jumped into the hull, picked up our cooking pot and started bailing too. After a few more hectic minutes, the hull was finally emptied. We resumed our positions and laughed with sheer exhausted relief.

I said, "Sorry about that guys… my fault." And Job laughed too, in his characteristically good-humoured way, "You *cannot* go out on the outrigger when we are sailing like this." I had done this twice now and, hopefully, there would not be a third time.

When we had caught our breath, Sanakoli eased and lowered the sail and, with the help of Job, rolled it half way up and tied it off. Then we resumed sailing with a storm sail half the size of the original, which made the ride a lot more pleasant — but still at good speed. Sanakoli handed me the sheet and told me that it was all right and that I just needed to slack it off if the outrigger rose too much. I liked the sharp pull of the sail in my arms and the burn of rope between my palms; it felt good to be in control and not be a mere passenger. We had just had another near capsize and we were only one hour into the expedition but on the positive side, the bilge pump had done its job and we had all performed well during our first crisis.

Half an hour later, the security dinghy came up to the side of us. It was hard keeping the two vessels aligned in the high seas but their fuel gauge read below half empty and they had to return. I yelled to Paul, "Did you get a cover photo for *Australian Geographic*?" Paul answered, "I don't know, the grey light is difficult but there might be a few good ones in between." The security boat almost bounced into the canoe as we briefly shook hands and he said, "Good luck." "Thank you for all your help," I answered, and looked at Paul and wondered if this would be last time we would see each other. His eyes looked like he was thinking the same thing. The crew and the driver exchanged salutations and blessings, the guards hooted and we waved them all farewell. Then the dinghy's engine noise became more and more distant. We were on our own now, dependent on skill and wit — and fate.

The sea and the canoe found a gentle syncopated rhythm. We ate some hard caramels and salty crackers and washed it all down with green cordial. The wind calmed as the afternoon sun shone through the clouds and lit the coastal mountains in a golden glow. The storm sail was rolled out again — just in time for a pod of curious dolphins to surface in our wake, have a good look at us, and disappear. We studied the map for a suitable settlement to make landfall, as I hadn't made any plans of where to camp this night or the following nights. There is little information on the coastal communities anyway, and I had no idea of how many miles we could cover in a day, so the best option was to embrace the adventure and leave the 'rest and recovery stops' ahead to find us. As it looked now, we were far off shore and there were no villages in this area: it would be unsafe to land on an unpopulated coast, so we continued northwards through the night.

Back in the tent

The day's videos were uploaded. I turned off my head torch and the tent was illuminated by the fire outside. The crew stoked the embers with more logs, and I could hear some laughter. I didn't retrieve my sleeping kit from the canoe when we went ashore. Job told me not to unpack anything while other people were present. His words of warning were, "You hide your things properly, when they see white man, they think money. If they see your camera, they will rob us; we don't know these people." But I was too exhausted to worry anymore about *raskols* or comfort; now I just needed sleep. It felt warm enough with my jacket outside my damp T-shirt, and the waterproof camera bag made a decent enough pillow — even though it was covered in sand and salt, just like my hair.

The conditions on day one of the expedition had been far beyond 'beginners' level.' I certainly couldn't sail the canoe on my own in such weather but I was learning, and we covered a good distance. So far, so good. I listened to the low voices, the sound of the waves and the crackling of the replenished fire. But now, suddenly, there was a raucous laugh — was it a good laugh? The sailors seemed genuine, the locals helpful; but who could be certain? I have been wrong before. I made one last check — head torch around my neck, knife in my pocket. I wanted adventure and I got it.

Chapter Two

The Fellowship of the *Tawali Pasana*

I crawled out of my 'cocoon' and wiped my salt-encrusted eyes. The bay was echoing with native birdsong and the distant crowing of roosters from further inland. The sun was still low on the horizon although the light of the clear sky warned of a hot day. It had been an uneasy sleep. I had woken up many times listening to my surroundings and checking that no one was trying to get into the tent. Now that I looked around, I realised that my fears of *raskols* were unfounded. The three sailors were sleeping on the ground, right next to my rain fly, under a sheet of plastic that we kept as a backup sail. My tent was pegged under an enormous mango tree to which our canoe also was also fastened with a long length of aged rope. The canoe was resting in shallow water halfway up the beach next to some dinghies swaying in the gentle inshore swell.

There was a young man, about 20 years old, blowing the ambers to ignite a fresh bundle of kindling. He looked at me with drowsy eyes, "Good morning uncle, I have been sitting up all night looking after your canoe and telling stories with your friends." I asked him when did the sailors go to sleep? "Maybe three… maybe later, I don't know, I have no phone. I will boil hot water and we can make tea," he answered. As the kettle was boiling, Sanakoli cut a swatch of the plastic he had been sleeping under and began to hand sew a patch over the long rip in the storm sail. As soon as we had eaten, we made a quick exit.

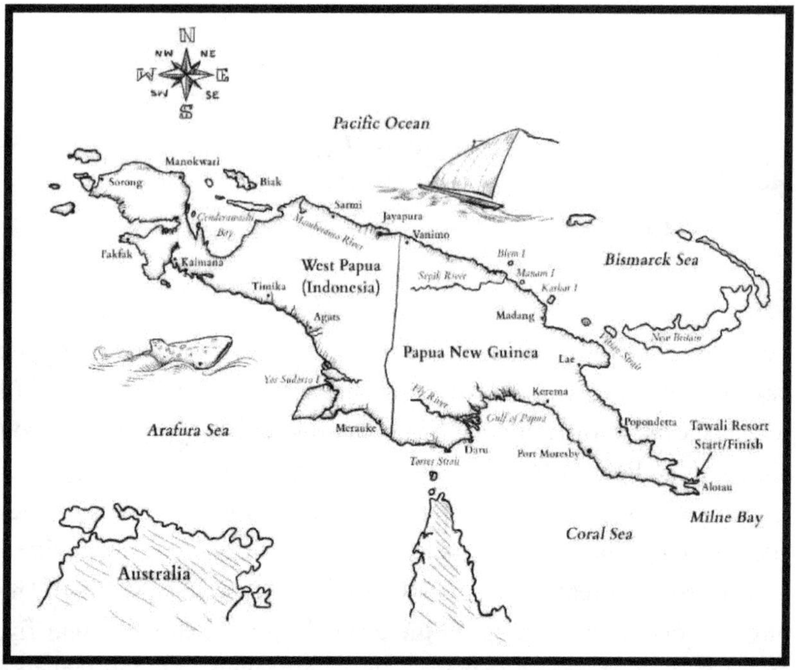

The planned route of this great circumnavigation started on the easternmost tip of the island, in Milne Bay and followed a counter-clockwise route up the PNG coast. After crossing the international border near the logging town of Vanimo into Indonesian West Papua, we planned to go around Sorong and then southeast back across the Gulf of Papua back to Milne Bay. This route fitted beautifully with seasonal wind patterns. These winds blow steadily from the southeast from May until November, and then change direction 180 degrees and blow from the northwest from December until March. My plan was to spend three months sailing the 3,000 kilometres to the westernmost point of New Guinea and then sail the remaining 3,300 kilometres over three months in return. It was paramount that I kept to this timeframe because, when the seasonal winds are blowing, they only blow one way and with considerable force.

I remember telling my grandfather about my plans. He had been a sailor his entire life. At the age of 60, he sailed around the world in his yacht, accompanied on certain legs by my grandmother. My grandfather's response to my idea was, "When you tell people about something like that, they will think that you are insane!" Indeed, it was a voyage associated with considerable risk. First there are the geographical challenges. New Guinea is the second largest island in the world with a coastline that is both diverse and dramatic. The topography of the north coast can be very steep with typhoon swells from the South China Sea crashing onshore, making landing in many places impossible. In some areas, active volcanoes rise precipitously out of the sea and earthquakes and tsunamis are not uncommon. To add to this, the northeast coast of PNG has the highest rate of lightning strikes in Melanesia. The south coast has its own challenges too. Steep offshore swells and dangerous currents are punctuated by long stretches of shallow tidal flats, knee deep dense grey mud, and mangroves full of saltwater crocodiles, which makes travel and landfall perpetually difficult.

Then there are the human obstacles. Most people in New Guinea live in rural communities, some of which are very remote, and it's estimated that there are over 1,000 distinct languages and dialects spoken across the island. In addition, one regularly hears stories of tribal wars and 'pay back' killings, particularly in the PNG highlands and the capital city of Port Moresby, which is ill-famed as one of the most dangerous cities on earth. However, as a sailor, my biggest worry remained coastal piracy.

I hadn't found any published accounts of piracy on the Indonesian side of the island, but I'd read about the Indonesian military's operations against the Free West Papua Movement (*Organisasi Papua Merdeka* — OPM), which had led to certain areas being declared off limits to tourists and other visitors. I had also received contradictory information on how to enter West Papua in a sailing canoe, so I was unsure about what would happen when I arrived at the border. My biggest concern was that the Indonesian authorities might not allow a canoe to travel around the whole island — and especially not if they found out I was making a documentary film. But at this point in the expedition, my preoccupation was to organise my crew and get the *Tawali Pasana* to the border without capsizing or running afoul of brigands.

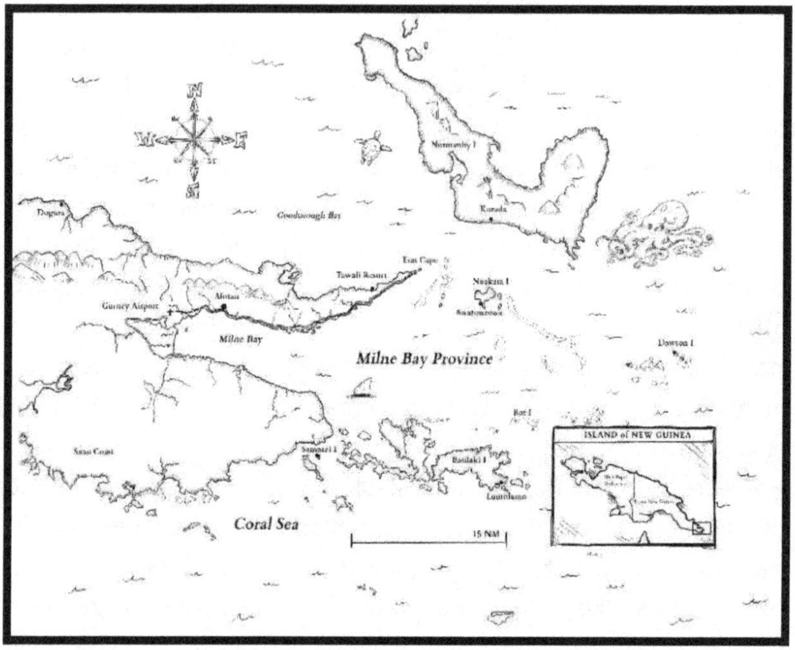

Milne Bay is the ‘sailing canoe capital’ of PNG. In the rest of the country, most coastal and offshore travel is undertaken by fiberglass dinghy. This modern mode of transport has also caught on in Milne Bay. Despite this, traditional sailing canoes are still being used for fishing and voyaging throughout the more than 600 islands and atolls dotting the province. It was also here that I met Job Siyae. During my first visit to PNG in November 2015, I travelled to Alotau, which is Milne Bay’s provincial capital, to experience the yearly National Kenu (canoe) and Kundu (drum) Festival. It was essentially a reconnaissance trip to see if it was even possible to sail a canoe around the island and, if so, whether I could find someone to do it with. Job was participating in the canoe race with his *sailau*, named *Boy Boy*, and had come in third place.

Job had what you would call 'good energy.' He was my age and was very talkative. We went out on his canoe together and I asked him if he thought we could sail around the island and if so, could he teach me. He said, "Yes, this is a good canoe, but it is very old, so we need to build a new one." We shook hands and agreed that I would come back the next year. I gave him a basic cell phone so that we could stay in touch.

When I returned in July 2016, it was with two 30 litre watertight plastic barrels filled with a first aid kit, a tent, snorkelling gear, a bilge pump, a roll of navigational charts, a few books, an eclectic collection of things to be given away as gifts and my communication and camera gear. But as I soon discovered, just to find Job was an expedition in itself. First, I had to travel from Alotau by four-wheel drive through the jungle on gravel 'roads' for two hours to East Cape — the easternmost tip of the island of New Guinea.

East Cape works as a connection hub for all the north-eastern islands and atolls in Milne Bay, and the main mode of transport to those remote places is by small fiberglass dinghy with a 40 or 60 horsepower outboard motor. I was to find the dinghy *Home Alone II*, which was anticipating my arrival. (Job had instructed me to be careful at East Cape because it was full of *raskols*). Luckily, I found my contact straight away, however, to my great regret, the dinghy didn't leave for Normanby until that afternoon, or when there were enough passengers. I didn't have the funds to hire a boat for myself, so I had to wait. The skipper then told me he would stay at East Cape overnight but pointed me in the direction of the neighbouring dinghy and said, "This man will take you." I took his word for it and packed all my stuff into the bottom of the boat.

I found a comfortable place in the shade of a big tree with an outlook to my dinghy. I was the only *dim dim* (the local word for white person) there but people were friendly and talkative. It wasn't hard to communicate; although most people in Milne Bay are fluent in a selection of local languages, almost all speak English as well.

A young man named Toby asked me where I was going.

"To Normanby to meet my friend — Job Siyae," I answered.

Toby didn't know of a Job but when I mentioned that he was a canoe sailor and described him as, "Bald-headed and smiling all the time," Toby became excited.

"You mean Wensis! Oh, my brother, he is a very good sailor. He sails alone. Sometimes he even paddles his small canoe to East Cape." I remembered that Job had mentioned that Wensis was his nickname and I was, of course, happy to hear that he had such a good reputation.

Toby ran one of the small stalls that were spread out under a tree, selling biscuits, *bruce* and betel nut to the dinghy drivers and passengers. Betel nut, or *buai*, is a popular local (and national) intoxicant. I observed a constant commotion as passengers peeled the green husk of the walnut-sized nut and mulled it around in their mouths. But that is only part of the pleasure; the chewer then dips a stem of 'mustard' into a bag of lime powder, before biting off the lime-tipped stalk and chewing it together with the nut. This concoction creates a chemical reaction that gives the chewer a subtle energy boost, or, as some people call it, 'a high.' The downside is that it causes excessive, bright red salivation, which stains the gums, teeth and lips. The chewer must then constantly, even obsessively, spit out *spelches* of blood-like saliva. And, by looking at the people of East Cape and the ubiquitous red stain splatters, I had certainly arrived at chewing central Milne Bay.

It was late afternoon by the time the dinghy was finally full, mostly of *buai*-chewing women and their children, weighted down with bags of shopping for the hour-long crossing to Normanby. The island was huge — elongated and rugged, and it seemed to shoot straight out of the sea. As I was sitting on the floor of the uncomfortable dinghy, I watched the island growing larger, which fired my imagination and filled my heart with the thrill of adventure. This was everything I had hoped for. The island looked dark and mysterious with its jungle-covered mountain sides surrounded by clouds. It was only a few years ago that two new species of frog were discovered here. One could only imagine what other wonders were lurking in the jungle. It looked and felt like I was entering Skull Island of *King Kong* fame; and, as I was later to learn, the skull reference wasn't too far off the mark.

I arrived at dusk but the dinghy operators already knew who the *dim dim* had come to see. One of them said, "*Dim dim* you come with us… we take you to our sister." The dinghy operator, together with some of the other passengers, picked up my belongings and escorted me up through a rough trail. The thick slippery darkness resonated with the nearby croaking of frogs as well as strange calls coming from deep in the jungle. After 15 minutes, we came to a cluster of huts on stilts with a small fire burning beneath one of them. The huts belonged to Job's mother. She was a very friendly woman of about 50 years of age. After a courteous greeting, she explained that Job lived far up in the mountains and that I could not go in the dark. Instead, I was shown to a room with a mat and mosquito net where I could spend the night. The next morning, I got a better look at the island; it was truly a 'real jungle island.' Everything was so lush and green, with many clear, fast-flowing small streams, continuously fed by heavy rain from the perpetually cloud-covered mountains. There were no paved roads and all the houses were elevated off the ground, most of them with thatched roofs and walls of cleaved palm trunks or rough wooden planks. The only exception was the Kurada station area where there were some shabby concrete buildings with rusting tin roofs, including a school, a church, a medical aid post and some government offices — typical of mission stations found throughout PNG.

A group of Job's female cousins helped me carry my kit to his house, far up on the side of the mountain — a steep 45-minute climb through gardens and jungle tracks. Even though I was in good shape physically, the heat and humidity soon took its toll and I had to stop for frequent rests. As we were nearing, the cousins yelled something like '*ooou ooou*' — sounds that were soon answered as long echoes from the forest. The first person we met was Job's six-year-old son Archean, who was on the track wearing only a pair of shorts. He had a great grin like his father and ran in front of us for the last stretch, expertly navigating the roots and sharp rocks with his bare feet.

Arriving at Job's house was quite a revelation. There was a great clearing on the mountain side. An open field of broad taro leaves spread down the slope with tall trees forming a jungle backdrop. This ended behind two traditionally-built huts elevated one metre above the ground overlooking tapioca gardens and the sea below. As I felt the breeze cool my sweaty clothes, I thought that Job must have one of the best views anywhere in the world. Across the water you could see East Cape and, to the left, numerous small islands and coral reefs dotted across the azure Solomon Sea to the horizon — like stitches in a marine tapestry.

Soon I was introduced to Imelda, Job's young wife. Her face had subtle features, with brown curly locks of hair. She was carrying their one-year old son, little Job, on her hip. Holding onto her skirt was their four-year-old son Messi. "Hello Imelda," I said, "So good to meet you and thank you for having me here in this beautiful place." I tried to say hello to little Job too, who was naked, but as soon as I looked at him, he started crying — clearly fearful of the *dim dim*. Imelda and the other bystanders just laughed.

Imelda spoke very little English but one of the cousins helped me translate some courtesy phrases. Soon Job arrived, bush knife in hand, walking barefooted along one of the tree trunks laying across the taro field. He had been clearing some jungle and was wearing only a pair of shorts but pulled on a T-shirt from a clothing line and gave me a big smile. I think we both felt a bit shy but I was thrilled to finally have found him. We shook hands.

"So good to see you again," I said.

Job nodded cheerfully and then pointed at the jungle hillside behind me. "We have water down there if you want to wash and you can put your belongings in this house here."

Job and Imelda had cleared their bedroom for me to stay but left their mattress. This was the biggest of the huts and was connected to their kitchen. They had moved into their old hut some twenty metres away where they stored yams and tapioca roots. Job had told me that

Imelda had been worried about having to accommodate a *dim dim* as they had none of the modern conveniences that white people were used to. So I made sure to compliment her on my hut and ensure that she knew I was grateful to be their guest; and this was true — this was beyond doubt the most beautiful place I had ever seen.

Besides being a generous host, Job was also a hardworking man, as I would later witness when he took me on a tour around his land. In fact, his mother was the customary land owner — as land tenure is largely matrilineal in Milne Bay. This means that Job's mother had given him the right to stay and plant gardens on the land. Job had started clearing ground a few years ago, and then moved his house from the village to this spot where he had prepared a large plot to grow vegetables. It was an impressive garden, especially considering the enormous, sharp rocks that were lying everywhere in the red soil. Besides tapioca and taro there were also yams, papaya and bananas, pineapple and a few betel nut palms; even one or two coconut palms were struggling to shoot their way up.

This little family could not possibly eat all the food they produced and they often donated their surplus to other families. Job explained laughing, "When people are too lazy to grow their own food, they come to me for tapioca and yams." But his face soon became serious as he looked at me and said, "We are good Christian people; we work hard, and we pray. That's why we no longer live in the village — too much talk and gossip — and people come and sit and tell stories and interrupt my work. I was once very sick in my heart and lungs because I was drinking and chewing betel nut and acting big head (playing up); it made me sick, like a cancer but then I found God and he healed me. Now we live up here where there is peace and the air is clean; and here I can live long, and my heart can be happy."

I totally understood him. Although his was undoubtedly a hard life — toiling in the rocky soil, cutting back the ever-invading jungle and carrying water up from a hillside stream twice a day — Job had chosen a beautiful site. It was so peaceful, with a fresh breeze keeping mosquitoes and flies at bay, and much birdlife, with no disturbances — except the odd adventurous Dane, not unlike Tolkien's Frodo Baggins, coming to take him away on a great adventure.

As the last light of day disappeared, the cicadas increased their cacophony. Job showed me into the kitchen hut that was just high enough for he and Imelda to stand up in. With my short stature, I didn't have a problem either and, as Job pointed out, "Lucky you're size 28 like us or else you cannot fit." I chuckled and said that I thought that it was the perfect-sized hut. (The people of Milne Bay are known for their short stature and referred to affectionately by their fellow countrymen and women as, 'Size 28' — a reference to the presumed average waist size of their trousers.)

There was no furniture in the hut, only a little shelf where Imelda kept her kitchen utensils together with some leftovers from a previous meal. We sat down on mats woven from palm fronds. In between us was a big plate of different tubers. In a pot was some noodle soup, with thinly sliced tapioca leaves and tinned mackerel. The noodles and mackerel were something I had brought with me. Job told me that normally they would just eat roots, leaves and cooked bananas, and if they needed protein, he would hunt for possum or go fishing.

We all bowed our heads and Job said a prayer, then we served ourselves and ate with spoons from tin plates. It was a cool evening. Little Job was even dressed up for the occasion in a jumper and some pants. He was still wary of me but was otherwise preoccupied with using both his hands to devour a slippery tapioca. The taste was very bland, but I was hungry and shovelled it down like the rest of the family, while greatly complimenting Imelda on her cooking.

The hut was now lit by the solar lights that I had brought with me from Port Moresby on Job's request. It was a smart set up and cheap too — well, at least for me. It consisted of a solar cell, a battery unit with two USB ports, and two led light bulbs, each on three-metre cables. Job and Imelda, and not least the kids, were thrilled with this new technology — and, at the same time, Job could charge his mobile phone. Job showed me their otherwise only light, which consisted of an open bamboo tube perfectly fitted with three large batteries connected to a small light bulb and a phone charging cable. Job said that It worked all right but it wasn't bright enough to read by and the batteries didn't last for very long. The solar light changed all that.

After dinner, we had a cup of very sweet tea while the oldest boy Archean was using the crayons I had brought for drawing in his school books, with his younger brother Messi looking on. Job was sitting with little Job, while Imelda was cleaning the dishes by the fireplace. We talked about the adventure ahead, and the fact that we didn't have a canoe — or "Sail," as Job called his *sailau,* which was too old and rotten. We both agreed that there was no time to build a new one, as this would take at least a month. Job said, "Not many people will sell their sail, so we must talk smart and grease our mouth and tell them; 'like this, and like this' — that is what we call *Kula.*"

Job though for a bit and said, "We need one or two boys for the sail."

I asked, "Can't it just be you and me sailing and then you teach me?"

"No," he replied, "We must at least be one more — it is hard work sailing a canoe and you don't know how. Maybe we need two more boys to help us." Then he mentioned a sailor named Sanakoli who lived on an island not too far away and who had an uncle who might be willing to sell his canoe. I asked about this Sanakoli character and he explained that I had met him at the canoe festival the previous year and that he had come first in the race. I didn't recall meeting a Sanakoli but thought that if he had come in as number one, he must be a very capable sailor.

As I was lying under the mosquito net that night, I reflected on the events of the day and what Job had told me about his substance abuse and ′big heading.' I recognised something that reminded me of my own 'colourful' past and I thought about how he had turned his life around and how well he had done for himself. At the age of 34, he had three healthy, happy children and a beautiful wife, as well as a plentiful garden in the loveliest of places. I felt a pang of guilt taking

Job away from all of this, and I promised myself that I would make it worth his while.

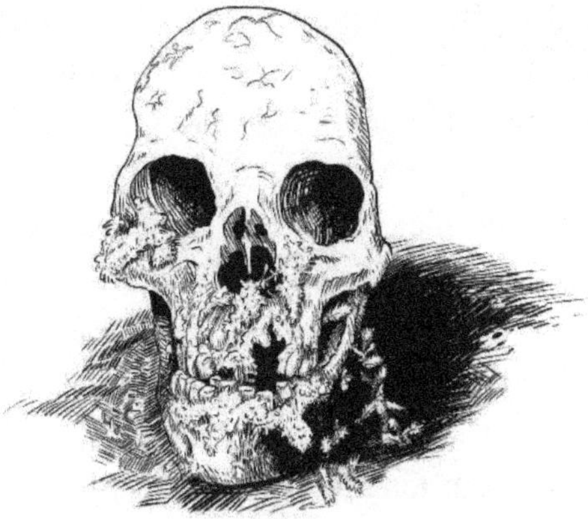

Early the next morning, thick cloud covered the island — and the seas were not favourable for an inter-island crossing. We had agreed that, when the weather improved, Job would sail to Sanakoli's island of Nuakata and engage him in our quest. But as I soon learned, you can't make any firm plans in PNG, and things will always take longer than expected. This was, of course, frustrating as I wanted to get the expedition underway, but at least I could do some filming in this amazing place.

After a breakfast of flour buns cooked in oil, Job took me into the forest to show me a cave. We walked along fallen trees, climbed a minor slope with steps of old roots overgrown by green saplings. After clearing a bit of vegetation, we turned on to a small trail leading up to a big rock pointing out of the hillside. Underneath was an elongated chamber about half a metre in height and one and a half metres deep. In the shadow of the rock were scattered around 40 moss-green and ivory-coloured adult human skulls. Some of the skulls close to us were overgrown with small ferns.

Job cleared the vines from around the cave entrance and started counting. “One, two, three… eight rows, eight generations.” He continued, “Maybe, I just guess, I am the number fifteen generation.”

I asked him if the cave was regarded as a sacred place.

Job explained, “Not for me but for some people, yes. Normally we don’t take people here. But you can see their teeth are clean. In the old days, they didn’t chew *buai* and eat mustard. These were strong people, cannibals and warriors.”

(Although stories of cannibalism in PNG persist, this practice has long vanished, with the last reliable report from the interior of the island dating back to the early 1960s).

I asked him if there were any legends about who the skulls belonged to.

“No, they are from long ago. We don’t know but, in the forest, you can see where they have been living. There are stones here. Also, in my garden, there are stones. And there are also two more skull caves but they belong to other clans.”

As we were about to leave, I asked if there was a ceremony we should perform, to show our respect for the dead.

Job looked at me, considered my question, and then laughed. “No, we just go.”

As we walked back via the rough path we had navigated on the way up the mountain, I imagined that Job had resettled land that had been inhabited by some distant forefather. It made sense that he would recognise a good piece of ground with a water source nearby, just as ‘people from the old days’ had done centuries, or even millennia, ago. But there was no doubt that Job’s skull — and hopefully the rest of him — would find its final resting place in a Christian cemetery and not in a cave. Clearly some things have changed.

Next morning the weather seemed to be clearing and Job got ready to head off to find Sanakoli. I wanted to go on his canoe but he said that I was to stay back and look after my things. I then offered him a small drybag to keep his phone and belongings safe on the canoe.

He just guffawed and said, “I’ll take this basket,” and picked up a black nylon compression bag that belonged to an old sleeping bag I had brought him.

“But that’s not waterproof,” I explained.

Job just replied, “Me, I hang it on the mast. No water will spoil it.”

Job packed a few things in his new ‘basket,’ including a folding knife that was a present from me to Sanakoli and a bit of cash for himself. We ran through our plans and agreed to keep in contact by phone. He pointed out a four-metre-high dead tree standing by his house and said, “When I don’t want to go downhill to get phone reception, I climb this tree.”

We said goodbye and, three hours later, Imelda excitedly pointed out to me, far in the distance, a small triangular sail out on the vast blue ocean on course to Nuakata Island.

The Fellowship of the *Tawali Pasana* is established

Two days later I was back at East Cape. It was about ten in the morning; the sun was hot, and I was sitting in the shade of a big tree. I had spent the last couple of hours looking at the dinghy drivers chewing *buai* and chatting. I almost felt that I belonged here as it seemed all the dingy drivers knew who I was and that I knew Wensis. So, it didn’t surprise me when a stranger pointed out a sail and said, “That’s your friends coming in.” And sure enough, soon the turquoise-coloured canoe dug into the sand and I could see Job jumping off together with some other men. I waved at him and we met under the scorching sun. He introduced me to two of the sailors, they were each carrying a white plastic bucket, the type you use for paint. They were scruffy looking with their holed T-shirts and stubbled beards. They introduced themselves as Justin and Sanakoli.

Sanakoli had a friendly face with long eyelashes and some red-stained crooked teeth. He was quite talkative and eagerly answered my questions. Justin, on the other hand, was more of a ‘strong silent type.’

Although he was the same height as the rest of us, he seemed bigger with his tank-like build. He had a square jaw and clinched eyes and didn't say very much, instead he just continually puffed on a *bruce*. Sanakoli confirmed that their uncle had a canoe that he was ready to sell and all we had to do was, "just go and get it." I suggested that we should meet and decide if the new recruits were 'up for it.' We found a suitable place on the beach away from bystanders. On the way I learned that Justin was 40 years of age while Sanakoli was 37. They were brothers — raised together in a family of ten children (not an uncommon size for a PNG family) on Basilaki Island. Now they were living on different islands, each with their wives and own children.

I recognized Sanakoli from the year before; I had even shaken his hand and congratulated him on his great achievement in coming first in the race. I didn't recognise Justin, because he hadn't competed at that festival, although by reputation Justin was a renowned canoe builder and famed for sailing solo to the outer reefs and returning with many turtles. I was a bit worried about having to feed two extra people instead of just one, as I had initially planned, but what is more, this Justin character looked a bit scary — even a little menacing. Then again, I thought that perhaps this wasn't such a bad thing after all, especially with the prospect of sailing through pirate-infested waters. I reasoned that at this stage it was more about getting the expedition underway. It wasn't even guaranteed that they would all join me for the entire expedition.

As we sat down together on the grass by a broken sea wall, my heart started pounding and I became apprehensive. This was where I had to convince these two strangers that they should leave their families and join me on a long, difficult and dangerous voyage into unknown territory — and all of this in return for a small monthly wage and the far-off promise of fame and glory. I believed that my best chance of talking them into it was to appeal to their 'sailors' honour' as I had little money to offer them. I introduced myself as a kayaker and film director who wanted to make an important documentary that would show the world what Milne Bay sailors and their canoes were capable of.

I showed them a map I had drawn of the island and pointed out the route we'd be undertaking and the challenges that lay ahead. I asked how I could best support their families and communities while they were away and agreed that I would send a monthly wage home, so they wouldn't have to suffer financially during their absence. And I reassured them that this wage would increase as we gained both fame and donations through social media. But underscoring all of this was that they would return as famous sailors and that I could help them get a job in tourism. Job and Sanakoli had absorbed my pitch with great attention. This was followed by comments and questions; but all this time Justin had just been sitting smoking his *bruce* looking at the sea, his demeanour made me a bit uneasy. I finished my speech with, "You are all here today because you are some of the best sailors in PNG. I would be honoured if you would teach me your sailing skills and join me on this historic voyage."

Justin turned his head slightly and looked towards me, and at that moment I knew he was 'hooked.' Encouraged by this subtle sign, I boasted something like, "Money will come and go but the stories about your achievements will never die." I surprised myself with my oratory skills.

I paused for effect and looked at my audience and then asked them if they were all 'in.' Job agreed and Sanakoli said, "I'm in!"

When I asked Justin, he looked thoughtful down at his *bruce* and replied in a low tone, "Yes, we can do it."

To my great regret I hadn't filmed the meeting. So afterwards I conducted a short interview, asking the sailors why they wanted to undertake this journey.

Job said, "I am not doing this for me. I want to tell my children that I was one of the great sailors who travelled around, so when I get old or die, then my grandchildren will know that I travelled around Indonesia and Papua New Guinea." He reflected briefly and continued, "And the Panaeati people, they want to show up, so we must put them down." Sanakoli and Justin burst out in great chuckles, and Job continued, "Basilaki and Normanby People must go around Indonesia and Papua New Guinea. That is all." And they all burst into laughter again. When I asked who the Panaeati people were, Job explained that they were considered the great sailors of Milne Bay. Panaeati is one of the islands in the Engineer Group, 200 kilometres east of mainland PNG. "So," Job continued, "They must be put down." And then they all laughed again while nervously looking around as to see if any bystanders had overheard their cocky exclamations — especially people from Panaeati. Like Sanakoli, Job wanted to leave a legacy for his children. Justin didn't feel like talking to the camera and instead opened his bucket and took out some lime and mustard and chewed *buai*.

As we stood up to leave our meeting place, Sanakoli asked what they should call me. I asked him what did he mean?

Job explained, "Now we work for you, so now we are your boys. And if we are older than you, we are still your boys. That is how it is like in Milne Bay."

Sanakoli followed up, "So do we call you? Boss or Mister or how?"

"Just call me Thor," I said a little befuddled.

"Just Thor?" Sanakoli questioned.

"Yes," I replied. "We are all in this together, so I'll just call you by your names and you just call me by mine… if that is okay?"

Then Sanakoli said, "Okay, good… just Thor," and he and Job laughed while shaking their heads at what they must have thought was a very odd *dim dim*.

A PMV to Alotau

We all jumped on to a PMV, or local bus which is more like an army truck with an open back, and travelled to Alotau where we went shopping for expedition equipment. We also hoped to meet a tourism officer Job knew from his church who could help us apply for PNG passports. As we were sitting on the wooden benches in the back of the bumping truck, I congratulated myself on having the sailors on board. And why wouldn't they be involved I thought? They had been sailing their entire lives and were in their prime; and then an adventurer shows up with the proposition of testing their skills to the limit on the ultimate canoeing adventure, a voyage through far off places with the reward of going into the history books as the greatest sailors Milne Bay had ever produced. I would have jumped at that offer if I was one of them. But then again, they also had families including small children to think of and they all played important roles in their respective communities. This placed a lot of responsibility on my shoulders, but I firmly believed that this adventure was a once in a lifetime opportunity for all of us to create something spectacular that would improve our lives and inspire future generations.

After about two hours of bumpy roads and a few river crossings, the PMV scrambled over the low iron bridge and into Alotau. The town of Alotau looks 'rugged' in most parts, although its green cloud clad mountain backdrop and the beautiful waters of the great Milne Bay gave the provincial capital its own distinct charm. We jumped off at the bus station, which was a dusty field with some long tin roofs providing shade for rows of benches. It was a busy place with locals loitering around, greeting relatives, chewing *buai*, and carrying heavy loads with bus drivers yelling out their destinations. There was a steady flow of PMVs and mini buses off-loading people and their market goods, and in return, on-loading homebound villagers with their bags of rice, sugar and jerry cans of fuel. About 30 metres away from the bus station was a marketplace where people would sell their garden crops, coconuts and fish. In front of both structures was a great grass field with a tall traditional hut and an integrated stage down by the beach. It was on this great arena that the canoe festival was held every year. From the waterfront there was a beautiful view across the bay and the distant blue mountains.

We walked up towards the centre of town, me carrying a waterproof backpack and camera bag, Job with his 'basket' on his shoulder and the sailors with their plastic buckets in hand. The centre of town consisted of one main street with a handful of Chinese-operated supermarkets and hardware stores, together with two banks. I noticed the wall of one of the stores featured a collection of 'WANTED' posters, the sort you might see in an old cowboy movie (although some of these were printed in colour). Each poster featured a 'mug shot' with the name and description of the renegade *raskol,* together with the details of a cash reward for his arrest. The poster didn't mention if the terms were 'dead or alive' — I had no time to investigate this, as we had a long equipment list to fill consisting of lifejackets, signaling flares, provisions, a 30 metre x 30 metre tarpaulin for the sail, ropes, paint and nails amongst many other things to buy. But first we had to go to the provincial tourism bureau where I was to meet an officer named Moda Andrew.

Job had already told Moda about our plans so, when I was introduced to him at his office, he seemed ready to engage in the project. Moda was about my age, and size 28 — of course — from the Trobriand Islands. He had white teeth like Job (meaning he didn't chew *buai*) and looked like an office worker with his ironed shirt, leather shoes and clean haircut. The only thing that gave away his cultural roots was a tattoo on his cheek, which wasn't an uncommon sight in PNG. After a brief introduction, Moda gave a long speech about how important tourism was for Milne Bay and then offered to help us create national identification cards for Job, Sanakoli and Justin. With IDs we would be able to obtain passports for all three sailors to travel through Indonesian West Papua.

The ID thing, however, turned out to be a long and tedious process as the sailors had never held so much as a birth certificate. So, we started by filling out the forms with details that included the birth place and age of their respective parents as well as their clan affiliation and so forth. This all had to be either recalled from memory (or guessed). The initial paperwork would end up taking several days — just to start the process — and, as I was eager to move things forward, I left Moda in charge and moved on. As we walked out of the office, I said to the crew, "He seems like a good guy that Moda but he talks a lot!"

Sanakoli laughed and said, "Yes Trobriand people are the people who talk the most… oh, you can never stop them."

As I left the tourism office a curious thing happened. I was approached by an inquisitive, fast talking man, who shook my hand and held on to it. He was basically 'interrogating' me about my plans and whereabouts. It felt very suspicious not least because Moda had just warned me about telling people about our expedition — because if pirates got wind that there was a *dim dim* furnishing a canoe, with all sorts of goods, we would be robbed. I pulled my hand away and left the stranger in a polite but stern manner without revealing our intentions.

Expedition Log 12 August 2016

12:20 hrs. Alotau, Sanderson Bay Harbour. Now as I write, Job is leaving to see his wife. Justin, Sanakoli and I are sitting amongst our shopping at the harbour where we are waiting for a dinghy to take us to their home island of Basilaki. It is there that we will secure the most essential piece of kit required for the expedition — the canoe.

Chapter Three

Dim dim over board

Expedition Log 31 August 2016

> 07:40 hrs. Departing Dobura. Wind 6-8 Knots from S-SE. Calm seas, the second day of the expedition is starting well.

As the sun rose, the wind picked up and our freshly repaired storm sail eagerly pulled the outrigger out of the water and although the wind seemed strong, the conditions were much better than the previous day. Despite this, Sanakoli didn't want to hand me the sheet. I understood why. There was a lot of power in that sail and, after all, my traditional sail craft apprenticeship had only just begun. Job went to the open green plastic container and said, "We put the lines out and get a fish." He took out a round plastic reel with some nylon line, complete with a squid bait on a jack hook and threw it all over the side, tying it off to the mast. Then he took out a thicker nylon line and threw the attached 'rapala wobbler' lure overboard from the outrigger and sat himself in front of the mast.

Justin was standing on the back steering the canoe with Sanakoli operating the sail. There was a clean swell and *Tawali Pasana* easily cut through the waves. We were covering a good corner of the bay, perhaps a crossing of about 18 nautical miles, aiming our bow at Cape Vogel. I was very happy with the pace. I sat myself on the reeling with my back to the ocean and my bare feet planted on the deck planks as I had seen the sailors do. The sun was shining bright and warm. After a rough start, we were now on our way to a successful circumnavigation.

I thought, maybe later in the day the wind would back off, like on the previous evening, and I could do some more sailing.

I learned the basics of sailing as a child thanks to my grandparents — spending every summer on their little yacht. As an adult, I had crossed the Atlantic and sailed in the Caribbean. I had extensive experience of kayaking and canoeing as well, firstly having completed an outdoor instructor's course. Later I lived in Venezuela for two years guiding kayaking tours and staying with the Warao Indians in the Orinoco delta. I was even taught how to build a traditional bamboo raft in Cambodia. So, for me, this was another challenge that I would in time also master. However, it was essential that I learned as quickly as possible. My crew had never undertaken such a voyage, and certainly they had never been so far from home. My 'plan b' was that if I could sail the canoe myself then, if necessary, I could pick up a new crew at the border of West Papua, in the capital Jayapura, which would include Indonesian-speaking Papuans.

We were already far out in the bay and, as I was sitting in the sun contemplating my sailing capabilities, disaster suddenly struck. It happened in a split second. The canoe hit a wave. I lost my balance and I fell back into the ocean. In my fall, I grabbed the gunwale but the sea pulled me back and the canoe slipped from my grasp as the end of the stern passed me by. Then a wave broke over me. As I resurfaced, I saw the canoe flying away. I was fumbling with my hat and sunglasses, which I had been quick enough to hold onto but in that same instance, I remembered the great sets of barbed fish hooks that we were trolling behind us and I looked down in the hope of avoiding them.

The black sail slackened off. I started swimming as fast as I could towards the canoe. Fortunately, there was a gentle swell; but now my mind was preoccupied with the idea of sharks lurking in the deep waters beneath me. When I finally did reach the stern, I looked up and saw the shocked faces of my crew. I pulled myself up on to the platform, relieved to be out of the water and said as I caught my breath, "Thanks… for… waiting up…. guys."

Sanakoli said, "Oh, sorry."

Job followed in a lecturing tone, "Now you stay down in the canoe, no crawling around. You always hold on to something when we sail." Job didn't seem angry, just cautionary. For my part, I was reassured to see that the sailors didn't want to lose the *dim dim* on the second day of the voyage. As the canoe resumed its wild ride, I sat inside the hull and poured a cup of water. I noticed that my hand was shaking. It was a near miss — but it could have been much worse, especially if I had fallen into the ocean at night or in rough seas. I took out my GoPro and started filming. I wanted to tell the camera what had happened and how I felt but I couldn't find the right words. I stared at it for a bit and then turned it off. Perhaps the expression on my face told a better story.

Then I realised that my iPhone had been in my pocket. I pulled it out by the lanyard that was secured to my pants. It was in a waterproof case but to my great disappointment I discovered that it hadn't kept tight and my phone was dead. This was a huge problem as the phone was my connection to Facebook where I had planned to share the adventure 'live' with a (hopefully) growing number of followers. The phone was also how I was connected to my emergency satellite transmitter. This little waterproof device allowed me to connect with the outside world in places where there was no phone signal. With these two I was able to make calls, send emails, receive weather forecasts and upload posts on social media. Now, with the phone dead, the only thing I could do with the transmitter was to post our location or send a SOS signal.

Cape Vogel

It was early afternoon; the canoe was carving through the waves at high speed and my clothes were long dried after my dunking earlier in the day. We had crossed the bay in good time and now we neared Cape Vogel. Patches of turquoise revealed themselves amongst the waves. "Hoo, reef. Now we catch fish," Job yelled. He was standing with his bare feet spread across the platform holding the rapala line ready for a strike as Justin steadily steered the canoe past some swallow shoals where waves were breaking. But there were no bites. As we neared the stony outcrop of the Cape, Job ordered the lines to be pulled in, and in good time, for the seas were high.

There were two big islands, Goodenough and D'Entrecasteux, both lying about 17 nautical miles off the Cape, which together created a bottleneck of long, powerful swells. I was thankful that we were still running on the small sail, because as soon as we hit the first rise, I could tell that we were in trouble. The swells were like a long moving liquid waterslide that the canoe surfed down — one swell after another after another. It was starting to feel like the same sequence of events that lead to the incident of the swamped canoe on our first day — but on a much larger scale.

Now we were surfing some considerably larger waves, and the danger was that, if we gained too much momentum, the bow would outrun its own wave and dig into the wave building in front of us — and then we would be flooded. I was sitting behind the mast with one hand on the reeling and one hand around a rope. Saltwater sprayed from the bow and the sailors were all yelling excitedly to each other in their local languages. Job was in the hull constantly bailing,

Sanakoli by the sail slacking and pulling in syncopation, with Justin standing at the back end of the canoe controlling our course. It was amazing to watch Justin at work, keeping his balance while lifting and sinking the heavy hand-held rudder through the high seas. His only support was his big flat feet planted on each side of the reeling and a piece of rope that was fastened from the top end of the rudder to the outrigger.

It was the first time I had seen Justin cut loose and abandon his reserved nature. He had a wild expression on his face and yelled, "*Hiiii Tawali, hiii Tawali Pasana*!" every time he steered our dug-out tree trunk down a new wave and then, at the last second, steered it off, thus avoiding digging into the wave in front of us. It was mayhem and Justin was in his element. If I hadn't been so busy clinging to the canoe and wishing it would end well, I would probably have been ashamed of my arrogance in thinking that I could match such skills in a few months. What I was witnessing here was the pinnacle of a lifetime of canoe sailing. It was such an impressive sight and I was full of awe. After a harrowing 15 minutes of close calls, clenched teeth and white knuckles, we had finally passed the Cape and were out of the swell. *Tawali Pasana* steered inside a long succession of reefs where the sea was clear and calm, and the bottom was a dark turquoise colour with silhouettes of coral. There was a joyous atmosphere on board. The sailors seemed relieved, although they didn't say it in words.

Then the coastline changed character. The mountains gave way to lowland mangroves spread as far as the eye could see.

"This is *sniper* country," Job said, sitting hunched in the stern steering with the rudder.

I asked him what he meant.

"*Sniper, sniper*, ha." Then his grin turned to a more serious expression, "Crocodiles. You don't see them... before it's too late. That's why we call them *snipers*." He gestured what I assumed to be a figurative bullet mark on his bald forehead. "They are very clever. They can lay like you think they're dead with the tongue out!" Job kinked his head to the side, stuck his tongue out and rolled his eyes in a very animated way.

Sanakoli eagerly joined in. "They cry like a chicken or a pig, or like a human baby to trick you. You hear them in the mangrove and say, 'Who's that crying?' But when you come close, they eat you!" And with that, Sanakoli clapped his rough palms together and said, "Just like... that!"

After pirates and bad weather, ocean swells and dangerous currents, crocodiles were probably the greatest danger on the voyage. I had read the literature and knew that they lived in great numbers across most parts of coastal New Guinea. Saltwater crocodiles are clever swimmers. They use ocean swells and tidal currents to travel between islands. One study recorded a 4.8 metre male travelling 590 kilometres in just 25 days. Another study from neighbouring Cape York Peninsula in Northern Australia described how three male crocodiles were captured and relocated. All three animals found their way back to the original capture site. One animal had been flown from the west to the east coast of the Peninsula where it spent almost four months before swimming back to its capture site, covering 400 kilometres in 20 days.

The amazing navigational capabilities of *Crocodylus Porosus,* along with its diverse choice of habitat, explains why they are the most widespread species of the crocodile family, covering a range from Northern Australia up though the islands of the South Pacific and all the way to India. It is a magnificent animal, the largest reptile in the world. It can grow to more than six metres in length and weigh up to a ton, with massive jaws that deliver the strongest recorded bite in the animal kingdom. Of course, six-metre crocodiles are a rarity but a three-metre crocodile could just as well pull you under. Despite their name, these reptiles are most commonly found in freshwater and are known to frequent rivers and estuaries and… mangroves.

Job's voice started to tremble as he told a story, "Oh, one time on Normanby, a little boy had gone missing. He was playing on the beach and next thing he was gone. People say, 'crocodile on the reef,' so me and my cousin we go diving for it." Job and his cousin found it all right but when they realised how big it was, they hurried out of the water. After the initial shock, they mustered their courage and returned with spears. Job continued his story, "When the crocodile sees us, he go deeper; too deep for our spears. So, we get shark hook on a strong rope." After several attempts Job gaffed the great beast in the side and with the help of the other villagers pulled it ashore.

When it was on land, the father of the lost child came with a bush knife and said, "You killed my son you monster, now you die!" But the blade just deflected off the crocodile's head. Job said with big eyes, "We tried the axe on the skull but nothing could break it — it was like the strongest steel — the steel of God." In the end, the father cut the belly open to retrieve the remains of his son, "To give him a Christian burial." After the story was told we all became quiet. Who knew what was lurking in those mangroves that ran for miles along the coast. We were sailing between 300 and 1000 metres offshore but the sun was setting and sooner or later we would have to anchor somewhere to sleep and, so far, we had not seen a village.

An accident waiting to happen

"*Kisooo*!" Job yelled. *Kiso* was a shout the sailors made when there was a fish on the line. We had hooked something big; the strong line tightened for a long second and then broke. "Big fish," Job said. I was disappointed that we had lost one of the expensive rapalas, let alone a good meal but we immediately tied a new rapala lure on and threw it out. Soon after, there was a bite. Job pulled the line in rapidly while feeding the excess line onto the floor of the platform. Everyone hooted as he landed a beautiful blue Trevally. He threw the wiggling fish into the front hull of the canoe and the hook was set again. Justin started cleaving firewood for cooking and soon there was another big bite. This time it was a coral trout, a deep Bourgogne red-coloured grouper-like fish with white pointy teeth and bright electric blue dots.

The sun was setting and the fire was burning in our little stove. This simple cooker was made from an alloy saucepan with sand in the bottom and the fourth side cut out to feed in firewood. Although ingenious in its simplicity, this stove was an accident waiting to happen. It had long pointy spikes sticking through from two sides to create a grill onto which we could rest a pot. Since day one, I had expressed concerns about having these rusty grill spikes on the canoe but it didn't seem to bother the sailors and I hadn't been able to bend them down with my multi-tool. We cut both fish into chunks with a bush knife as the sailors discussed something in one of their languages.

Job came to me and asked, "How do you want us to cook, we only have one saucepan. So, you want us to cook rice first and then we eat that, and then we cook the fish? Or how?"

I looked at him for a bit and then said, "Can't we just eat fish and forget about the rice… if that's okay with you guys?" They all laughed.

"Yes, that's what we want but we thought that white people couldn't eat fish alone."

"No, no," I said, "I am here to learn from you. I can eat anything, and I'd much rather eat fish than rice."

Sanakoli nodded approvingly. "That is good. Us sailors, we eat anyhow."

The fist-sized chunks of flesh were boiled in fresh water and the pieces that wouldn't fit in the pot, like the heads and tails, were smoked over the embers for later consumption. As we sat with our plates of fish and cups of fish soup, I thought that this was the adventure fantasy of a 13-year-old boy come true. It was just what I had dreamt of — being on a great adventure like Mark Twain's Huck Finn: flowing with the current, not having to wash and eating whatever you wanted, whenever you wanted, following the rhythm of the journey.

As we sat and ate, we began to talk about the Indonesian part of the island, or West Papua. We discussed how strict they were with travel permits and visas and that I was hoping that the tourism officer in Alotau would help get our passports processed on time. Job mentioned that they had met with Moda before departure. Moda had informed them that, because they were traveling with a *dim dim,* they would be representing Milne Bay. It seemed that, amongst others, he had told them that they should make sure I was 'looked after.' As Job talked, I realised that Moda had instructed the sailors as if I was an ordinary tourist that they would need to 'babysit.'

Job said, "If something happens to you it will fall back on us and our families, and then it will fall back on Moda and on the tourism people in Milne Bay." He finished by repeating a warning, "From now on, no more going to the outrigger or sitting on the side of the canoe. You must stay inside the canoe."

And then it struck, that they had totally missed the point — that we were an *expedition team* out to create a great world record. I didn't know if I should laugh or cry or tell them to get lost. I took a deep breath and tried to focus on the positives — I was grateful that the crew were worried about me getting hurt or drowning and they were committed to the circumnavigation — but on the negative side, this totally changed the dynamic and contradicted my grand vision. I was here to learn to live and sail like a real Milne Bay sailor and, as comrades together, we would make history.

As I sat hunched with a plate of fish between my bare feet, I thought that there was also a hard reality to consider; we had almost sunk on the first day, twice, and I had fallen into the sea on day two — and we had just made it around Cape Vogel because of the incredible experience and skill of the sailors. So, for now, I was virtually a passenger on a canoe that I could not sail and it would take more than a few months to learn to do so. This meant that I was dependent on three sailors who didn't share my vision of fellowship. Instead, it felt like I was the oddball tourist who they had to humour to get paid.

Chapter Four

Bay of Pirates

Expedition Log 1 September 2016

> 00:50 hrs. We have anchored in the mangroves near a tiny coastal hamlet. The crew are anxious about this strange village, so we stay on the canoe — ready to sail off.

We sailed off at first light, after an awful night! We had slept, or tried to get some sleep, wrapped up in damp rain coats and plastic sheets, while fearing *raskols* and crocodiles. It had been a wet cold night but soon the sun was warming our bones and we made a good pace towards Tufi — a beautiful peninsula of long deep fjords and white sandy beaches fringed by coconut palms. I knew this because I had a book at home about the area with the very telling title *Beautiful Tufi*. I also had a contact there — a local man named William, who was recommended to us by an Australian kayaker named Sandy Robson.

Germany to Australia

I had heard about Sandy from reading her account of being attacked by a Saltwater Crocodile in North Queensland, Australia. The reptile had bitten the back end of her fibreglass kayak. This forced the Australian to paddle towards the beach — understandably — with all her might. Sandy then spent all night stoking a big fire to keep the lurking giant away. Later, I learned that she was undertaking a kayaking adventure, retracing the route of the German adventurer

Oskar Speck, who made his epic voyage from Germany to Australia in the 1930s in a foldable double kayak.

At the time, Sandy was on the last leg of a five-year voyage, now navigating through Indonesia and West Papua, paddling in the opposite direction of my intended course. I had contacted Sandy for advice on the West Papua coast and she immediately offered her support and promised to share details. A week later, I received a long list of contacts and coordinates for places to camp, and she promised to share more experiences as she progressed. Luckily, Sandy reached Alotau the very same day as I came in with my crew. We agreed to meet for a beer. I was excited to learn more about the conditions ahead. I had heard that she had encountered some unwelcoming locals and that there had been challenging seas on some sections of the route. I met her in the afternoon in a hotel garden. The 43-year-old adventurer walked in with a limp, wearing a quick-dry T-shirt, kayaking shorts and reef shoes. Sandy had short blond curly hair and a great smile. Under her heavily-tanned right arm she was carrying a waterproof map case.

Sandy was full of advice and stories — most of them cautionary. She told me about an incident that had made her decide to get a support dinghy for the remaining voyage through PNG waters. Sandy had been in the country less than two weeks when a group of men stalked and harassed her while paddling. Then there was another incident near Ali Island close to Aitape where she had been chased by an ill-intentioned fisherman in a small sailing canoe. Luckily, Sandy had a sail on her kayak too and could keep her distance but the chase lasted for over seven kilometres. She said, "After that happened, I thought, *shit*, I can't continue unless I can solve this problem because my journey is not worth someone injuring or killing me." So, with the assistance of local government and sponsors, Sandy engaged a dinghy and crew for the remaining three months, from where she would cross over onto the Australian Island of Saibai and complete her voyage. But as she said,

"It's also different for me because I'm a woman and they see me as an easy target."

Of course, she was right. I had the benefit of travelling with seasoned PNG sailors, as well as being a man, and the whole idea of our journey was to deliberately engage the locals. Sandy also reminded me that the people of PNG are mostly welcoming and friendly but, "When they see a white person, there is always a chance they'll think you've got a lot of money. So, they will be looking at what you've got and what they can sell it for — cameras, video equipment and all that stuff; you *gotta* keep all that well hidden."

While talking about my delayed departure, Sandy expressed concern. As the weather would be getting harder with the changing season, she specifically mentioned the strait that ran between the mainland and the island of New Britain. "I think the most dangerous part is the Vitiaz Strait, because you've got really tough sea conditions — big swells and strong currents — the sort of place where dinghies just sink and people can't come out and rescue you because the sea is so rough. And onshore, in some areas, there are villages that people have told me are very, very unsafe. I had to heed the local advice and skip a part of that section. And when I was there, the wind was blowing 32 knots and the swell was absolutely huge." Sandy then asked me to show her my map. I unfolded it on the table and she took out a ballpoint pen and ran me through the most challenging sections of our route while circling the communities where she had good experiences, as well as underscoring the best outposts to buy provisions.

Finally, I asked her, "Do you have any advice about what to do if I hit *rock bottom* and don't want to go on?" Sandy thought about my question and then smiled. "I recommend that you go to the shop and buy yourself a block of chocolate and wrap it in newspaper to keep it from melting and put it in the bottom of one of your bags. And when you come to crunch time — which is always going to happen — and you think you are at the lowest of the low... then get out the chocolate," she laughed. "But remember, what if this is just training and it is going to get even harder." We both laughed at her encouraging philosophy and agreed that it was time for a beer.

I was quite concerned to think that Sandy had been paddling around the world solo for five years but after two short weeks in PNG she needed a support dinghy for security. I was grateful for her help but I was also worried about getting too many details concerning what was lying ahead. It was clear that Sandy had some impressive organisational skills. This included planning everything two weeks in advance, such as distances, places to camp and rest, and people to meet. But it wasn't the way I wanted to do it. My idea was to follow the seasons and the weather and the seas and take things as they came. Nonetheless, meeting with Sandy also gave me a sense that my adventure could be achieved.

The Tufi coast looked stunning. It was just as I had imagined — steep cliffs topped with lush jungle and pure white sandy beaches surrounded by coral reef. The midday sun was burning bright and the water was crystal clear. We were all tired from the cold night on the canoe and were eager to make landfall but the tide was low and, in most places, the barrier coral was resting just below the surface. Closer in, we spotted a patch that looked a bit deeper. As we steered slowly through the keyhole and over the reef, which was barely possible, I watched some small blue fish swimming for their lives as the bottom of our canoe crashed through the skyline of their aquatic metropolis. Fortunately, we made it inside the reef without breaking too much coral and Job steered us towards the first shiny white beach. It even had a small island at one end. Some young girls were fishing from a canoe by an isolated stand of mangroves. When they saw that we were coming in, they hurriedly paddled ashore and ran up a small palm-clad hill and disappeared in the direction of some huts.

As *Tawali Pasana* touched the sand, a group of women of all ages came down to the beach. A middle-aged woman wearing a bright dress greeted me. The sail was hanging freely from the canoe and the crew had sat down to chew *buai*. I explained to the woman where we had come from and that we were looking for a place to pull the canoe ashore. The older woman gave an order to the girls who then also disappeared up the hill. Meanwhile, the other women gathered around the canoe and asked us all sorts of questions, as the girls that had been sent off came back with four coconuts for us to drink. Soon after, a man arrived. He had a small moustache and was wearing a blue polo shirt and a grey cap. He presented himself as William.

"William?" I said. "Do you know an Australian Kayaker, Sandy Robson?"

"Yes, she stayed with me," he confirmed with a broad welcoming smile. I told him that this was a great coincidence and that Sandy had recommended that I find him. William was very happy to hear this. He made a sweeping motion with his right arm and welcomed us to Tufi and said we could stay on 'his beach.'

He then invited us up to his house, which was situated on top of a hill overlooking the sea. The ground here was covered with the loveliest short green grass. Tall coconut palms randomly dotted the land and provided welcome shade. William gave us a tour of the property and then showed us his relatively new guesthouse, which could accommodate six tourists. I was impressed by his design, which featured a communal area with sand on the floor and a shower room. He explained that occasionally he hosted foreign visitors who wanted 'a village experience.' Besides being a part-time guest house manager, William worked for the Tufi Dive Resort about 30 minutes' walk away. I could detect that he was also expecting to accommodate me. So, I explained that I had very little money and I'd rather stay on the beach. Instead, I offered him a small sum for letting us camp. He seemed understanding and said that he was happy to help us with our voyage.

In the afternoon, William offered to take me to the dive resort. The route led us through his village. Although there seemed to be kids and chickens and dogs running around everywhere, it was a very neat and tidy place — and very lush. Every family had one or two traditionally-built sago-leaf-roofed huts standing elevated above the ground on high stilts. Most of the huts had fishing nets hanging on the walls. As we made our way down towards a small secluded bay, we saw several anchored canoes. To reach the dive resort we had to get on an outrigger and paddle across a minor fjord. From there we scaled a steep hill and walked through some tall sward. Suddenly, we were on a landing field of low stubby grass looking across to sloping ground and some aged permanent buildings; this was Tufi station. Across the open field was the dive resort, which had a beautiful outlook over a deep fjord with jungle spilling over the sides of steep cliffs.

William presented me to the managers, a blond-haired Australian couple in their 40s.

"Where did you come from?" the husband asked more than a little surprised. He looked at me like I had popped out of the ground, which was a reasonable enough assumption given my scruffy appearance.

"In a canoe," I answered.

"In a canoe!" the husband exclaimed, only to be interrupted by his wife who equally exclaimed, "In a canoe from where?" I gladly told them about my adventures, including the accident with the phone and my immediate need to get online.

They nodded with a mix of sympathy and wonder and then the husband said, "Normally the only visitors we get here arrive by air from Port Moresby. But we'll give you a hand. We have good WIFI and a table on the outdoor terrace, and we'll even serve you a beer."

I thought, what a luxury! I was so happy to be in such orderly surroundings. Although it had only been three days of sailing, time at the dive resort was a much-needed break from the dangers of the open sea. I placed both my cap and my ambitions of becoming a 'real' Papuan sailor on the table, took a healthy quaff of the ice-cold beer and opened my laptop.

Since I had lost my mobile phone overboard, I hadn't uploaded any accounts from the trip. I made up for that by sharing photographs in a post, thanking the Australian couple for their hospitality. I also spent some time trying to figure out how to get a new phone, which brings me to the greatest of all my problems — a lack of finances. (I didn't even have enough money to pay the next months' wages for the sailors). After an hour, William came back and said it was time to return to the village before it got dark.

Packing the canoe

We had an easy morning. After breakfast we packed the canoe. My idea was that we'd push out by midday and do some safe and enjoyable sailing up what promised to be a scenic coast and stay in another village on the peninsula. There were more than a few things to repack and, contrary to my ideals of a simplistic trip, I must admit that we had a lot of 'stuff.' I had given one of the blue barrels to Job and Sanakoli to use for all their belongings. Justin had been given his own bag for clothes. And if you considered my blue barrel as well, we had already occupied half of the hull. Besides this, there were rice bags with bananas and coconuts and, of course my video bag, laptop bag, solar charger kit and First Aid bag — all of which competed for the remaining space.

During the repacking, we discovered that some of the food and clothes had gotten wet, so they had to be dried. And then there were repairs to the canoe that needed to be attended to. In all there were plenty of things to do. Justin and Sanakoli were helping with all the usual tasks but I noticed that Job wasn't there. When I asked where he had gone, Sanakoli said that that he had taken off in a dinghy with some locals to go fishing. This annoyed me a little, as I was keen to get the canoe sorted. I was repacking the inverter and the foldable solar panels and asked Justin to stow our spare battery in its Tupperware box and seal it with duct tape. As I was stuffing the drybag, I noticed that Justin was taping the box in an inefficient way. I interrupted him and said, "Hey Justin, I have been working in an exhibition hall where I had to tape every day. Let me show you how to do those corners." He gave me the tape and I kneeled and started work, while eagerly explaining the technique. Justin sat for a short time, then he stood up and walked away. I was quite into the whole taping thing and I didn't notice that he had disappeared and now, I was doing his job. This made me really annoyed and I thought to myself, "What is wrong with these people, why would you walk out of a job in the middle of it?" Then it dawned on me that he might have walked away because I had tried to tell him, a 40-year-old man, how to tape a Tupperware box. What was even more stupid was that I had other tasks at hand that only I could do and, now, there were only two people to organise this whole tree trunk. What an idiot I had been.

At about one o'clock, Job returned in the dinghy. They had caught a metre-long Spanish Mackerel. I told him in a polite manner that I'd wish that he had stayed back to help organise the canoe as we had talked about instead of going fishing. He just smiled in a funny way and just said, "Yes," and walked off. Meanwhile Justin had returned to the canoe and was now sleeping on the platform with his green towel over his head. Sanakoli was standing by the dinghy chewing *buai* with the fishermen; he didn't look like he was going to sea anytime soon. It was ridiculously frustrating that these guys didn't appear to want to follow the plan. I didn't know if this was premeditated, or if it was something that had just happened but it was clear that they had no desire to hoist the sail and set off. So, I gave up. It was already past midday. I guessed that we might as well stay in this spot for one more night and get some rest. Instead, I collected my film gear and went up to the village to poke around and see if I could at least get some good shots.

There was a great atmosphere in the village. Colourful lorikeets were screeching from the palm tops and blooming bushes were growing alongside all the small huts. The women were all wearing loose-fitting colourful dresses. The older women had tattooed faces, which was the customary way of signalling that a girl was ready for marriage. But it didn't look like the tattoo tradition had caught on with the younger women in the village. The men, on the other hand, didn't have any facial tattoos. They were wearing shorts with T-shirts sporting different logos. Everyone was smiling and even the kids seemed well behaved. It was obvious that the villagers were used to tourists and I felt very welcome.

The Tufi Peninsula is pretty much cut off from the outside world as there are no access roads, so the only way to get there is either by aeroplane or by dinghy. This had both advantages and drawbacks. The isolation meant that it was easy for the locals to regulate misconduct, as 'troublemakers' didn't have anywhere to run or hide. But with about 70 nautical miles to the nearest town of Popondetta, the locals would have to travel by dinghy for medical treatment or to sell fish or garden produce. Despite all of this, the village looked prosperous compared to other places I had visited in PNG, not least because the dive resort brought in tourists. It was interesting to compare this place to Milne Bay, which was also isolated but a much larger geographical area. In Milne Bay, international cruise ships disgorge thousands of tourists several times a year, there are two dive resorts and multiple hotels and guesthouses — but that didn't seem to generate a lot of wealth for the locals. On the contrary, both poverty and crime were increasing. As the journey progressed, I was learning about the diversity and inequality that made PNG such an interesting and challenging place.

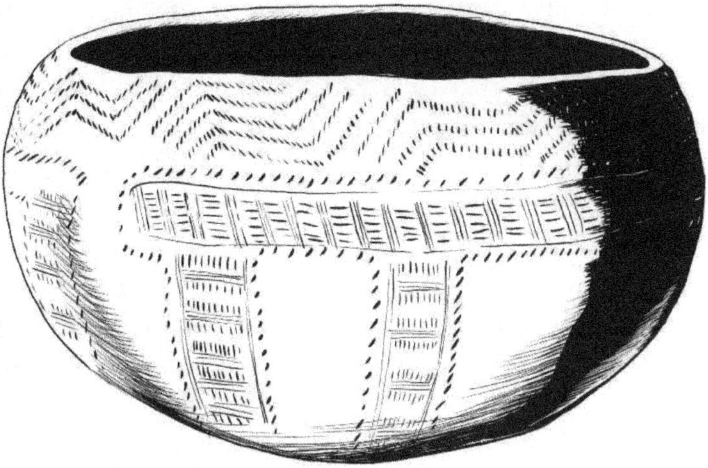

One of the villagers who was engaged in the tourist trade in Tufi was an old lady who I met on my walk. She was sitting in her open hut sewing dry palm leaves together. Her face was tattooed with black stripes running the length of her forehead, chin and cheeks. On closer inspection, I could see that she was making mats. She invited me up on to her platform and showed me how they were crafted. Long broad strips of sago leaves were double layered and sewn together vertically — leaf by leaf — until the mat was about 160 centimetres in length. Then the sides would be cut with a pair of scissors and sewn vertically with a needle and bark twine so that they wouldn't fall apart.

The tools were modern but the materials were ancient. These mats were very different in style from the more stiff and sturdy woven mats you would normally see on the floors of most huts in PNG. They had a lovely smell to them, like fresh dried grass, which gave the whole hut a pleasant earthy aroma. The old lady had lots of interesting things in her hut. Heavily patinated woven baskets with snail houses and shells were hanging from the ceiling. On the floor there were more shells collected in half coconuts. She explained that these were for making necklaces.

By the fireplace, I noticed a bowl-shaped clay pot amongst her aluminium utensils and plastic boxes.

"Do you use this for cooking?" I asked.

She confirmed that this was a traditional cooking pot and then yelled at a young kid who ran off and soon re-appeared with a newly made one, nicely decorated with patterns along the rim. She explained that they sometimes still used such for cooking taro or rice as they made the food smell fragrant.

She said, "When I was a young girl, I carried this one for water." She gestured that she would carry it on her head. I tried to balance the new clay pot on my head without holding it but soon grabbed it again in fear of dropping it. My clowning really cracked her up and she expressed some long '*hi hiiiii*' giggles while patting the clay pot as I held it in my hands.

The old lady told me that she normally sold her mats to tourists. She would charge 10 kina (one kina is about $US 0.30) for the small ones and 20 kina for the larger ones. She explained that they were very warm and could also be used to protect yourself from both the sun and rain. Besides that, they were light and could be folded in the middle and even rolled up. They were really cool. I thought back on the cold night that we had spent in the mangroves. I had felt bad about not providing the crew with proper sleeping kits. Sanakoli used a one-piece orange construction jumpsuit and the other two just had hooded jumpers to sleep in. So, I commissioned three mats to be made.

"Do you think you can have them ready for tomorrow?" I asked her.

"When do you leave?" the old lady wanted to know.

"Early morning" I answered.

She replied, "When I finish, I can take them down to you in the night." That sounded fine to me but then she added, "Or you can come up and give me cash, then I can work fast."

I laughed at her proposition and said, "Okay, so you can work faster if I pay you now?"

"Yes, of course," she answered with a business-like expression on her face. I gave her the 20 kina that I had in my pocket and we agreed she would get the rest when she came down later that evening.

We got up at daybreak and gathered around the warm glowing embers from the fire on the beach. We roasted some green bananas and boiled a pot of rice. Just as I asked if the guys had seen the old lady, she arrived with mats under both her arms and a *bilum*, a traditional woven bag, around her neck. She was very happy to see that we hadn't sailed off yet. The old lady handed Justin and Sanakoli a couple of betel nuts from her *bilum* and explained that she had been up all night working. And, when she was finally finished, she fell asleep straight away. As she woke, she said to herself, "Oh, it's already daybreak. No good, these people already might be sailing off." So, she'd hurried down to the beach. I showed the mats to Sanakoli who gave me an approving nod and, while chewing his *buai* said, "That is the best mat for sailing — rain cannot wet us. When the rains come, we just go inside." He then made a gesture of having a roof above his head and continued. "This is much better than these new woven mats we use in our huts. This is the traditional way." The old lady giggled again, flattered by Sanakoli's recognition. She had even made an extra one for me, which I was thrilled about as I had made a conscious decision to leave my yellow inflatable sleeping mat back in Denmark.

Leaving a safe harbour

Although we had only stayed in the village for two nights, it was an emotional departure. A lot of people gathered on the beach as the crew had made new friends and exchanged contact details and promised to stay in touch. The kids were excited to help push the canoe off as well. I thanked William and his wife for their hospitality and, in return, they both wished us good luck and said we would always be welcome in Tufi. The women gave us concerned looks as they bid us a safe journey.

We got on board and pushed off but no sooner had *Tawali Pasana* departed than a man called us back. A lady came running down along the beach with a large plastic bowl balanced on her shoulder. She handed it over to another guy in the water and he handed it to Justin. The bowl was full of green bananas, taro and a big chunk of sago, which is a lump of dry starch laboriously processed from the sago palm. Justin emptied the bowl and handed it back to the man in the water. Sanakoli pulled the sheet and our sail caught the wind as we waved goodbye.

It was such a beautiful place and such lovely people. We were all touched by their hospitality and kind wishes. But there were other emotions at stake. We had enjoyed a welcome break from the uncertainties of the sea but now we were leaving a safe harbour to undertake a journey into some reportedly very dangerous waters. And not just the sailing conditions. The locals in Tufi had warned us about pirates roaming the waters around the capital of Oro Province — Popondetta — so we were now wary of the serious risks ahead. The plan was to follow the coast of the Tufi Peninsula and then make a crossing of Dyke Ackland Bay and thereby avoid the waters around the towns of Enoro and Pongani which are connected by road to Popondetta. After the crossing, we would hopefully find a village before nightfall. But all this was a worry for later, the weather forecast looked good and the wind was steady, so we steered out of the turquoise shallows and into deep blue sea, leaving a shrinking coastline behind us.

"*Kisooo*!" We had a bite. And then we hooked something big. It was around midday and Job had great difficulty pulling in the line. I excitedly studied the thrashing white silhouette of the beast as it came up from the deep — it was a shark! The crew were all very excited. Justin reached for a bush knife. Although the shark was only a metre in length, it was too dangerous to pull aboard alive. Job was holding both the line and the bush knife trying to *whack* the shark on the head. He made a swing at it, then another. He missed both times. Then Justin took over. He waited patiently, while the shark kept banging into the canoe, biting the air. Finally, the shark was in position and Justin hacked the blade across its spine with a thumping sound. It was still. He pulled it aboard. It looked like a silky shark. It was such a beautiful creature and I felt bad about killing it, especially considering that 80 per cent of the world's shark population has already disappeared and sharks are important for the health and biodiversity of other fish populations. But on the other hand, I wasn't in PNG to impose my Western conservation values. This was life for my crew and they weren't involved with super trawlers and longlines with hundreds of baited hooks. As Sanakoli explained, he would catch sharks, eat the meat, and sell the fins to the Chinese.

Despite all of this, I couldn't help asking Sanakoli if it would be possible to unhook the shark and release it alive. Sanakoli looked at me befuddled and answered with an annoyed tone. "How you want us to get your hook out of its mouth when it is biting everywhere?" Fair enough. From his perspective, there were plenty of sharks in the sea so, of course you'd rather kill the shark than risk losing the expensive lure. Job carried the fish in both arms to the bow and dumped it in the front hull. We threw the line out again and soon hooked a mackerel and later a small barracuda as we passed some offshore reefs. Soon the blood from the dead fish coloured the water in our perpetually-leaking hull. We reeled in the lines and the catch was cooked together with green bananas as we were sailing along. Despite our luck with fishing and the good stay that we had had at Tufi, there was a gloomy mood on board. No doubt the stories of piracy were running through the minds of the crew because they were certainly preoccupying me. I considered whether I should tell the crew of my own experience of crime and seafaring. Although this story may have eased the mood on board, I was hesitant to tell it. I was worried that Job and Sanakoli, with their Christian beliefs, would disapprove of me. Maybe there was also a part of me that wasn't reconciled with my past. So, I kept it to myself.

Thor's story

But I'll tell the story here. It was the start of summer in Denmark. I was about 14 years of age, and one of my best friends, Christian, had bought a small outboard engine from a dodgy character in the southern part of Copenhagen's industrial harbour. We just needed a boat, and then we could cruise around the waterways of Copenhagen all summer. We didn't have any money, so one evening the two of us and another classmate named Gustav got in a car and drove up the north coast, where all the big villas and mansions litter the shoreline.

We were all too young to hold a driver's license but as long as the police didn't stop us we would be fine. About 20 kilometres out of town we parked on a quiet, dark street and walked through a random garden, following a pathway through lush bushes smelling of lilac. We soon reached the beach. It didn't take long before we found what we were looking for. In the bright moonlight an aluminium dinghy was resting on the sand. It even had a set of oars but, unfortunately, it was locked. Luckily, we had brought a set of pliers and with eager hands I slowly cut through the wire bit by bit. With our youthful communist ideals, we didn't have any scruples about stealing this dinghy, as we assumed it belonged to some rich capitalist that easily could afford a new one. We believed what Marx said, 'That all private property is theft,' which of course made us feel fine about being thieves ourselves.

We were strategic by thieving so far up the coast, as we minimised the risk of someone recognising the dinghy in Copenhagen. We collected the outboard motor from the car, together with a jerry can of fuel, some bottles of water and some chicken-flavoured crisps. We packed the dinghy with provisions and pushed the boat out. We used the oars to silently row the dingy well off the coast and then mounted the motor. The plan was to motor the dinghy back to Copenhagen under the cover of night, while smoking joints and munching crisps — it was such a glorious plan and we were so excited.

The houses on the shore looked quite small now and there were no lights to be seen from them. This indicated to us that no one had detected our mischief. Christian pulled the engine cord but nothing happened. He tried again but still nothing. Gustav and I were eager to give it a go, and get out of there but then Christian remembered to turn on the choke. He tried again. Now it sounded like something was happening. After yet another pull, the engine came alive. Success! We congratulated each other with excited but hushed voices and pulled the ores in. It was still dark ashore, no one had heard us.

When we were all ready, my friend turned the accelerator handle and the motor hummed loudly but to our great surprise, nothing happened.

"Turn it some more," I suggested — but again nothing.

"Have you turned off the choke," Gustav asked.

"Yes, everything is good," Christian whispered loudly.

We were all eager to get the hell out of there but the motor just created a lot of noise and bubbles with no propulsion whatsoever. It was still dark in the houses. Gustav and I asked all sorts of agitated questions as to why the thing didn't work but Christian was just as frustrated as we were and said he had no idea. He verified that he had seen the motor work in a big oil drum full of water. Finally, we decided to tilt the engine out of the water and there we made a terrible discovery. The propeller was gone! Apparently, it had fallen off as we started the engine — what a disappointment. The idea of rowing the dingy all the way to Copenhagen was way too laborious a prospect. We cursed the 'capitalist running dog' who had sold us the faulty motor. So, we rowed back in and pulled the dingy back to its original place. Luckily, it seemed like no one had woken up and we carried our things back through the dark garden and drove home to Copenhagen disappointed to have let down Karl Marx.

It was getting late and we were halfway across the bay, which lay wide and flat at the foot of a massive blue mountain range with rows of dreary clouds cascading down its sides. "This is cowboy country," Job said with a stern grimace. And this was true. The area had a bad reputation for lawlessness and there were a lot of weapons around. This can be traced back more than sixty years to the Second World War and the Kokoda Track Campaign, where Japanese forces made landfall in Dyke Ackland Bay on 21 July 1942 with the objective of crossing the Owen Stanley Range to attack Port Moresby on the south coast. Australian soldiers engaged in what was to become a series of bloody jungle battles to defend the then Australian overseas territory. When the Japanese retreated, they abandoned their weapon storage bunkers. Some of these stashes had recently been excavated. This meant that there were *raskols* with-high powered firearms running around robbing people.

As evening fell, we were running a good pace and had already made it halfway across the bay. It was strange grey weather. We started to see the lights from the harbour and the main town further inland. But just as we most needed the wind, it dropped. We had the big sail up, although it was barely holding. Occasionally it would give an insipid flap that, together with the grey hazy weather, just made the whole situation even more eerie. To make things worse, when there was no pull in the sail, I could feel the now waterlogged weight of the outrigger. If you stepped out on it, it would dip in deep. Job would say, "Don't go to the outrigger." I stepped away and it slowly rose again. It seemed like this outrigger needed more than a day of drying in the sun to become properly buoyant. The crew seemed nervous. As we were sitting there, I could see that they were talking about something out in the distance. Suddenly Job said, "Dinghy is coming this way, you get down!"

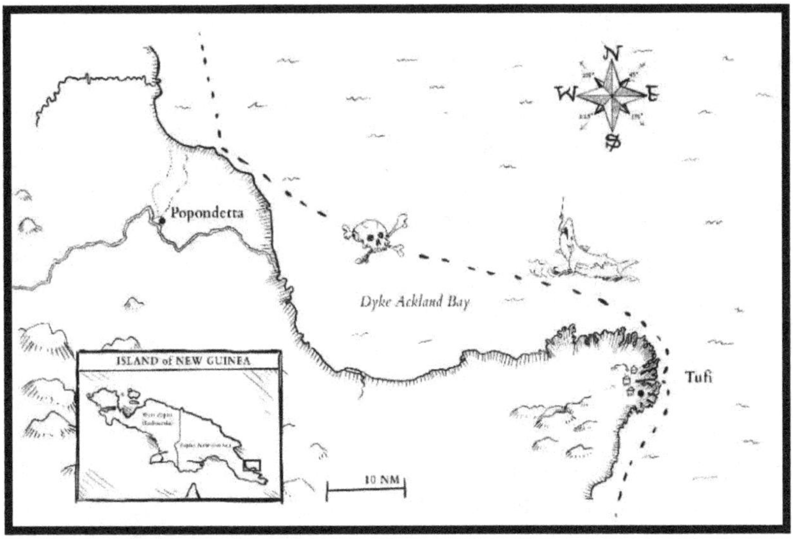

There wasn't much space to hide in our little canoe. The only thing I could do was to lay down flat on my back on the canoe floor, looking up at the limp sail. I could now hear the motor of a dinghy coming towards us. The crew were talking in low, tense voices. I was thinking that I would only be able to hide as long as the dinghy didn't come too close. I wondered what they would do if they saw me and what we would defend ourselves with? We had two bush knives and a long spear and the mace that I was holding firmly in my jacket pocket — not that mace could do much against a machine gun. The motor was running close now and the crew was sitting in silent anticipation. I hoped that the people on the dinghy didn't find the canoe too tempting with all the boxes we had lying on the deck.

The engine noise now sounded closer than ever and I cursed myself for being so naive as to have thought that a sailing canoe would be a discreet way to be travel around the island. These canoes were only seen in Milne Bay and we had left that region on the first day. The rest of the island was now using dinghies so, everywhere we would go, this canoe with its bright colours would be a curious sight. From my coffin-like position I zoomed in on Job's yellow eyeballs. They followed the course of the engine noise as it ran parallel to us and then passed our bow. The three crew all looked in the same direction. It sounded like the dinghy continued its course.

I kept down and listened to the sound of the motor. Was it going away or changing direction again? Sanakoli then popped open his bucket and took out some *buai*.

I whispered loudly to Job, "Hey man, are they gone?"

Job laughed at my question and said: "Yes, yes, they are only fishermen, out fishing. You can come up now."

I took my hand out of my pocket and got up. It was even more foggy now and I could see the suspicious dinghy as a dark shape disappearing into the grey mist. As we were drifting about, several other dinghies were coming and going, some fishing and some seemingly on their way inshore before nightfall. I felt like we were sitting ducks. But none of the others came too close. As the night slowly devoured us, a warm wind started blowing from the mountains and we slowly continued our tack across the bay.

Chapter Five

A sinking outrigger

Sitting in the canoe next to Sanakoli, looking at the black outrigger, I could see green patches of thin seaweed gently swaying as we glided through the waves. There wasn't much wind this morning and the lack of forward motion made the canoe rock wildly. It was clear that the outrigger was waterlogged and becoming a liability. We had already moved our storage boxes and stove into the canoe, and Job had again made it clear that I was not to venture out on to the platform.

I looked at Sanakoli and asked him, "What do you think of the outrigger?" Sanakoli was quiet. I could see Job, who was steering behind him, force an uneasy smile.

Then Sanakoli said with a long, concerned tone, "Oh my head is paining, we want new outrigger. Our outrigger is really heavy and now we have the wind behind so even more weight go to the outrigger."

"It's not too dangerous to go sailing today?" I asked.

Again, there was a long pause. Sanakoli looked up the coast and answered my question with a question of his own. "You say the place you talk about is close by?"

In the same instant, Justin yelled something and quickly untied the rope holding the sail, standing ready to lower it. I asked Sanakoli what was going on.

He warned, "Mountain wind. It's changing around."

We weren't far from the coast, actually in a kind of bend where the mountains of Cape Ward Hunt started to become lowland again. The canoe kept its unhurried but unsteady course, while we waited in suspense. If we got a strong breeze from the wrong side of the sail, then we would most likely tip over as there was almost no buoyancy left in the black outrigger. It was six days since we left Tawali. We spent the previous night in a secluded fishing camp and the night before that we stayed in a dodgy village — neither suitable places for pulling the canoe on land.

It was very unsettling and we were all eager to get to a safe village to dry the outrigger or even cut a new one if we could find the right sort of wood. Sandy Robson had recommended a place called Mambututu where there was a man called Peo who could host us. I had tried to call him several times but with no luck. Still, if everything went well, we would be at Mambututu by the afternoon. The coastal topography flattened more and more, and the beaches became grey and littered with blackened timber. Further inland you could see mountains against a gloomy sky. I enjoyed experiencing this new type of coast, a mixture of swamp and delta. It was a great contrast to the postcard-like beaches of Milne Bay and Tufi. This was the gritty New Guinea few people would ever experience. This was what I had come to see first-hand — the diversity, uniqueness and remoteness of the world's second largest island. Fortunately, the wind seemed to be behaving and, after about fifteen minutes, Justin tied the rope to the mast and support branch and we did a *yaya-towa* and continued up the coast in a slow tempo while looking for signs of a settlement.

We passed some smaller estuaries and noticed a scattering of fishing shelters along the beach. Some were empty and others were occupied by families. We were sailing close enough that we could see the puzzled expressions on the people's faces. Our unexpected arrival had stopped them smoking fish and sorting their nets. It looked like a tough life. Their clothes were holed and their open triangular shelters were built entirely of forest materials, and there weren't any dinghies. A pack of eager emaciated dogs chased us along the beach barking as we sailed past. The people seemed friendly and waved excitedly at us as we waved back.

At around 3 p.m., we came to the entrance to what we assumed to be the Mambututu River. The bright grey sky gave the water an odd greenish-brown colour. Far across the river mouth we noticed some houses behind a row of coconut palms. The outflow had created a large flat sandy shoal where poles were planted to support gill nets. We were struggling to stay clear of the shallows. The current was strong and there wasn't much wind. A man and a child in a canoe were tending to one of the nets. The man waved at us and I yelled back, "Hello, is this Mambututu?" The man confirmed this with a nod of his head and waved us in as he began to move ashore. We had to paddle with all our might to beat the current, only just making it around the sandbank. The man and child gestured us towards a small black river running diagonally to the backside of the dunes.

As we entered the calmer water, I jumped ashore and approached the man. He was in his mid-forties, tall in build with a shaved face and head. He was wearing a rolled up black woollen hat. I presented myself as a Danish adventurer attempting a world record with three

Milne Bay sailors. He introduced himself as Tomas. "Is this Mambututu?" I asked hopefully.

"Yes, the village is on the other side," he replied as he pointed across the river.

"Great," I said, "We are looking for a guy called Peo. Do you know him?"

Tomas nodded eagerly and confirmed with a big smile, "Yes, yes, that is me — that is my other name!" I couldn't believe our luck.

I continued, "Ok, so you were the one that sailed the dinghy for Sandy Robson — the kayak lady?"

Tomas nodded again, "Yes, I was in the dinghy from Lae all the way here. She stayed with me."

"Wow, what a great coincidence," I said excitedly and continued, "So Tomas, do you think that we could stay with you and maybe pull the canoe up on your beach?"

He looked serious but nodded reassuringly, "Yes of course my brother, you come and stay at my place. I am a policeman, so you are very safe in my house. No one will touch your canoe."

The crew and I were thrilled to hear this and all shook his hand. We were relieved by the prospect of getting the canoe on dry land. But first, Tomas suggested that we have a wash in the river as there wasn't much fresh water in the village. I looked into the slow flowing water, which was almost black with tannins, and asked him if there were any crocodiles in there. He smiled and said reassuring, "No, no my brother, no worries, they only come out at night." It had been three days since we'd had a wash in fresh water, so we took the chance — but stayed close to the canoe. Afterwards the sailors changed to their dress shorts and Justin put on a new red T-shirt with PNG graphics on it. I put my dirty clothes back on in an attempt not to look too well off.

After our ablutions, we boarded *Tawali Pasana* and together with Tomas and his son, crossed the great dark Mambututu River. Our two passengers were clearly excited to be on board such a vessel. Tomas told us that he had been working as a police officer in Popondetta. Now he had returned to look after his land because his parents were getting old. His dream was to attract more tourists to his village and build a guesthouse. He told me that the village had hosted a national game fishing event one year as there was good fishing for Papuan Black Bass — a sought-after game fish renowned for its ferocious strike and strong fight. He was hoping that more fishermen would come but so far there hadn't been any.

We landed the canoe directly in front of Tomas' house. Most of the villagers had seen us from afar and were now gathering around the canoe, inspecting it and asking questions, while kids were jumping and playing excitedly in the water. When they heard that the sailors were from Milne Bay, they eagerly confirmed that there was a man from Milne Bay in the village who was married to a local woman. The sailors seemed pleased to hear this, especially Justin and Sanakoli, as everyone was giving them betel nut to chew. When the commotion eased, some of the villagers helped pull the canoe up on the beach. Although there were about fifteen adults involved, it still felt like hard going. When well above the high-water mark, we lifted the outrigger while Sanakoli and a few boys stuck small logs underneath so that it could rest with air circulating under it.

Mambututu seemed to be divided into two villages and Tomas' family had their land positioned in the middle of the two settlements. Tomas' land consisted of three traditional huts and two large low-lying and open-sided platforms with a thatched roof on top. A small brim of bushes and a low fence divided the beach and the land, and behind the houses, the jungle began with coconut trees planted amongst other tall trees.

Tomas introduced me to his parents who appeared to be in their 60s. Tomas presented his father as, "The great Chief of the land." His father was a nimble, friendly man with short, grey, curly hair and black freckles spread across his wrinkled face. He had grey, slightly-crossed eyes, giving the impression of weather-beaten innocence. Tomas's mother seemed younger than her husband and was stouter. She had a wide nose and square jaw with a friendly smile and two enormous front teeth that had such a gap between them that one could speculate that she might be missing a tooth or two — or three. They both greeted me, and I told them that I was honoured we could stay on their land and that we were grateful for their help.

The couple suggested that we take all our things out of the canoe and bring them up to one of the open huts. They said that the crew could lodge there and that I would sleep in a room in Tomas' brother's hut on one-and-a-half-metre high stilts. Tomas guided me up a stairway and inside the hut. On the wall there were some faded election posters and a bundle of clothes and rags. Tomas gave me the first room, which didn't have a door but a curtain hanging in front of it. On the floor, there was an old thin mattress. There were no windows and, of course, no electric light but the room was well lit from all the cracks in the walls and a solitary window in the corridor. To some, this might seem like very basic accommodation but for me this was luxury. I was thrilled to get a room to myself out of the black sand and away from prying eyes. Here I would have a chance to get my batteries out and charge the cameras, but most importantly, backup the filming from the last three days.

Now it was a good time to negotiate a price. It was clear from my earlier conversations with Tomas that the fishing tournament with its outside visitors had given him high expectations of the income he could gain by hosting a tourist like me. This worried me a great deal. I only had 350 kina in cash left and we had at least four days of travel to reach Lae, PNG's second largest city. I emphasised that we were on a tight budget and had very little money left to pay for accommodation but in return I offered to draft a tourism plan for him. He seemed to accept this, and we negotiated three days for 200 kina — a high price. But I was also cautious about not ruining the cordial atmosphere, and the deal still left me with 100 kina to pay for a tree for a new outrigger — and 50 kina for provisions. We also agreed that we would share food.

I had suggested that we would cook for ourselves, "Not to put too great a workload on his family" — but the real reason was that we had just enough rations to sustain ourselves to Lae.

But my feeble excuse was gallantly put aside with Tomas emphatically declaring, "No we can't do that. You are our guests. We all eat together."

I could do nothing but gratefully accept their custom and shake hands. As I unpacked my things, it also occurred to me that the family was enjoying the prestige of hosting outside visitors and it would probably make them look bad if they didn't feed their guests.

That same night, we all had dinner together in the big open hut. The women had created a menagerie of colourful metal plates and bowls — one with boiled tubers, another with boiled sago wrapped in leaves, and yet another with noodle soup and boiled rice, complete with a little plate of fried fish. I had suspended a torch from the ceiling and the crew and I were sitting cross-legged in a circle together with the Chief and Tomas. The Chief had been a Christian Pastor most of his life. He lowered his head and began, "Let us all pray." We bowed our heads and folded our hands while the Chief said a prayer in his nimble raspy voice. We all ladled healthy portions on to our plates. It still amazed me what enormous portions the sailors could eat, and Tomas — who was a large man — served himself likewise. But what surprised me even more was that the old Chief served himself the biggest portion of all.

We all ate with a great appetite, although I ran into a speed bump with one of those sago things wrapped in a palm leaf. Sago is basically starch from the trunk of the Sago Palm. It is derived through a laborious and time-consuming process. First, the men will fell the rock-hard spiky tree trunk and 'beat' the insides in to a pulp. Afterwards, the women will scrape the inside 'meat' out and squeeze it until the sap runs. The liquid is then collected in a fine mesh bag and turned into starch. When dried, it has a 'funny' texture — at least for a Danish palate — kind of like flour but with dry chunks. When it is boiled it becomes gooey and, if it is heated over a fire, it becomes hard but with the centre retaining its chalk-like texture, which can make you gag unless you have plenty of fluid to flush it down with. After choking on a dry clump of sago, I tried my best to avoid it altogether.

Over dinner we told Tomas and the Chief about our voyage and the associated perils. The Chief said that, "God must be looking after you." I am not religious but I agreed with him and mentioned the good fortune we had arriving into Tufi, looking for William, only to find that it was his beach we had landed on. And now we arrived in Mambututu and the first person we met was the person we were looking for: Peo — or Tomas. The Chief nodded knowingly. Tomas asked if we wanted any more. We all replied that we were full and grateful. This was the old Chief's cue to scoop up the remaining rice and noodles as well as the last piece of fish, devouring it all with near-miraculous determination and speed.

As I came down the steps the next morning, I met Tomas. He looked rough. His eyes were red and swollen. "How are you doing Tomas, are you all right?" I enquired with concern.

"Yes, thank you but I have been up all night looking after you and your canoe," he replied.

"So, you haven't had any sleep?" I said a little surprised.

"No, you are my guest, I must protect you as long as you stay in my house," he explained. I felt a bit bad for Tomas but also appreciated his concern and suggested that he and his brother at least took turns. He said, "No, I must do it. That is our custom." I then went to see to the sailors. They had all slept well and seemed happy in their hut. I was a bit worried that they might feel it was unfair that I had been accommodated in my own room but to them, it seemed obvious that I should be billeted in this way and perhaps they were actually relieved to have the *dim dim* kept safe for the night.

Tomas and I had a long program planned for the day, starting with going to the morning garden food market, which was only held two times a week in the northern end of the village. Then Tomas was to give me a tour around the whole village. After lunch I had planned a meeting with the crew, then I was going to help Tomas with a tourism plan. After dinner I wanted to show one of my kayaking films on the laptop. However, most of all, I had just wanted 'a day off' but I was also eager to get my camera out and film some real village life.

The southern part of Mambututu village was very lush. As we entered the area all the villagers started echoing, "*Oro, oro, oro, oro,*" in a continuous rhythm. Tomas explained that *oro* means 'welcome' in their language — and this is why the whole province was called Oro, I guess. It was a very pleasant way of being greeted, as it wasn't just individuals who told you that you were welcome but the entire village. For an outsider, it also gave the impression of social unity. I responded with, "*Sipo dave,*" as Tomas had taught me, which means 'good morning' in the local Binandere language. This seemed to please everyone and also triggered some giggles.

I felt like a novelty as I was shown around by Tomas. Most of the villagers came out of their houses and took my hand with both of their hands and shook them firmly while we both bowed making sure to avoid eye contact. I greeted a couple of middle-aged women in long, colourful, floral dresses. I noticed that they both had tattoos on their right arms.

I asked Tomas if it meant something.

He explained, "It is a tattoo — just for decoration. I can make you one."

I said laughing, "Maybe not, let me think about it."

He responded in a matter of fact tone, "Okay, it is very painful."

We passed an extraordinarily long house on stilts. Tomas explained, "This is the young boys house. This is where the boys stay until they get married. The young girls will stay with their families but the boys must stay in this house. If the young boys stay with their family, they will get old without getting married." I later learned that these houses were called *oro,* just like the greeting, but said with a different pronunciation.

The rule was that there must always be a fire burning outside the *oro* every night. The young boys would put out mats, called *taro,* and old wise men would come and sit by the fire and share knowledge about customs and their traditional way of life. When a young man got married, his clan would help him build his own house where he and his wife would live. It was interesting to think of the great differences in culture between myself and these men. I was 35 years old and living as a bachelor in my flat in Copenhagen. I never had a desire to settle down and get married, as this seemed like a great restriction. But to these young men, getting married probably meant more opportunity and higher social status. With a woman, they would be able to build their house, grow a garden and start their own family.

The Magistrate

We continued down to a backchannel that was running behind the village and were greeted by a group of men standing together with a couple of women. The scene that played out puzzled me. A man with a shaved head presented himself as a 'Magistrate' and said in a sort of jesting but authoritarian tone, "This is a surprise visit, did you have any contact?"

I smiled and answered, "Yes, it is a bit of a surprise. I had a phone number but nobody responded. I think you don't have a lot of phone coverage here?"

"Yes, yes," the group agreed in unison as I continued.

"So, we had to try and find it. But the first person we meet was…" and I pointed at Tomas and continued, "What a lucky coincidence! Because you know I know Sandy Robson the kayak lady."

"Yes, she came and slept with me," the Magistrate said with great eagerness.

"Ah, really …" I said, trying to disguise my surprise.

"Yes, she stayed in my house and she told me that you were coming."

"Really?" I said as I tilted my head sideways.

The Magistrate continued, "Did she give you the contact?" I started to feel like I was being interrogated. Something wasn't quite right.

I answered, "Yes, she wrote on a map. Go to Mambututu and call this number." I didn't want to mention the name Peo as I felt that this could result in trouble for him.

The Magistrate shook his head. "You send text!"

"Text?" I asked for clarification.

"Yes, you send a text! Wake up! Are you back in year 2000 now or even the 1990s?" the Magistrate continued menacingly. The bystanders all laughed, and he shook his head with an expression of feigned grievance.

The Magistrate continued in his half-blaming, half-humorous tone. "There was supposed to be people in traditional clothes welcoming you and saying welcome. Thor, you missed out."

The bystanders all laughed and I gestured that he was right and apologetically replied, "Yeah but I am here to learn about your culture and your customs and now I am learning about texting as well." They all laughed again, and the Magistrate shook my hand. This seemed to ease the tension.

I said that the *oro oro* welcome had been very touching and we had been made to feel welcome. "Ohh Thor, it had been much, much better if we had known you had come," the Magistrate droned on.

I was getting a bit tired of his whole repetitive argument and tried to seal it off in a diplomatic manner by saying, "Yes, we can't change the past but we can work towards the future."

The magistrate agreed and said, "Anyway Thor, my name is Ishmael Peo and I'm the Magistrate in this village and I was very upset that you were very silent about coming. I hope that you accept that."

"Yes, and I hope that you accept that I came in silence," I said with an apologetic, disarming smile.

"I am doing that right now," he said, and we gave each other a hug.

A first meeting with the crew

After lunch, the crew and I gathered in a second open hut further away from other houses to have a private meeting. The crew had spent the morning with the man from Milne Bay, trying to figure out if the right type of tree to craft an outrigger was to be found in this area. Now they were sitting in a line with their backs up against a plank of wood — Sanakoli in his old green polo shirt, Job wearing my white cap with a thin wool shirt that I had given him and Justin with his green towel over his left shoulder. None of them seemed very comfortable. I was busy installing my two cameras and an audio device to record the meeting. When all was in place, we could get started.

"The reason I have called for this first weekly meeting is so that we can talk about what's going to happen next week and what has happened in the previous week. We can also talk about things we can do better or things that annoy us. Because we are going to be together for many months in a small canoe, we might build up some tensions."

Sanakoli smiled at this and said, "Yeerh."

I continued. "So, I think it's a good idea to have these meetings so everyone can voice their concerns. Does this sound like a good idea?" I unfolded my notebook with a list of bullet points.

Job was looking up at the ceiling, Justin was looking at Sanakoli, and Sanakoli looked at my book and said "Yes, it sounds like a good idea."

"Should we start talking about the outrigger? What do you think we can do?" They were all sitting in silence. I continued, "So what do you all think? Tomas is fine with us staying until the day after tomorrow, so that gives the outrigger two days to dry. How dry will the outrigger become?

It looked like they were all thinking, then Sanakoli took the initiative, "It depends on the weather. If suns shining its going dry quickly. But if raining you know it's wet. The sun is shining today. So, let's see tomorrow." There was a pause, "But for the new outrigger we can't succeed for new outrigger, because the trees are different from what we want."

I thought for a few long seconds and looked up, "So we might risk that we can't find a proper tree… also further up on this trip?"

"Yeerh," Sanakoli pipped up. Justin who now had turned towards me grunted and nodded. This was of course a big problem that I hadn't seen coming. What if this tree we needed only grew in the Milne Bay area and we couldn't find another with the same properties? Then we would be in real trouble.

We talked about if it was possible to make one out of fiberglass, or if they knew of another type of wood we could use. I then suggested an idea that I had raised before. "But what if we suspend the outrigger over some hot rocks or embers, then maybe we could dry it out quicker? Sanakoli's face turned into one enormous embarrassed grimace and even Job and Justin were smirking and shifting the weight off their seats. I continued, "But guys, I am just thinking solutions here. Don't you think it could work?" Sanakoli said something to Job in their language while half laughing. Then they all smiled to themselves and Sanakoli said, "Yes but it looks funny to us. That's why we are laughing away." And with that, they all sat giggling shyly to themselves. Sanakoli was the first to speak, "Because you will make fire along the outrigger and be drying it like ... fish… he he he."

I tried to hide my frustration and said, "But I am just trying to find solutions, as many as possible. And we have to do something."

"Yes, Yes," Sanakoli agreed and nodded. Then there was a pause and we at least agreed that the crew would go on a walk into the bush to see if they could possibly find the right sort of tree and, if not, then we would have to continue with the old outrigger and put it on land to dry every time it became too heavy.

We then talked about arriving into new villages. We agreed we would aim to always arrive in daylight and always leave our sleeping kit and food for dinner and breakfast ready. I corrected the camera and then Job finally spoke. He was clearly agitated, "When people they see white people, they say money, and when they see that," he nodded at the camera and continued, "and all the expensive things, they will think, 'we can sell that and get big money.'" Sanakoli agreed.

"Just to remind you," Job said and looked at me seriously.

I nodded, "Yes I am aware of that but I am also making a film and I have to take that camera out sometimes and film."

"Yes, that's the one," Job's eyes opened, and he excitedly pointed at me.

"I just remind you that they will see it and come and take it and what can we do?" Job repeated.

I didn't like to be reminded of the obvious risks and tried to manage the annoyance in my tone of voice. "Yes, if they do that, then that's how it is. I have already said goodbye to my camera and I have already said goodbye to my laptop. I have already said goodbye to everything." They all laughed heartily. It clearly appealed to their fatalistic sense of humour. I smiled in reconciliation. "So, if the *raskols* take it, then that's how it all is. What's important to me is that we are all safe."

They giggled nervously, and Job said with a serious smile, "Yes but I don't want them to…" he made a pistol shooting motion to his leg, "One leg down and I can't work garden. I got kids. When *raskols* come they are *gonna* shoot us. What can we say?" He pulled his shoulders up and showed the rough palms of his hands, "If we say 'oh, oh like this' bush knife will cut us." Job made a cutting motion with his hand across his neck. "We are scared, and we are three men. One thing is important that we are not scared. So, if it's God's will, we are safe."

I nodded and said, "I think it is a good way to see it. If it is God's will it happens but until then, we should hope for the best."

We moved on to other topics such as me not falling off the canoe and firewood and water. I also asked them to engage me more in the actual sailing when they thought it would be safe. Job complained about the colourful bag that we were using for our lifejackets. I didn't understand why this was a problem and he explained, "When they see this big colour bag, they think… 'ahhh… good things inside'." It was hard for me to understand that these bags could look valuable.

Job seemed frustrated that I didn't get this point and ploughed on excitedly, "I am not concerned about me. I am concerned about you. You are a white man."

I was agitated that he would bring up these gloomy predictions again and I answered, "I knew that when I came to PNG. I knew I was going to a dangerous place!"

Job continued in a sharp hushed voice looking down. "I know how people act. They come, and they cut us. They shoot us, and we die. It is not safe. I know how Papua New Guinea people do."

Job's predictions made me very uneasy but I had to dispel the mood before it festered in all of us. I quickly said, in a more comforting and reasoning tone, "But so far we have been lucky, and people have been very nice."

"Yes, thanks God's plan," Job added with an earnest expression.

I continued, "And this next stretch they have sea police. They have police going by motorboat, patrolling and shooting *raskols*. So, Tomas says it's quite safe."

"This side?" Sanakoli asked and pointed in our sailing direction.

"Yes. And they are patrolling up here in Morobe and all the way up to Lae, so we will definitely meet them." The crew nodded and seemed to agree on this. I ended the meeting by asking them if they had any preferences for the food and if there was something they thought we were missing or if there was something they didn't like.

They sat in silence for a while and then Justin said something to Sanakoli in *Bwana Bwana*.

"Ohh," Sanakoli said and laughed, "Justin says, tell him to get rice and biscuits!" And we all laughed, except Job who had pulled his legs back up under his chin. He seemed like he had already left the conversation.

I thought it had been a productive meeting. I hoped that we all felt a bit more like a team cooperating on mutually set goals. Job's sharp preoccupation with robbery and death had tied off a knot of uneasiness that had been growing in my stomach since we departed from Tawali. But there was no time to think of this now. I had promised Tomas that I would help him with a plan on how to start a business in tourism. And then I was going to show one of my kayak films. It was a lot of work being in a village. I couldn't wait until I was back in my room under the mosquito net — away from people.

Chapter Six

A missing Magistrate

The next morning, we went into the bush; we were looking for a tree to use for the new outrigger but there was no sign of the type of we were looking for so, after a couple of hours roaming around in the backland of the village, we gave up. I was worried that this tree might only be found in the Milne Bay area. We could have launched a longer expedition into the interior but then we would have had to pull the whole tree trunk back to the beach, so we decided to try our luck on our route up along the coast.

On the way back, I told Tomas about my idea of having the canoe decorated with traditional motifs. I asked if he knew of a skilled wood carver or painter that could fashion a traditional Mambututu design on the canoe — maybe the *tapa* cloth design that his people were known for? Tomas assured me that he knew the man for the job — if I could just supply the paint. That pleased me. We hadn't acquired any designs on the canoe yet except a Milne Bay flower and a butterfly (the symbol of Oro Province) crudely cut by a teenager in a fishing camp.

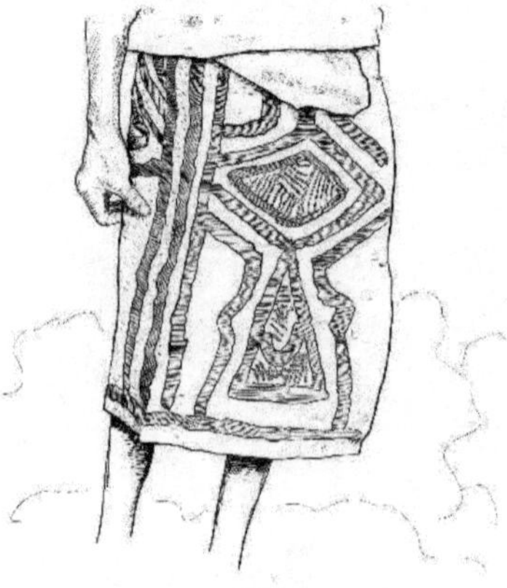

After lunch, Tomas unexpectedly came into my room. I had all my electronics laying around charging and he clearly looked fascinated by what he saw. It really was a lot of valuable items to be carrying around, even for Tomas who had been working as a policeman in Popondetta, so I explained to him, "Sorry that there's so much stuff. Most of it is not mine but things that people have sponsored so we can make a good film."

Tomas shook his head with a troubled expression. "Oh Thor, when I saw all your things, I was thinking 'has he left his house and brought all his things with him.'" He wanted to negotiate payment for the *sing sing* (a traditional dance in Papua New Guinea — the purpose and type of dance varies from tribe to tribe). I only wanted them to do a *sing sing* for us because they wanted to or because their custom called for it. But to back out now would be rude, so we agreed that the dance group would get my last 100 kina note and some small gifts. I pulled my gift bag out of one of the blue barrels and poured the contents onto the floor. I had already given a lot away — like a piece of amber embossed in silver with a ring for a necklace. I had given that piece to Job's mother who got so excited that she asked her husband to sew it onto her chest. But there was still something left of my knife collection together with several packages of ukulele strings.

Tomas was fascinated by the knives. I realised that all this stuff must have looked like a treasure trove and I immediately regretted showing him. I said that he could pick a knife and a bag of strings.

He handled the knives several times and then said, "Maybe I take two, for the group?" I realised that with all the knives out I couldn't tell him to only have one, so he selected one for himself, which was a lock back folding knife with a handle made of brass and dark hardwood, and another knife of similar design.

Sing Sing party

It was late afternoon when the *sing sing* group finally arrived. I had been prepared for a while with my camera set on a tripod while looking to the grey skies hoping it wouldn't rain. There were ten people all in their 40s and 50s gathered and ready. I asked Tomas if there were no young people interested in the *sing sing* and he said that they were all busy elsewhere. The dancers were beautifully outfitted in customary ornaments. On their heads, they were wearing clusters of feathers from the white cockatoo and different species of lorikeet.

Both men and women had bare chests with necklaces — especially the women who had garlands of shells draped across their naked upper bodies. On their arms and ankles and waists the dancers had tied green palm fronds. This was completed by a type of belt embellished with seashells and a *tapa* cloth (a fabric-like bark, light in colour with traditional designs painted with red dye from a special leaf), which is unique to Oro Province. Some of the dancers were holding wooden carved *kundu* drums, a traditional instrument that varies in size around New Guinea, but the hour-glass shape is always the same, wide at the ends and slim in the middle with one end covered in stretched goanna skin. Some of the men were holding long spear-like sticks decorated with feathers on both ends.

After a bit of coordination, the ceremony began. There wasn't much singing, mostly drumming and dancing in the form of a shifting formation back and forth while raising and lowering their backs with high knee lifts made in a repetitive movement, while the tall feathers in their headdresses swayed up and down. After ten minutes, the dance was over and there was bit of a standstill. Then Tomas's mother took the stage and said, "Thor, thank you for taking a photograph and being with us today and seeing our culture dance." Then she added that one day they hoped that they could visit me, "There," and she pointed in an upwards direction in an approximation of where she believed Denmark was.

I complimented them for being such good hosts. I thought they had great potential and I wanted to help them achieve this but their biggest challenge was to find someone who could bring tourists to their village. They all said thank you and then Tomas' mother gave me a white necklace made of carved corals with some black rings which she tied around my neck. I presented them with my remaining guitar strings and two knives. They seemed happy with this and we shook hands again. Later, as I was packing up, Tomas came back and said, "Thank you for putting my mother's culture group on the internet."

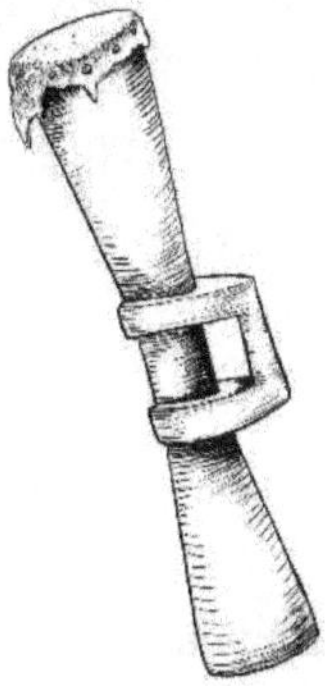

After dinner, I went to my room to charge my equipment and backup the latest recordings. I was tired from a day of filming and socialising. It was hard having to be 'on' all the time — being polite and interested in all the people who wanted to talk to you, especially because I am a rather introverted person. But it wasn't long before Tomas called on me again. I assumed he wanted some more paracetamol for his mother. I was cursing to myself while thinking of all the people I had already supplied and that we would have to restock soon. But as I came down the stairs, a group of men arrived. They were standing in the blue light of a LED torch and they all looked serious.

The wind was funnelling between the dark stilted huts as the group of village leaders told me that the Magistrate had gone out in his canoe the previous evening and that they feared he had been blown out to sea as he had been missing for more than 24 hours. So, they wanted to know if I could use my GPS to find him. This story gave me an eerie feeling. The tops of the coconut trees were rattling now and this wind would be much stronger out on the water. I told them that I was very sorry to hear this but explained that the GPS couldn't find people, rather it was something you used to know your own location and navigate to already fixed positions.

I asked if they had sea rescue authorities in Popondetta. Tomas thought for a bit and said that there might be but he didn't have their telephone number. He explained that the rescue efforts the village had set in place were to send two boys by foot up the coast to another village to ask to use their dinghy for the search. I asked how long this walk would take and Tomas said, "They'll be there by morning."

I was rather tormented by this new knowledge and in some considerable doubt about how I should engage in the search party. I couldn't make any calls through my satellite device as it was linked to my iPhone that was now corroded and useless. We could push *Tawali Pasana* out and go looking for him but going out in the night would be like finding a needle in a haystack and the weather wasn't good. I concluded that it was too risky, and we had trouble enough already ourselves and we were only nine days into the expedition. So, I went back to packing my things and had an uneasy sleep.

Sailing out

I got up at first light and found Tomas half asleep against one of the stilts under the house. He woke with a surprised jerk as I passed him.

"Good morning," I greeted him back. I was happy for him that he would finally be able to get some proper sleep when we were gone. The crew were up already and I could see Sanakoli walking quickly up the beach towards the hut. It looked like he had been down at the canoe. When he came closer, I could tell he wasn't happy.

"Thor, have you seen how they have spoiled our canoe?"

I replied that I hadn't.

Sanakoli continued very excitedly, "It looks like children have painted their graffiti, like they do on back of the shops in Alotau." I was surprised, as Tomas had sounded like he had an expert artisan at hand. We took a couple of bags each and walked down to investigate.

Even from a distance you could see the new 'art' that covered almost half the side of our canoe. Sanakoli had been very accurate in his description. Black block letters spelled out: 'Mambututu, Oro Province,' and then someone had made a simple motif that I guessed was a *tapa* cloth pattern, although it had none of the charm or integrity of the ones I had seen on the dancers the day before. In short, it was sloppy work. It looked terrible and did nothing to honour the ancient traditions of the *tapa* design or Mambututu in general. I was disappointed, but I didn't have enough energy left to deal with it now. So, I told Sanakoli that we would paint it over as soon as we arrived in the next village. This seemed to ease Sanakoli's temper and we got on with packing of the canoe.

When the canoe was provisioned, we had our breakfast of buns and tea. While eating, I noticed one of Tomas' young sons hacking purposelessly into a muddy log with one of the knifes I had given to the culture group. As we were eating, more and more people gathered by the canoe to see us off. Some of the women had brought us bananas and taro and the man from Milne Bay presented Justin with a wide brimmed hat woven in palm fibre. The men from the Counsel were there as well. They told me that the dinghy was now out at sea looking for the Magistrate and that they had been in contact with some of his family members who had advised the authorities. I told them that we would, of course, keep a look out for the Magistrate as well. The villagers wished us a safe journey as we paddled the canoe out in to the current of the great river.

The outrigger was rising and sinking out of the greenish brown sea but the algae had been scraped off and now it seemed to be floating more than sinking. I was happy to be out on the water again, away from people. It was hard work having to navigate the odd dynamic of 'being a guest' from the richest part of the world; but that was what I had chosen to do and that was probably how it would be for the next six months. I was also becoming concerned about the cost of staying in villages. We had come to Mambututu with 350 kina and left with 20 kina, three bags of rice, a hand of ripe bananas and a lump of sago bread — all of which might last three to four days, until we reached Lae. And, hopefully, we would be catching some fish.

Around midday, we ate. We were joking about how much food the old Chief could eat and Sanakoli said laughing to me, "Yes, I was looking at him eating, eating, and then I looked at you and your eyes were big, just looking at him." I laughed as well and said,

"Yeah man, I almost got a bit sad that he didn't want to share with his grandchildren." We all laughed again. But then we came to talk about the missing Magistrate. This put a dampener on the mood, maybe also because it reminded us of how fragile and alone we were, when out at sea. But there was more to it than that.

Then Job laid out the whole truth about our stay. He said, "Your man Tomas wasn't telling the truth. It was the Magistrate, Peo, Sandy stayed with, not Tomas. It was the Peo who followed her in a dinghy from Lae."

"How do you know all this?" I said with surprise.

"Our uncle from Milne Bay told us. If you had stayed with Peo in the big village, then you would have a big *sing sing*. Those people you stayed with, they operate for themselves, they don't share with the big village." I looked with a puzzled expression at Job and then at the others.

I asked Job, "If you knew this why didn't you tell me sooner?" Job didn't answer but just looked at the rocking outrigger. Sanakoli and Justin also sat in silence. I shook my head in frustration. "Hey you guys, next time you find out something is up then please tell me, OK?"

I was disappointed that the sailors hadn't shared this with me earlier. Obviously, there was little feeling of brotherhood amongst us. But I was most angry with myself and my naivety. I had let Tomas fool me. After that meeting with Peo the Magistrate, I had a strong suspicion that Tomas was having me on but all our things were in his house, so I had just ignored it. I had a pretty good idea of what the crew thought; you wouldn't have had to spend much time in a Papua New Guinean village to know that there wouldn't have been any accidents if we had stayed with the right host.

Chapter Seven

Who's steering the canoe?

It was late afternoon. We had made good progress since we left Mambututu but our plans of making landfall before dusk were not looking great. We were at least five nautical miles off the coast, which was blocked from us by a fringe of steep rocky islands and shallow reefs. Somewhere behind those islands was the village of Bosade where Tomas had a given us a contact — but to make matters more difficult, the sun was setting and the wind had dropped.

We had two options: should we continue outward and north around the largest of the islands named Mindrugutu and then tack back towards Bosade or sail down through the smaller islands and reefs east of our destination. I looked out at the point. There were some big seas out there and we had almost no wind. We all looked at the maps and tried to figure out what to do. One of the crew suggested to paddle down through a gap between the steep cliffs of Mindrugutu Island and a smaller neighbouring island. We could see a breaking swell (probably from a reef running between the islands) but it looked like the fastest way to get in to the coast — so we lowered the sail and started paddling. It was hard work. We felt the reflecting swells from

Mindrugutu rocking the canoe. I looked up and could see the cliffs and the black jungle above.

The air was thick with high pitched screeches. The treetops were alive. It looked like the canopy was dissolving into a thousand black dots fluttering upwards and into the graphite sky. It was a huge colony of fruit bats flapping towards the coast to spend the night in the treetops of the dark interior, feeding on fruit and drinking nectar from flowering trees. The colours of the day had disappeared as we neared the passage but the white foam of the break looked more daunting and dangerous than ever.

I asked the crew, "Are you guys sure about this? Those breakers look quite big for us to pass through." There was silence. The wind had started blowing from the mountains and I turned around looking at them and asked, "What about we hoist the sail and tack back towards where we came from and then sail into the coast from there?" The was still silence. And then the men started discussing it amongst themselves in one of their languages. It seemed that they really couldn't agree. I looked at the white foaming breakers in front of us and said, "Hey, let's take the safe option and sail back and around." The men discussed this for a minute more and then they pulled in the paddles and turned the sail.

As soon as we had made a little distance towards Mindrugutu, the canoe got up to speed and the outrigger started skating on the waves. There was no moon and now it was hard to distinguish the sea from the horizon. The only firm objects were the black silhouettes of the islands in front of us. We were quickly passing one island after the other. Then we started to make our way in between them and some low-lying reefs. We spotted a tiny white light marking the entrance to Morobe Bay, an old station that was once the administrative headquarters of German New Guinea.

The mountain winds were blowing with force now and Justin was talking in an agitated voice from the back end where he was steering. It was almost pitch black and we were running in between reefs and rock islands. The reef was giving way to white foam. Some of the lower lying coral heads could only be detected when we were harrowingly close. I wished we could slow the speed of the canoe; this was like navigating a maze of potentially devastating corals and rocks at high speed. It was pointless trying to use a good torch either, as the beam would only reach what was immediately in front of us and ruin our night vision.

I was sitting in the canoe clinging to a rope with one hand while fumbling with my waterproof torch in the other. If we were going to flounder, or if I was to fall overboard, then I wanted to make sure my light was working. Job was standing by the mast pointing out obstructions and reporting them back to Justin as we were flying along. I started to doubt my decision of taking this route and thought that the crew might have had a better idea. After a terrifying 20 minutes, we had made it inside the reef and the sea immediately became deeper and calmer. We tacked and ran up along the coast in good speed now that we were safe inside the islands. After a couple of hours and a rain shower, we made landfall at Bosade, where we found Tomas' friend — who was drunk.

The morning came with a clear sky and the sea was easy. The bad first impression from the night before had evaporated and we had the loveliest morning in the village. Bosade serves as a rest hub for coastal dinghies travelling to and from Lae, as there is no road. A dinghy operator told me that they always try to sail in pairs or small conveys to avoid piracy. The betel nut sellers transporting sacks of *buai* for the market in Lae were at the greatest risk — as this 'essential' commodity doubles or sometimes triples in price when they are sold in the big city. And, if the *buai* merchants didn't get robbed on the way, they would still risk being robbed when returning to their villages with thousands of kina in their pockets. When I asked the operator about police patrols along the coast he said, "We never see them."

Expedition Log 9 September 2016

> 10:30 hrs. 10 knots of wind. Speed 3-4 knots. I have already had to hide from two curious dinghies.

Mid-afternoon, we passed the northernmost point of the greatest of the coastal islands, Lasanga. I knew there was a larger village on the island but I'd had enough of people and villages and the wind pushed us over to the smaller island of Zumbale. We agreed that we would try and find a place to camp there. I was dreaming about finding a fishing-camp or maybe even a deserted beach. A big turtle dived as we turned towards the northern point of Zumbale. On the other side of the point we noticed something strange. A big blue metal frame was lying half submerged up against the rocky coast. We continued further down the coast and saw another large elongated white metal frame perched on a sandbar in front of the island.

We crossed through some small breakers and found ourselves on a wide flat coral reef that connected the sandbar to the island. The rocky shore slowly transformed into a palm-fringed beach — again with an odd structure on it. The light was rapidly dying as we made landfall. Next to the odd structure we could now see what was a decently build hut with a metal roof. We had found a fishing camp — and it was empty!

The fine-grained sand slipped under our barefoot soles as we pulled the canoe as far up as we could and then tied it off to a coconut palm. Then I had a look at the beach. It was everything I had wished for — deserted, beautiful, with even a good roof to sleep under. Sanakoli had already started a fire. We went to the canoe and pulled out a bag of rice together with our plates and cups and the lunchbox with a sparse selection of day-snacks, cordial and tea.

The crew were very happy with the place as well. Job had inspected the house and came back and said with a content smile, "This is a very good house. I will make bed here tonight." The fire was cracking as the rice started to boil. We were sipping on our cups of tea while watching the blood-red sky colour the sandbar and its brilliant white metal frame in salmon pink. This was a real camping experience with my crew, away from the crowded village and curious looks — away from drunkards, mangy dogs, crowing roosters and crying babies. Now we all had a chance to relax and just enjoy each other's company. This was the way I had envisioned our evenings together would be. The evening air was warm and the swell rolled lazily, bubbling onto the shore, gently sieving the course purple sand. I blew the steam off the tea and smiled to myself.

We all just sat there in silence taking in the evening atmosphere, when suddenly, Sanakoli broke the spell with a low hushed voice, "Somebody's coming!" We all stood up and saw the silhouettes of two small outrigger canoes paddling around the beach. I went to the canoe to pack my camera away and put my GPS in my pocket. Justin had the big bush knife by the fire and I pulled out our smaller knife and had it laying ready in the canoe. I sat down to anticipate the arrival. I was weary but felt more annoyed than anything, 'Why couldn't we have just one bloody night to ourselves!'

A few minutes later the canoes made landfall. It was two young men, both less than 20 years old. They were astounded to see a white man but very friendly and excited. We all shook hands and I politely explained who we were and where we were going. The one who spoke the most was named Kim. He was wearing a green rugby shirt, denim shorts and had a beard. He explained that this was his island as he was son of the Chief in Buso village on the mainland but we were very welcome to stay there.

We all sat down and Kim explained that they had been watching our strange vessel from the village. "We saw your ship and said what is this kind of ship, and when we saw it disappear behind Buabo and not come out on the other side we thought — *aye* — they must have stopped at our island. So, me and my friend, we paddle out. And then we meet you." Kim looked at me with amazement and shook his head while laughing. He just couldn't fanthom that a white man had come to his island in a sailing canoe.

We served Kim and his friend a plate of rice each and, as we all sat around the fire and ate, Kim said, “We stay with you tonight and look after you. We can sit up and tell stories.”

I nodded with my mouth full, slumped down with resignation, and replied, “Thank you very much Kim. We are very grateful for you having us here on your island.”

After dinner, I washed our plates in the swell and excused myself to Kim and his friend explaining that I was very tired and needed to sleep — if they didn't mind. They nodded understandingly. Then I went to the house and strung up my hammock under the curious looks of Kim and his friend. As I lay in the hammock, I wrote some notes about my frustrations before nodding off.

A grand feast

The next morning, I got a clarification of the elongated metal frames; it was obvious now in the light. Kim took me down the beach and showed me yet another of the framed structures. It was a shipping container! He explained that one morning they had found many such containers washed up on the island. Everyone was of curious to know what was inside but the containers were all locked, so they went to work on them with their axes. As they cut through the outer layer, they found some insulation foam; and, as they penetrated the inner membrane behind the foam, a gush of chilled air hit them — they were freezer containers, and to their great joy they discovered they were full of food.

The first container was full of frozen chickens, another with dairy products and yet another with frozen green vegetables. The village didn’t waste any time and instantly began one long, gluttonous feast. But soon they realised that there was more food than they even could possibly eat, so they invited other villages to share. When the food was eventually all gone, the villagers turned to the containers themselves. The metal sides were used for roofing and walls of their huts and the cooling engines inside were dismantled and sold for good money to a big company in Lae.

I told Kim that it was a great fortune that they had gained, but I couldn't help but wonder what tragedy proceeded this. I asked, "Do you know where the containers came from? They must have come from a ship — right?"

Kim nodded seriously, "The Bobongara Reef."

"Where is this reef?" I wanted to know.

Kim pointed north to a distant point of the end of the Gulf of Huon that we were in. "Big reef out there. Very dangerous. Many ships sink." I assumed that Bobongara reef was near the Vitiaz Strait which Sandy had warned us about. Kim didn't know any specifics about the boat that had lost the containers or what had happened to the crew but one could guess that it might have been one of the coasters freighting goods from Lae to the next big town of Madang, about 160 nautical miles further up the coast.

After breakfast, we said goodbye to Kim and paddled out across the colourful reef, past the great sandbank with the container frame that was lying like a picked over carcass. There was no wind, so we paddled for a good two hours and then had a break. The sun was already scorching and there was no shade. The blue sea looked too inviting so I pulled off my shirt and jumped in. As I was hanging on to the canoe Sanakoli said in an agitated tone, "Stop fooling around, you get back inside."

I pulled myself back on board and asked him, "Why can't I swim, we are not moving?" He didn't answer and we picked up the paddles and continued. But then I thought of it. I had never seen the crew jump in the water while at sea.

Perhaps I sensed the reason for this before I expected. Soon we came across a big school of fish feeding on the surface. Job shaded his eyes with a hand, "Ohh, yellowfin." As we paddled closer, you could clearly see the big tunas jumping out of the water as they were feeding on a school of fish. A few frigate birds had joined in from above, diving in to get their share. Suddenly, we saw a triangular fin breach the surface and a big splash from a vertical tail. A monster of a shark had now joined the feast. Now I understood why the sailors didn't swim in the deep waters. The feeding frenzy moved out of our path so we missed the chance for a tuna steak.

Expedition Log 10 September 2016

> 12:30 hrs. 6-7 knots of wind. S. We have spotted a lonely drifting outrigger canoe. It is covered in white bird droppings. Could it be the canoe belonging to the missing Magistrate from Mambutu, Peo Ishmael?

I looked at the crew, the whole lost at sea story, together with the risk of piracy, had cast a bad vibe over the expedition, and now it had come back again to haunt us. They were all studying the canoe. Justin had climbed halfway up the mast for a better outlook. "Hey guys, do you think this could be the Magistrate's canoe?" The crew was talking together in one of their languages and then Sanakoli said, "*Maski* (never mind) we don't know."

"We should sail closer and have a look," I continued.

Job was standing by the rudder, "No we already passed. We don't want to turn the canoe." I had a bad feeling about this whole thing but thought it was our duty to at least check that there was no one in the canoe and see if it there were any names or signs that made it recognisable for a later investigation.

So, I said again, "Hey, let's look at the canoe. We need to find out if it belonged to the Magistrate."

Job was agitated, "No, we go."

I argued, "If this was the Magistrate's canoe, then his family should know."

Job said fatalistically, "If you had gone to stay with the Magistrate then he would be busy looking after us and he wouldn't go out fishing in bad weather."

Before I could answer, Sanakoli turned to Job and said in a blaming voice, "Job, don't you put that on our man here." We all turned quiet and the lonely canoe slowly disappeared behind us.

I felt guilty and annoyed, not so much about Job's comment but more that I hadn't insisted on turning the canoe. Who knew, this canoe could just as well have drifted from another village although the bird droppings indicated that it had been floating for a while and the current could probably have carried it all the way from Mambututu. I could, of course, try and call someone from my phone but there wasn't strong network coverage and I didn't have a number. I knew that the Magistrate's brother lived in Lae, so I planned to try and get his number when I was back online and call him.

Cutting a piece of the gulf

The wind picked up and we started to move further and further out to sea. We were now in the gulf of Huon and distantly approaching Lae. Lae is known as an industrial city from where a lot of food products are produced and shipped to the rest of the country. Another thing the city is known for is its high crime rate — and, not least, piracy. We had earlier talked about not sailing directly into the city, as to avoid detection and instead stop in a village before Lae and then motor in by dinghy to get provisions. But now we were getting further and further from the coast. Job was still at the rudder and I asked him if we were crossing the bay or what was happening? He spoke with his friends. "We can cut across, straight across," Job said and did a cut upwards with his arm.

I said annoyed, "Hey guys, if you make such decisions you have to talk to me. We make it together." They didn't answer.

I took out my map case, it was waterproof and transparent. In it I had two types of map, one side showing a topographic A3-sized map that I had printed from an American military survey from the 1960s, the other side had a present-day nautical chart of the area. By combining these two types of map, I could both read the inland topography and coastal waters with buoys, shipping routes and lighthouses. My plotting instruments were the same as I used when kayaking — a small brass passer and a square plotter. The square plotter is an ingenious and simple instrument; it is basically a square ruler about 13 by 13 centimetres with printed 360° markings — North, South, East and West. In the centre, I had drilled a hole and fastened a string.

I looked at our charts and found our approximate location. To take a bearing, I placed the centre of the square plotter on our position, making sure it lined up with the grid marking on the chart with north pointing upwards. Then I pulled a line with the string to our desired destination, a bay east of Lae. I looked at the compass markings on the plotter and saw the string intersect on the 10° north northeast. Now I knew our course. I kept hold of the string where it touched the bay. By measuring the length of the string, along the grid on the side of the chart – where I knew the distance between each latitude grid line was 60 nautical miles — I could read our travel distance. This was about 30 nautical miles. On my GPS, I read that we were sailing with a speed of four to five knots. This told me that our crossing would probably take about six to seven hours.

The sea further out didn't have any white caps. I said to the crew, who were still sailing outwards, "Hey guys, if you keep this direction then we will be across the bay just as it gets dark. Do you think the weather looks good for the whole afternoon?" Job and Sanakoli made a few short comments to each other but then Justin cut through with his sharp voice and fast words. I didn't understand anything except a couple of times he said, '*Bolibolimai*' which is the name of the south wind. He talked a great deal while pointing at the sea with a smouldering *bruce* between his fingers, while scouting the horizon with his 'Clint Eastwood hang em' high eyes.' The other two listened and, when he had finished, they both nodded. Sanakoli turned towards me and finally translated, "We go." I immediately forgot all about being annoyed at the crew as the blood pulsed in my temples and my heart pounded with excitement. Our first great crossing!

The wind picked up as we came further out into the gulf. The swell wasn't too big and it was very pleasant sailing, with a high sun and little drama. We came by another giant fish feeding frenzy with swooping frigate birds, diving boobies and jumping tunas. Job was looking longingly at the spectacle while sighing, "Ohh, yellowfin," but we were too far away and there were no hits on the rapala lure. Still, I enjoyed everything about the open water, the sharp reflections in the blue abyss, the drying salt on my chin and the wind blowing past my ears.

I thought back to my kayaking days in Venezuela, where I worked as a tour guide for a company offering three-month packages consisting of Spanish lessons, volunteer community work and adventure travel. The students were mostly young Europeans on gap year, predominantly girls — the best job I had ever had. But after a couple of years, I realised that by guiding tours for other people, I would never challenge myself to the limit. I enjoyed the privilege of being able to share my experiences with others, but this was when I realised, if I started making films, I would be able to share my adventures, challenge myself and maybe even turn it into a living.

I set myself the goal to make the world's best adventure film. Although I was not short of grand ambitions, I still had enough grounding to know that I wouldn't be able to do this first go. Back in Copenhagen I tried to break in to the film industry by doing unpaid labour while supporting myself as a technician in an exhibition venue. My spare time was spent making videos for YouTube about sea kayaking. I felt vulnerable publishing videos of myself online but people liked them, so I went on to make three sea kayaking films. During this period, I didn't have any money or free time; all my energy and resources were spent on filmmaking. The efforts paid off and in 2013 I won my first film prize — I was on the right path. In 2014, my buddy Kay and I, paddled 1200 km around Denmark. The wind was against us three quarters of the way, and it ended taking us 38 days instead of the 25 days that we had aimed for. It was a tiresome trip that put our friendship to the test, yet after this, I knew I had to do something bigger.

Arriving at night

At 8:00 p.m. we found ourselves in a pitch-black bay. We were well past Lae and now needed to find a safe village where we could stay for the night. I started to smell the vegetation and noticed a moth passing by. The shore was dark with irregular dots of light, mostly from fires. As we came closer to land, the wind dropped completely and the outrigger started to pull downwards. So, we lowered the sail and began paddling. Sanakoli said, "When we go in, you go ask for the Magistrate and he will look after us."

Job added, "If dingy come you hide in the canoe."

As we came closer to what looked like a village, and we could see a big fire on the beach, we could also hear a lot of men yelling — and they didn't sound the least bit sober. Instead, we changed course and paddled towards some bright industrial lights on the west bank of the bay. It looked like a station building but it was hard to make it out in the dark, and a row of coconut palms in front obstructed the view. "Maybe they got a guard there," I said and Sanakoli agreed, "Yes they can look after us." But the beach was too steep and the surf too large.

It was around ten o'clock now and we were all tired from paddling the heavy canoe. Then we spotted the silhouette of a man and a woman sitting in a canoe in the bay. "We go and ask them to tell us where to go in," Sanakoli suggested. But as we approached the canoe, the man and woman seemed to move away from us, so we paddled faster and then they paddled even faster away. In the end, we got close enough to tell them that we were from Milne Bay and needed help and they came around.

It turned out that it was a couple out fishing on a reef. When they saw us, they became afraid, as they had never seen such a vessel before. But when we did meet them, they were very eager to help and said that we were lucky to come to Bucava village as there was a lot of good people there, so we followed them into a flat outcrop and pulled the canoe halfway up the beach. The husband and wife then disappeared and soon returned with a 50-year-old man with a long beard and tall build. He presented himself as Asalem and said that he was the village policeman. He told me that I could sleep in his hut and that the canoe would be fine and we wouldn't have to worry about the drunkards further down the beach — as they were just kids.

Chapter Eight

A merry band of axe-wielding villagers

It was still early in the morning as I was being guided along a small dirt path that ran along the beach. The boy I was following led me past a structure that I assumed must have been the one we saw the previous night with the bright light. The elongated building was constructed on the ground, with the walls covered in traditional mats but with a shiny new metal roof. The empty window frames made it appear to be in its last phase of completion and there were some locals already at work on it.

The boy took me to an old traditional house. Out of one of the doors emerged a lady in her mid-40s. She didn't look like the other local women as she was wearing a T-shirt and a pair of jeans. I shook her hand and she presented herself as Marina; then she yelled something over her shoulder. A man about her age came around the corner. He was wearing a white T-shirt, board shorts and a pair of flip-flops — and he was brushing his teeth. He smiled and then turned sideways while raising his hand in a 'just a moment gesture.' He rinsed with a bottle of spring water and proceeded to introduce himself.

"Hello bro, welcome to Yambo, Bucava Village, my name is Leo," he said with a big grin on his friendly round face that looked like it had been sculptured from a habit of healthy but not excessive eating. "You want some breakfast? Please… sit down," he continued. I pulled up by a wobbly round table and Leo asked his kitchen lady for three cups of coffee. Leo then informed me, "I went down to your canoe last night; some kid came and told us that there was this ship that had landed in our village. But when I got down there, you had already gone to bed?"

I blankly admitted, “Yes, sorry about that. We have been travelling for 12 days now and I was really tired, so I couldn’t be bothered with too many people.”

Leo gave out a deep laugh and said that he understood. He then explained that he and his wife lived in Lae but were building a guesthouse here in his village and he pointed to the new building next to us. I told the couple about our journey and the trouble with our salt-water-pickled outrigger.

Leo said that they would be more than happy to help us on our quest and Marina nodded eagerly, “You can bring all your things to our house, they will be safe there.”

And then Leo added, “And you can put your canoe on our beach here if it is not too steep — sorry I haven’t built a wharf yet but it will come!”

And then he added, “Actually, we are going into Lae this morning — so if you want to come to do some shopping, then you are more than welcome.”

I was thrilled to hear this and thanked him, jumping right to the point, “I’ll just go to the canoe, get my things and then we can get going.” There was a silent pause and Leo looked at me with an odd expression. I thought shit, I must have stepped out of line. I tried to save the situation. “Sorry, I’m in such a hurry. I need to slow down. It has just been very hard work getting us this far and I am really worried about our outrigger.”

Leo’s chubby cheeks rose again and he laughed heartily, “That’s all right bro, first we eat, then we take you to Lae.”

Leo the *Bigman*

In PNG, there is an expression: *Bigman*. In former days, a *Bigman* would be a great warrior, with knowledge of tradition, have had rich crops and many pigs and been able to share his wealth during festivities — a chief or a village hotshot.

Leo was a modern version of a *Bigman*. He had inherited a significant piece of land from his father and made a good income as a divisional manager of a tyre company in Lae. Despite living in the city, he had started a couple of projects in his village. In addition to building a guest house, he was raising funds for the local school through a charity organisation. His engagement in his community also generated wealth for his family and friends in the village. He was supporting his elders and employing his auntie as a cooking lady, as well as four young men who worked directly for him.

We were served a rich breakfast of fried buns and eggs with pieces of sausage — it was heavenly. As we ate, Sanakoli joined us. After breakfast, we went to Leo's beach but it was too steep and Sanakoli suggested that we should keep the canoe where it was. Job and Justin had already had breakfast when we came back. I told them that I was going to be in Lae for a couple of days to do some shopping and, most importantly, to follow up on our passports and papers. In the meantime, I suggested that the sailors should get some rest and try to find out if there was the right wood for an outrigger here. Leo had brought enough food to last the sailors for the next couple of days. He also offered them his house to sleep in but the sailors were happy where they were, not least because several women had already brought them food and they had met another man from Milne Bay who was married to a lady in the village. I asked them if they had any shopping requests and Job responded, "You get me them lollies that taste like *Colgate.*" I nodded and wrote 'mint pastels' on my shopping list.

It took an hour to motor to Lae by dinghy, and it was a great ride. The coastline flew by as we passed one river estuary after another staining the sea a café au lait colour. Beside Marina and Leo, we had three boys aboard who were operating the dinghy. One of them spotted a fish feeding frenzy and we veered towards it. Marina and Leo immediately took out a fishing rod each and cast their squid-baits in to the sea. Leo was talking loudly over the noise of the motor, "This is our thing. We started fishing maybe two years ago."

Marina joined in, "When we get the chance, we go out fishing every weekend. The kids are big now, so we can go out on our own." We motored over the feeding fish a couple of times but soon the tuna stopped jumping, we pulled the rods up and continued along the coast that was now getting flatter with an ever-increasing number of estuaries.

As we arrived in the harbour, I saw that avoiding sailing into Lae was a good decision. It was a very busy but crude harbour, full of dinghies and people coming and going. Even if the crew and I had anchored the canoe inside the protected fence of the local yacht club, there wouldn't be a dinghy driver in the greater Lae area who wouldn't know that a white man in a sailing canoe was passing through their waters. Our dinghy hit the sand and we waded the last five metres through a thick soup of putrid debris and plastic trash up to where some of Leo's family were waiting in a four-wheel drive pickup truck. After the boys finished off-loading garden produce from the dinghy onto the truck, Leo and Marina drove me to a guesthouse. The check-in process was easy and the barbed wired protected compound looked nice. So, after Leo and Marina had made sure I was settled, they took off with the promise of taking me shopping the following day.

The guesthouse was run by a church group called SIL. This was one of the many hundreds of Christian organisations in PNG whose main purpose was to translate the Bible into as many native languages as possible. The guesthouse was open to any visitors and was clean, and cheap and, most importantly, safe. After a good long shower, I spent the afternoon charging and backing up my film. But now that I had phone reception, I was faced with the unpleasant events surrounding the disappearance of Magistrate Peo — who must have been lost at sea for six days now.

Through Sandy's help, I had secured the number for the Magistrate's brother who worked in Lae. I didn't know if he had heard the news. I also felt guilty about not having made efforts to try and get in touch with him sooner, let alone regretful about not insisting on investigating the empty canoe. I thought of the old survival proverb —

you can last three weeks without food but only three days without water — and I doubted that a fisherman would bring water with him when going out at night. I walked outside my room and felt the neatly cut grass prickle the soles of my feet. I dialled the number.

"Hallo, Henry here," a distorted voice sounded.

I introduced myself and explained, "I am very sorry to bring you the news… but your brother Peo from Mambututu has been lost at sea for six days when he went fishing in the night and I don't know if they have found him yet."

There was pause as though there was a delay on the line.

But then, a loud voice sounded, "Ahh, don't worry bro, he was found after drifting four days at sea, more dead than alive but he is doing all right now." It almost sounded like the brother was laughing. "He's just taking it easy now, getting his strength back." It was like a stone had fallen off my chest. I suddenly felt silly having dramatised it all. I thanked the Magistrate's brother for the good news and hung up. What a relief.

After this, I was full of optimism. I called the Immigration Officer in Alotau who was helping us process our passports. But I was barely half a minute into the conversation before I detected that nothing whatsoever had been done to get our requests to Port Moresby. Annoyed I hung up and called 'our' Tourism Officer instead. He was disappointed and embarrassed about the situation and promised to help us process the passports while we were travelling to Madang. I agreed to transfer him money for his efforts.

The next morning Leo picked me up from the guest-house. "Morning bro, how was your night back in the real world?"

"Oh, I had a great sleep and the best part was that there were no roosters to wake me up at four in the morning," I answered while jumping into the front seat.

"Ha ha. Where do you wanna go? I have taken the day off so just let me know what you need and we'll get it." My grandparents had transferred me a cash donation, so there would be money in my account for some equipment upgrades and food. So, first I mentioned that we needed some new fishing tackle and ropes for the canoe. "You got it — I know just the right place," Leo nodded to the guard as he let us out of the compound.

On our drive, I got a better impression of Lae. It was a very lush city, with a lot of rain coming off the mountains and, although the roads had more holes than asphalt in many places and there were a lot of run-down buildings, it all seemed quite charming compared to dry and dusty Port Moresby. As we were driving around, I asked Leo about the reputation that Lae had as a dangerous place. "Well you know bro, there is of course some bad things happening here but for us locals, we just go by with our business. Just keep your car door locked and stay away from the bad neighbourhoods; then you will be fine."

Since both Leo and I were keen fishermen, he first took me to a kind of a 'secret tackle shop' situated in a building dealing with something completely different, local transport or something like that. After being led in by a secretary who walked us through a large office space, we entered an elongated room with shelves and walls stocked with all sorts of lures, hooks, line, wheels and rods, as well a plethora of outdoor items. All of it dirt cheap! Leo introduced me to the 'CEO' and explained that he was a keen fisherman himself who just wanted to do his part in promoting the big game fishing scene in Lae. So, every time he was in China, he would bring new items home for his shop. Leo and I were like kids in a candy store and I laughed to myself about how excited the sailors would be to get some new lures.

Afterwards, Leo drove us to a marine shop where I got a new sheet and a pulley and two extra signal flares. Then we went to a food wholesale store where I stocked up on staple items as well as some smaller things, such as shampoo and sachets of coffee that we could give away as gifts. Leo also took me to a TNT office where I picked up a package from Sandy containing her old topographic maps of the coastline we were about to travel, as well as a couple of sponsor items she had gotten from Consort Shipping and, not least, an assortment of instant outdoor meals.

In the evening, I was invited for dinner at Leo and Marina's house. They lived in what you would call a good middle-class neighbourhood. There was a high fence around the house, which was built with modern materials but still standing on stilts with space beneath used as a garage and for storage. Upstairs, there was a spacious living room and kitchen that contained everything you would find in a European home — a flat screen TV, a big couch with a coffee table and holiday photographs on the walls. Marina served us a lovely steak dinner which I devoured while Marina and Leo talked about their life in Lae.

Marina had grown up in the city and was now working for her family's company that was developing and selling electronic solutions. Leo had spent his early years in Yambo, moving to Lae to study, then later to Port Moresby. It was in Port Moresby that the two had met. Now Leo was working as assistant manager for a tyre company situated not far from where Marina worked, and they would often meet for lunch. I was really enjoying this family setting. It was a welcome break from small village hassles and I was sitting in a 'real chair' with no mosquitoes, learning about the lives of modern Papua New Guineans.

The next day we took the dinghy back to Bucava. It was a beautiful ride. Near Cape Arkona we passed a great fish feeding frenzy. The sea was boiling with jumping yellowfin. As we were trolling back and forth, we suddenly spotted a huge whale shark that had joined the feast. Within minutes, we had caught two nice tuna and aimed for the village. And we came back to some great news. The sailors had been out in the backwoods with Aslan and found the right type of tree for our outrigger. This was a great relief and I complimented Aslan and the sailors for their good work.

Leo was very excited about the news as well and, the next day, he gathered together a group of men with sharp axes. It wasn't hard to find a willing workforce because everyone was eager to help us with our voyage. Job stayed back with the canoe while the rest of us walked along the bay passing behind the great rocky point of Cape Arkona, which Leo had named his guest house after. On the way, we came through several small villages — all part of greater Bucava. In every village, we had to introduce ourselves and tell the story of what we were up to. At every stop and chat, there seemed to be new axe men joining in what was now becoming a procession.

When we came to the last village, I was introduced to the Chief. He was wearing a red polo shirt with the sleeves cut off so that you could see his long burly arms, formed by a life of hard work in the jungle. He greeted us informally and I explained what we were looking for. He nodded, "No worries… we'll help you." And then he turned to the group of men and said something in their local dialect, which made the whole circle of men crack up with laughter. Leo wiped some blood red *buai* off his lips and explained, "We are just cracking jokes. He just said…" pointing to the Chief, "We help him build his canoe and then I'll sail with him and meet his family and get married and stay there." As Leo finished the sentence the whole group, Leo included, burst into laughter again.

I joined in and I shook hands with the Chief, "Yeah, we can do that… it's a deal!" I replied

The chief grinned and then theatrically raised his eyebrows and surprised me by saying, "Nice one."

And so, our band of axe wielding villagers made it into the forest, with the Chief leading from the front. The forest was flat and swampy with low dense foliage punctuated by taller trees. The sound of breaking waves soon disappeared and the echo of birdsong and the buzzing of flies took over. The men spread out through the almost vertical rays of light that penetrated the forest and, although they went out of sight of each other, they all stayed within earshot. Leo didn't search but was followed by one of his boys who was carrying a water cooler. As we walked, Leo confessed that he had been nervous about approaching the Chief as this was his father's original village and he hadn't been there since he was a child. But the Chief and the villagers greeted him and they all said that it was good to have him back.

After ten minutes, there was a call. We gathered around a tree with light bark and an open crown with far reaching branches holding light green foliage. The spear tip shaped leaves were sitting in rows on each side of a green stem. It was the right species (known as *Yayauve* in the Basilaki language). There was no question of that. The trunk was straight but too thin and short to match our needs. The search continued as the bush rapidly became hotter and damper in the morning sun. I contented myself by noticing that there were only a few mosquitoes about.

After exploring for half an hour more, we finally came to a tree with the right proportions. Pearls of sweat were forming from Sanakoli's forehead as he looked up at the crown. "What do you think Sanakoli?" I asked in anticipation

His rapid shallow breathing betrayed his exhaustion. "I think that the length is all right but the top there, right up at the top it is too small." He wiped a stinging insect away from under his eye and continued. "We'll just see what Justin… what will he say to us." Justin soon came and, after a couple of minutes of walking around and studying the specimen from all angles, he nodded. The tree had a diameter of about one metre. The sailors weren't completely satisfied with the tree, as the stem was branching out into two parts but they hoped that the straight part of the tree was long enough for our purposes.

Soon the forest boomed with the rhythmic blows of steel chopping into wood. One man would be swinging his axe for about three minutes and then another would take over the chopping with his axe. Meanwhile, the rest of the group would sit and talk and chew *buai* while sharpening their axes. I had a go myself. It was fun. I had never tried to fell such a big tree. It was very hard work in the humid heat and I understood why the men were taking turns. After 20 minutes the tree fell with a loud cracking sound that tore a rip of sunlight through the rainforest canopy.

Now that the tree trunk was laying diagonally with one end still elevated above ground, you could really get a sense of how long it was. Sanakoli measured out five arm lengths (nine metres), the length of our canoe, and added an extra length before marking it off. Some of the men started cutting off the crown so that we could get the trunk down to the ground, while others worked on the branches. I also had a go at cutting off the crown, which was quite a difficult prospect. I had to balance on the tree trunk, a metre above the ground, swinging the heavy axe in the scorching sun while the colony of red ants that had been inhabiting the tree were attacking my bare legs like a determined legion of enraged soldiers. Soon my back began to ache.

The work reminded me of my years as a roof thatcher in Denmark. I started out by joining my father during summer holidays. Later through my teenage years and early 20s, I worked for him full time. Working on a roof with natural materials was tough and laborious. The hardest part was when the house was almost finished and I had to walk up and down aluminium ladders carrying two sets of 15-kilogram cleaved oak logs on my shoulders. Often, bark crumble would get in to my eyes. When reaching the ridge, I would continue stepping along the crest, temporarily blinded, balancing precariously without safety equipment, with one hand out and the other wrapped around the logs that were cutting into my shoulders. Under these circumstances, there wasn't much time to enjoy the Danish countryside; all my attention was focused on each step along the slippery hay covering the ridge. At the end of the roof, I would hand the first set over to my Dad, who would be sitting with one leg on each side of the ridge. He would position one set for each quarter metre of roof and I would return and collect the next two from the pile. Although I enjoyed the outdoor work and the companionship with my Dad and his thatcher friends, I didn't want to do this kind of backbreaking labour for the rest of my life.

Since then, whenever I was daydreaming in some far-flung corner of the tropical jungle, sitting in a tree full of biting-sucking-stinging insects or carrying a heavy backpack up a steep muddy trail in 35-degree heat and 99 percent humidity, I would think back gratefully on how thatching taught me to keep my focus on the job at hand and ignore the physical pain. A youth of hard work in the outdoors had indeed prepared me well for a life of adventure.

Standing on that tree trunk in the coastal jungle of Papua New Guinea, I felt a familiarity with this type of cutting work, although wearing shoes didn't seem to help my balance. I looked at some of the other men, their bare feet naturally gripping the trunk seemingly ignoring the biting insects. There was sweat in my eyes, a wobbling tree trunk under my feet and savage red ants at work. How long had I been cutting now? It seemed like an eternity. I had had enough. My groin seemed to be on fire. I handed the axe back to its owner, slid down the trunk and ran out of the clearing; and when there was no one in sight, in the privacy of a shrubbery, I pulled down my pants and plucked off the collective of ants that were drilling into my testicles. I suppose Danish roof thatchers are human after all.

By the early afternoon, the tree trunk outrigger was starting to take shape. The forest floor was littered with fresh white wood chips. Sanakoli and Justin would stop chopping from time to time to walk around and instruct the other men about where and how deep they could cut. I filmed the process but most of the time I would sit with Leo and the other men and talk. A man with sprinkles of grey curls, a short-brimmed hat and a friendly face with a tiny nose had also joined us. He had a giant left foot that was swollen with Elephantitis. Although he had brought his axe, it didn't look like he had come to work. It seemed he was more there to just hang out and crack jokes. It may have been hard work but it was also something of a social event and Justin and Sanakoli really bonded with the other men.

I was concerned about what the price would be for all these men's labour but Leo reassuringly whispered to me, "Just give them 50 kina for rice, tobacco and sugar, so they have a big meal after work, then they'll be happy." I was surprised how cheap the labour was and told him so. When we were preparing the canoe back in Milne Bay, Sanakoli asked me if I wanted a new outrigger on the canoe, because there was a kid on his island who had a big outrigger tree growing in his garden, but he wanted 600 kina for the tree so he could buy himself a touch phone. I had spent most of my money, however, Sanakoli said that the old outrigger would last us all the way to the Sepik River. I then went on to explain how wrong I had been and realised that Sanakoli had had no idea how far away the Sepik was, as he had never been there. Leo laughed, "Well bro, we saved you 550 kina, and the boys here are happy that you now have an outrigger from Bucava."

By the afternoon, we had a subtle banana shape and it was time to transport the great trunk back to the village. It was still a big piece of wood, so we tied several ropes around it and pulled towards the coast. One or two men would walk in the front with bush knives to hack down any obstacles and furnish our path with any leaf or stem that could ease the friction, while the rest of us pulled and pushed. It was slow and hard going. After a while, we reached a small muddy creek covered in low foliage. Now that the log was floating, the work became a bit easier, although the creek had some sharp bends and turns. Finally, we reached a larger river and then an elongated lagoon that led out to the sea. On this stretch, our new outrigger had its maiden voyage as one of the men got up on the log and poled it with a stick until the lagoon ended behind the beach. I had no wish to get into that murky water but the other men seemed to show little concern. It was late afternoon when Leo's dinghy finally arrived. We pulled the log into the rough surf and one of Leo's boys swam the log out past the breakers. We were waiting for him in the dinghy, tied the log to the boat and we slowly motored it to its new home — *Tawali Pasana.*

The next day was dedicated to 'sharpen the outrigger,' as Sanakoli called it. I had been looking forward to documenting and participating in the cutting as well but I was occupied in Leo's house helping write up a plan for tourism in his guesthouse. As we were sitting working, Job came by. "How is it going with the outrigger?" I asked.

Job was looking at his flat bare feet and then up towards us, "Me, I cut it my own way but them they do it their way. They say I don't know how. But I have built many canoes." His eyes became hard and he made a chopping motion with the edge of his hand in to his palm. "I know how to cut, so I just let them do it their way."

I was busy doing the plan with Leo and it looked like Justin and Sanakoli knew what they were doing, so I told Job, "Okay, just let them do the hard work then, maybe you can make some other improvements of the canoe. What about that new rope I got? Can you tie that to the sail?"

"I just go up the beach," Job replied in an uncharacteristically low voice as he continued in the opposite direction of the canoe.

By midday the next day, the new outrigger was finished and the *patotos* connecting the platform to the outrigger that had been recycled from the old outrigger were hammered into the ivory coloured pontoon like pegs into the ground. The canoe was resting on the beach with a brand-new outrigger and the ground around the canoe was littered with wood chips. There were a handful of villagers hanging around and a constant exchange of people coming and going. I noticed that there was now a raised a fence around the canoe, fashioned with our long stern line and some branches.

Sanakoli was tying some of the *patots* to the *kialos* by recycling some old fishing nylon and using the new where the old wouldn't suffice. When I asked about the fence, Sanakoli said looking down at the handy work, "Our friend the policeman made this fence for us. Too many people coming asking questions and telling stories. How can we finish when people are telling stories?"

I agreed that a fence was a good idea and asked Sanakoli to show me how to tie the nylon. It was a straightforward pattern but the key was to keep the line tight until it was finished off. When I had done my first one, Sanakoli nodded and said in a long tone, "That's the way. Now you make the next one there. You see the nylon is old on this one, too old. You use the new nylon on this one." I liked the mentality of these sailors. We had more than enough new fishing nylon to replace all the old. But why should we if the old was still working? But pulling and tying the 130-pound nylon line was hard on my fingers.

"Argh, this is really hard for the hands!" I exclaimed.

"Ohh, my hands pain too but you must tie properly. If one *patoto* come loose or break, one more will break and soon the whole outrigger will break off," Sanakoli said with a serious expression. I asked him about Job and if he had been helping cut the outrigger, "No, he don't know how to do it properly, he makes it his own way." I suggested that they could include him in how they were doing it but Sanakoli just scoffed, "We want to make it properly and we know how."

I noticed that the old outrigger was lying by itself, cleaved into larger pieces. I also noticed some round tunnels bored deep into the waterlogged wood. 'Dammit,' I thought aloud, the outrigger had been full of ship worms. I felt disappointed that I hadn't noticed this before as I had always wanted to taste one. Shipworms are not a worm but a type of clam that eats rotten wood. The holes give away to a small two-part white clam shell but the whole long worm-like body is actually inside the wood.

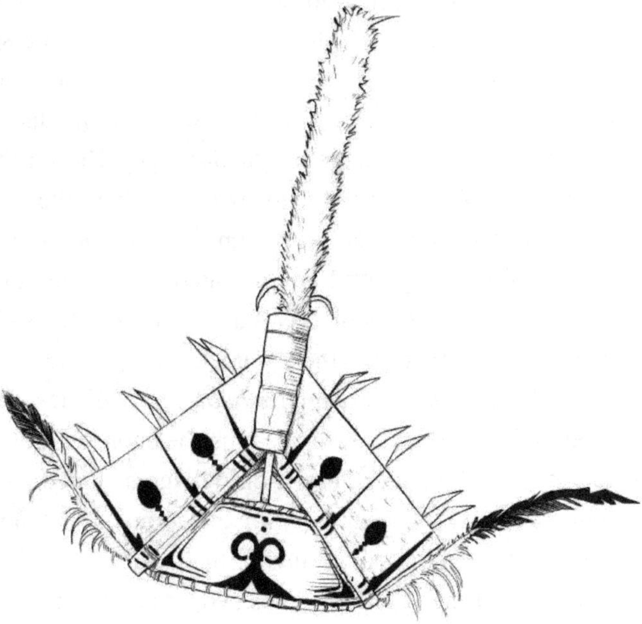

With the new outrigger ready, it was time for us to continue our journey. Before we could go, however, the village wanted to host a *sing sing* for us. After sunset, people gathered on the beach by the canoe. It was a great jamboree of villagers who came in shapes and sizes. Some of them had brought LED torches to light up the dance circle. The dancers were all adult men and women, elaborately decorated with necklaces and green palm fibres tied to their arms and legs. Some of the men were bare-chested but most of them were in T-shirts with the women in dresses. The men were wearing their traditional headdresses, which were white triangular hats decorated with white Cockatoo feathers. Back in the day, the whole hat would be made of white feathers but nowadays there are mainly constructed from cardboard, painted white and decorated with black markings and white and yellow feathers. The men were either wielding *Kundu* drums or spears, and the women formed a choir.

There was a great atmosphere of anticipation and excitement as the *Kundu* drums started to take off and soon the night filled with the high-pitched nasal voices of the female choir as they were swaying beside each other waving small green twigs. The men were drumming and dancing in different formations in the circle created by the audience. During the many songs, bystanders joined in on the parts they knew or liked. At times the elder women joined the choir and sang along, recounting a popular tune from their youth. All the songs were in their local language but Leo translated for me when I wasn't filming. There were songs about everyday life in Yambo — sowing the garden or getting married but the all-time crowd pleaser was a song about going to the mountains looking for *buai*. The audience went wild with laughter and all joined in with gusto on the choruses. It was very moving to witness the connectedness the villagers shared — stories that not only united the community in the moment but now also connected them to the past and, in turn, to the future.

There was a pause and the circle opened up and formed a kind of a corridor that continued out into the darkness. We had come to the last song that was about chasing the devil away. The drums started to drone in a monotonous beat and everyone was looking into the darkness. Slowly a figure came out of the black night. It was the captain of the dance group slowly making his way nearer. Occasionally, he would break up the dance to jump forth and scare one of the bystanders. This made everyone scream with excitement. There was a face-off in the end between the spear and drum wielding men and he — the devil — was defeated and the scene was over.

After the dance, there was still a buzz of excitement. Leo told us to get in line because the community had some gifts for us. But Job didn't want to be involved with the rest of us. His attitude really annoyed me. It seemed quite rude. So, I tried to wave him over while saying, "Hey Job, come and join us."

But then Sanakoli poked me in the side, "He cannot do this, his church do not allow this." As Justin, Sanakoli and I were standing there in line, Leo expressed a few words of gratitude and well-wishes and then he said that now the villagers could come and give us a goodbye present if we wanted.

There was bit of stir but nothing happened. Then I took the initiative and said something like, "Thank you all for this beautiful farewell *sing sing*. This is the most beautiful *sing sing* we have ever had and we are also so very grateful for your help cutting the outrigger. Thanks to you we can now continue our world record. You are all part of this journey now. The canoe is from Milne Bay but the outrigger is from Bucava." There was quiet after this, and then slowly one by one the villagers came forward to shake our hands or put a *bilum* bag or a necklace around our necks. I felt a bit odd about receiving all these gifts, as I didn't have anything to give back; we had already received more than we could ever dream of from this village.

Expedition Log 17 September 2016

> 09:30 hrs. Departure Bucava. Five knots of wind. S-SE. The sun is already burning. The whole village is standing on the beach and they are getting smaller as we sail. It was an emotional farewell.

The canoe felt so much more stable with our new outrigger. Our pantry was well stocked with gifts, such as coconuts and root vegetables and the man from Milne Bay had given us a giant bunch of green bananas. Sanakoli, who was splitting the bananas into smaller clusters so they would pack better, said, "It floats well, now we are stable. But it is still green inside, so we have to make it dry later somehow." He packed the last of the bananas in a rice bag next to the firewood by the mast. He then reported, “Our man from Milne Bay told us to look out at the Bobongara reef after Finschafen — very dangerous place. They say a witch live on the reef — sometimes man and sometimes snake. So, when we go there, no play up, we must be very smart.”

Job joined in. “Bobongara reef, that where the Rabaul Queen sank, many people died. Very dangerous place.” This was the same reef that Kim on Zumbale warned us about. The reef seemed to be in the Vitiaz Strait between this peninsula and the island of New Britain. Sandy skipped this section as the seas were too big and some of the communities were unwelcoming. But there was no way to avoid this piece of coast if we wanted to continue our circumnavigation. It was probably going to get rough but at least we had a new outrigger and access to a good weather forecast — and of course bananas enough to last us half the way around the island of New Guinea.

Chapter Nine

Half-man half-serpent

I woke under the canvas. It was early morning and we were anchored near Finschhafen, in a small lagoon surrounded by high walls. As I waded ashore, I was constantly balancing like I was intoxicated, trying to find a steady-not-too-sharp foothold, and of course I ended up cutting my toe. Soon after we started the breakfast fire, a couple of men appeared on the beach. They were the local landowners and we invited them to eat with us. The men were very happy that we had anchored in their lagoon and we were too because it was a special place. Natural rock walls circled this little pool of about 200 metres wide, punctuated by a narrow entrance. And the entire place was surrounded by 10 metre-tall cliffs, with jungle vines spilling down the sides. After breakfast, our hosts showed me a small spring in a rock wall where we could wash and fill our water containers. It was such a privilege to have the chance to collect spring water instead of the often contaminated well water or stagnant mosquito-larvae-infested tank water which we would normally have to boil before drinking.

We were all tired from the night before and weren't in a hurry to get out on the water again, so we spent the entire morning hanging out with the locals. When we asked them about the conditions ahead, they got very excited.

One of the men named Benny said, "The Bobongara reef is magic. There is a snakeman living there." I looked at my sailing companions. They were all listening eagerly. Benny continued, "So, when you go there you must be very quiet, no throwing trash in the water or *pis pis*, no swearing or singing or talking loud. It is a very dangerous place." Benny looked deadly serious and the sailors nodded understandingly.

I spread out the map and pointed to our location and asked about where it would be good to go in. I had been looking at a lagoon before the coast changed to cliff again and the reef began. They identified a good place to rest. The village of Wandokai after the reef was also suitable, but Benny warned, "People up there all the way to Wasu can be tricky people, so you look out." We planned to take our chances and sail to the last lagoon before the ominous reef and then spend the night there and next morning. When the wind was fair we would pass the reef and go to Wasu.

"No drama," I confidently responded.

Before departure, Benny's wife cooked us a good lunch and, as we said goodbye, they gave me a *bilum* bag, and in return I gave them a tin of mackerel and a bag of rice. Job had been complaining about pains in his chest, so Benny gave him a pill sheet of amoxicillin, "You drink one a day," he said with ill-informed authority. As we sailed out, I advised Job that it would be better not to take the antibiotics and instead wait until we found a doctor but Job was certain that it helped him — so I laid off.

The sea was dark blue and the wind soon picked up in velocity, gusting between 12 and 20 knots. We were running with a speed of about seven knots and Job was at the back steering our lively canoe as she dove through and then surfed through the waves. Sanakoli was at the sheet and I could tell that the conditions didn't allow him to hand over the sail to me anytime soon. Justin was sitting in front of the mast with his white bucket, chewing *buai*. The coast looked lovely with white beaches, coconut palms and low mountains. I heard Job utter a sound behind me and then I heard a splash and Sanakoli yell. I turned around. Job was trailing after the canoe. I turned to grab our casting rope and throw it to him but then I realised that he was clambering to the rudder that was tied to the outrigger.

Sanakoli slacked the sail and Justin was on his feet. The canoe lost speed and Job pulled himself back up onto the canoe. His wet shirt was sticking to him like a dishrag and his hat was hanging around his neck.

"Are you okay?" I asked.

"I'm all right, just slipped my foot," Job replied, although he didn't seem to be himself. Justin took the rudder and steered in towards shore while I was looking at our map for a place to rest. After 20 minutes, we came in behind a rocky outcrop where the water was relatively calm. We rolled down our big sail and threw out the anchor.

The tall black rocks gave us a welcome break from the wind, although there was still a bit of chop. I made us some biscuits with peanut butter and topped up our ceramic cups with 'dirty watar' as Job called our cola-coloured cordial. But there was no one cracking jokes today. Instead, there was an odd mood onboard. I had an eerie feeling that Job's accident was a bad omen and that we had to be extra careful now. I didn't mention this to the sailors and they didn't express it either but still, there was something in the air — something bad was going to happen and it was as if we all knew.

After eating, I laid the map across my salt spotted shorts and measured our distance. "We don't have long to get to the safe lagoon before the reef so let's go there and continue in the morning when the wind is calm." I pointed out the lagoon that was surrounded on the map by a yellow pattern, which indicated sand on the coast. This was the last suitable landing spot for a while, as the map legend also indicated steep cliffs from there on up the coast. The sailors agreed. Then Justin untied the main sheet from the yard and we changed to the smaller black storm sail.

It was quite a manoeuvre to pull the small sail and spars half way out over the water and pass it onto the other side of the mast and then pull it back in again so it would rest on the deck where it would be tied to the mast rope — but it was even more backbreaking to do the reverse manoeuvre with the mainsail and pull it back into place on the platform next to the strake. As I was jerking the two nine metre spars rolled into our main sail, I congratulated us all on our new stable outrigger.

As soon as we left the protection of the black rocks, we felt the pull of the sail and the power of the winds. It had picked up and felt like over 23 knots, which seemed to be the limit of responsible sailing. The sea soon drenched *Tawali Pasana* and her four souls onboard. There were a fair few white tops and the sea seemed even darker than usual. Something was about to happen. We were doing some long tacks well outwards until the sea started to become too big and then we would tact back inwards until we reached the chop created by waves returning from the shore hitting the open sea waves coming in.

On one of our outwards tacks, I noticed that the shoreline was getting steeper. I looked at my map and then at the GPS. I couldn't believe it — we had sailed a lot faster than I had calculated. We had already reached our lagoon. I showed the GPS to Job who was in the hull bailing.

"Hey, we missed our lagoon, we need to turn around," I said in a loud, strained yell over the roar of the wind and crashing waves.

Job said something to Sanakoli who was standing with one foot in the canoe and the other on the platform controlling the sheet.

"We cannot turn around now, wind is too strong, we must go anyhow," Sanakoli yelled back. "But guys, this is the only place we can go in, from here there is only steep cliffs and the reef."

Justin spoke a few fast words while looking out to the sea. The sky had a strange dead light to it with few clouds and there was nothing to see on the horizon other than some Frigate birds hovering far above. The sharp black silhouette of their wings reminded me of flying foxes.

Sanakoli said, "We make the sail small and go anyhow."

Sanakoli slacked the sail that was now whipping and flapping and Job gave away a metre of main sheet and re-tied the remainder to the mast. With the sail lowered, the three of us — with great effort — rolled some of the sail around the boom and tied it off. Meanwhile, Justin was keeping the canoe straight in the bouncing waves. We let go of the sail. Job jumped back into to the hull to resume bailing. As Sanakoli pulled the sheet, *Tawali Pasana* took off like a racehorse out of a barrier. Although the sail was now smaller, the canoe ran at an unprecedented and unnatural speed.

What happened next was overwhelming. I recall a feeling, not so much fear but more a strange sadness. Along the coast a white wall started to grow taller and taller, seemingly quarantining the wild turmoil of the sea from the lush green hills that rose and sank with rolling undulations. These cliffs continued as far as I could see. I considered whether I should put on one of our lifejackets — but I also wanted to feel free to move around on the canoe. Instead, I released my waist-pack that was secured around the mast. In it was my camera, GPS, notebook and a knife. I hastily clicked it across my naked upper body. Then I double checked that our map was secured with a carabiner and that my navigation bag with the emergency kit was well attached and all pockets were zipped.

The Frigate birds were still with us as we turned the flapping sail into the white tops that frothed like icing on a deep blue sponge cake. We made our way inwards. The wind only seemed to increase in velocity and our old canoe was skating down the swells. As the waves started to become higher, the sea changed colour to a cloudy turquoise.

We were on the reef. The sailors were talking to each other in excited language. I could see the white walls along the coast increasing with spray from the waves crashing at their feet. If we had an accident here, there would be nowhere to go ashore. I understood why Sandy had avoided this piece of coastline in her kayak.

The long swells and the bow catching up with the waves in front was just like a bad déjà vu. As I was sitting behind the mast holding on to the gunwale, an anger rose up in me that was directed towards the sailors. Why had we gotten into this situation? Why hadn't we turned around? Why hadn't they at least rolled up the sail halfway as we had done on the first day? But it was all too late. We were already in a mess and my emotions turned to weird kind of fatalistic sorrow. We were utterly alone — in the hands of lady luck and at the mercy of the sea. So, I did the only thing I could do. I took the waterproof camera out and hit the record button. I was ready. And sure enough, our luck ran out. Everyone yelled. The nose dove into a wave and *Tawali Pasana* was flooded in a second. The sail gave out a gruesome lashing sound as Sanakoli released the sheet.

"Get on the outrigger. Get on the outrigger!" Justin bellowed. A wave from the stern was pushing the canoe sideways and downwards. We all jumped to the outrigger to release the sinking bow from an invisible death grip. The black sail was now thrashing uncontrollably like it wanted to shake the whole canoe apart. As the outrigger came into the sea, Sanakoli jumped to the top rope and the sail fell into the sea. In the madness, a strange distraction came over me. In my mind, everything slowed down and almost stopped. I could see a Frigate bird above me — so close that I began to imagine that I could see the world as he saw it.

‘The wind is strong this afternoon. Turbulence vibrates through my wing feathers. The tumult of the waves below should push fish to the surface any time now. I turn my head sideways and through my black pearly eye I see the mountains. I see the long white cliffs. I see a vast open plane of turquoise uproar. The reef is angry. This is not unusual. But today there is something out of place. This is not common driftwood. It is a platform almost submerged and there is a black shape floating next to it. This is not a time for man to fish. The waves are telling them this. There is a strong man pulling a big oar. He wants to keep the platform in the same place but the reef does not agree. Now the other humans are moving. They are all yelling in their strange call. A man with no hair runs to the front. He is catching something that is floating. Not food; it is wood and plastic. The black-haired human now moves next to the man with the oar. The white human runs to the mast.’

I stuck the camera between my teeth. The saltwater burned in my eyes. I grabbed the pump handle, stuck it in and started to work the bilge pump. Dammit! The strokes were hollow. There was no resistance and so no water blowing out of the pump. I looked at the 38 millimetre hose running into the hull. I shook it and tried again. It was like fighting to wake from a sleep paralysis. Nothing happened. I thought for a second, then I placed my wet hands around the top lid and turned it with all my might. It gave way and I pushed my fist to the inside. The rubber diaphragm moved and so did the handle. I re-sealed the lid and pulled up the handle and, on the down stroke, I now felt the merciful resistance. Yes! And now a hard pull up and a strong push down. The tube rumbled, became stiff and sea water started to spew out of the exhaust tube. It was alive! Harder and stronger. I found my rhythm. We are not going to sink today.

I looked up. Job was standing in the front hull. He looked oddly out of place with the water up to his waist. He had salvaged the floor boards onto the platform and he was now bailing with our saucepan.

Sanakoli was in the back, mirroring Job's hectic motions with the plastic helmet. I took the camera out of my mouth and positioned it on the floor pointing at me and then swapped arms. The sea was pushing us inwards and Justin was fully occupied keeping our dear canoe from broadsiding on the swells coming from behind. But now, the balance on our nautical bank book was starting to look good again. More water was leaving the canoe than was coming in and Sanakoli shifted focus to the floating sail and started to salvage it with the help of Job. They wrapped it all together in a great bundle, tied it off with the sheet and manoeuvred its heavy bulk up onto the gunwale.

Water was spilling out of the black plastic as the sail was rested securely on the canoe. Finally, the pump's exhaust pipe started to cough and I congratulated our bilge pump on a job well done under extreme circumstances. With the hull empty we could focus on secondary matters and with hectic movements we placed the water containers back into the hull and put the floorboards back in place. Our storm sail was still taking up most of the space in the canoe but we didn't dare raise it or try to manoeuvre it onto the platform next to the main sail. It was just too dangerous in these conditions. With the canoe now empty and things back in order, our confidence grew, although there was no safe landing ground in sight.

Job picked up an oar and started paddling. Sanakoli burst open one of our spare plastic sheets and I helped him tie the fluttering life-form between the mast and one of the riggings. It immediately functioned like a small two metre by one metre sail. Then he grabbed a paddle and started digging into the sea in front of Justin who was using all his considerable might to keep the canoe straight in the swell. My camera was still recording. I yelled to Sanakoli, "What are we doing now?"

Sanakoli quickly took a finger to his lips and looked around with eyes wide open. "Shush… now we be quiet, no talk." The message was clear. It was time to be humble. There was no landing in sight and the reef was still frothing and spewing and convulsing. So, I took up a paddle and started paddling as well.

Humans on the cliffs

We continued like this for what felt like an eternity. The sea was incredibly beautiful in its destructive power. The looming grey skies, the stoic white walls and the sizzling foam gave the water a most intense turquoise glow that seemed brighter than the sky, a glow so vivid and sharp that it felt serenely deadly. We were all sitting in a row with bowed heads as we dug through the clear liquid, stoke by stroke, desperately trying to break up the dark silhouettes. When I looked around, there was nothing in sight to comfort my troubled mind. Waves were breaking everywhere on a never-ending reef and, when we looked ashore in the hope of finding a small beach or protected backwater, waves would explode there as well, as if the sea spray painted the wall with great running block letters that spelt out, 'abandon all hope ye who enter.' So instead, I bowed my head again and listened. I listened to the flapping sail, the clash of water against the hull and the regular rush of a wave cresting behind us.

The sound of these waves was the worst. Every time I felt the grip of a big wave lifting the canoe, an eerie thought ran through me like being forced to look at a reopened wound. Would this be the one to tip us over? But Justin always managed to wedge us out of the ocean's grip and let the hull skate off at the last second as the foam crashed down onto our brave outrigger in a hard, vengeful pull that yanked the whole canoe and made the rigging whip. It was an awfully tormenting situation to be in but there was nothing to do but paddle steadily and let the wind and the waves push us along the coast. I tried to get a few shots of the beautiful and harrowing scenery. Most importantly, I reminded myself that, should we end up in the water, we would still have a canoe to hang on to and from there, there would still be a few more dance steps of disaster to go through before the reef would claim our lives.

It was late afternoon when we started to notice the tops of coconut palms above the cliffs. A little later, we spotted the first human. They waved, yelled and whistled at us but they were too far up and we just waved back. Soon after, we started to see what looked like the wall turning and slowly but steadily a wide lagoon started to come into sight. Hope and relief grew in my chest as a quarter of an hour later we rounded the wall and came into the calm water of the most beautiful bay imaginable. The rays of evening light slowly melted the grey clouds and punctuated the grass mountains which slowly rolled into forest and spilled out on a white cobblestone beach.

This whole incredible landscape was framed by a bright turquoise bay. It looked otherworldly. I had never expected to experience such geography in PNG. So, I broke the silence. "What do you say guys, isn't this beautiful!"

"Yes," Sanakoli replied. "Sooo beautiful and they got cows in those mountains," and he pointed to some white and brown dots high on the mountain side. I was happy and proud that we had made it past the ominous reef that had fostered so much dread and despair. In my mind, I was already planning to make the sailors a good meal of rice and noodles — with not one but two tins of mackerel for dinner — and then we would all have a good talk about the events of the day and congratulate each other on how well we had handled the near disaster.

As we paddled nearer the shore, people came from all directions to meet us on the beach. There were women on their way back to the village carrying firewood and garden food in big *bilums* on their backs and there were men with long slim bush knives and hide whips. As we came ashore and shook hands, I noticed that many of them were wearing colourful necklaces of tiny plastic beads. And here, the men's *bilums* looked more like shoulder bags made out of jeans or whatever cloth they had at hand. The people said we were welcome and that we would be safe on the beach. A man started a fire for us while the rest of the crowd helped pull the canoe up on the white rocks.

As the evening sun turned the beach pink, people slowly dispersed — but a handful of locals stayed back to chew *buai*, tell stories and look after us. We had shared tea and biscuits with our new friends but now the rice was boiling and there was still a lot of people around, too many to feed. I didn't want to flash too much wealth around so I only took out one tin of mackerel. I knew that Sanakoli and Justin weren't keen on eating in front of strangers and, when I told them that dinner was ready, they just encouraged me to go ahead. This wasn't the first time we had been in such a situation and it annoyed me a great deal. I knew they would be starving and needed the energy. Job had left us as soon as we reached shore and was now was sitting 100 metres up the beach with his own little fire burning, talking to a local. I went up to tell him that dinner was ready but he just said, "I'm all right, you eat."

I kind of understood why eating in front of others made the sailors uncomfortable and I also knew that after dark they would sneak down and make themselves a plate. But I was hungry and too tired of their shenanigans, so I just served myself and climbed onto the canoe where I could eat in privacy. The last rays of the day coloured my face and the big plate of rice went down very quickly. It struck me that now I was eating the same size portions as the sailors. If you don't know when the next meal will present itself, then you might as well get as much onboard as possible.

I sat looking at the contours of the island of Umboi and the larger mass of New Britain across the strait. There was a warm breeze from inland, flowing with the scent of the green hills. All day I had the scream of hissing wind and waves in my ears, now the only sound coming from the ocean was a gentle swell across the turquoise lagoon, kissing the white round pebbles on the beach. The ocean was a formidable entity. And what a beautiful ending to an almost disastrous day. I laughed out loud with contentment at the feeling of wearing dry clean clothes. I laid down on the rattan platform with my hands resting behind my neck and closed my eyes as I recounted the events of the day. It had gone so fast, except the paddling from the reef to the lagoon. I felt that we should have a meeting tomorrow on the canoe, when offshore. It would be good for all of us just to talk about what had happened and how we could avoid such situations in the future but, most importantly, it would be good to congratulate ourselves all on having performed well. But as I was laying there my thoughts were suddenly interrupted by loud yelling.

I rose up and saw that the noise came from a group of boys that had been hanging out a few metres from the canoe. Was it about us? Everyone was yelling in the group and in the dim light they seemed to my eye like just one black mass. Suddenly the circle widened as a wild scream was heard and one guy lashed out towards another. The target didn't seem as willing to fight but desperately kept the attacker away with his bush knife. Soon blades were flying back and forth, one in defence and the other in attack. The attacker was wild with anger and screamed in rage as he swung his long thin blade in fast cuts, forcing the other guy into the water. It was clear that somebody was going to get seriously hurt. Luckily, the bystanders had the same notion and tried to break up the combatants while avoiding the sharp knives themselves.

When a couple of men finally came in between the two rivals, the man in defence took off at a high pace across the beach and disappeared into the bushes while the attacker was cut off by his friends. I looked at Justin and Sanakoli and a couple of local men who were standing next to the canoe watching the whole thing. Sanakoli explained, "Our friends tell us that that running boy was seeing the other boy's sister and he didn't like it." Sanakoli looked serious, "If he hadn't made '*sixty*' (the Milne Bay slang for taking off or running fast) into the bush, he would cut him." One of the locals who was wearing a 'US GI jungle hat' said in a consoling voice, "Don't worry friends, you are safe here. We will stay with you on the beach." I told them that we were very glad to hear this and thankful for having their company. Then I helped Sanakoli pull our storm sail down onto the beach and make an open shelter by resting one end of the bamboo boom on the platform and the other in the wedge of two paddles stuck between the stones and tied together in an 'X' shape. The plastic sheet was our roof and the wooden yard kept it suspended.

As we were working Sanakoli said to me, “You pack your things properly before you sleep,” and he nodded towards my swim shorts and underwear that was hanging to dry on the outrigger. I complied and we finished the shelter quickly. I rolled out my sleeping bag on the warm stones and took out my notebook. It wasn’t even necessary to use the head-torch as the full moon lit up the entire beach in a beautiful white light glow. After recounting the events of the day, I repacked the dry bag and put it next to my head. I snuggled up in my sleeping bag and instantly fell into a deep sleep.

I woke. It was like something had passed by my head. What time was it? It felt like night but I heard the low plonk of stone against each other as they were being stepped on. My eyes were itching from salt. The moon was still up and the round pebbles on the beach were shining like millions dying light bulbs. I was alone in the shelter. That sound again. I turned my head and then held my breath; 20 metres in front of me was a person. It looked like a young man but he was hunching while making slow sneaking steps towards the bush. He was barefooted with a white T-shirt on and a *bilum* over his shoulder. In one hand, he had a 50-centimetre long bush knife, thin and rounded, and in the other hand he was carrying my dry bag!

I jumped out of the sleeping bag and said in a loud voice, “Hey man, what are you doing!”

The first reaction of the robber was to make an almost comical shocked jump. He dropped both the bag and the knife and, with a loud clang, he took off. My shoulders fell but instantly rose again as the robber suddenly turned around and picked up his knife. My split-second reaction was to take some rocks and throw them at his face. However, as soon as the guy picked up his knife, he turned on his heels and made *'sixty'* into the bush.

'Bloody hell' I thought. I was shocked but most of all annoyed. I just wanted to have a proper night's sleep with no more dramas. But I kind of understood the guy as well. People here had very little material wealth and he had seen an opportunity. I walked over and picked up my dry bag. There wasn't even anything of value in it, except my Batman Diary and a book. I went up on the side of the canoe and woke up Sanakoli and told him what had happened. And then I went to the fire where the other men were sleeping and told them. There wasn't much we could do, so we all just went back to sleep.

The moon was still up when morning came. I went to the canoe and downloaded the weather report for the day. It didn't look good. The wind would be picking up by midday, just as we probably would be rounding Teliata Point where the two seas meet. But on the positive side, there was quite a few places to call in, although we had been warned about some of the communities in this area. The sailors got up and villagers started walking by on their way into the mountains. As we were packing, I discovered that some of our clothes were missing from the drying line. I had forgotten to pack it away before going to bed. By this stage, I was pretty fed up with the place and just wanted to get out of there.

Tawali Pasana slid easily off the beach and into the flat bright sea and we started supporting the sail with with our paddles. Sanakoli was arranging our small solar cell on the platform to charge his phone.

I said to Job, "Hey man, they nicked my underwear and shorts from the canoe last night."

Job wasn't his usual expressive self, as he sat there with the now dwindling beach behind him. In a moody mumbling voice, he said, "They took my hat too and Justin lost his slippers. These people are not good. *Raskol* people they steal. They are not like Yambo, Mambututu, Morobe, Tufi, they are good people. We must know this next time come here, they are not open people, some people are good, some are bad."

I nodded, "Yes but the elder people seemed kind of nice."

"Yes, they were good people," Job nodded in synchronisation with the canoe.

Sanakoli had gone on to cut firewood and now he had placed a pot of rice on the smoking stove. I turned to him and asked what he thought of the events of the previous day.

"It was so lucky that we make things quickly. If you make things easy, easy and slowly, then you can get into an accident."

I nodded and replied, "It was actually quite scary, I thought, wow this is bad but I think the worst part was when we got the small sail up and I was seeing the waves crashing into the outrigger sometimes. Could they have pulled it down?"

Sanakoli made a confirming shake with his head, "Yeah, yeah, they can pull it down but our outrigger is new and strong enough. I was thinking that if we had come with the old one then we would definitely get accident yesterday." He paused and looked on to the map. "So maybe on our way we have to get some place to dry our outrigger. I think if the outrigger gets dry in three days, or two days, it will float more than now. If it is really dry, I think four of us can stand on the outrigger."

"Should we try and see how many can stand on it now?" I asked jokingly.

Job cut in and corrected me. "If you go on the what now, the outrigger can't sink because we have the sail up."

"I am just trying to make jokes," I said in a disarming tone.

Sanakoli laughed agreeably, "Yes, you are trying to make us happy! Yes, the outrigger cannot sink when the sail is up."

I replied, "Yes we are sailing."

Sanakoli continued in a high singing voice, "Yes, because we are on our journey!"

Job didn't partake in the cheering but just sat hunched by the rudder. I asked Sanakoli, "What did you mean when you did that 'shush' on the reef. Why was that?"

He became serious. "That was because the Finschafen people said that this was the death point. That's the dangerous point. So, they said if anything is wrong don't talk a lot or shout or speak in different languages. That why, when you ask me explain what's happening, I said 'shush.' Our safety is more important than explaining."

I was hoping that Sanakoli would say something about the snake witch but instead I confirmed, "So we actually passed the most dangerous part now."

"Yeah. We are past the point and now we are on good travels again."

I faced Job and asked him if he wanted to say something. He shook his head in an avoiding way, "No, I want to wash my eyes."

"Are they burning?" I asked.

"No, yesterday I fall into the sea and I didn't rinse my eyes, my eyes always do like this if I don't wash them. So our eyes don't make itchy, like something is scraping them." But Job interrupted himself, "Ay somebody ringing!" A faint ringtone was heard from Sanakoli's red phone. But then the battery died.

I turned off my camera and looked at the map. The next big town was Wasu. Sandy had recommended that we go in there and, at the same time, she had warned us to stay well away of Long Island, which was an intriguing looking round island with a crater lake in the middle, just off the coast. Apparently, Long Island was home to some of the worst pirates in the area, making the coast to Madang a risky proposition — not unlike most of the coastline in PNG.

Chapter Ten

Infections

Late in the afternoon, we came into the bay of Schlangen Harbour. We could see Wasu in the bottom of the wide bay but it seemed like the sailors just wanted to continue past, although they didn't say this to me, which annoyed me a great deal, so I said, "Hey guys what is the plan? Either we sail through the whole night or else we go in here now. Remember that we all agreed that we didn't want to arrive in a village in the middle of the night." The sailors discussed this amongst themselves. I was feeling a bit dizzy, maybe from being in the sun all day, and the last thing I wanted was another night of drama and uncertainty. Sandy had recommended this small outpost as a good place to go in.

Then Job turned to me and said rather annoyed, "OK we go in and you go straight to the Magistrate and ask him to look after us." I agreed to this and the sailors said *yaya-towa*, which was their word for turning the canoe. Wasu looked rather developed from afar, it had a great concrete pier but no ships around it.

As we got closer, a great school of tuna suddenly started jumping in front of us. "Oh, yellowfin," Job said with an excited voice and the other sailors also became all fired up. We hadn't had any fresh fish since we left Bucava, so this opportunity was too good to be true. Job scrambled through our green plastic container with fishing kit and cordage, found the plastic spool with the 25-pound line with the squid bait, quickly threw it out and trolled it behind the canoe as we all watched in anticipation. Job would sit with the circular plastic spool in one hand and softly jerk the 25-pound nylon line with his other hand. "Kisoo!" He yelled out, as the thin nylon made a sharp tug into the blue deep. Job jumped up as the fish aggressively forced him to slacken metre after metre of line. It was a delicate fight, the line was way too thin for the strong fish, so Job spent some nerve wrecking five minutes of giving and taking the line before he could start pulling in again.

As we started to see the light blue torpedo shape wriggle of the creature below, we all hooted in excitement but the fish suddenly dug under our canoe as if it had heard our death chant. Job quickly steered the line over the head of Justin by the rudder and handed the line to Sanakoli who was better positioned on the platform. As soon as his hands were free, he went to the outrigger and took up Justin's long barbed spear. The fish was getting tired and Sanakoli steadily pulled the big tuna close and, as it gave side, Job thrust the spear into the sea. There was an instant explosion of splashing water. The whole of Job's upper body was shaking as he tried to keep hold of the long spear that was about to be jerked out of his hands. Justin and Sanakoli yelled and screamed with excitement. Job was shaking all over. In a slow hard lift, Job got the fat fish up on the rattan. The sharp tail whipped in death spasms as thick red blood pumped out onto our deck. It was a beautiful yellowfin tuna of about seven kilos, expertly speared just above its long black side fins. We all hooted excitedly and congratulated each other on the great catch.

The arrival at Wasu was like so many others. We were instantly surrounded by curious locals, they were all over the small beach, some of them even wading out into the water to hold on to the railing and look at or equipment, meanwhile, screaming kids were playing around in the water. I was feeling quite dizzy but kept up my welcoming countenance, as my philosophy was: the better people know you and what you are about, the less likely they are to rob you.

So I started shaking hands with as many as possible while saying the usual phrases: "Hello, we come from Milne Bay and we are sailing the whole way around the island of New Guinea — both Papua New Guinea and West Papua Indonesia." Curious eyes everywhere, red betel nut smiles, rough stiff hands, polite nods, sweat and *buai*, shuffling bare feet. "My name is Thor, I'm from Denmark, Europe… Yes, far up north… yes, very cold. That's why I like Papua New Guinea, such a beautiful place." Sanakoli and Job had gone ashore too and were shaking hands, giving out blessings and answering questions. After a while things settled down, a fire had been lit and the atmosphere was good. I was introduced to one of the local politicians. He said that we would be all right here but there were some bad characters from other parts of the coast, so he promised to arrange for two fully-armed security guards who could help look after us and he invited me to spend the night in their Local Level Government (LLG) compound. I thanked him gratefully and he said he would send one of his boys to pick me up later.

After the most important things were sorted, I climbed back onto the canoe with weak legs. There was a bit of surge pulling the canoe back and forth but we didn't want the canoe hived up on land, as then there would be people all around the canoe and, by having *Tawali Pasana* afloat, we could also make a quick exit if needed. As I rose up on the platform, I felt a feverish sensation roll in. I looked down at my swollen toe and it felt like it was pounding. I assumed that it was the infection that was giving me fever, although it might as well be an outbreak of malaria. I looked around, smoke was stinging my eyes as Justin was trying to light our stove with some wet firewood. I knew that we didn't have any antibiotics in our small first aid kit on deck, all our special medicine was well stowed away in an orange dry bag under the floorboards and, with this circus of people around, I didn't want to start displaying all our luggage. I went to Job who had come aboard to collect his basket, "Hey man, can you give me some of your amoxicillin?"

"I don't have," he said in an avoiding way.

"But I know you still have some, they are in your pocket or the basket you are holding. I'll give you some new ones tomorrow."

"Enough," Job said and jumped onto the beach and walked through the crowd.

Cold pearls of sweat were forming on my hot forehead, although the wet shorts and damp T-shirt were chilling me. But inside my chest, I felt a fire, not of sickness but of rage. I tried to shake the anger off me and ran the palm of my hand over my face in an effort to think clearly. I thought: The sun is almost down, I'll wait till it's dark, then most people will go to their houses and I can dig around for the medicine box without too many bystanders. I sat down behind Justin to have a break from people; he was now chopping up the tuna with the small bush knife. After a little while, Sanakoli came back aboard and said, there are two mothers here who want to cook for us."

"What do they wanna cook?" I asked, as I woke from my own thoughts.

"The fish, they feel sorry for us, we give them the fish and garden food and they go to house cook and come back and we eat."

"Wow, that's the best news ever" I said, just give them a bag of rice and as many bananas they want and the fish." Sanakoli made a face of profound contemplation and then said: "Me, I think we give them half the fish and Justin smoke the other."

"Even better, good job! Then we can have fish for breakfast." My mood instantly improved at the thought of such a wholesome breakfast.

The sun was almost down and I told Sanakoli what had happened with Job. "Yes, I heard him. I thought hey, I don't like the way he speaks to our friend, that is no proper way to speak." I agreed and asked him to sit in front of me to screen off the view of the onlookers. When he was in position, I opened the floorboards next to him. I shuffled a rice sack and found the orange bag in the dark. I pulled it out and took out our waterproof medicine box. On the inside of the lid, I had taped a list of our medicine stock and a short description of what it was for — flucloxacillin: Skin and soft tissue infections — 500 mg — two tablets — every eight hours. Eureka! I found the package, stuffed it in my pocket and went ashore to greet the two security guards who had had come to look after us. One of them had an old rifle and the other one a baton. I guessed that it would be better than nothing and we negotiated that they would get 12 kina each to look after us, and then I added a piece of tuna to the bargain, which seemed to make them happier about the job.

Swearing

Now that the safety was sorted, I felt the jobs for the day were done. The young man who was to show me to my bed for the night had arrived. The prospect of getting away from the spectacle of people on the dark beach far exceeded my desire to wait for a hot meal cooked with love by two Papua New Guinean mothers, so I picked up my sleeping kit, a package of biscuits, a jar of peanut butter and said goodbye to Justin and Sanakoli. At the edge of the beach, I passed Job who was sitting by himself looking at his phone, I knelt down next to him and asked if could just have a word with him:

"Hey man, I think it wasn't a very good way you spoke to me on the canoe, when I ask you for help it is very impolite to say 'enough.'"

Job had been looking sternly at the ground while I was talking and then he answered: "That is the way we talk."

I got agitated. "I am sick and I was asking for medicine and then you just shoved me off! This makes me really hurt and sad."

“But there were many people so I couldn’t give you!” Job answered in a rapid angry voice.

“But that was exactly why I asked for your medicine instead of having to pull everything out of the fucking canoe to find it!” I hissed in a loud voice.

Job replied in a hurtful tone: “If you swear at me, then I leave. Then I go home.”

I realised that I had made a mistake then, and said: “Sorry Job, but I wasn’t swearing at you, I was swearing at the canoe. I am just disappointed that you told me ‘enough.’” Job didn’t react, he was just sitting with his arms around his knees looking at the dirty sand between his feet. I rose up, paused for a second to let the vertigo pass and then followed my guide up through a wide dirt road with no lighting, which was the main street of Wasu.

There were houses that had been built with modern materials long ago and they all had high fences around them. As we walked, I thought of the conversation with Job. From his Christian viewpoint swearing was really bad. In the broader Papua New Guinean public, you never heard swearing either, maybe a ’shit’ once in a while but that was as bad as it normally got. Personally, I didn’t like to use swear words either, as I believed one should be able to master one’s language powerfully without resorting to the use of obscenities. But now, when the ‘shit hit the fan,’ my high ideals didn’t hold up. After ten minutes, we came to the local government office compound. The main building was newly painted timber and elevated a metre above ground. To the right there was a small barracks-like building that I was shown into. It looked like the place was being renovated; there was nothing in the dark room besides a pile of building rubbish in one corner and a couple of bunkbeds.

I was given one of the beds, which I soon furnished with mosquito net and sleeping bag, and then I was left alone. After a dry meal of chicken flavoured biscuits and peanut butter, I swallowed my antibiotics and rinsed my swollen toe with iodine. I regretted that I didn’t have any of that tuna, my body was struggling and needed some protein. Protein and salad, that was what it needed. But I was now so thrilled finally to be on my own as I lay down to get a proper nights' sleep. The room smelled like mould or maybe it was my sleeping bag. It was greasy and humid, that was for sure, but it was so good to finally have a rest. I thought of Job; what a mess, poor guy, we would need to get him back in the game. The mosquitoes were bouncing off the net. I hoped it wasn't malaria and just an infection. In Venezuela, I nearly died of dengue fever and definitely did not want a repeat of that. My strings of thought slowly dissolved and I floated blissfully into space, but was suddenly pulled back down to earth as I heard people enter the room and bright lights shone at me.

At first, I was shocked, but then understood that it was the police. I got out of my sleeping bag and humped towards the men. The police captain was a very sturdy man, about my height, with the rough facial features of a highlander and was in his mid-forties. He had a black mustache and presented himself as Captain Korop Bako as we shook hands. He said, "I just come to check up on you and see if everything is all right, and you didn't have any trouble."

I told him I was fine and that the canoe was being looked after by two local guards.

The captain nodded: "I just wanted to check up on you, because we just caught two young men this evening, they were in a stolen dinghy, not out to do good things."

One of the police officers was still blinding me with his torch, I held my hand up over the eyes.

"Good to hear that you are keeping the coast safe," I said in a complimentary tone.

"Yes, you people take care on this coast, too many rascals around here," he said, looking tired.

"At least you have some good firepower and some tough looking men," I said while trying to look encouraging in the spotlight.

The captain seemed to ignore this and instead he picked up his red plastic phone, the same as Sanakoli. The display gave his rough face a blue hue: "You take my number and if you get in trouble you call me and let me know where you are." I thanked him and he continued. "I'll have a couple of my men patrol this area and make sure no one disturbs you." I thanked him again, we exchanged numbers, shook hands and they all left.

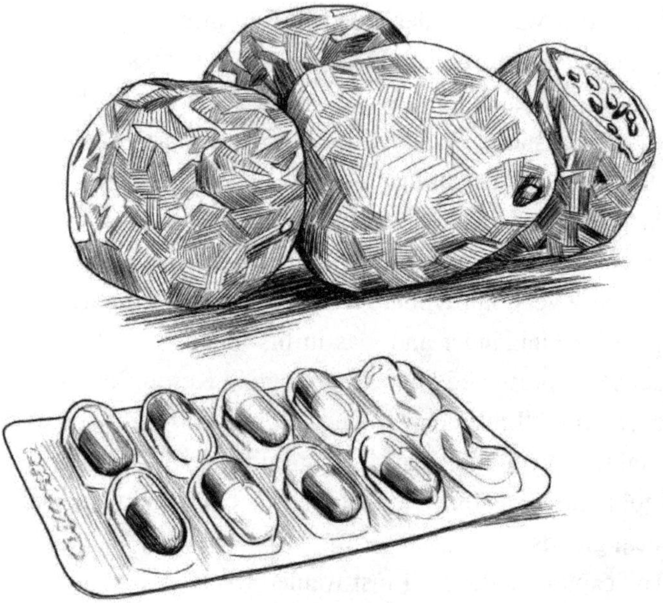

After an uneventful night in the barracks, I returned to the canoe in the morning. The two hired guards were sitting by a fire on the beach and all seemed to be in order. My fever seemed to have subsided, so I reckoned that it was just the infection that made me ill and not a mosquito-borne illness. I was starving, so after greeting everyone good morning, I eagerly asked the sailors where the smoked tuna was. Sanakoli looked sad, "There is no more tuna, the dogs ate it all. Your man Justin there put it in the saucepan with a lid but the dogs, they what, they stole it in the night."

"What, how did that happen?"

"They climb on the canoe while we sleep. We didn't see them. They come and steal." I shook my head in disbelief, my body was craving protein to battle the infection but instead I made do with some chicken flavour biscuits from our lunch box. Then I remembered the passionfruit I had bought on the way through the town and cut one of them open. Slurping down the liquid pulp was so revitalising and I instantly realised how much I had been missing vitamins.

Justin and Sanakoli were preparing for take-off but Job was sitting by himself on the beach, so I walked over and sat down next to him. Job was feeling sad that I had sworn at him. I tried to make him see our controversy from my perspective. But he was hurt that I had sworn at him and wanted to go home from Madang. I gave up on trying to convince him that I hadn't sworn at him. I ran my hand through my greasy hair, and said, "I'll happily buy you the ticket home but I think it would be a great shame, you are very important for this expedition, it is a very hard journey but if we just find a good way to work together then we can make it."

My voice then started to crack, "I am very grateful for our friendship Job, we cannot give up now, we have to keep fighting together." Job was very moved by these words, although he didn't look up. My eyes were wet too, I couldn't bear it anymore and stood up. Ten minutes later Job untied the stern line, washed the sand off the rope and jumped on board.

Expedition Log 20 September 2016

07:30 hrs. Departing Wasu. 4-6 knots of wind. It is quite a busy place and now all dinghy drivers in the area know that there is a canoe with a white man going to Madang. It would have been better if we continued past Wasu yesterday, as the sailors wanted to do. The sailors are on edge, the guards have been feeding them pirate stories all night. I keep our map and my phone at hand all times, ready to call Captain Korop Bako if a fast-moving dinghy should approach.

Chapter Eleven

Kidnapped

In the late afternoon we sailed into Nima, Gali Parish. The village looked like any other but one hut stood out amongst all the other bush material huts, and that was the one with a parabola on the roof. It was the first time I'd seen this in PNG. The following morning, I woke in the hut with the satellite dish. My room had a big whiteboard with some community stakeholder diagrams. On the wall were posters with infographics and team-building tables. The hut was owned by a man in his 50s of Anglo-Australian and Papua New Guinean descent named Shannon. He used to work as a consultant for several mining operations around PNG. Now he lived in his wife's village while she was teaching in Madang.

Shannon took me on a tour around Nima and explained, "You see, this is the trail that leads down to the creek. It is a long walk down there to get drinking water. Oh, you saw it last night yourself, maybe 15, maybe 20 minutes through the bush. I have been trying to organise these people, set up a council so that we can apply for funding and build a well in the centre of the village. There is freshwater down there you know and we could even run it on an electrical pump, but you can't organise these people, it is like they don't see the idea."

He looked tired. So I tried to comfort him by saying that I knew the feeling of being with companions that not are on the same page as you. The village seemed very dry and flat with sand on the ground, nonetheless there were pretty flowers planted around the houses, an elementary school, and at the edge of the jungle there was a grassy well-maintained soccer and volleyball field. We walked to the beach that was already shimmering with heat. In front was a large inshore reef and further out you could see a few white crests, indicating where the reef drops and the deep begins.

Shannon shaded his eyes, "When I came here as a younger man, the reef was full of fish. People would paddle out in outrigger canoes with hooks and catch only what they needed — good fish you know. Now they are using torches in the night and have spears and take everything they can get near. The fish they catch now are small. Maybe it also has something to do with climate change. Back in the day, the beach was much further out and there were huts where we are standing now — but the sea has eaten it all away."

We waved goodbye to Shannon and the villagers of Nima as the wind slowly carried us up along the coast. There was little breeze out further, just like the last couple of mornings. Job called to me from his position by the rudder, "Thor come, now you steer." I walked over to the back of the platform next to Job. He was squatting in the back end of the canoe with one foot on each side of the railing supporting the rudder, or *yabby yabby* as he called it, with both hands. A rope was fastened to the top of the long paddle and the other end had a loop that was tied onto one of the outrigger sticks.

Job started to explain and instruct, "You just keep the *yabby yabby* like this. If you want to go left you push like this." He pushed the back edge of the paddle blade with his foot outwards and the canoe instantly started turning left. "Now if you want to go, what, right, you pull the *yabby yabby,*" and he pulled the long blade almost out of the water and the canoe started veering right. "Now you try." Job stood up and I carefully stepped over and behind him as he quickly stooped under the rope and jumped into the hull — and, just like that, I found myself steering the canoe.

I was standing with one foot on each of the railings holding the *yabby yabby* with one hand and gripping the support rope with the other. I was surprised how stable the great rudder felt. The motion of the water running past the hull pushed it firmly into the side of the tree trunk, which easily kept it in place thanks to the counter pull of the rope connected to the top shaft of the rudder.

"Wow, this is great!" I exclaimed with nervous excitement.

The sailors laughed and Job said, "Now you push the *yabby yabby* with your foot." I positioned my toes and the palm of my foot on the blade and slowly pushed outwards. There was a lot of resistance and my toes started to hurt. But the back end of the blade angled away from the side and the canoe turned. I quickly let go again but the sail felt like it was pulling too much wind.

Job said, "Not too much. Pull up the steer. You turn too much." I pulled the heavy piece of rosewood almost out of the water and felt how all my support disappeared and I almost lost my balance but regained it by pulling counter to the support rope tied to the outrigger. The canoe now slowly turned back on course and the sail started to lose its pull. "Now you put it down again, we don't want to sink," Job laughed. I pushed the heavy thing into the sea and slowly got us back on course. Now that I knew the extremes, I would just have to learn how much adjustment was needed to keep the canoe in trim.

It was like making an even, bold line with a spray can — you need to have a constant distance to the wall and then be careful not to move too fast or the line becomes weak. But not too slow either, because then the paint runs. It's about finding the middle-way and you only learn how to master this through many hours of practice. "That's the one," Sanakoli said with his mouth full of *buai*, dipping the stalk of green mustard into his lime container. "Now you learn how to sail and we can have a rest." I was standing in full concentration, focusing on our course and how the sail was pulling and keeping my balance.

I glanced at the joking sailors. "This is really painful for the toes. How do you do this all day?"

Job lifted his left foot and pointed it at me grinning. "We sailors we have tough skin but we pain too, you must harden your skin so it will grow tough." I didn't last more than 15 minutes before both my feet, my lower back and my left arm were aching. I handed the rudder back to Job who made yet another funny remark.

The wind picked up around midday and we started to make some good miles up along the coast. We got the stove burning and put a saucepan on with a kilogram of rice. We were all eager to get to Madang, which we would probably reach the next day. Madang is a large town that is renowned for its charm. And it is a very good place for wreck diving since it was occupied by Japanese forces during World War Two. Because the Japanese never had air superiority, most of their resupply boats were sunk *en route* from home ports and now rest at the bottom of the sea.

Job had spent some time there when he was younger and even had family in a village further up the coast. He didn't talk a lot about his time in Madang but said that there were many *raskols* there and we would have to be careful. Sandy Robson on the other hand claimed that Madang was an easy-going place, so I didn't take too much notice of Job's doomsday predictions. Madang was an important port of call for us. I needed to follow up on our passports and not least my visa for

Indonesia. The outrigger also needed to dry out thoroughly because, as Sanakoli put it, "It still green inside." The problem was that we needed a safe place to put the canoe on land, so although I hated to ask for help, I had contacted two of the major resorts in Madang in the hope that one of them would host us for free. I felt nervous about this because I was afraid of rejection.

Our stove was burning well despite splashes of sea water from the running canoe raining down on the embers, and soon we had a pot of rice ready. We were low on conserves, so I pulled out one of Sandy's outdoor meals from the hull. "Hey do you guys like spaghetti Bolognese?"

"What, what is that", Sanakoli asked from the stern.

"It is spaghetti, an Italian dish; it is famous all over the world," I explained while filling the aluminium-lined bag with hot water.

"We don't have that in Papua New Guinea," Job said.

"You are in for a treat then, it is really good," I said excitedly. Four metal plates were spread out on the platform. Justin divided the rice evenly and I unwrapped the spaghetti bag and poured the hot Bolognese sauce onto the rice. The smell was terrific. It reminded me of Europe.

Sanakoli picked up his plate and poked the contents with his spoon. "Eeey… what is this?" he said with an air of great scepticism.

Job lifted the spaghetti with his spoon and giggled loudly. "This looks like the worms from the belly of the pig!" Everyone cracked up and he laughed. "When we cut pig, this is what we find in the stomach." Despite their hesitation, the sailors ate the spaghetti and meat sauce, although they weren't too impressed. I was hungry but I couldn't eat all of my rice.

Sanakoli noted this and said, "You give me what you can't finish and I'll eat it — like old man Mambututu." We all cracked up again and I handed him the plate.

A black bay

In the late afternoon, the clouds over the land had an odd yellowish grey colour. I asked the sailors, "Have you guys ever seen a sky like this before?"

Sanakoli took off his sunglasses and said, "Eey, I've never seen clouds like that." We were still a good day's travel from Madang and starting to look for a place to land. According to the map, there were a few villages along this coast so it was just a matter of choosing one that looked like it had a protected beach to land on. We were about two nautical miles off the coast and had started to make our way inwards when the wind suddenly picked up. A strong squall ran down from the mountains ripping the sea surface up as it rolled over us, stretching every wire and rope on the canoe.

The big blue sail aggressively pulled the outrigger out of the water as we shot off up and along the coast. This was way too much force for the canoe and the sail was stretched to the limit. There was nothing we could do but hold on and run with it. Job and Justin climbed to the outrigger to counter-weight the pull of the sail. I was in the hull bailing and Sanakoli was holding the rudder, bouncing up and down as we skated over the waves. Foam was splashing in from the bow and the hull steadily filled with water. Every time it was above my ankle I would bend down and start bailing again. "Always empty your bucket on the platform," were Sanakoli's words of instruction, "Because, if you do it on the other side, a wave can catch your bucket and then you lose it." I had no intention of losing our bailer and flushed the platform as best I could.

The light was dimming and the mountains were now silhouettes; and this revealed the reason for the dirty sky. Up on the slopes, we could see the distinctive flaring red lines of fire. It was most likely the locals who were practicing swidden agriculture (a process of cultivating and fallowing land) to prepare new gardens or grassland. I thought to myself, as if my present situation wasn't dramatic enough, being on a leaking canoe that was being pushed uncontrollably by a

squall into the night, up a coast known to be thick with pirates — hey, why not add fire and billowing thick smoke just to top it off. I shook my head as I thought back on the events of the last few days: The near disaster on Bobongara reef, the knife fight, the robbery, the pirates in Wasu, the fever, the risk of losing Job, and now this. But I wasn't about to break. Instead I focused on the mechanical art of bailing while appreciating the apocalyptic inferno along the coast.

As the sun set, the wind lowered its velocity. About an hour later, we made it into a large bay and the wind dropped completely. The water was calm and dark as ink. We took up our paddles and slowly made it inwards. The moon wasn't up yet and the contours of the mountains were just one black mass. It was hard to distinguish how deep a bay we were in, but as we came closer to land, we could see white lights along the shore. But it didn't look like village lights. "Fishermen," Job whispered, "They are out in their boats catching fish with their lights." We didn't have a light on the canoe as we thought it wise to avoid detection. But we needed to find out where there was a village to go to, so I found the map, sat down in the wet hull and turned on the red light on my head torch. By comparing maps to my GPS reading I soon found our position — but there were no settlements in that area. It all just looked like mangroves along the coast.

Job interrupted me with a sharp whisper. "You turn off that red light, it burns my eyes. You use normal light."

I whispered back, "No, that's the whole point of using red light, you don't lose your night-vision."

Job wasn't convinced. "That is devil's light, the devil sees the red colour."

I was now getting annoyed by Job's wacky beliefs. "So, you would rather be blinded by the white light?" I whispered even more annoyed.

"You two be quiet, someone's coming!" Sanakoli said in a low strained voice. I turned the light off and raised my head out of the canoe. We all sat still, listening. There was a motor in the distance and then we saw one of the lights moving. I quickly put away the GPS and hid the most valuable looking things. Justin reached for his long bush knife and laid it in the canoe next to him.

Soon the dinghy came along side with its blinding white light. I had my jacket and hat on but there wasn't really any point hiding as they would see me anyway. Sanakoli and Job stood up on the platform. "Hello we come long Samarai — Milne Bay," Job said. He was speaking in *Tok Pisin*, which is a form of pidgin English that is spoken in most parts of PNG. The dinghy came up on the outrigger side and bounced carelessly into the fragile poles. One of the men onboard held on to the outrigger. There were four men on the dinghy and now they were scouting the canoe with their sharp torch.

Justin, who was sitting next to me, put his hand on the bush knife and said quietly, "If they touch you, I kill them." There was no doubt that he meant this and it felt strangely comforting.

The fishermen became very excited when they discovered that there was a white man onboard. I just waved at them and said, "Hi guys, how are you doing?" trying to look as casual as possible. Immediately they escalated their interest in the random encounter. They were bouncing around in the wobbly dinghy — and talked amongst themselves with slurred voices. It became evident that they were drunk. Then they asked what we were doing and where we were going.

I stood up next to Job and Sanakoli told our story. The fishermen concluded that we were lucky to have met them and said they wanted to take us to their village. The four of us assured them that this wasn't necessary and we were just waiting for the wind to sail and they should just continue fishing. But there was nothing we could say to convince them otherwise — now that they had found us, they were going to take us ashore. We could probably have fended them off but there was likely a whole bay full of their motley friends who would come to their aid should we 'attack them.' Anyway, they had a dinghy with a 40-horsepower engine; we had a sail and no wind. Two of the fishermen grabbed the side of the outrigger, the motor started and, before we had time to protest, they started to pull us along.

We went on like this for about 20 minutes — out of the bay and in the direction from where we had come. I thought, at least we were being motored backwards as this circumnavigation was intended to be undertaken by sail and paddle power only. But my biggest worry remained — where were these guys taking us? Back to a remote fishing camp where they could rob us undisturbed, together with the rest of their gang? Or were they taking us to a village as they claimed. For now, we couldn't do anything but to play along and hope for the best.

Soon the motor powered down. We approached the side of a small dark outcrop that had a little light glowing in the trees above. We slid ashore on a cobblestone beach buffered by a small swell. The sailors pulled the canoe in the last bit but kept the hull in the water and only tied off the front. The fishermen staggered ashore and pulled the dinghy up next to our canoe. It was pitch black on the beach, but by the torch of my headlamp I soon started to see people sort of crawling down a small jungle trail towards us. We greeted the first of them and the fishermen started to tell the amazing story of their unusual catch.

A fire was lit and, in the flickering light, I saw more people crawling down the hillside. I made sure to greet as many as them as possible. It was only about eight o'clock in the night, so obviously there were people about. I was looking for a Magistrate or a Chief or some other community leader — but there weren't any. The people seemed friendly, although they were clearly concerned about what to do with the loud drunken fishermen on their beach. It seemed that, although the fishermen had family in the area, they weren't from this village, which I learned was named Salial. The only leadership figure they had in the village was a Pastor, so they sent a couple of kids after him.

The fire was burning high now and there were people — men, women and children, all around the canoe inspecting it and asking questions about the different components and equipment. Justin hadn't moved since we came in. He was just sitting in the back of the canoe, smoking a *bruce*, observing the unfolding scene, vigilant. It was a stressful situation. We didn't know how welcome we were. Some people offered to help us pull the canoe on land, but we said that we'd rather just keep it in the water for now, although it was rolling back and forth with the swell and the side of the dinghy was constantly bouncing into our outrigger.

Finally, the Pastor appeared. He was a man in his 40s, wearing a buttoned shirt and long pants. It looked like he had just gotten out of bed — he didn't seem very authoritative, nonetheless, he ensured us that we were welcome and that we could pull the canoe up. There was a bit of a standstill. We still weren't sure of how we should go about things but then it looked like the fishermen were getting tired of hanging around and wanted to go out to sea again. I went to the big fire to smoke off some of the sand-flies that were eating me alive.

A little after, one of the fishermen came up to me and said, "The dinghy owner wants you to pay him 50 kina for helping you."

"What?" I said shocked, "We didn't ask for your help. You dragged us here."

"But we saved you and we sailed a long way."

"I don't have 50 kina," was my immediate response. I stuck my hand in my pocket, where I knew that I had 20 kina. "Here, this is what I've got. Please give this to your Captain and say thank you very much." The fisherman took the wet bill and went back to the dinghy. I had barely turned my back on him when I heard a long wild roar like the sound of a wounded animal. It was the dinghy owner.

He had jumped off his boat and was now staggering towards me as he wailed, "20 kina, 20 kina, we saved your life! 20 kina!" He picked up a great elongated coral block and lifted it above his head as he ran towards me. I had little time to think — I prepared myself to fight but at the same instant, the entire congregation of villagers encircled the drunkard and held him back while another group stood up in front of me. The dinghy owner was still screaming — like a madman — but was pushed back to his boat.

The Pastor said, “Oh I’m so sorry, they shouldn’t treat you this way.” The owner was still carrying on hysterically from his boat. I thought it best to defuse the situation — I found a 50 kina bill in my secret pocket. I asked Sanakoli to call over the negotiator and asked for my 20 kina back before I would part with the 50. The Pastor said, “No you don’t pay that man anything.”

But I just answered, “Let’s just get those people out of the way and hope they don’t come back.” When the transaction was over, the drunk fishermen pushed off and disappeared into the night and *Tawali Pasana* was pulled ashore.

Chapter Twelve

An unexpected flight

Expedition Log 22 September 2016

16:21 hrs. Approaching Madang. I am feeling nervous. I have been hiding from dinghies all afternoon, but they were all passengers travelling to town.

I was sitting in the canoe looking at my phone, we had a bigger worry than pirates right now — we had to find a safe place to stay in Madang. I typed in the telephone number of the assistant to the manager at Madang Resort and took a deep breath I was about to ask him if we could stay there with the canoe for free. I hated it!

I have always been envious of those outward-going types who just try their luck with whatever, and just succeed. Those people who seem so unaffected by criticism and rejection, those seemingly-carefree social people who enjoy striking up a conversation with a random stranger. I am quite aware of my shortcomings in this regard, not least because I had failed so miserably in gaining funding for this project.

Leading up to the expedition, I had applied for a grant through the Transglobe Expedition Trust (TET). Their motto is 'Mad but marvellous' and they supported only the wildest of expeditions. They had come back with an email asking me to elaborate on certain points. I replied the same day but a couple of days later, I learned that the email had bounced back. I tried to resend but the same thing happened again. I was busy with preparations and I think subconsciously I was afraid of their reply — so I just ignored it. A couple of weeks later, when in PNG, I followed up and the TET Secretary told me that they hadn't received my answer and already had their meeting. I had lost my chance.

I know that the remedy to this impasse was to keep trying and get used to rejection. My näive assumption was actually that, if I just put myself in a position where I needed to ask for help, I would grow into the task; but I haven't been very successful at that… so far. I sighted the glow from the famous lighthouse of Madang. We would be there within an hour. I needed to find a solution. I then thought, 'Damn those sand-flies.' They really nailed me last night and had started itching. Then I snapped out of it. No more procrastination. Here we go. Calling…

"Hello this is Madang Resort, Sibona speaking."

"Hello there, this is Thor Jensen, Danish adventurer. I wrote you an email yesterday about the possibility of visiting your resort with our sailing canoe? We are approaching Madang..."

"Oh yes, Mr. Jensen, you can berth your canoe in our lagoon, you know where it is? You can give me a call when you arrive and we will escort you in."

"Thank you so much Sibona, that sounds great. We are looking forward to visit your resort."

"Thank you, Mr Jensen. See you soon."

"Thank you Sibona." Success! I rose up in the canoe and spread my arms in triumph. "Guys we'll be sleeping in Madang Resort tonight. I just spoke with them and we are welcome!" The sailors nodded approvingly.

Meeting Sir Peter

We were woken the next morning by a loud noise. On the great green lawn in front of us, I saw a caucasian man of sturdy build, in his late seventies, wearing khaki pants and a light blue polo shirt riding a sit-on lawnmower. Job poked his bald head out from under the tarpaulin and excitedly announced, "That is Sir Peter Barter. He owns Madang Resort. He is a *Bigman* around here." I tried to greet the great man with a wave of my hand but after a few attempts, I realised he was probably ignoring me, so I crawled back on-board the canoe.

Tawali Pasana was berthed in a small artificial lagoon centred in a fenced-off lawn precinct below the resort. There was a marvellous waterfront vista and across the small bay we could see buildings and what I assumed must be the centre of town. The waterways were busy with overloaded passenger dinghies connecting the approximate islands with the town. It was a very beautiful area with a relaxed air of provincial charm. The water was clear, the sun bright and the coconut palms were swaying in the gentle trade winds. Outside the lagoon, the resort had its own jetty where its luxury motor yacht — the Kalibobo Spirit — was berthed. Besides cruises to Alotau and the Trobriand Islands, the charter also took tourists on week long 'expeditions' up the mighty Sepik River, which has its outlet 124 nautical miles along the coast from Madang.

The Sepik is the longest river on the island of New Guinea and home to some very elaborate traditional cultures, the most famed of which is the Chambri tribe — or the crocodile people — a community that still practices scarification. As a rite of passage, teenage boys are cut with sharpened bamboo or razor blades on their backs and chests in a pattern resembling crocodile skin. There were actually quite a few woodcarvers from the Sepik region who hung out in front of the resort, selling their crafts to passing tourists. They were very friendly. I noticed that their psychical features were different from the locals. They were slimmer and taller and their facial features more elongated.

It appeared as if the carvers had their own little colony and one kind fellow pointed me to a water post on the resort ground where they washed themselves — and I could too.

After a good rinse, I got into my only pair of jeans, found a clean shirt I was saving for special occasions and walked up to the resort. There was a cluster of bungalows and two buildings with rooms, as well as swimming pools, a restaurant and a cafe. I found the owner of the resort in the open cafe overlooking the main channel into Madang. Sir Peter Barter was a white-haired man of Australian descent. He had spent most of his life in PNG and was a successful businessman and one-time Governor of Milne Bay. He was speaking to another Australian man working for a local company. I presented myself and thanked him for letting us stay with the canoe.

Sir Peter asked me few questions about our voyage but didn't seem that impressed. He said, "Yes, we haven't had that good an experience with you adventure types here. The last bloke we helped came here in a sailing ship. He just needed a couple of days, he said, and ended up leaving the boat here for more than three months." He took a sip of his coffee.

I tried to turn the conversation onto a more positive track. "But won't it be great exposure for Madang Resort to be part of this world record circumnavigation?"

The old man looked at the sea. He had seen it all before. "Nah. It's just a great expense for us and we never really get anything in return, but you can put your canoe up on our ramp. Speak with Miso he'll know what to do." I thanked him sincerely and promised that we would only need three nights. But my audience was over and it looked like the Sir Peter Barter had turned his attention elsewhere.

I returned to the crew who were waiting for me by the canoe. I was carrying three chicken burgers and a fish burger from the restaurant. It was still morning but we were all starving. To my great surprise, the sailors didn't seem that enthralled with the burgers and French fries, and Justin only ate the fish patty from his burger meal. While we were sitting with the sailors poking suspiciously at their breakfast, we had a meeting. We needed to go shopping and together we compiled a list that included caps for Justin and Job, a four metre by five metre tarpaulin to use as a tent on the canoe, 20 metres of rope, and white paint to cover the Mambututu graffiti properly.

"And also, we need music, like a radio," Job said with an air of great importance.

Sanakoli agreed. "Yes, to make time go fast on the canoe. The Chinese will sell them." All the sailors nodded.

Then Sanakoli added, "And you, you know what to get me, you get that flex card. I need credit so I can call my missus!"

I agreed that this was important. "I'll give you all some money so you can make your own purchases and call your missus' to see how things are at home."

With the shopping list out of the way, I told the crew that I needed to spend time on my computer fixing up our passport application problems and extending my PNG visa and, in return, it would be their job to do repairs and paint the canoe. They all seemed to agree on this but then Job made a sign of having something important to say. This made me nervous. Job had been feeling unwell for weeks and this had been the elephant in the room since we left Wasu — and he wasn't getting better. He said, "Me, I want to go to church. I want to go to church and pray."

I made a silent sigh of relief and said, "That sounds like a very good idea and then maybe you can make contact with the family you have further up the coast, so that we can stay with them?" Job nodded compliantly and the two other sailors seemed to understand the importance of him going to church. I gave them all some petty cash and they left via the big resort gate — Job to talk to God and Justin and Sanakoli to buy flex cards and betel nut.

At midday, Miso arrived. He was a man about my age and height who came from the Trobriand Islands. He had a round, kind face and was wearing a sailor's uniform. He seemed to be in charge of the resort's vessels. Justin and Sanakoli instantly clicked with him, as they were all from Milne Bay, and thereby practically related. We soon learned that most of the staff in the resort were from the Trobriands, except the guards who all looked like sturdy local types. We got to meet most of them, including the Sepik wood carvers, because everyone was excited to help pull the canoe ashore. After half an hour, *Tawali Pasana* was resting well above the high-water mark on a steep concrete ramp, well protected inside the big lawn area. It couldn't have been a better set up. We were secured by a high fence and, just outside, we had our new friends the woodcarvers to look out for us and conveniently, a bit further down the water's edge, was a small day market where they sold fruit, fried fish and betel nut.

I was in doubt about where we would sleep but Justin and Sanakoli soon arranged the sail so that we had a shelter on the canoe. I had offered the crew a night in a room with a bed, and had inquired about the price of a cheap guest house across the channel but none of the sailors were interested in the offer. We spent the afternoon resting and stayed the night on the canoe. Next morning, the resort owner came down to inspect the canoe. He was riding a three-wheel scooter — like the ones that pensioners use in Denmark. He was accompanied by two great German Shepherds that didn't leave his side. He had a camera with him and took several pictures but he still wasn't that talkative, although he did ask the sailors some questions about how the conditions had been and about the voyage. Later in the day, James, the Operations Manager, came down and offered me three nights in a bungalow, which I was thrilled about, as this gave me a chance to back-up my recordings and charge batteries but most importantly, it gave me a timely break from the voyage.

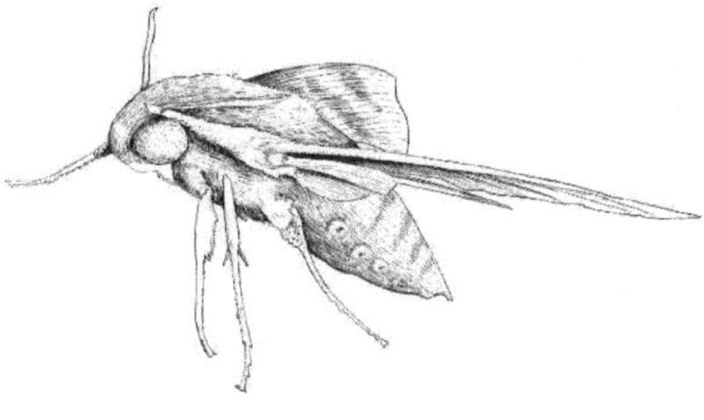

I wish that I could say that we sailed out of Madang after three days at the resort, but, as I said before, things never work out as you plan in PNG. And I suppose wise old Sir Peter knew that better than anyone. In fact, we ended up having the canoe on land in the resort for 14 days. The main reason for this was that I had to fly to Port Moresby and renew my visa and, at the same time, get the passports processed once and for all. The one positive outcome of this was that I got to meet Sandy Robson again.

Sandy had reached the capital about the same time and invited me to join her for a goodbye dinner at the Royal Papua Yacht Club. This gave me insight into how she managed her relations with sponsors and government people alike, who all helped her on her journey. Sandy was charming, engaging and very energetic — and she knew how to work a room. I must admit that I was nervous about having to dine with all these strangers but it turned out really well, in no small part because of Sandy's introductions.

There was a great atmosphere at the function and Sandy introduced me to Immigration officials, the manager of the yacht club, a lady who ran a resort in Wewak further up on my route, as well as another lady who lived in the border town of Vanimo — all people who could help us with our voyage. The connection to Immigration soon paid off as the visas and passports were processed in record time. I found out that our applications had been sitting in the Immigration office for almost a month without being processed — because our friend Moda hadn't paid the handling fee. When I confronted Moda about this, he excused himself saying that he didn't trust the immigration workers with the money.

The whole Port Moresby experience was a costly affair for me. Luckily, I had again received some cash from my family but even better, I had finally sold the sea kayak I had in Copenhagen and now I could transfer the monthly wages to the sailor's families with the remaining cash to be spent on a cheap iPhone. After a hectic week in Port Moresby, I boarded a plane.

As I looked out through the double plexiglass window, I came to think back on a conversation I had with an old Papua New Guinean pilot in a hotel bar. We spoke about the shape of the island, which is often referred to as in the shape of a bird but this old aviator protested, "No, I have always seen it as a dragon. It is wild; the mountains are like thorns, the tail is long and pointy, the head is spewing flames and underneath, you know Yos Sudarso? — the island." I nodded as to confirm we were on the same page and he continued, "That's the claws." I loved this description and thought, 'If anyone should be an authority on this matter it must be an old pilot from PNG'.

Volcanoes ahead

Back in Madang, I met Miso as I entered the compound. He was dressed in traditional attire consisting of a leaf pouch covering his groin, flossed greenpalm and traditional black, white and red Trobriand body paint. "Hi Miso, are you going partying or what?" I joked.

"Nah, we just have a new group of tourists arrive — Germans, I think. Every time they come, we have to dress up and make a *sing sing*." Although he didn't say it, his expression told me he'd rather not be naked in front of complete strangers wearing just a leaf instead of working on a boat in his smart sailor's uniform.

Miso showed me into the employee compound where he was living with his wife and two small children. It was a little colony of houses and dorms built with modern materials where the predominantly Trobriand staff lived with their families. I asked what it was like having so many people from Milne Bay working at the resort. "Peter Barter, he like Trobriand people, he is from Milne Bay himself," Miso explained. It made good sense to hire people from the 'Trobes' as they spoke English well and have a very gentle nature. The staff seemed to thrive in their little colony. Miso showed me into the house next to his, where the sailors had been living while they were waiting for me.

It didn't seem like the sailors had been up to very much while I was away, except Job who had met his uncle and frequented his church. But I sensed that the three sailors were all weary of hanging around in Madang, so I called a departure meeting in the hope of rekindling their spirits. I started something like this: "Friends, while I have been away, many good things have happened but the best thing is that you now have all got your passports." And with that I handed them each their documents, which they all opened with a combination of awe and excitement. "Indonesia here we come!" I said.

"Wohoo!" Sanakoli exclaimed.

Then I turned their attention to the new maps Sandy had generously given me. "Guys, I have been calculating our journey and we are actually traveling much faster than I had expected. Our only trouble is just the delays that we have experienced with cutting the outrigger and now this delay in Madang." I opened my log book. "If we look at the days we have actually sailed then it looks pretty good. Tawali to Madang — we have covered 513 nautical miles. Although we have been away for 37 days, only on 15 of these days have we sailed. So, if we calculate the sailing days, then we actually travel an average of 34 nautical miles per day — which is really impressive. If we can keep this pace up, we will be in Indonesia within a week to 12 days!"

Justin and Sanakoli seemed to get this, although Job didn't pay much attention. I then ran them through the route up to the border town of Vanimo, pointing out the different villages Sandy had recommended and which I had plotted on my GPS. Job had lost interest by then and was sitting looking at his phone. I got annoyed by this and asked him to pay attention but he only replied, "No I don't need to." This reply really made me angry — he was supposed to be my right-hand man and, now that I had finally gotten him the passport, I felt the least he could do was try and be interested.

I cooled myself and said, "That is really disrespectful Job." He didn't answer and just looked at his phone. Instead I focused my attention on the two other sailors and continued to explain our course.

I have always been fascinated by maps. Those colourful plates with gridlines, curves and symbols convey to the reader and observer the conditions of a certain area or part of the world. But the real reward is when you finally experience a given place first hand, and it always turns out that no matter how vivid your imagination or how much experience you have with a map, you will always be surprised — for better or worse. The upcoming route was no exception. There were several active volcanic islands dotted along the coast, and inland, the Adelbert Range could potentially help us with a good offshore breeze before turning flat and calm as we neared the mighty Sepik River basin.

The outflow of the Sepik River was a concern. Sanakoli shared cautionary stories they heard from Miso and the Sepik carvers and, in return, I recounted Sandy's struggle in those treacherous currents. The whole inland course of the river looked exciting and, initially, Paul and I had talked about going up the Sepik River in a dinghy but the season was now against us and our time was limited (and a canoe would be too hard and slow). I pointed out the Schouten Islands to Justin and Sanakoli — a string of volcanoes about 21 nautical miles off the Sepik coast. Since my first preparations in Copenhagen, I had dreamt about visiting those islands and one in particular really caught my interest — Bam Island.

Bam is an active volcano projecting 600 metres out of the sea with no beaches. I had wondered how life would be on such an island. But now that we were looking at the route, it was evident that we would just need to cover as much ground as possible before the Northwest Monsoon started to blow against us. As we were repacking the maps, Job came back into the conversation. He said that we needed a police escort leaving Madang. "Now every *raskol* know we are here and that we are going to Sepik with a *dim dim*." I was getting a little tired of Job's paranoia but I knew it meant a lot to them, so I promised to look in to it.

Expedition Log 7 October 2016

> 10:00 hrs. Finally departing Madang after 15 days ashore with three freshly printed passports and an outrigger that is dry as a bone. I didn't succeed in getting the police to follow us out. They had no fuel for their dinghy. But we got an even better escort.

Miso was driving the resort speedboat while a cameraman from EMTV (PNG's largest TV station) filmed us. This had all been arranged by Sir Peter Barter, who was also on board with his camera. The speedboat was now buzzing around us as the old gentleman climbed around the boat snapping one photo after another — to the great consternation of the Trobriand deckhand who was hired to look after him.

Although we had spent too long here, it was a good stay. *Tawali Pasana* felt like new, with a buoyant outrigger and a fresh paint job. The sides had been decorated with new carvings by our Sepik friends, beside the old decorations — the flower from Milne Bay and the butterfly from Oro Province. And now, we had a *tapa* cloth pattern from Mambututu, the *Tawali* logo, Cape Arkona and the snake man from Bobongara reef. From Madang, we got a carving of the lighthouse with a fruit bat and, finally, a blue orchid — the logo of Madang resort — a fitting acknowledgement of Sir Peter's hospitality.

All these carvings represented people who have helped us along this journey. And considering Sandy's guests in Port Moresby, and not least Sir Peter Barter and all his staff, it was becoming clear to me that people really enjoyed being a part of a great adventure. In the end, one of the main objectives of this journey was to tell a balanced story about contemporary New Guinea. I thought, 'Maybe I shouldn't be so afraid of asking other people for help' — although I still hate it.

Chapter Thirteen

Volcanoes and paint fumes

The canoe was berthed next to a weathered wooden pier at Ululan village, one days' sail from Madang. It was 6:40 a.m. and the sky looked moody. Justin and I were in the canoe and Job and Sanakoli were sitting on the pier. I had just downloaded the days' weather report and it looked dodgy, but I was keen to cover some miles. I had already learned that the sailor's senses were the most reliable indicators when it came to predicting weather, so I asked Job and Sanakoli if we could go sailing, "Hey guys, what do you think of the weather?" None of them answered. This annoyed me greatly, not least because I didn't have the sailing knowledge to make these assessments myself. I tried again.

After a pause Job finally said quietly, "Maybe, we wait and see." And so, it was to be a rest day.

Later I got to speak with Sanakoli one-on-one, "Hey Sanakoli, what was going on between you and Job this morning? Why don't you guys want to tell me if we can go sailing or not?"

Sanakoli looked embarrassed and then said, "Eh, it is Job who must tell you to sail… in our what, custom, it is like… Job is the boss to us. He says, 'You come with me and the *dim dim* on a travel.' So, in our tradition, he is above us and we must follow him."

I scratched my head. "But it doesn't look like he is doing too well, he seems very stressed."

"Yes, Job is not well." Sanakoli paused to consider his words. "It pains my heart to see how he treat you the day before, he don't want to look at the map, talking back to you. Not good."

"Yes, that really pissed me off," I replied.

Sanakoli frowned and added, "And on the canoe, me and Justin do all the work."

I gave Sanakoli a friendly tap on the shoulder. "Ok I'll go and have a chat with him and see if we can figure it out."

After looking around, I found Job sitting with a couple of villagers. It looked like he was preaching about God. I walked up and politely asked if I could have a quick meeting with him. The villagers courteously gave me their seat on the fallen tree trunk and walked off. "Hi Job, I just wanted to talk to you about the trip. This morning was a bit funny. How come you guys didn't want to tell me to sail or not?" Job just looked straight ahead. When I saw that no answer was forthcoming, I continued. "I was thinking, maybe you could be in charge of the navigation. I could teach you how to use the GPS and plot a course on the map?" Job sat for a bit like he was considering my proposition, but there was something else inside of him struggling to come out. He finally spoke.

"Home in the village I am a *Bigman*. Here these two are bigger than me, so I cannot tell them what to do."

"What do you mean bigger? Like they are older?" I questioned.

"Yes, they are older so I must listen to them."

"OK," I continued, "But you and I planned this trip… remember — it is thanks to you that Justin and Sanakoli are here. So, you are the boss!"

But my argument was quickly turned around. "I take them on big travel. If something happen to them, the blame will come to me." He hit his chest with the tip of his fingers. "Their family and brothers will say, 'You took our brothers to Indonesia and they did not come back. You must pay pigs and money… Everyone will say, 'Oh sorry, there is Job who lost his friends,' and me, I will be put down." I could see the worry in Jobs eyes and tried to calm him with the argument that nothing was going to happen — and, if indeed something should happen, I could pay. But that didn't seem to do much, as what he was most worried about was the social stigma that would follow.

The next morning, the same scene played out although the weather forecast looked better and the sea smooth. I asked Job and Sanakoli, "Hey, is it looking like good weather for sailing today?" Neither of them answered.

Then Job spoke in a defiant tone, "You ask him," and nodded towards Sanakoli. Sanakoli avoided eye contact and nodded back at Job, "You ask him."

I shook my head in disbelief, jumped into the canoe and spat out the words, "Guys, I am fed up. I have wasted 15 days and I don't know how much money on flights and documents so that you could get your stupid passports. I don't have any more energy for your bullshit. So, whatever it is between you two — you guys figure it out." Job and Sanakoli both sat on the pier looking with embarrassment at the canoe, while Justin helped me prepare to sail.

We departed at 6:30 a.m. There was no wind. At nine, the breeze crawled up to ten knots and we slowly rounded Cape Croilles. The PNG coastline never fails to amaze and this day was no exception. We were passing through the Isumrud Strait, with the mainland on the port side and on the starboard towered the volcanic island of Karkar — a massive green pinnacle with the last of its 1,839 metres disappearing into a cluster of cauliflower-shaped white clouds. Through this passage, we entered a new type of coastline and started to feel the long swells of the South Pacific Ocean mixed with the calmer waters of the Bismarck Sea. Soon we would be sailing along the exposed northern ridge of PNG where long swells crashed directly on shore after rolling thousands of kilometres past the Hawaiian Islands and fanning across the largest ocean in the world.

The sea wasn't rough, although the sailing didn't feel smooth. The small swell was steep and every time we tipped over a crest, the sail would jerk up and down. I asked Job something regarding how the sail reacted, but he just ignored me. It was like having an obstinate teenager on board — I know because I had been one. Justin broke the odd silence with a goofy laugh, maybe to ease the mood. Sanakoli at least seemed more relaxed than Job, but there had been a strange vibe on board all morning. Now that I had time to reflect on what Job had told me, I better understood the mental pressure he must be feeling — being responsible for two other sailors while harbouring a justified concern about pirates, combined with a fear of capsizing — and on top of this, he had to navigate the conflicting social hierarchy between himself and the two older but more experienced sailors who didn't even trust him to repair the outrigger — and, not least, he also had to 'look after' a *dim dim*.

I needed to do something. I stood up on the bouncing canoe and grabbed the mast for support. I raised my arm to the sky as to enhance the magnitude of my words. I spoke aloud, "Friends, we have now sailed 1000 kilometres already and we have a long and dangerous adventure ahead of us. It is important that we are all willing to adapt and maybe make some personal changes to make it all work." I swung my arm out as to embrace them all and continued. “We come from different cultures but if we want to make it around this mighty island, we will have to work together — like one big family.” I looked at my audience. They were all sitting looking to themselves. As usual, I didn’t get any feedback. All I could do was hope they agreed with my ‘preaching.’ I sat down and we continued our ‘wobbly’ course in silence.

After a little while Sanakoli said, “Why are we sitting in quiet, we have music now.” I had totally forgotten about the radio they had bought. Job pulled it out of a dry bag. It was the craziest piece of consumer electronics I have ever seen. It was called a ‘Super Stereo Radio’ but it wasn’t bigger than 30 centimetres. It was strangely decorated with brown foil to resemble wood and had one round loudspeaker in the middle. It ran on batteries and could both play AM and FM radio bands as well as MP3 files from both a USB and an SD card. The only thing it didn’t have was a volume button. It had one setting — ‘loud.’ Job took out the Micro-SD card from his phone and stuck it in the machine and turned it on. A loud, overly trebled PNG pop song in fast tempo started playing. But that wasn’t all. About 50 tiny light bulbs decorating the device were now blinking in different colours like it had its own little internal disco party going on; and there was no way to switch it off.

“What madness is this!” I said, “The thing uses more battery on blinking than on playing music!”

Job giggled, “Oh Chinese, they put lights on everything.”

Sanakoli laughed too, “Ha, ha, ha, that is how the Chinese listen to music.” Justin pointed at the radio with a pistol finger and a sneaky grin, “Me I take them lamps off and build me a big light torch.” On board was a Danish Filmmaker, three Papua New Guinean Sailors and a blinking Chinese radio with a life of its own. *Tawali Pasana* was rocking towards the Pacific Ocean, leaving a trail of Gospel songs, Dolly Parton, and *pidgin* pop in her wake.

Tell the story

We had spent the night in a dodgy village outside of Bogi — the last big station before the Sepik. Now I was having my morning tea on the beach whilst running through my notes. Suddenly, I realised that we had been invited to stay in a lodge there. I had completely forgotten. I thought, 'Man, I'm wasted. We could have had a night in a quiet and safe place, probably with a great meal as well.' What a shame. Suddenly a huge crowd of kids and young people gathered around me. I wasn't really in the mood for company but although I tried to ignore them, the kids didn't go away.

After a while, something funny happened. A young man asked, "Excuse me mister, but when will you tell your story?"

I looked up, "My story?"

"Yes, why are you here with the canoe?" Then I understood what they were are all waiting for. I got up and began telling the tale of our voyage. The kids screamed with laughter when I told about me falling overboard and their eyes grew big when I narrated how the half-snake half-man witch had almost sunk us at the Bobongara Reef. In the end, I summarised that we wanted to make a world record and show how important their traditional knowledge still is today. To make all this more understandable to my young audience I used the canoe as an example. "This canoe is like Papua New Guinea, it has some modern materials, like nylon string and plastic for the sail but it is also built from bush materials and with the same design that your *Bubu's* (Grandparents) built." The crowd stood for a moment to digest the words and then they looked at the canoe.

Expedition Log 11 October 2016

13:00 hrs. Departure time. The wind is blowing 10-12 knots at best and is carrying us outwards towards Manam Island, a great volcano standing 1807 metres above sea level and mysteriously blue in all its might. We are slowly entering the Sepik region and the locals in Bogia haven't been short of warnings about the Sepik people whom they say are 'untrustworthy.'

Around mid-afternoon, the lazy wind began to blow us towards Aris, a small island next to Manam.

"Hey guys, should we discuss what we are going to do, like where we want to stay tonight," I asked. It was a hot afternoon and the sun shone bright reflecting off the map case as Sanakoli unfolded it.

"Wind is not good for going into land," he said. We all looked at the maps. The alternative was to go backwards into Manam or try and land on Aris Island. "We can go there?" Sanakoli pointed towards a small island straight north.

"That's Bam Island. It is an active volcano about 21 nautical miles out to sea," I answered and continued. "It looks like a really exciting place but there's no beach."

Job looked over Sanakoli's shoulder. "We go there, too many *raskol* on the Sepik."

I looked at him. "But isn't it a bit dangerous? The wind is very unsteady and we'll be lucky to get there before midnight."

Job then said with a serious tone, "We sailors, we know."

Justin said something in their language and they all looked towards the small blue triangle on the horizon. I recognised a spark in the eyes of my Milne Bay companions and felt the rush of adventure running through my veins — we were going to Bam Island!

As the sun set over the Sepik River basin, the wind started blowing. *Tawali Pasana* was making good miles by rhythmically digging into the dark sea. It was a bold plan. We wanted to entirely avoid the Sepik coast and the great river mouth by sailing out to Bam Island and from there follow the chain of small volcanic islands westward and across to Wewak on the mainland, the capital of East Sepik Province. The downside of this strategy was that we would be very exposed to the open sea and we had no idea of what awaited us on those remote islands.

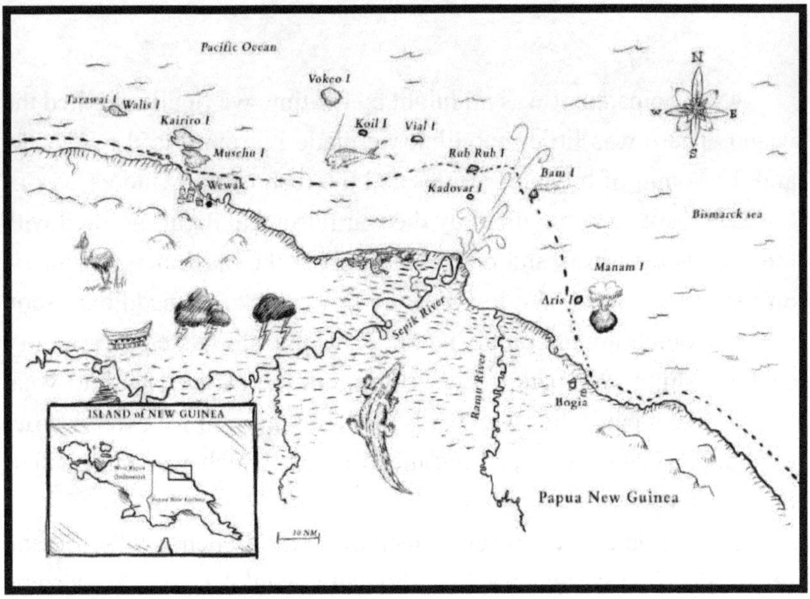

Looking at our topographic map, Bam didn't seem to have a beach, let alone a barrier reef around it. It was basically the top of a submerged volcano (and one of the most active in PNG) with steep sides shooting 685 metres up from sea level, ending in an open crater that last erupted in 1960. But according to our old map, it looked like there could be a village. The sailors seemed both confident and excited about going out to these islands. I suspected it reminded them of voyaging amongst their own islands and atolls at home. For my part, I couldn't be happier with this mix of anxiety, anticipation and the unknown. I had been studying this island on Google Earth from my little flat in Copenhagen, and now I was actually sailing towards it.

The island stood on the horizon like a grey hazy pyramid with a top covered in a wide cluster of smoke. I looked over the outrigger, there was Manam big and dark, with the summit enveloped in thick orange glowing fumes. Inland, over the Sepik basin, we regularly saw white flashes, the area living up to being the most lightning struck in Melanesia. The wind was perfect and blowing from behind, strong and steady. It was as if all the forces of nature had been set in motion to make this dream come true.

As anticipated, it was midnight by the time we finally reached the island. There was little moon but we made it around to the lee side, and the sound of breaking waves and the rush of the wind eased off. Suddenly, we were engulfed by the warm tropical night — filled with the sounds of insects and birds calling from the black mass of jungle on the cliffs ashore. We lowered the sail and started paddling. Soon we saw something out on the point, it was the silhouette of a man in a canoe, fishing. We paddled up to him and he showed us into what looked like a bay. The swell wasn't too bad there so we extended our rope and Sanakoli dropped the metal block, which was our anchor, into the deep.

The whole canoe, ourselves included, was drenched with salt and sea spray. We were all tired, but I thought it would be good to eat some rice as we hadn't had any dinner and wouldn't know what tomorrow would bring. So, I asked Job, "Hey man, do you think you could help me make some rice."

But Job answered, "Enough, you eat biscuits and sleep." Yet again he was really irritating, but, instead of letting it get to me, I started cleaving some wet firewood with the bush knife to get into the dry core and build a fire. Despite all my best efforts, I couldn't get the fire started. I then asked Job to help, but he just continued to ignore me. I gave up and handed the pot of cold rice to our local fisherman friend and said he could have it. He offered to have his wife cook it for us but I just said, "You keep it." Then I made my bed on the wet canoe and dozed off — cursing Job.

Life on a volcano

I woke in my damp, dank sleeping bag. The light was still weak and the ocean calm. There were a couple of cone-shaped islands on the horizon and, towards the southeast, I saw a weak blue line that revealed the mainland. I followed the sound of waves rolling onto rocks and turned around. The canoe was anchored in a very exposed half-ellipse-formed bay with a steep black cobblestone beach. Cliffs and boulders were stacked above us, as if the whole island had been built by a giant who had finished off the creation with a handful of jungle on the side. As I was studying the massif above us, I noticed there were some small outrigger canoes resting between the rocks, secure from the sea. Something was moving in the left-hand corner of my eye. I turned my head and discovered that the cliffs were alive with people — all sitting and watching us, their skin had the same tone as the cliffs but their coloured T-shirts gave away their presence.

After washing my face in the sea, I devoured a packet of biscuits and put on my jacket. The sailors weren't that interested in going ashore so we agreed that they would look after the canoe. The three then paddled me into the beach where all the Bam men had gathered in anticipation of my arrival. There was too much swell for a landing so I grabbed my camera bag, waited for the right moment, and jumped ashore as the sailors pushed off. The first to greet me was the fisherman from the previous night. His name was Jerry and it turned out that he was the village Pastor. He was in his late 50s and had a friendly red smile which revealed that there was no shortage of *buai* on the island. His face was covered in grey beard stubble and framed by large reading glasses. He had a very polite nature. Jerry showed me up a path along the boulders, leading past a curious rock with names scrawled all over it.

I was followed by a tail of men and, as we reached higher ground, the sound of roosters crowing and dogs barking increased. We passed some coconut palms and banana palms and entered a village. All the huts were built from bush materials and there were no signs of plastic rubbish. I suddenly realised that I was quite alone, surrounded by strangers, so to ease the mood I started presenting myself and asking all the young boys for their names. Some of them were more eager to shake hands than others but none of them seemed ill-intentioned.

As we got further into the village, I noticed some ransacked old huts that were constructed with modern materials and several houses built of timber cut by chainsaw. There were also some plastic rainwater barrels standing around. I was taken to the Chief's house and men, women and children gathered around. The Chief's son came forward and explained that his father was away but I was welcome and he gave me a carved model of a wooden canoe as a gift. I bowed and thanked him sincerely, while blaming myself for not having thought to bring a gift. Then I thought that, at least I could entertain them with our story. I began by excusing the fact that I didn't speak *Tok Pisin* or know their local language. They all said it was all right. I spent half an hour on our story and everyone seemed to follow it, at least they laughed and shook their shoulders in fear at the right time. Afterwards, there were comments and handshakes before the people dispersed to attend to their daily chores.

What I really wanted to do was to scale their 685-metre-high volcano but the top was covered in clouds and there were a few lightning strikes that made the naked kids scream with fear. So, while we waited for the weather to clear up, Jerry took me on a tour around the village. It wasn't that different from the other coastal villages we had visited. He explained that they were about 2000 people living on the island and they had a primary school. There was no electricity and they got their drinking water from small creeks or by collecting rainwater in the big green plastic tanks that had been donated by an NGO. In the dry season, they had suffered from drought and they had to rely on a navy ship to supply the island with water.

I then asked how it was to live in such a remote place. He explained that, if they wanted to travel to the mainland, they would usually take the only motor dinghy on the island and sail to Wewak but this cost 100 kina per passenger and took five hours. The steep price meant that there was no financial incentive in selling their garden produce on the mainland and, as a consequence, people lived off what they could produce in their gardens and what they could collect from the sea.

Around midday, the sun broke through the clouds and I started ascending the volcano accompanied by Jerry and a man about my age named Josef who offered to carry my camera bag. It was hard work and the jungle was wet and slippery, but, after 20 minutes, the forest receded and we continued up a steep path through a series of gardens where some women were working the fertile soil with their back to the ever-expanding ocean. It was fascinating to see how they cultivated the steep slopes. I noted that they hadn't divided the land into terraces by piling up rocks, as I had observed in other parts of the world. Maybe it was due to the unstable history of the volcano.

As we struggled upwards, Jerry told me that there was no superstition surrounding the volcano but he explained that the old people said, "When green grass starts to grow on the top then the volcano is about to erupt." He paused for a breath and continued. "We also have experts coming from mainland, maybe once a year but they never tell us anything." We huffed and puffed and finally the grass gave away to a red hard-packed soil with steaming cracks leading upwards. As we scrambled over the top, I realised we had been walking on the lee side because now the wind rolled in over us, cooling our sweaty faces. There were a few bushes amongst the rocks but mostly the place consisted of bare red rocky soil. But the most exciting thing was the view. There was Manam Island smouldering to the southeast, there was the mainland to the south and, running westward, we saw the two neighbouring islands, neither of which had open craters — the smaller Kadowar Island and the somewhat wider and bigger Blup Blup Island.

I was corrected by Josef who said that the local name for Blup Blup was actually Rub Rub and Bam Island was actually called Biem. He explained this, "Maybe some German missionaries came and didn't understand what people were telling them, that is why you now see the wrong name on the map." I agreed that the local names sounded better. On the top, I noticed yet another rock covered in names, or 'tags' painted with different colours.

This surprised me and I asked, "Is it tourists who's been writing on the rock?"

Josef huffed and said with a disapproving air, "No, that's the local kids." After following a 200-metre-long ridge, we finally arrived at the crater. It looked like something very ancient and very alive at the same time! The inner walls were steep and rugged and the cone let out a smell of sulphur with white vapour coming up from deep inside the earth.

I again came to think of Sisyphus with the rock, with whom the last two months had made me feel very much akin. I had now reached the summit of my mountain and I was having one of those truly spectacular experiences that are rare but never forgotten, one of those times when it dawns on you that a great dream has come true. The adventure was materialising. From sitting in a European capital city on the other side of the planet looking at a dot on a screen, now I was actually standing on this sprouting rock off the coast of New Guinea — I felt like the luckiest man alive.

After a few minutes, the breeze cooled me down and I realised the volcano was also a destructive force that could cover the entire island and its gardens and houses with rocks and lava in minutes and with little or no warning. I turned to Jerry, "How do you feel standing here? Isn't it scary living on the side of a volcano like this?"

The Pastor looked around. "It is very beautiful up here."

"But what if it erupts?" I continued.

"Then I think we will get some kind of sign, a glow or something, before it erupts," he said and shrugged his shoulders with a smile. What we didn't know then was that the neighbouring island of Kadowar, which didn't even have an open crater, would suddenly erupt on 5 January 2018 and the population of 500 islanders would be evacuated to Rub Rub Island, leaving half their island covered in lava and ash. The People on Biem were evacuated as a precaution but have since returned.

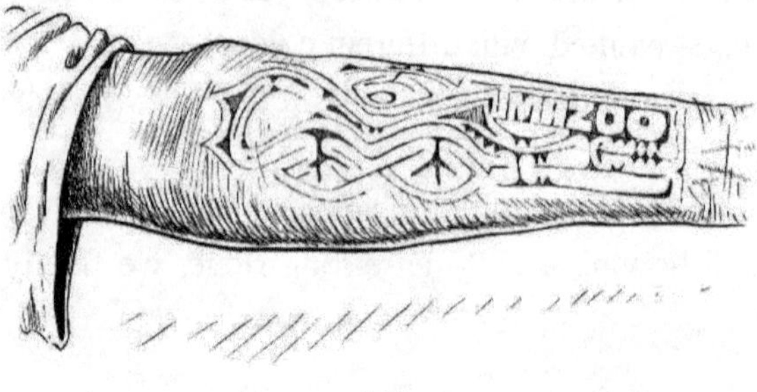

From the top, we scrambled down the loose rolling rocks steering towards the village below. As we came closer to the community, we had a short break to catch our breath. I was pretty happy about this because my left knee was really hurting. It was clear that two months in a canoe had taken a toll. Josef looked at a banana palm whose trunk was covered in graffiti tags — *Leeloh, scrafix, kagz, the one, ka,* and *solax* — scraped into the soft stem. Josef wrinkled his nose, "Look at the young people, they destroy the palm with their writings. I think the owner want to take them to court because they are making a lot of rubbish. That is why I don't want to see graffiti on a new coconut or banana like this." I couldn't help but laugh to myself about this comment, considering my own past. But this graffiti phenomenon was something I hadn't experienced in any other village in PNG and I was curious to get to the bottom of it.

As we walked back through the huts, I noticed a teenage boy with a short sharp haircut, shorts and a colourful T-shirt. On his arm was drawn a pattern. He showed me a blue ballpen drawing with the letters 'Mazoo' written, surrounded by what appeared to be traditional motifs. I asked the kid if this was his style name and he answered, "Yes." I told him that I used to write graffiti too, in Denmark, when I was his age. He seemed quite shy but agreed to write his tag in the sand with the point of his bush knife. A village leader named Lucas, who had joined us, read out aloud 'Mazo' (pronounced Maju). I was a bit afraid that I might have exposed the kid's secret identity but he didn't seem to mind.

Jerry and Lucas and I sat in the shade. After a healthy dram of fresh coconut water, I started interviewing them about this graffiti trend. Jerry was sitting in the sand with his back up against a small tree. He said, "To me it is unnecessary." I asked if they were trying to stop it. "Well we could try but it is a thing that young people are very interested in. But this kind of activity can spoil other people's property, like coconut, betel nut, they write their names on the young coconut."

"But why do you think they are doing this?" I wanted to know.

Lucas, who was squatting next to his Pastor, answered, “Graffiti is very common in our community. They realise themselves as they are some kind of heroic action person.” He explained that amongst the kids there was a kind of rivalry (much like the US-inspired graffiti scene). “Let’s say, if I was writing comments, somebody would come and swear at me by writing any comments against me. And when the owner of the item, the coconut or betel nut palm, he don’t want to see this so he shall chop it away. And sometimes those kids involved in such activities will end up in court. So our leaders here are discouraging it.” He explained that the family of the kid would have to compensate the owner of the tree with food items — although he felt that the sentence had little effect as a whole. “But it won’t work because every time new ones start writing.”

“But when did it start? Ten years ago?” I asked.

Lucas, shook his head, “It is not new here. Because the older ones that have done it has passed away and the younger ones coming up are getting into it.”

Jerry explained, “When the missionaries came in 1965, I think it was, they taught us to write. We didn’t know before then but when we learned to write our name we started to write everywhere.” Now there was only one question that hadn’t been answered. I looked at Lucas,

“What about you? Did you do it when you were young?” Lucas paused for a second — as if he had been caught red-handed.

“Yeah,” he replied.

I then turned to Jerry the 59-year-old pastor. He smiled like a school boy and gave out a low, “Yes”, as well but added, “When I grow older, I realise it is unnecessary.” He then revealed that his style name was ‘komx.’ I asked how he came up with his tag. He replied, “My name is Komes, so I change the ‘s’ with an ‘x’, you see — to make it style.” I told both of them that I thought this was great and then we three generations of ‘taggers’ took turns in writing our style names with a bush knife in the sand: ‘Komx,’ ‘Lukz’ and ‘Pexes.’

The afternoon was sunny and hot. We spent our time in the open bay, swimming and diving with the locals. There were kids floating around on flat wide pieces of balsa wood, screaming and splashing, and fishermen in their small canoes inspecting their boat and chatting. I found Job and told him that I wanted to sail to the neighbouring island of Rub Rub. The wind was perfect for the 13.5 nautical mile crossing, but Job said he was fasting and didn't want to come with me. In a fit of pique, I bluntly told him that he should consider whether he wanted to be on the canoe at all or stay on the island. (It was not my proudest moment). Back on the canoe, the two other sailors didn't seem to want to sail either. Justin quickly disappeared into the deep with his spear, so I gave the idea away — I needed to rest my legs anyway.

No good going sailing and being cross

There had been some heavy thunder over the Sepik all night and, when we woke up, our little half-moon-shaped bay was full of water hyacinth and driftwood. The islanders were all out in their canoes, digging through the debris, collecting what they could find. I asked a young man about it and he said, "We find many things, like wood and bucket and rope and sometimes canoes. The people on Rub Rub even got two dinghies from the sea, one of them with a motor on it!"

The wind was good for sailing now and we couldn't stay anchored much longer, as we didn't have much lee from the waves and logs kept on bouncing into the canoe. The problem was that only Justin, Sanakoli and I were on board. I hadn't seen Job since our quarrel and, by what Sanakoli told me, it sounded like he had taken my words to heart. Sanakoli explained, "I spoke with him yesterday. He says to me that he'll stay and find his own way home. He is not going with us anymore."

"That is ridiculous," I said and continued. "He has no money to get himself home. We need to get him back on the canoe and then I'll give him a flight home from Vanimo — that is if he *really* doesn't want to continue."

Sanakoli looked troubled and then said, "Job is a sick man, he is not doing well." He chewed some coconut and continued. "Me and Justin we worry. If Job go home unhappy, his brothers will get cross and come after us."

"How will they come after you?" I asked.

"We don't know when but they have guns and they will kill us." Sanakoli made a worried frown. I had met one of Job's *raskol* cousins and knew Job had a past of his own, so I understood the concern.

To calm them down, I told them what my firm belief was, "The best thing that Job can do is to continue on this voyage. I don't want him to give up and go home. It is hard now but we will figure it out and when we reach the finish line, he will be happy that he pushed on."

Sanakoli seemed to agree with this. We paddled him ashore and he disappeared up between the slippery rocks to bring Job back. Now it was Justin and I on the canoe and we spent the next hour moving *Tawali Pasana* around as waves started to come in and clusters of logs and water hyacinth threatened to entangle the outrigger. As we were having a dry break under the plastic, Justin did something that he rarely did, he spoke directly to me. "You, you talk to your man Job, on a canoe, no good going sailing and being cross, you must talk to him." I weighted Justin's words carefully. Of course he was right and I promised him I would do so. A part of me secretly wished Justin and I could just continue on our own — he seemed so wonderfully uncomplicated, just wanting to sail and chew *buai* and fish.

When we finally saw sign of our comrades, people had started to gather on the small beach, some wearing banana palm leaves as umbrellas. A small outrigger canoe had been put to sea with Job and Sanakoli on-board and it was now navigating the islands of weed and logs that had invaded the bay. When Job climbed on-board, I said, "*Heeey*, Job, my friend so good to see you," and I actually meant it.

Job just said "Yes, yes," while smiling. He looked happy to be on-board. We made the canoe ready and the rains ceased as we were ready to take off — but there was one last thing to do. We paddled the canoe as close to shore as possible and I dove into the sea, under the belt of debris that was guarding the shore and scrambled up onto the beach to shake hands with Jerry, Lukas and Josef, and all the other good people of Biem Island. It was very dramatic and the gesture was not lost on anyone. Soon the sail was up and we made our way out of the bay to the spectacle of a large group of waving new friends on a beach, leaving them with a memory — their big rock had a new tag: *Tawali Pasana 2016.*

Our good sailing wind eased around 2 p.m. The sun came out and the sea became placid, like glass. We were still far from Rub Rub and I started to feel the Sepik current pushing out towards the open sea. The only thing we could do was to grip our paddles and start digging. It was hot, hard work. I considered suggesting that the sailors paddle in intervals, one hour paddling, then five minutes' break, just as I used to do when kayaking but then I reminded myself that I was there to learn their trade and customs — so I took a break whenever I felt tired, just as they did.

New Year's battle

It surprised me that, despite the intense heat, none of the sailors drank anything. It was three hours of sheer physical exertion before Sanakoli had a cup of water, although we had about 18 litres left on board. The sun was setting and the island was still far off. No wind had revealed itself. I wrapped some PVC tape around my fingers where the skin was coming off and then took up the paddle again. As we laboured in silence my mind drifted back to Biem — standing at its smouldering, majestic volcanic peak. I broke the silence, "Hey guys, I'll tell you a story from my teenage years." I could see that they were all listening. The story I was about tell the sailors was definitely on the edge, but if

I had learned one thing during the last few months, it was that Papua New Guineans loved a good story. So, I began.

"I used to paint a lot of graffiti at home in Denmark as well. I started when I was 12 or 13 years old. Of course, it is illegal to paint graffiti on walls and trains in Denmark but we did it anyway. We thought — if there can be a billboard with commercials, then our painting deserves to be on display too. I became quite well known, because I did a lot of painting and I had my own style. But it was… of course… against the law and this story is about how one day everything went wrong." I looked up. I had the sailor's complete attention.

"Yes, you tell," Sanakoli urged me on, paddling mechanically.

"I was part of a graffiti group called a 'crew.' We were five friends painting together. One year we agreed to have a 'battle' with another crew — not a real fight but a friendly competition to see who could make the most paintings during all of the month of December. We agreed to a point system, with different types of paintings on different places awarded different points… so at the end of the month, the crew with the most points would win."

"The battle was tough but even. On New Years' Day, we decided to do a *whole train* which is four wagons of 13 metres each, entirely painted on one side. This would settle the battle once and for all. Of course this was a risky affair as the train yards are patrolled by guards and dogs and to paint a *whole train* takes time and a lot of paint. We took a train to one of the Copenhagen's outer suburbs where there was a big rail servicing yard. We arrived in the afternoon, the winter darkness was already descending as we climbed through a hole in the fence and scrambled under some stationary trains with our duffel bags full of spray cans."

"We were three persons painting and the service ramp was soon covered in clouds of fumes. With hectic but systematic motions, my crew covered the train in fast-flowing chrome paint. We had to be quick and finish before the guards came back. After filling out the letters and the background, we started drawing the black outlines, before finishing the masterpiece off by adding white highlights and second outlines to make the letters 'pop.'"

"As I was cutting one of my lines, I suddenly saw a dark figure at the end of the ramp. I didn't know if it was a policeman or a guard. I yelled, "Guard," and we all started running. We climbed the barbed wire fence and increased our speed through a maze of small walkways. There hadn't been anyone at our heels, so we stopped to catch our breath and consider what to do next. We had barely stopped before a police officer on foot appeared at the intersection of the small pathway in front of us. "What are you guys doing here?" He said in a deep voice. It was clear that he was looking for graffiti painters. My two friends acted as if they were drunk and said that we were on our way to a party. There was no way he believed this. So I bent down, tied my shoelaces and, as he was almost in front of us, I jumped the nearest garden fence." The sailors were spellbound.

"The last thing I saw was the Police Officer grabbing one of my friends who was struggling to get free. The other friend disappeared into the night. I landed in a garden, dashed across the lawn and over another small fence and landed on a brick barbecue. The grill flew off. I rolled onto the grass and got on my feet. I exited the garden by a gate and sprinted across a quiet road through a suburban neighbourhood towards the next row of gardens. I looked to the left and down at the end I saw a policeman running parallel with me in same direction while yelling into his radio — but he didn't see me." On *Tawali Pasana* there was complete silence — the sailors had even stopped paddling as they anticipated the climax of my story.

"I made it into the darkness and finally dug down behind a wall of firewood next to a house. My heart was beating out of my chest. I was heaving for fresh cold winter air. I slowly calmed my breath and tried to listen beyond my pounding temples. A car with a flashing light was racing up the road and dogs were barking. A whole police squad was out looking for us and, no doubt, they hated city kids coming to their town vandalising their trains. I thought that my best option was to stay put. It was a good hideout and no one knew to look for me here.

But as my heart rate slowly dropped, the icy winter temperature started creeping in through my jacket and chilling my sweaty body. I put on my hood and coiled up in a ball — but it helped very little. Then I started to hear voices next to me." All three sailors were nodding in syncopation as if to non-verbally say — don't stop now!

"I looked over the pile of firewood and realised that it was close to a kitchen window. It had been opened by a lady inside and I could smell the warm air from the pork roast in the oven and hear happy voices and laughing. Then I heard the party shushing each other when the Queen of Denmark's New Year's speech came on the television. After sitting there for nearly two hours, my feet were numb. Remember… it was winter in Denmark. I don't know if you guys have experienced this but when it is really cold your hands and feet start paining and you lose all sense in them.

"I hadn't heard any cars or dogs for a long time and the first New Year's rockets were starting to explode in the cold sky. I decided to get up. I had paint on my jacket so I hid it in the wood pile and snuck out of the garden and started walking into the centre of town. I didn't want to take the train back as the policeman had seen me and I feared the authorities might be looking for me at the station. I found a phone box in a busy Indian restaurant and called a friend named Christian, who came in a car from Copenhagen and picked me up. It was about 9 p.m when I finally got home. After a long hot shower, I went to the New Year's party — but none of my crew showed up."

The three sailors had resumed paddling but in complete silence. After a few seconds, Sanakoli asked, "So your friends… they went to the *calabus* (jail) but you got away?"

"Yes, that's right Sanakoli," I said, "Everyone at the party was asking me where they were and I had to tell them that they had been locked up — it wasn't much fun partying that night."

"But you won the what… competition?" Sanakoli asked.

"Yes. we won." I answered.

“That’s… the-eee… one-eee,” Sanakoli said with a singing tone. Justin and Job giggled. Sanakoli then continued, “We don’t want you sitting there saying nothing. When we travel we want to hear stories.”

Chapter Fourteen

On the wrong side of the border

Expedition Log 21 October 2016

02:00 hrs. We have reached Vanimo Bay! Now we are drifting, outside on the ocean, waiting for daybreak before we can safely navigate the breakers.

It was early morning as we made it inside the big breakers by Lido village (some of the same waves that make Vanimo one of the best places for surfing in PNG). The trip had been surprisingly smooth sailing; the last two days had felt incredible. We had covered 162 nautical miles. *Tawali Pasana* was finally running on the same good energy that she had at the beginning of the trip. After a quick handshake with our local host Steve Tekwie, I packed my documents and got on a small minibus full of locals in their best work clothes and smelling of shampoo on their way to town.

We passed several logging sites and a great pier where timber was loaded onto enormous metal prams that transported the costly hardwood out to Malaysian cargo ships anchored offshore. Then we flew by a roadside market and a beautiful sandy beach before rolling into the dusty centre of town on the southern side of the bay.

Vanimo town consists of flat one-story buildings, mainly Chinese-run supermarkets and hardware stores, built like tanks in metal plate. There are also some wooden houses, a bank, some government buildings and a post office. The local market has shaded stalls where people buy and sell garden products. Curiously, they were also selling imported Indonesian cigarettes, solar sets and Bluetooth music players. The centre of this town is a study in contrasts. On one side there is a beautiful blue bay with the lush green mountains in the background, and on the other side there are dusty roads and open gutters full of rubbish, splattered red with *buai* spit. I checked my phone. The 3G network wasn't working.

It was the second time I had been to Vanimo town. The first visit was in 2015, on my recognisance trip, but this morning I was too tired to feel any excitement. There was no time to waste, we had already been spending too much time on bureaucracy and canoe repairs; the winds were changing and I needed to finalise the visa application process for Indonesia. This meant a lot of printing and filling out of forms. Sandy had warned me about the complexities of the Indonesian bureaucracy. I was nervous about applying for our visas. What if we weren't granted entry or just given a one-month visa?

My greatest concern, however, was that our journey could be perceived by Indonesia as an activist initiative in support of the OPM. In 1963, the then Dutch Colony of Irian Jaya was handed to Indonesia (after intense international pressure) pending what was called the 'Act of Free Choice,' where the people of Papua voted on whether they wanted independence from Holland or integration into the Republic of Indonesia. Both the Sukarno government and, in turn the Suharto military junta, wanted to retain control of the resource-rich territory. After what the UN considered a 'mock election,' West Papua became the 26th province of Indonesia. Since then there has been almost continuous clashes between the Indonesian Army and the OPM. Regular military raids mean that some areas are kept off limits to outside visitors. I had also read accounts of journalists 'going missing,' and although the Indonesian Government now wants to open up the region, journalists and most film crews are still denied access.

We were about to sail through territory occupied by the Indonesian Military. To ignore this might sound cynical, as our voyage put me in a position to document the conflict (although most of the operational areas are inland). On the other hand, by engaging in the

Papua struggle, I risked the end of the expedition — and then there would be no story to tell at all. My strategy was to stay well out of it. For these reasons, I had toned down my website content about, 'being a filmmaker wanting to make a modern portrait of the people of New Guinea.' Instead I geared everything towards the circumnavigation, which of course it was, and as Sandy had said to me,

"The Indonesians will love that you are making a world record."

I filled out the visa application at the Indonesian Consulate. Now it was all up to the authorities whether to grant us passage or not. When I returned to the canoe, our host Steve was standing on his beach in shorts and a white singlet. He was holding a fishing rod. Steve probably had one of the best locations in the entire village. His traditional house was large and wide and standing on sturdy one metre stilts, overlooking the lagoon and the breaking swell on the outside reef.

Steve was in his 40s and seemed quite worldly. He was the President of Sunset Surf Club and had been part of a small group from Lido village to start the sport in PNG. He and his wife had eight children together, half of whom were adults now (and they all looked like Steve). "Catching anything?" I asked.

"Oh, the adventurer is back from town!" he replied as he shook my hand and looked to the sea. "Nah, only small fish nowadays but the waves man, the waves are getting bigger." He reeled in his fishing rod. "You haven't seen it when the Northwest Monsoon is blowing. We get some crazy big waves here."

"So, you want me to get out of here quick?" I joked.

"Yeah man, or else you'll never leave. Nah don't worry, in May the sea will be completely like a mirror again. You will probably have built a house and found a wife by then!" We both laughed and I walked over to the canoe that had been pulled up on the beach about 15 metres from his house. It was a good place with fine sand, shade and with no danger of falling coconuts.

The sailors were all sitting under the tarpaulin on the canoe, ready for our meeting. I started by thanking them for their great effort and said, "We are doing really well. We have covered 1,700 kilometres in just 53 days! That is already a record in itself and then take into account that we have spent 29 of those days on land, not sailing. Imagine how fast we can travel now that we don't have to worry about the outrigger!" Then I talked about finances.

Job immediately changed the subject and said, "My worry is going to Indonesia. We are going there and they all ask too many questions and we don't know their language, so how are you going to get interpreter? If we don't know their language… we are gonna use these." He made some funny hand signs, which made the other sailors giggle and then continued. "This country is not like our country, so if you make mistake they…" He paused and then made a gesture of slitting his throat with his finger. "They put you in *calabus* — for how many years. There are people from here, Vanimo people, they are still locked up over there. These people tell us, 'Make white man do it good and then go across.' We don't want to lose our life over there."

I told him that, during the preparations for the trip, I had been in contact with two English speaking people from the other side — an Indonesian diver and a Papuan man who had both shown interest in joining the canoe but now that we were here, they had both stopped answering my emails. I then tried to calm Job by saying that if we just behaved well, we would not be arrested for anything. I looked at them and said that our biggest risk was to be associated with the OPM, and that when somebody started to talk to them about that, they should just change subject and say that they were just here to make a world record.

They all agreed and I was happy to see that they hadn't been told much about the OPM by the people in Vanimo. I thought the meeting was over and said, "Finally, I would like to thank you all for being part of this trip, and it is my great hope that you finish this great adventure with not only something to your name but also a good chunk of cash and business opportunities as well. And please tell me if there is something you aren't happy about and I'll do my best to sort it out — to make you happy."

They sat quietly and then Sanakoli spoke. "Yes, that is my concern about going to Indonesia. I don't want to eat one packet of chilli." He laughed at his own joke and then became serious. "Also, what we see from you is that you are under pressure, so we want to make sure that you also make it properly, and we have a break on the way. Maybe from Sorong or from Daru."

Sanakoli was right about my exhaustion, however his talk about 'a break' made me uneasy, "What do you mean by 'break,' like going home?" I probed.

"Yes, we must go home to see our families — for two weeks." The idea of going home on vacation surprised me, as this was not part of our deal. I told them all that I understood. Now the most important task was to reach the end of the island and the town of Sorong before the winds turned against us. This would give me time to find finances for a flight and then we could see if it was smartest to go home from there or from Daru, after we re-entered PNG from the southern border. Justin and Sanakoli seemed happy with this, although Job looked like he had resigned himself to his own thoughts.

After six days in Vanimo I picked up our Indonesian travel documents. They were special 'Social Visas.' I was so happy that they had been approved. Now we just needed to get them stamped in Jayapura and then we would be able to travel through West Papua, hassle free, for the next two months, and after that we could renew in-country and stay for a maximum of six months! I estimated that we would only need half that time. The day after, on the 27th of October 2016, *Tawali Pasana* launched towards West Papua. Steve, Julia and the good people of Lido village waved us off as we steered the canoe out of their protected lagoon and sailed up along the coast 36 nautical miles towards Jayapura, the capital of West Papua.

There was a good mood on-board, we were all excited and even Job cracked a few jokes. Around midday, the wind started blowing from the steep, remote coastal mountains and we got caught in a heavy downpour that lasted for half an hour. As the haze cleared, we glimpsed the old Dutch lighthouse high amongst the clouds — we had crossed the border into West Papua! We were all excited and celebrated this significant moment with a lunch of spam on toast. After washing our plates in the sea, we hoisted the Indonesian flag and Justin changed his black, red and yellow PNG T-shirt to a more neutral green one.

Sailing into Jayapura was magic. The sun was setting as we neared a big round bay surrounded by steep mountains. It was obvious that we were entering another country. Outside of the bay, we saw some strange boats anchored. They had one main hull and, on each side, there were two large platforms with a thin outrigger at each end. The platforms were supported by hundreds of riggings connected to masts in the middle of the hull, with the platforms covered in thousands of spotlights. Later we learned that the platforms held giant nets that could haul up thousands of squid attracted by the lights.

Jayapura looked spectacular in the gloaming. The mountainsides were dotted with a tapestry of house lights, car lights and colourful flashing billboards. On the top of the highest mountain was written 'Jayapura' in great red neon letters. It was like entering another world. The sailors' eyes were as big as teacups and they eagerly documented the entry with their small mobile phones. There was a fair amount traffic of smaller boats passing us, so we put up our lantern for the first time on the journey. We navigated in through a series of small islands, one of which had a big glowing crucifix on top, and then sailed towards the eastern part of the harbour where I knew Customs and the Harbourmaster had their offices.

It was night by the time we drew near and the waterfront was lit up by anchored wooden Indonesian fishing boats. We could hear the traffic in land and smell gasoline. I was supposed to be guided in by my local contact Fernando but my PNG sim-card didn't work here, so we ended up berthing the canoe on a long wooden pier that was connected to a great colony of low houses on stilts. I had walked on this pier with Fernando back in 2015 and remembered the people there as friendly. There was a row of other boats berthed, mostly typical Indonesian dinghies with slim wooden hulls and bamboo outriggers on each side. We also recognised a couple of the PNG-style fibreglass dinghies. These familiar dinghies seemed to inspire a bit of confidence in the sailors, who otherwise had no desire to go ashore.

Despite none of us speaking *Bahasa*, I talked with some teenage boys who took me to the nearest house. It turned out that the owner, who was a very fat Papuan man, spoke *Tok Pisin* well, and he was more than eager to let us stay at his pier. When the sailors heard him call to them in one of their languages, they came ashore. The big Papuan man invited us all into his house and, to this day, I can't help smiling as I remember the looks on the faces of my companions as we walked from the dark pier into his brightly-lit veranda. It was a bombardment of the senses — even to me it looked crazy.

The floor was covered wall-to-wall in patterned linoleum. The walls were a luminous pistachio green and the window bars that encircling three quarters of the veranda were painted in red and gold. Above his main door, which led into what looked like a living room, were skilfully painted Christian figures — Jesus, Mary and Joseph. A great television set was playing a Hindi soap opera and the loud nasal voices and high-pitched music streamed out to the veranda together with a smell of perfume, spices and incense. I looked at my companions who all had a nervous have-I-died-and-gone-to-heaven expression on their faces. I said, "Hey guys isn't this great, we are in Indonesia!" They all nodded with distant smiles. We were shown to some big red couches and then the man's boys brought a big tray of tea and cookies. It helped a great deal that the owner spoke *Tok Pisin*, and we learned that he was making a living smuggling petrol from Jayapura's gas stations to sell in PNG for a tidy profit.

We spent the night on the couches and were awoken by the 4 a.m. Muslim call to morning prayer echoing through the city. The sailors were befuddled by this. I explained that it was because Indonesia was predominantly a Muslim country, actually the most populous Muslim country in the world. From our pier, we could now look across to the centre of the city, with the old colonial hotel Jasmin in view. Further down along the harbourfront, past numerous restaurants, was the new Swiss Bell Hotel.

We paddled across the harbour, where we met Fernando. He was a Papuan in his 20s and a photographer and computer technician. He spoke English well and had promised to take me to the Harbourmaster's office to get our papers approved. Meanwhile, the canoe stayed berthed with the sailors on board. I had told them not to go ashore as our visas hadn't been authenticated and promised that we would go out celebrating in the afternoon when it was all sorted. I put on my waterproof backpack full of documents, jumped on the back of Fernando's small motorcycle and we made our way through the Jayapura morning traffic.

The smell of fumes was intense as we raced past traffic lights and tall glass buildings, and then stopped for a red light behind rows of scooters, cars and taxis. This was such a difference from the dusty logging town of Vanimo. Everywhere you looked there was food on offer, street vendors selling colourful drinks, countless small open restaurants selling noodle soup, fried chicken and the national dish *Nasi Goreng*, not to mention the supermarkets that had everything your heart desired — and at a fraction of the price of PNG. It seemed like we would be living like kings here in West Papua. After five minutes, we drove into a hot concrete parking lot in front of the Harbourmaster's big white building.

Mr Lucky

Here I would love to tell you that I had prepared everything back in 2015: spoken to the Harbourmaster, Customs, Immigration, the Police and, thanks to all these preparations, our check-in went smoothly. On the contrary, back then, I never visited any of these offices. I was simply too paranoid that they would refuse the idea and thought the best strategy was to engage as little with the Indonesian bureaucracy as possible by just entering quickly and silently, which in hindsight wasn't such a smart idea. Instead, I had spent my time in Jayapura trying to find an English-speaking Papuan who would join me on the Indonesian leg of the voyage but that plan didn't succeed either. So, as we entered the Harbourmasters office, I was understandably nervous. This was 'make-or-break' time. This was where I would know if they would allow a canoe with three Papua New Guineans and a Dane to sail around West Papua.

The Harbourmaster's office was a large government building, and after asking around, we were introduced to Mr Lucky. He was a fit, light-skinned Indonesian about my age. His uniform was ironed and his head was shaved. He spoke English fluently. He studied my papers and asked for our sailing permit, also known as a 'CAIT.' I had read about this permit, and there was quite a lot of confusion about it posted on various forums. CAIT was the old permit system, which was expensive and took a long time to process, as well as needing to be renewed every second month. Then there was the new electronic system that could be filed out online in one day and which had fewer restrictions. My strategy was to claim that I didn't need either as I wasn't travelling in a yacht rather an open canoe, just like Sandy Robson had just done — and she hadn't needed a CAIT either.

I laid out this argument to Mr Lucky.

He just shook his head and said, "If you sail here you need a CAIT and you need a registration number on your boat and a customs clearance from PNG." He flipped through my passport and sternly noted, "And your visa hasn't been stamped yet."

I tried to argue a case for my traditional canoe, the 1700 kilometres we had covered, how Mr Lucky was ensuring the success the world record, and that what we were doing was practically almost like hiking just with a canoe we'd need to push into the water every day.

He just said, "It is all very good, Mister Jensen but you need a CAIT before we will let you leave this harbour."

I then asked if there were some other government organisations that I could consult, that might help us circumvent the CAIT.

He looked directly at me and said, "Oh, I can call the Army Special Forces right now, and they will take very good care of you."

My heart dropped and I laughed nervously, "Ah, that won't be necessary." I had clearly crossed the line and it was time to leave the office. I thanked him for his consideration and said I would stay in touch.

What followed next was a very long and stressful day of visiting government offices and then a meeting with the Papua New Guinean Vice Consul, who tried his best to help us. When I returned to *Tawali Pasana,* the evening prayer was sounding and the sun was setting. I was to deliver some bad news.

I told my crew, "Guys, they won't let us in the country. I need to get us a sailing permit and that will take 14 days to process, and since we don't have any stamps in our visas we have been ordered to sail back to PNG and return when our papers are in order." There was silence.

Sanakoli was the first to speak. "So, we, what, have to sail back, now?"

I shrugged my shoulders. "I think we can wait until tomorrow. I am really sorry for this. It is my fault. I didn't do my homework properly." The sailors didn't say anything — so I broke the silence. "Hey, let's go for a spin tonight anyway. We can all shower at Fernando's place. He will look after the canoe while we go out."

The sailors just said, "All right," and started digging out their clean clothes from the hull.

We walked up along the busy harbour road leading up to a giant shopping mall — *Mal Jayapura*. It was newly-built and bore a great resemblance to the fancy malls you see in Europe. For my three friends, it was yet another culture shock — from when they made their first hesitant step onto an escalator, to the shining shops and the kids fun land with computer games and colourful giant plastic animals. They all huddled together and didn't walk far from me.

Sanakoli asked, "So they are all open, you just walk in?"

I waved them into a clothing store. "Yes, you just walk in and if there are some clothes you like, you try it on and buy it. You just help yourself."

We walked in through the gentleman's clothing department and were greeted by some smiling Indonesian ladies. I tried to hold up a white shirt with a tie under Justin's chin, which they all found funny. The sailors became a bit more relaxed but didn't wander off on their own, let alone spend any of their money. After a while, we found a trendy cafe where we sat down and ordered food. The waiter hid her nervous look with a smile as she handed menus to my three weather-beaten companions. The sailors didn't know what to eat and asked me to decide, so I ordered a selection of different European dishes. I was excited to have the opportunity to share a bit of my culture with them. Job giggled when he was served his coke in a tall glass with paper tissue wrapped around it. Beside the fizzy drink, the glass contained ice cubes, a slice of lime and a straw. "What is all this?" he said, touching the paper tissue.

"It is so you won't get cold and wet fingers when you drink your coke," I explained. They all seemed to find this ridiculous — which I suppose it is. They enjoyed the food though, not least Justin who normally only ate fish but loved his lasagne.

We sailed out of Jayapura by first light. I was eager to get the canoe back across the border as I didn't want to create another hassle with the authorities. The weather looked fair and we were making a good pace on the morning breeze. I was of course incredibly disappointed, let alone exhausted. I had been pushing this canoe to get forward, to motivate the crew, to get their passports processed and we had been racing against the changing season. Now we had been blown back at least 14 days. The worst part was that I didn't have anyone to blame but myself. I thought I could push through despite the odds, like I had done since leaving Denmark three months ago. What a blow this was.

I needed to keep the spirits up amongst my sailors, so I said, "Hey guys, sorry for the disappointment. I thought they would let us in; let's use this time in Vanimo to get some rest and repair the canoe. Fernando will help us with the permits and before we know it we will be back in Indonesia."

It was quiet on the canoe, then Sanakoli spoke. "Eh, we want to say something," and he laughed nervously. "We want to go back home. We are tired. Traditional canoe is not machine it is operated by energy. We are already about two months now… so… we are kicked out of the what — country. So, we have to go back and see our families. And come back on the second trip."

I couldn't believe what I was hearing and then turned around and said, "Hey Job do you have any comments on going home?"

He moved slowly and his yellow eyes were wet. "I'm a bit worried about the travel, because if I go home, I don't know. That's the reason. If I will come back or not… I'm am a bit scared. We go travelling and we are gonna get sick and die, it's… my children are by themselves. I don't worry about the record." He made a gesture with his hand as to flick away an invisible fly and looked down.

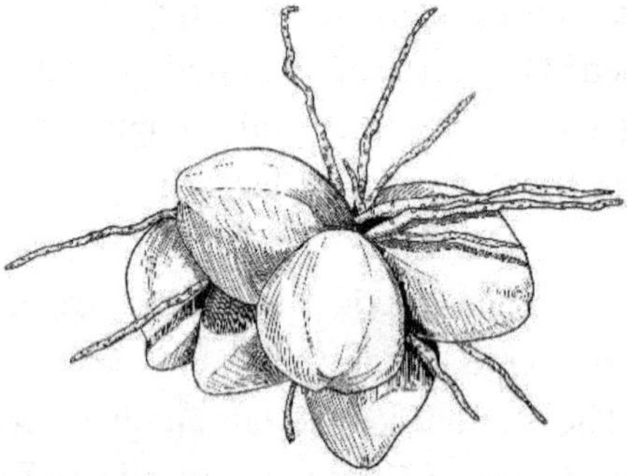

I said that I understood him and then we both sat in silence for a while. This was the ultimate defeat, and although Job had his own problems, I felt that it was my failure if he was leaving the expedition for good. I had dragged him into this with the hope of achieving something great, leaving a legacy for his children and starting a business in tourism. After I had regained control of my emotions, I looked at Justin and Sanakoli. "What about you guys? If you go home now, are you gonna come back?"

Sanakoli, pulled the sheet and said, "We promise. You fix your what — papers — and we come back."

I replied, "You know the wind will probably turn against us and we have to sail against the wind some of the way?"

Sanakoli frowned and wrinkled his nose, "When we come back. I don't care how bad the weather or how many years we will travel." I was happy to hear this grand statement. I also knew that it was easier said than done.

With the canoe parked well above the hightide watermark on Steve's beach, I could focus on getting as much film of the sailors as possible — in case I should never see them again. In an interview with Justin and Sanakoli, Sanakoli had repeated their vow of coming back. When I asked if they wouldn't risk getting into trouble from Job's brothers, Justin took the cigarette from his mouth and answered, "Me, I can be *raskol* too." So at least Job's brothers wouldn't be a hindrance. However, Job's interview was the most interesting — and revealing. He had a lot on his mind and he clearly wanted to get it out.

"On this trip I have been falling from God, that's why I'm feeling sick, arguing and calling names, that is why I must return home to find peace and God." I asked him what I could have been done better on the voyage and he started by expressing his frustrations about the uncertain structure of command on the canoe. "We must make thing properly from the beginning. You are the chairman, you are the committee and so forth. We are looking at this trip and we are thinking: 'One, the trip really important. Two, we see that it is not safety. Three, we struggle by ourselves. Four, we are thinking about our lives.'"

What he kept coming back to, were the finances and the lack thereof. I had been sending his family the equivalent of a senior officers pay — but to him it didn't feel like much, maybe because he had never held the money in his hands himself. "That is what we call bread and butter money," he elaborated. "In Papua New Guinea custom, we are not worried about big name, we are worried about people want to have benefit, we are not worried about breaking record, no. They want big money when they come home. That why I tell all people." He looked into the camera. "You must come with big money, not just small money. Not 100.000, no millions. Like these American or Australians, they got dollar."

Job had a break, collected his thoughts and then continued in an excited manner. "When you say no money, we think why is he doing this? In Papua New Guinea, you cannot say no money. In PNG, everything go down when no money."

I tried to argue my case. "What I wanted to do with this journey was to show that you don't need big money to do a big adventure."

Job raised his finger. "That is what makes people bump here. That is why Sana and Justin say in Indonesia, 'We go no more.' They say, 'Thor didn't make it properly, we must go back to Vanimo.'"

Before I had time to ask another question, he continued immediately with another thing that must have been bothering him and the other sailors the entire time, and that was our method of travel. "Thor is bossing us to move. In traditional canoes we never paddle canoes, we don't want. When we paddle we say, 'eh, prisoners.' In our custom, we do not paddle. If weather is calm, we just stay. You paddle kayak, easy-easy, this is a log, twenty people pull it up on the beach, not six-four people like dinghy. In your country, you will have machine to pull it up."

I asked him if he would consider joining the voyage again when I was back in PNG on the other side of the island, because then he could claim to have sailed around Papua New Guinea. He said, "I don't know. When Thor say you come back, I come back, I don't know. If he says 'no', it is all right. Only thing I am worried about is seeing the place, seeing Indonesia. I went and saw Indonesia, it is a good place. It is not a *raskol* place." Job sighed, his shoulders fell and then he looked into the lens and said, "That is all."

I was standing in the small departure hall of Vanimo airport with Steve and the sailors who were all lugging bags full of gifts for their families. I had given them all a chunk of cash that they had spent at the Indonesian border market, buying electronics and clothes. Justin had bought a solar kit and Sanakoli a mini DVD system with an integrated screen and Job a big music player for his hut. I must admit that it wasn't all out of generosity that I had given them my last cash for a shopping spree. My strategy was that, if Justin and Sanakoli's family saw them come home with all these gifts, they would be more likely to encourage them to go back and continue the voyage.

The gate opened and people filed in a line to show their tickets. It was quite emotional having to say goodbye to Job. On one hand, I felt I had let him down, on the other hand, I was relieved not to have any more conflict with him. He also seemed touched by the situation but most of all he looked happy to be going home. I told all the sailors that I was proud of them and shook their hands. Sanakoli was the last in the row and before he turned his back to board I said, "You guys return!"

The propellers were humming behind the departure hall as people dispersed from the airport. Where was I to go? I was stuck in Vanimo with a canoe I couldn't sail, only a quarter of the way around the island, and the Northwest Monsoon was knocking at the door. If things had ever looked bad it was now. At that moment, there was only one thing I could come up with. I jumped into Steve's cousin's taxi and said to both of them, "Now, let's get wasted."

"Woohoo!" the two cousins yelled and we drove off to the nearest bottle shop.

Chapter Fifteen

A dancing man (with a semi-toothless smile)

Expedition Log 6 November 2016

06:45 hrs. I have managed to crawl from the tent into a hammock swung between two coconut palms.

The light breeze was doing little for my heavy head. My brain felt like that big timber log Steve had anchored in front of his beach, banging around in the swell. We went on a bender the day before, after we had said goodbye to the sailors. It was actually a relief not having to be responsible for them, but this relief meant little compared to the doomsday feeling of loneliness the hangover had produced. But that morning I thought there was something else as well on my palate — disappointment was what I could taste, utter crushing disappointment and bitter defeat, even betrayal! I thought, 'We got kicked out of Indonesia, and yes, that was my fault and what do the sailors do, they run home to their wives and kids.'

'Ok, maybe that's a bit rough. It's thanks to them that we made it this far. What are the sailors going to do now, go back to their normal lives? And then will Justin and Sanakoli *really* consider coming back when I get the permits? Was I the only one who felt the magic — the *Tawali Pasana* magic? Man, when we sailed out on that first day from the Tawali Resort, it was awesome. The best day of my life… no… there was an even more important event before that — that was the best day of my life — the day I bought the canoe.'

As I laid there in the hammock snoozing and oozing off my anger, defeat and regret, I tried to turn my thoughts to something positive, back to the pre-expedition days in Milne Bay. I had just met Justin and Sanakoli and we had been shopping in Alotau. I said goodbye to Job and took a dinghy out to their birthplace of Basilaki Island to buy the canoe. It was a four-hour ride southeast but it felt like leaving almost every sign of the latter-day world in our wake as we berthed on the ancient jungle island in the late afternoon. The arrival itself was uneventful although Sanakoli had explained that he hadn't see his mother, Lena, in seven years.

When we pulled up at her beach, the two only exchanged a few words and I was shown to a hut on stilts that some of her five other sons were in the process of building for her.

The next morning, I climbed down the ladder and saw Lena in her kitchen hut. Justin and Sanakoli's mother was a light-skinned lady of about 70 years of age. She had grey curly hair and wore one of those long, coloured, fashionable dresses most women now wear in PNG. She seemed strong and vigorous; and I guess you had to be, to raise ten children. The kitchen hut was small and dark, and elevated just high enough so that chickens and dogs couldn't stick their heads in. She was sitting in the light of the entrance, stoking the fire that was blazing under a big black kettle, while a scrawny-looking kitten rubbed itself against her knee.

Lena wasn't alone in maintaining her place. A nephew of hers, a boy of around 12 years of age, lived with her and helped keep house. I greeted her with a 'good morning' and she nodded in a friendly manner and said, "Oh Tol, Tol." (I think she meant 'Thor, Thor' but I wasn't sure as she only spoke the local languages). Her place, Lumo Lumo, as it was called, was protected by mangroves on each side from the beach, with a view towards a large channel and an elongated island some 500 metres across. She was the only one living there but people would, from time to time, turn up in their canoes to fill drinking containers, as there was a trail behind her hut that led to a small freshwater swamp-like creek.

Sanakoli was still in his orange sleeping jumpsuit as he walked over to me. "Morning, morning," he said.

"Morning Sanakoli," I replied. I have been dreaming about sailing canoes all night, when will we see it?"

He laughed at my boyish eagerness. "Ho, ho! You don't worry. You see over there. Not the last but the second last bay we passed with the dinghy yesterday. That is where we are going." He gestured west, across the small secluded bay of Lumo Lumo, past the mangroves and over some small mountains.

"How long will it take to get there?" I asked.

Sanakoli rotated a *buai* nut lovingly between his fingers, "We walk, maybe an hour? Justin has already left to bring word to our small father, our what… our uncle, that the *dim dim* is here to buy his canoe." I rubbed my pale hands with excitement. After 13 days in the country, I was finally about to secure the most vital piece of equipment needed for the expedition. I wanted to suggest that we'd skip breakfast, pack some crackers and get going but then I remembered Lena who was already at work in the kitchen preparing something. I controlled myself and instead climbed upstairs to set up my film equipment.

After breakfast, we could *finally* take off. We paddled across a small bay into a muddy harbour. The barrier trees were slim and tall.

The sound of the ocean had died and the mosquitoes were buzzing like fiends. The canoe was tied off and we climbed up onto a great fallen log. "This is like a highway. I cut this," Sanakoli said and pointed towards what I learned was a pattern of fallen logs creating a path through the mesh of mangrove roots in the swamp.

I took off my shoes and started following him. "Are there any crocodiles here?" I asked nervously.

"Yes, maybe... but they are very shy. When I was a small boy there were many. Now they have all gone away," he answered. I looked down. The tide was going out. So much of the bottom was mud and the only thing moving were the small Signalling crabs waving their sand-coloured claws like warning flags.

After a while, we made it out of the swamp and in to a beautiful long bay with white sand and picture postcard bending coconut palms. We passed a hut and briefly greeted a couple of Sanakoli's cousins. As we continued up the beach Sanakoli said, "This place is too beautiful, do you think it would be a good place to make guest house?"

"Yes, it looks fantastic," I replied. "It is very private and you can go snorkelling on the reef out there. What about freshwater, do you have enough for people to shower?"

"No that is our big problem on this island, we had a big drought last year, many crops died and people suffered. The government had to come with water supply but it took long time," he elaborated. It was such an amazing island, exactly something for a tourist brochure but it was hard for the locals there to make money. I learned that the most common income on the island was from copra production. (Copra is dried flakes of coconut). Making copra is a long and tedious process and the per kilo price is low. There weren't many other opportunities there, except perhaps when outsiders came to the island on some business venture or another.

As we climbed the small mountain range to the second bay where the canoe was, we came by a small logging site where big timbers had been cut into heavy planks. Sanakoli explained that this was hard and dangerous work and, despite this, it wasn't very well paid. He knew this because he had worked on a sawmill in Alotau when he was younger. He then talked about a *dim dim* who had tried to start a seaweed farm on Basilaki. And then there were the prospectors talking about excavating gold from the mountains. Although there seemed to be some possibility of making an income from the land on Basilaki, it didn't sound like any of it would benefit the locals. Except for the seaweed initiative, these projects ended up leaving the island in a worse state.

Dancing man

The sweat was pouring from our foreheads as we made our way down the other side of the mountain. We had a break and Sanakoli, who was gasping for air, said, "So you asked me what our small father was doing for work — he is a dancing man."

"Like a professional dancer?" I questioned.

"No," Sanakoli explained, "When he hears music he starts dancing and he cannot stop." I must have looked befuddled as Sanakoli elaborated further.

"Let me tell you a story. One time my small father sailed to Alotau with eight bags of copra. He sold them and made big money. Now he was so happy and then he heard music playing in the street. Many people were standing around and he got excited and wanted to dance, so he gave his *bilum* to a stranger and started dancing and dancing to the music; he could not stop. After long time, when he was finally finished and got his what… senses back… he went looking for his *bilum* with all the money in but the stranger with the *bilum* was gone."

"So, he lost all his money?" I enquired fully engaged with his story.

"Yes, that guy just ran off with his money."

"Was your small-father drunk?" I asked.

"No, he is a dancing man. When you see him, you will know if he is happy. If he is happy, he will dance."

We saw a couple of great birds taking off with loud screeches. They were hornbills, a fruit-eating bird with a giant beak and a very distinctive call. At last we made our way down towards the second bay, where the sand was grey and there was a small river flowing out into the ocean. Behind a long brim of coconut palms was what seemed to be a larger gathering of huts. We walked in behind the village and found Sanakoli's uncle in a hut surrounded by a lush garden. He didn't speak English very well but what he could say was, "My name is Sebastian Petuweli. I am born on 26 June 1935 before Second World War." Although the man was 81, he seemed to be in good shape and high spirits. He was my height, maybe smaller.

He was wearing a red cap and his black curly hair stuck out from underneath it. He had very inquisitive eyes and a great smile, although half his front teeth were missing. He had a red sleeveless T-shirt, and his dark arms looked toned and sinewy. His wife, who had silver coloured hair, also seemed youthful. She offered Sanakoli and I a big plate of fresh papaya. I asked him, "So you have a canoe we can buy from you?" Sanakoli translated and he nodded with his semi-toothless smile. Then he spoke to Sanakoli and I learned that the canoe wasn't in the bay. It was elsewhere but his partner in the canoe, together with Justin, had gone to fetch it. I must admit I was deeply frustrated by this delay but kept up a good front.

It was about midday when the canoe finally arrived. Sanakoli and I had just been treated to a meal of chicken and root vegetables by one of the other uncles when we heard a conch shell blowing. I grabbed my tripod and camera bag and made it down to the beach. It was a lot bigger than the one Job had and the sail was made of a lightweight blue tarpaulin — full of holes and patches. I didn't know much about canoes at that time but the woodwork seemed old and weathered, especially the deck, which looked like it was made of rotten sticks. The ropes for the riggings looked even worse; they were crude and badly flossed. The canoe was aged white in colour and the letters A.T.S were painted on the side.

My excitement was severely dimmed by the doubtful state of this vessel. I considered the possibility that the Papua New Guineans just wanted to make some quick cash out of the *dim dim* by selling a run-down canoe. So, I started asking Sanakoli all sorts of critical questions about the condition of the vessel, as if I was haggling over a used car. Poor Sanakoli did his best to assure me that it was indeed a good buy, and the restoration that was needed could be done in a few days with local bush materials.

He told me that the canoe was three years old and built by Sebastian, together with two other partners, and the reason the canoe was named 'A.T.S' was that it was the first letter from each of their names. The canoe had been used for shark fishing and passenger runs to Alotau but now the partners were willing to sell it for the agreed price of 6,000 kina. After all these explanations, I was convinced and felt embarrassed that I had acted like a cheapskate Dane. The island had just gone through a crippling drought and everyone was struggling — if anything, I should be paying more. It was time for the *dim dim* to seal the deal.

We walked back to the village and up into a dark hut where I sat on a woven mat with Sebastian and one of the other partners, Sebastian's nephew, a man was in his mid-20s. Sanakoli was acting as mediator. There was an odd moment of silence. Then the nephew checked to see if there were any eavesdroppers about. Sanakoli had told me that it was important that we were alone when we made the deal and that other people didn't know how much the canoe was sold for. The reason for this was that Sebastian feared people would get jealous and hire witches to cast a spell or put a curse on him, so he would get eaten by sharks at sea, "Or worse." I had heard that jealousy and witchcraft were a big problem in Milne Bay, so I was careful not to cross any customs. I turned to Sanakoli. "So, should I give them the money?"

"Yes," he replied without hesitation. "You give them the money now." I counted out the damp 100 kina notes in to six bundles of 1,000 kina each and laid each bundle on the mat. The two other men didn't move but just stared at the money.

I followed with an improvised speech to the two men. "I would like to honour your practice of canoe building by sailing around all of Papua New Guinea and West Papua and making a film about it, so we can show the whole world your customs and traditions."

The two men sat for a while and then Sebastian spoke. "I would like to thank you too for giving us this money because you give us the right amount. And we support you in your travel around Papua New Guinea. Thank you very much."

I likewise replied "*Tinani Bani*" (or thank you). They all laughed at my clumsy but heartfelt words.

Sanakoli then pointed to the two men. "They are already planning to build a new canoe." The two men smiled and we all got up.

Afterwards, the extended family gathered and we all had a big meal — which was customary after such a deal was struck. I was already full from the previous chicken and paw paw but I did my best. As we were sitting under an open tin roof, Sebastian came over to me and pointed at my phone, "You have music?" I looked up at him. He spread out his arms and with his semi-toothless smile he said, "Because I am a dancing man." I quickly ran through my playlist nervous about picking a tune he would like. 'This is the one,' I thought, and pressed play. It was the 80s disco hit, 'Party all the time' sung by Eddie Murphy and produced by the legendary Rick James. As the booming rhythm and the synthesisers started screaming out of my phone, the 81-year-old started to dance. His face was one big happy smile as his body spun and swayed gracefully like seaweed in the swell. Damn that man could dance! I could do nothing but join in and try to keep up, while Eddie Murphy sang about his promiscuous girlfriend going clubbing. The whole village seemed to enjoy the spectacle and, as the song came to an end, Sebastian clapped, shook my hands and we hugged. Now that the deal was done, there was nothing left to do but return to Lumo Lumo with our prize.

The villagers pushed us out and we hoisted the sail. Despite multiple holes in the blue plastic, the canoe was running fast. Sanakoli was steering and Justin was chewing *buai*, while one of their other brothers pulled the sheet. I was sitting with my camera, eagerly documenting everything but then strong emotions suddenly washed over me and tears welled in my eyes. It was the realisation that I actually had a canoe! It was rotten and leaking but it was *my canoe*! It had been so much of a struggle just to get here but now I had the coolest vessel you could ever own — no specked-out Maserati, private jet or luxury motor yacht could ever match this and had anyone at that moment offered me such modern machines in exchange, I would have laughed in their faces. I thought to myself: 'This is the defining moment,' now there's nothing to stop me from sailing around the world's second largest island.

Rooster in a basket

Back in Lumo Lumo, there was no time to waste. I had to meet Paul Kerrison in Alotau in just two days' time. So the plan was to sew a new sail overnight and then sail to Nuakata where Justin and Sanakoli would restore the canoe, while I took a dinghy to Alotau to pick up Paul. The next morning, the sail was ready thanks to three of Justin and Sanakoli's brothers. Then more relatives came by to see us off. There were a couple of Lena's sisters and brothers as well. In the party there was also a very talkative man in a camouflage jacket. He wasn't from the island but worked in the nearby village as a schoolteacher. He started to explain the significance of sailing canoes on Basilaki. "The canoe is, to the people here, a sign of good things. When they hear the sound of the conches sing, they all rush to the beach to help pull the canoe on land because they expect the canoe to come home with barter goods, or fish or garden food. Or maybe new people."

This was 'gold,' I thought. My first question was, "Do they use the canoes much nowadays, now they have dinghies?"

"Yes," he replied, "You see them making more now. They dropped some years ago when dinghy came but now people have realised how expensive *zoom* (fuel) is. So, they are using the canoe instead to go to Alotau. You pay 50 kina for a dinghy but can go by canoe for 10 kina." It pleased me to hear that the traditional canoe could compete with a modern dinghy.

Some 4,000 years ago, a wave of seafarers, the Austronesians, sailed from what is now the Philippines and populated the coastal areas of New Guinea. The islanders in the Milne Bay region stay connected through the Kula Exchange Ring, a system that establishes and maintains relations of reciprocity, which is still alive today. One of the tokens of this relationship is a shell necklace. Some necklaces are big and elaborate with shiny conch shells, while other necklaces are fine strings of red discs skilfully made of the inside of oyster shells. The most common ones I saw people wearing were these red ones called *bagi*.

A *Kula* object can bear the name of its maker, and travel from hand to hand, island to island over many years. A person can have one or more *kula* partners and through *kula* relationships people can exchange food, arrange a bride price or settle disputes. But as Job had told me, it was also about being a well-spoken and, maybe even cunning, negotiator. What I later realised was that the *kula* spirit was also part of our journey as we formed relationships across the island of New Guinea.

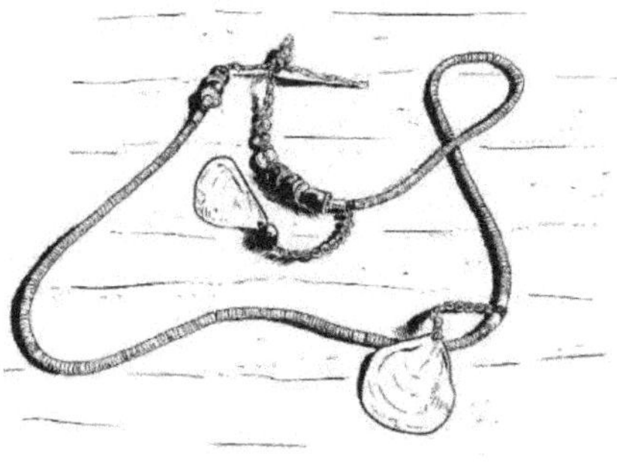

One of the sailors' uncles had brought a basket with garden food and a live rooster in it. Sanakoli cautiously asked if we might stay a bit longer to have a feast before we departed. I was rather tired of feasts and delays so I suggested we cook the rooster on Nuakata. Sanakoli agreed to this and we made ready to take off. We carried the new sail and spars down to the canoe and tied them on. The whole family had gathered on the beach but as we walked back to shake hands and say goodbye, something very powerful happened — Justin and Sanakoli's mother started wailing; so deep and painful a cry that I had never heard before. I was surprised by all of this because I hadn't experienced people showing strong emotions to one another in PNG before. Later I learned that displays of loud wailing is expected in these circumstances. Nonetheless Sanakoli and Justin tried to look serious and shake hands but they were clearly moved. As we climbed back onboard Justin quickly hoist the sail with red eyes, he hollered a loud, "Yehee!" The wailing followed us all the way out into the deep blue channel. The magnitude of this dramatic moment was not lost on me. Justin and Sanakoli were saying goodbye to their family to go on a long and dangerous journey — further than anyone from Milne Bay had ever ventured in a canoe.

We reached Nuakata in the afternoon. The sailing there had been smooth, and on the way in we passed some deep reefs where I caught a couple of good-sized fish — which Sanakoli jokingly claimed I had stolen from him as he had caught none. Nuakata was significantly smaller than Basilaki and, although it had a high mountainous inland, it looked tiny compared to Normanby, which was laying mighty and imposing and blue in the background. This was a perfect base for our final preparations. As Sanakoli said, "From here you go to East Cape in half an hour and bring back your photographer man… what, Paul."

As we entered the shallow waters in front of Sanakoli's village of Awatowtowa, the sail was let out and rolled down. Sanakoli jumped ashore and greeted his wife who was carrying their three-year-old twin sons. She was a young woman with smooth features and an elongated face. Both the sons climbed eagerly into their father's arms. "Thor, this is my wife Rachel and these two are my sons, Pati and Bani. This man over here, (pointing with his chin) is Rachel's father." A small man with puffy eyes and very little hair on his round friendly head said hello. The village didn't seem very big — built on a flat piece of land slowly sloping inland, sided by a low hill on one side and mangrove scrub on the other. There were only three huts. Rachel's father lived in a tiny house by the beach. Midway, on the best piece of land, lived the local Magistrate and at the end of the valley stood Rachel and Sanakoli's hut.

From the outside, the hut looked decently built in natural materials. It had a little patio and three rooms. We carried our goods into one of them. As Sanakoli put down a big rice sack the whole place bounced, "This is the best room but be careful, some places the floor is old," he cautioned. Next to the main hut there was a little kitchen shelter where Rachel would do her cooking. There Sanakoli introduced a girl of around ten years of age together with their two oldest boys, Kingsley and Jordis at seven and eight. Rachel and the girl were working in the kitchen, and while we were waiting for the women to prepare the fish, Sanakoli spoke about his life on Nuakata.

"Sometimes we go up to the garden in the mountains and work there. Other times I take the canoe and go fishing. We smoke the fish, and when we have an Esky (plastic cooler box) full of fish. I go to market in Alotau. When the fish is sold, I go home." To the question of how he got to live on Nuakata, he explained, "I met Rachel, so I must move to her land. Like it is in our custom. Her family is the poorest in Nuakata so we don't have much land but the fishing is good."

"Where does Justin live then?" I asked.

"He has a wife further out on Dawson Island but sometimes he has other wives. He is my older, so in our custom I must listen to him. He is not good with business, so he listens to me, so when I say we sail with the *dim dim*, he will sail." During his talk, one of the twins had been hanging around Sanakoli's neck. Sanakoli looked at his son. "This one is Pati, you see him always wanting to stay close, the other one… where is he, Bani, always get into trouble — like night and day," Sanakoli said as he shook his head while laughing to himself and stroking his child.

The following day, I returned to Alotau to pick up Paul and return to Nuakata a few days later. The canoe already looked better. We had help from eight young boys and men with the renovation of our vessel. A lot of the *kialos* supporting the outrigger had been changed and new *patotos* had been shaped in to spear heads and hammered into the old outrigger log. As Sanakoli pointed out, "These *patotos* are the ones that break when big wave hits so we must make them strong." While some men were working on the outrigger, others were sewing a new big blue mainsail on the lawn. We weren't short of cordage as Sebastian had given us a bag of nylon rope and string that he had 'acquired' from the seaweed project in Basilaki. Justin and Sanakoli supervised the work and participated wherever needed. Paul loved it, he walked around with his camera photographing everything while chatting with the workers.

I was torn between having to document the work with my video camera and participating in the actual build — I was, after all, here to learn to become a sailor. Nonetheless, I got to help sew some of the sail and tie the new rattan sticks that made up the floor of the outrigger platform. The mast had been taken down and Justin changed most of the rigging. Before it was put back up, Sanakoli hammered a wooden dove with a red flag into the top of the mast, like a weather vane. "The dove is our clan name," he explained.

The thing I found most fascinating about the whole building process was the communal nature of the work. In this culture, people helped each other whenever there was a big task at hand, whether you wanted to clear a piece of land, build a hut or make a canoe, the community would all pitch in, and in return you'd host a big meal for all of the participants and, of course, return the favour when other people needed it. Thanks to this system of reciprocity, we had the canoe ready in just three days and it didn't cost me anything except some rice, tinned mackerel, tea and tobacco.

On the last day, the workers got 10 kina each, which they were thrilled about. Sanakoli translated, "They are very happy, tomorrow Sunday, they are all going to the big village to see football match, our boys against another island. Now they got money for soda and smokes." I told them all that I was grateful for them being part of the adventure. One of the workers, an old man with a grey curly beard and a bucket hat, had brought a newly cut paddle with him and asked if I would buy it. It was beautifully crafted and perfectly symmetrical with a wide leaf-shaped blade, and on it he had painted *Eneta* in swirling gothic letters. In the local language this means — 'that's the one.' It was perfect.

Chapter Sixteen

The shadow

It had been yet another long day and I was back in the hammock at Steve's place in Vanimo. The reef was rumbling monotonously as wave after wave spilled over into the lagoon. Steve's big timber log had broken loose from its anchorage and was now rolling back and forth restlessly. I heard the call for dinner.

As I sat down by the table in the open tin roof covered house, I could see Steve was watching a film with all the kids on a laptop; Julia served me a plate of rice and tinned meat.

"Oh, thank you mother, you are taking very good care of me." I clapped my naked belly.

Julia proudly answered, "Yes you have gotten fat. Good." I was getting a bit of belly, probably from drinking all those sodas (and beers) and not doing any exercise except taking the bus into Vanimo every day.

I had been in Lido for more than a month and the cruising permit still hadn't arrived. A great thing had happened though; the Governor of East Sepik had approved funding for our voyage. But the excitement soon evaporated when it became clear that some of his corrupt employees had 'misplaced' my proposal. I was now fighting to have the papers 'found' and processed before the Christmas holidays.

After dinner I walked up towards Vanimo Surf Lodge, which was situated at the other end of the village where the asphalt road began. I had never been inside but I had stumbled across the Manager on the beach — a tall blond-haired Australian named 'Gordo,' who invited me to come by for a drink and meet some new people. I hadn't bothered as I had no energy to socialise with more people than necessary, but now, I was feeling that any opportunity to free myself from the inertia of waiting would be welcome.

As darkness fell, I considered the fate of the expedition. I didn't know if the sailing permit would ever be approved. There were no finances. The plan Paul and I had of getting funding through a magazine article had even fallen through. I didn't know if the sailors would return now that it had been so long, and the Northwest Monsoon was already blowing. Sandy Robson had suggested that I could go home to Denmark and return after four to five months, when the winds were favourable and I had raised some money. But to go back now would break the continuity of a great journey. I had briefly entertained the idea of just ending it here at the border. I already had had an amazing adventure and a good story to tell and our 1,700 kilometre journey was a record in itself. But I had also made a vow not to return to Denmark before the circumnavigation was complete. This inner debate, and the decision that followed, can best be explained through a fairy-tale by my famous countryman Hans Christian Andersen — 'The Shadow'.

A learned man travelled to the tropics. One evening he sent his shadow to investigate a mysterious house across the street, where 'the maiden of poetry' resided. The Shadow didn't return and so the man travelled home to Northern Europe — alone. Many years later the Shadow visited his former master, who was not doing too well. The Shadow, who was elegantly dressed, told the man that he had visited the court of poetry and then travelled the world and became rich and famous. The Shadow asked the man if he would like to travel with him and, in a reversal of roles, to serve as *his* shadow. It didn't end well — with a betrayal and a beheading — as nothing ever does when the right order of things is disrupted.

It is a pretty dark story but not that far from my reality. If I were to return home now, I would only ever be able to tell part of a tale — and be perpetually lamenting the amazing adventures that *might* have been but never were. Instead this regret would grow into bitterness that — like the man's shadow — would also destroy me. What the learned man in the story didn't understand, however, was that the Shadow was a liar who only ventured to the front-room of the house of poetry — it couldn't enter the glimmering, brightly-lit inner saloons without the man. Now, in Vanimo, *my* shadow was standing in the anteroom of my life and at this great turning point it was up to me to push aside the dark doubt — and by all means, paddle all the way around this island of New Guinea before I even dared to think about booking a one-way ticket back to fairy-tale land.

I was all worked up by these thoughts. It wasn't about commitment now but rather anger towards everything standing in our way. I had a sort of 'secret weapon' though, a philosophy which had served me well when passion for an adventure just wasn't enough. It goes like this: When I was making my kayaking adventure films, I embraced any kind of resistance, obstacle or danger as 'good for the story.' The greater the complication, the richer the tale.

I woke from my humid thoughts and found myself at the front of a great, almost medieval-looking, wooden wall surrounding the Vanimo Surf Lodge. There were no lights on and the gate was locked. I called out but no one was around. I could hear the distant sound of music, so I climbed the fence — a risky move in PNG. The landing was soft and I stood up. No one had seen me. The lawn was well kept with a few small palm trees scattered about. Down by the beach I could see light streaming out of a great, open communal hut. There was sand on the floor, wooden tables and benches and an elevated bar area with a kitchen. It looked pretty basic and reminded me of the jungle camp I had worked at in Venezuela.

The manager offered me a cold beer and introduced me to some of the surfers as, "Thor, the crazy Dane with the canoe." The clientele weren't the stereotypical 'surf bums' I expected but rather they all seemed to be educated Australian men from the upper middle-class on a sports' holiday. I came to speak with a bespectacled man in his 50s. At first glance I thought he had a prosthetic nose but then realised — with relief — that it was skin-coloured zinc cream. He introduced himself as Dr Rob Goodfellow, and then asked me a lot of interesting questions about our journey.

It turned out that Rob had lived and taught in Indonesia for years and had even worked under three Presidents and many of the Provincial Governors. On top of this, he was a well published author. He gave me some advice on how to work with the Indonesian bureaucracy,

"In Indonesia the best approach is that you must ask for advice and then follow that advice — and your supporting documents must be well presented and credible — and above all they have to *look good…* form is more important than substance." Then he gave me some suggestions about how I could better promote my expedition. When I walked home that night it was with a renewed sense of optimism.

Plan B

Over the next week I visited the surf camp every evening and Rob helped me put together a sponsorship proposal, sharpen up my promotional material and create a newsletter for my followers called, 'Message in a Bottle' — not original but very catchy. The basic idea for the newsletter actually came from Sandy, who had also given me advice on how to find funding. Sandy suggested that I have a visible 'donate button' on my website and that I could send it out to all my contacts with a short update, a video or photos and invite people to support me.

In the daytime, I would go into Vanimo and work from a government office where my local friend Imelda was employed. She was a highly-skilled office worker of around 50 years of age. Her competence and good work ethic would probably have brought her a much higher position had she been a man. Imelda and her sister helped me apply for 'PSIP funding,' which is a Provincial-level government-sponsored program for community projects and special events.

Meanwhile, I was beginning to consider a 'plan B' in case the sailors didn't return or I didn't get the Indonesian Sailing Permit. The plan was as follows: If I couldn't sail *Tawali Pasana* myself, then I could adapt one of the small paddling outrigger canoes from Vanimo. I would pack the bare minimum of supplies in one of the blue watertight barrels and attach it firmly to the canoe, that way I would have a vessel that could stay buoyant, not if, but when I got swamped. For propulsion I could cut a traditional Greenland-style kayak paddle. This would be good for long distance rowing against the wind. In addition, I would make a little mast for good wind days. On the way I would hopefully meet *Bahasa*-speaking local travel buddies who could paddle alongside me from one village to the next. I liked this idea — it would be rough but at least everything wouldn't be lost if 'plan A' didn't come through.

Steve had started surfing back in 1990. In 1995 he was part of the national team representing his country in the Pacific Games in Tahiti, French Polynesia. The team returned with a bronze medal which made the sport take off in PNG. But what really put Vanimo on the international surfing map was the documentary film *Splinters* made in 2011. Steve was now coach for the women's international longboard team, and every morning two or three women would pick up surfboards from his house and go surfing. I spoke to Marielle who was on the team. She was a two-time national champion and a single mother of five young children. I asked her how often she surfed she replied, "I train every day. In the morning, I make breakfast for my children and then I go out for a couple of hours. Sometimes I see good waves, I forget to make breakfast for the kids, I just go out." she laughed.

I had noticed that she had a sticker on her surfboard that read, 'Pink Nose Revolution: Surfers Against Violence Against Women, Empowering Women with Equal Rights and Opportunities.' She didn't seem to know much about it, so I asked Steve. He explained it was an initiative of the Surf Association of Papua New Guinea (SAPNG) to empower women in the sport and address the issue of gender-based violence.

Steve explained that when women began surfing in Lido, some of the older men protested, as there was a superstition that women on the reef would be bad luck for fishing.

"But it is not like this anymore," Steve reassured me. When I looked into the 'Pink Nose Revolution,' I discovered its origins. After the launch of *Splinters* a large number of surf boards were donated to SAPNG but all the boards were taken up by male surfers. This was called out by the female national surfing champion Leslie Umpa, who also appeared in the film. When the next donation came, half of all the boards had their noses painted pink, and were given to the female surfers.

December came and I moved into the Surf Lodge. Man, it was so good to have a break from Steve's screaming kids. Rob had flown home but we kept in constant contact. Gordo had gone too but before he left, he introduced me to the new Manager, another Aussie named Paul, who was just like Gordo with the same tall build, blond long hair and constant stream of expletives. His partner was a Dutch web-designer named Anna. They were just as friendly as Gordo and he let me stay at the Lodge at a very good rate.

On 8 December, all government offices were closed and Imelda, who was full of frustration and regret, said that we had, "Lost the Governor's funding," but that we could try and claim it back in March next year. I had had enough by then, and thanked her for doing her best. I wasn't the only one who was frustrated. There had been a whole mob of angry people in front of the government building three days before, who hadn't received their promised funding either. It started to get violent so the Police came and dispersed them. Meanwhile, I learned that one of the employees close to the Governor had a 20,000 kina (USD$6,600) claim for 'community soft drinks' approved.

I had Skyped with Paul the photographer about this whole mess. He pointed out, "To some it could seem a bit odd, that a Dane comes to ask a poor country to sponsor his adventure." I didn't see it like that. I was making a world record with Papua New Guinean master sailors — in a Papua New Guinean traditional sailing vessel — and the more ownership the country had of this project, the better. Besides, it was a small investment for Vanimo who, in return, would become a prominent part of the story and strengthen their significant potential in tourism.

I went to bed that night feeling more frustrated than usual. I was so disappointed with all those people who didn't understand the greatness of this adventure — from the TV producers in Denmark, to the government people in PNG. But the most frustrating part of this whole situation was that in the end I had no one to blame but myself. 'I had made my bed and now I had to lay in it,' as we say in Denmark. I thought, 'This is what you get when your expedition plan is built on die hard optimism and few means.' As I was tossing and turning on the uncomfortable mattress, an email ticked in. The screen was bright and sharp.

Dear Thor,

Herewith I am sending you copy of SY. TAWALI PASANA CAIT, please find it attached.

TAWALI PASANA CAIT is valid until 28th February 2017.

For further information, please do not hesitate to contact us.

Thank you for your kind attention.

Have a nice day.

Best Regards,

Yes! I had permission to cruise around West Papua, although it was only valid until 28 February. That was fine because once approved it was easy enough to apply for a renewal. Now I just needed some sailors. Job was out of the picture. The stress of being away from his family had taken a physical toll on him, in addition to the hierarchy issues, which had created so much conflict on the canoe. Now that they had all returned home, Job was no longer responsible for Justin and Sanakoli and could in theory re-engage in the voyage with the two brothers as his superiors — but that was never going to happen. Still, I hoped that Job could join us for the last leg from the southern border of PNG to Milne Bay. Only time would tell.

The next morning, I nervously dialled the number for Sanakoli, to find out if I still had a crew.

"Hey Sanakoli how are you doing?" I chirped.

"Oh Thor, you should have seen me the other day, I caught twelve tuna, they just kept on going around my canoe."

"Twelve tuna! Are you sure it wasn't sardines? I don't remember you catching anything last time we fished your reef?" I joked.

Sanakoli yelled through the speaker, "That was because you stole my fish, you got no luck!"

We both laughed, and then I told him the good news about the sailing permit and asked, "So are you guys ready to fly back to Vanimo for the next part of the adventure?"

Sanakoli nearly jumped through the phone with excitement. "That's the one I wanted to ask. People here keep asking, 'When you go back?' and, 'Oh you must finish!' — So, I tell them, 'Me and Justin we are ready to sail, we just wait for our *dim dim* to give signal.'"

I jumped up liked a coiled spring and punched a big adolescent hole into the air — but then I quickly calmed myself. "That sounds so great Sanakoli. I knew I could count on you. By the way, how is the weather there?"

He answered, "In Milne bay we got big wind."

Then I replied in a strangely ordinary way. "Here the wind is still strong but sometimes it changes around."

Then Sanakoli repeated the magic words I needed to hear again. "We go anyhow, you just tell us when to come."

The sailors were hungry for adventure — even their families wanted them to go. One problem remained, I still hadn't secured any sponsors or funding, although I had started receiving a few donations from Facebook followers. What really saved us was my mother. She was so happy to hear that the permit had come through, that she gave me an early, and very generous, Christmas present. This allowed me to buy flights for Justin and Sanakoli and start our voyage into West Papua. As a librarian, she wasn't a wealthy woman but she wasn't the type who spent her money on designer vases or foot spas either. I was so grateful for her help but also embarrassed to take her money. The Lodge Manager Paul, put my mind to rest by his wonderfully insightful, simple explanation, "I wouldn't think too much about it mate. When you have completed your sailing, who's going to care about things like that."

Despite all of this good news, things went slowly — as they always do in PNG — and I ended up spending Christmas and New Year in Vanimo. Justin and Sanakoli arrived on 8 January 2017. They both looked well. Justin was wearing a *bagi* necklace, that he thought he might trade along the way, and Sanakoli, who was always the most modest of the two, had invested in a new pair of rubber thongs. I must admit I had missed them. Now that we were going to have to sail against the powerful Northwest Monsoon along the most exposed coastline in all of New Guinea — from the 'horned shoulders' to 'the nose of the dragon' — Vanimo to Sorong, we had to strengthen *Tawali Pasana*, and Justin had a plan. Inspired by the canoes that sail from the outer islands of Milne Bay, Justin cut two triangular boards, one to cover each end of the canoe, so it wouldn't flood so easily when the nose dove into a wave.

As we were cutting the tarpaulin, I started to understand their motivation for continuing the voyage. Apparently, a host at NBC radio in Alotau had been interviewing Moda who was following our journey on Facebook. Every week he would broadcast an update on our latest exploits, both in English and *Bwana Bwana* (the traditional language spoken in Justin and Sanakoli's part of Milne Bay). And as Sanakoli explained, "So we arrive to Alotau on the second day of the canoe festival, and eey, all our friends already know about our travels, they want us to tell stories about, what, *Talwai Pasana* and say, 'You must continue!'"

I could have hugged that radio host when I heard this. The final touch was to mark the canoe with its new registration number. This number was required by the Indonesian authorities, but in PNG there is no registration of traditional sailing canoes. Nonetheless, the Maritime Safety Authorities officer in Vanimo, Mr Ivan, was very helpful and, after corresponding back and forth to his headquarters in Port Moresby, he got *Tawali Pasana* registered under the number:

PNG C0001. It was the first canoe ever registered in the country. Steve also left his mark on our now famous craft by carving a traditional head motif from Lido village on the strake.

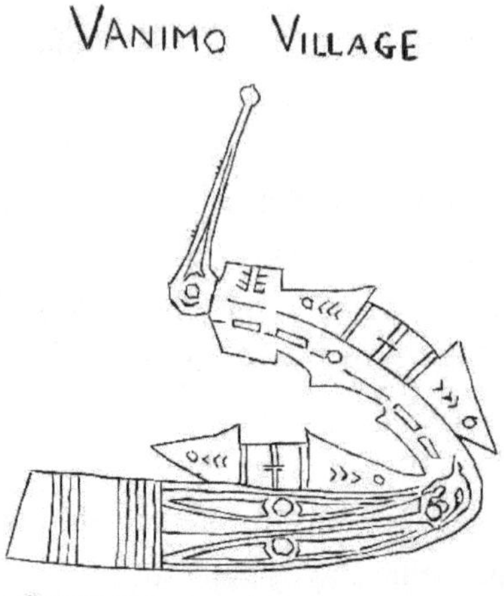

CANOE HEAD DESIGN

The day before departure I bought a pig and Steve's family organised a departure feast. It was a huge amount of work and engaged a lot of people — from killing the pig to burning off all the hair, then gutting it and cutting it into pieces. Some of the meat was cooked in an earth oven called a '*mumu'* — an elongated hole in the ground bedded with hot rocks and embers then covered in banana leaves. Then the root vegetables and meat are put in and it is all covered again and left to bake for several hours. My friends from the Vanimo Surf Lodge came by together with Mr Ivan and his wife. Before the dining began, Steve's sister Dorothy said some words, "Thor, we thank you for your visit. In our custom, when strangers come to our beach, we invite them in and give them food, when they leave, they will give back a pig or a gift. We thank you for the pig and we all wish you and your boys, good luck on your voyage around the island."

Early the next morning Steve's father came to the house. He was an old man that had lost most of his teeth and hair as the years gained on him. He walked slowly, supporting himself with a cane. He nodded to us briefly and then he sat down on a plastic chair in front of the ocean, where Steve's log was now laying half buried in sand. The old man started speaking to the sea in a local tongue. Steve whispered to me, "This is an old spell. He is making sure that you will have a good travel and you will have no trouble in Indonesia, so you can sail right through."

The old man's spells seemed to work because at that very instant the wind started to blow steadily from the east. We were eager to get the canoe in the water but before we could depart, we had to take a one-hour drive to the border and 'stamp out' of PNG and into the Republic of Indonesia. Steve's cousin had said he would take us but first he had to go in the other direction, into town to take his wife shopping. Two hours later he was finally back and we got in the taxi; now it was low on petrol so we had to go back to town first to fill up. When we arrived in Vanimo we had to wait for another guy to have lunch, take over the taxi and drive us up to the border.

The sun was in zenith and I was about to boil with frustration. We were losing good sailing wind and after 86 days in Vanimo — yes, 86 — I was more than fed up with the place. I was about to lose it when a shining white Toyota Hilux pulled up next to us. It was Ivan with his wife, and they offered to take us up to the border and back. We jumped inside the air-conditioned cabin and took off. After three hours we were by the canoe, our passports stamped and our blue plastic barrels packed with gifts. At four in afternoon of 14 January we finally sailed out of the lagoon for the second, and hopefully last, time.

The sail to Jayapura was slow but without drama and this time we came prepared. Inspired by advice from Rob and Sandy, I had acquired a fancy-looking leather folder for my papers, I had embossed business cards as well as printed and laminated ID cards for the sailors and I. But the master stroke was a quality print postcard that I had put all my graphics skills into. It featured a photo of the canoe, our route around the island, and not least an image of Justin, Sanakoli and I with 'official' name tags. On the card was written: 'The World's First Circumnavigation of the Island of New Guinea in a Traditional Sailing Canoe,' with my contact details printed below.

The postcard was the first thing I would give to officials as a 'special gift' — and it worked. You could see the bureaucrats faces light up with astonishment when they understood the magnitude of our crazy world record. Then I presented my business card, and after this I would open the folder with all the important papers in order. It was pure theatre and it had the desired effect. The two-day-long process included meetings with the Harbour Master, Customs, Police, the Sea Police, Immigration, various health authorities and finally the PNG Consulate. It all went smoothly and the Indonesian officials were all very helpful. Mr. Lucky from the Harbour Master's office looked pleased to see me back. Even his superior left his office to shake my hand and have a selfie taken. Before I left, Mr. Lucky said, "You have a long journey ahead, it will be much easier now that you have your papers in order." It was a good thing I had printed plenty of documents — including a whopping 250 postcards. Rob was right. It worked.

Now that we were in 'the land of milk and honey,' Justin and Sanakoli deserved a bonus for re-committing to the adventure, so they each got a smartphone. The sailors had never owned such a device before and they seemed nervous as we stood amongst the shiny glass cabinets in Jayapura Mall. "You decide which one, we don't know," Sanakoli said. So, I got them phones with good cameras. Then we went to the more relaxing environment of a restaurant and unpacked the new devices. As the colourful screens turned on, their faces lit up with excitement. Neither of them had ever operated something remotely like that before, so I helped them through the basics of setting up a web account so they could call their wives cheaply using Skype.

Emails and social media were a steep learning curve, not least for Justin who could hardly read or write. But if they could use these tools it would be a great advantage should they later set up a business in tourism. They quickly mastered how to play music and use the camera.

I really enjoyed the fact that I could teach them something, but there was also an ulterior motive behind giving them smartphones. Now that we were in West Papua, I had to be careful with filming, whereas smartphones seemed to be everywhere, so it wouldn't look odd if Justin and Sanakoli started recording, and not least I would be able to share their views of the voyage.

After four days in Jayapura we were clear to travel. The canoe was re-fitted and provisioned with a fully stocked pantry. The fellowship of the *Tawali Pasana* was now prepared to enter the innermost salon of mystery — and the sailors all came armed with smartphones, ready to snap a selfie or record a scene, should they the encounter 'the maiden of poetry.'

And as for me — my shadow was back in its rightful place.

Chapter Seventeen

The monsoon of doom

The first leg out from Jayapura was a tough one, and the first four hours were absolute mayhem — one of those 'I-wish-I-had-never-set-out-to-sea' situations. The Cyclops Mountain Range that protects the waters of Jayapura bay runs down the coast with steep cliffs constantly pounded by great oceanic swells. This energy is then refracted back to sea producing gut-churning surface conditions. *Tawali Pasana* was being hammered, twisted and tortured from all directions. One second she was on the peak of a wave and the next, the wave would be gone, leaving the canoe hovering in mid-air before free falling flat into a deep swell valley with a thumping splash. Nonetheless, she was in top form, and so were Justin and Sanakoli as they intuitively worked the rudder, the ropes and the sail like an extension of their own limbs, as the brothers and the canoe became one nautical entity, fighting for survival.

I was fully occupied in the hull, continuously bailing while praising Justin's new splash-board, which saved us from being swamped several times. Around noon, the wind dropped and we continued slowly up the coast. The morning's harrowing experience made me think of a discussion I had in the Vanimo Surf Lodge. One of the surfers asked why we didn't wear life vests. It was a good question, as in Denmark I would always wear a lifejacket when kayaking. My short answer was that if I were to be lost at sea, the sharks would eat me anyway. The more complex explanation was that Milne Bay canoe sailors didn't wear life vests. Even if they wanted to, they couldn't afford one, and anyway, to ask my crew to wear one would be to question their expertise. The same was true if I was to wear one. In the end, we were all in the same boat.

As night fell, we finally had a chance to go behind a headland for a nights' rest, but instead we decided to continue. We cooked and ate while slowly sailing throughout the night. Now that we were travelling against the seasonal wind, we had a new strategy. When the weather was fair, we would sail as far as possible, when the wind turned against us, we would rest ashore until the next favourable weather opportunity presented itself.

We were also under considerable time pressure because the sooner we covered the 561 nautical miles to the westernmost point of the island, and the city of Sorong, the sooner we would be able to take advantage of having the powerful Northwest Monsoon at our backs. In spite of the near impossible prospects of sailing against the wind, we had a 'hack' — we would "Go on the mountain wind," as Sanakoli explained. In theory, the mountainous coast would provide us with a solid draining side wind in the evening and early morning hours — 'the Katabatic Effect.' The first night, the theory didn't work very well but the next morning the wind came back with a lazy wisp, slowly cascading from the mountain, enough for Sanakoli to allow me take the *yabby yabby* — under his watchful eye, of course. It was awesome to be standing at the stern — like King of the World — with the canoe in front of me, looking down the ramp of a big turquoise swell.

Justin must have felt that the canoe wasn't sailing as steadily as it could because he woke from his nap in the front, looked up with one open eye and cautioned, "You make wrong turn, we tip," and then he pulled the cap back over his face. I was already nervous about steering so his comment didn't really help. Nonetheless, I kept at it until my steering foot was throbbing and my back aching. We were aiming to reach a small cluster of islands some 32 nautical miles up the coast. At this point, the inland vista became flat — framed by long white sandy beaches that looked very inviting, but this was not a luxury to be entertained. The great swells that rolled so gently under our hull in deep water changed character as they reached the coast and created such a thumping sound when they broke, as to strike fear in the heart of any sensible canoe sailor.

I asked Sanakoli if it would be possible to land on one of those idyllic-looking beaches. He replied without hesitation, "If you go in there, you never get out again." There were also several rivers running into the ocean, which we had hoped to be able to go up to seek shelter but, as we passed by the first and then the second estuary, it was clear that this wasn't an option either as the waves seemed to get more destructive as they collided with the river outflow, not to mention the random sand banks that were formed as barriers by these same conditions. From now on, all the way to Sorong, landing would only be possible in protected bays or behind islands and headlands; we would have to plan our sailing very carefully.

WAKDE / INSUMINAI

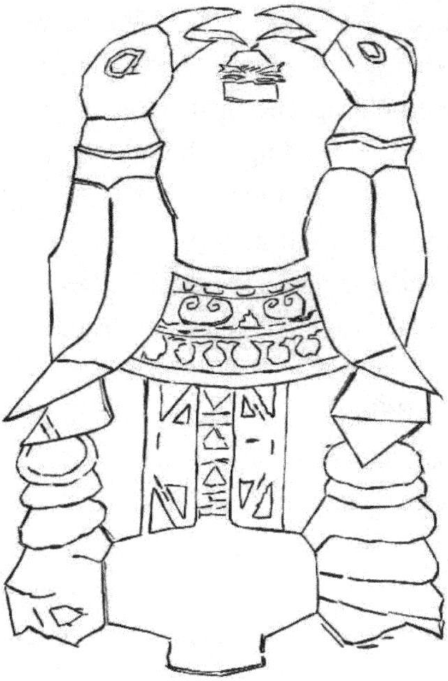

At nightfall, we reached the first island — Kaitjebo. It was too small to land on and was surrounded by razor sharp coral reef, so we anchored 70 metres behind it and spread the tarpaulin over the canoe. The firewood was too wet and the sea too choppy to make a fire on board so, instead, we ate damp biscuits with spam under the blue light of my head lamp while light rain drummed on the canvas. Although the canoe was wet and hard, it still felt cosy to be back under the tarpaulin with Justin and Sanakoli. I thought we should have a treat, so I took out a bag of jelly snakes I had bought in Jayapura. Sanakoli had crawled out in the rain to check on the anchor and I handed the bag to Justin, "What is this?" he interrogated me. Justin had a look of wonder on his face as he turned the colourful snake between his fingers.

"It is lolly — rubber lolly?" I held my laugh and told him it was made from gelatine and sugar and all kids loved them.

Justin stuck it in his mouth and chewed, while saying, "In the turtle arm, when you cut it up, you find the same thing."

Sanakoli came crawling back in, dripping wet and Justin passed him the bag. "What is this?" he also exclaimed in an astounded but sceptical tone. He held up one of the snakes and said, "This is like rubber!" Justin and I cracked up with laughter and Sanakoli joined in while shaking his head, "Oh Indonesia!" Exhausted from two days of hard sailing, we all soon fell asleep. It was a short-lived pleasure. I woke with a jolt under the dark plastic sheet and immediately felt that something was very wrong. I looked out from underneath and could see that we weren't in the same position as when we went to bed. The anchor had dragged bottom and we were drifting towards the coast! We hoisted the sail and, after an anxious hour, we came to the safety of the much larger island of Mengge. It was a close call — I shuddered at the thought of not waking in time and the life-threatening consequences of drifting into the breaking zone. After securing the canoe with both a stern line and anchor, we could finally go back to sleep.

The next afternoon, we arrived at Masi Masi Island, where my map clearly indicated a small village. As we paddled into the bay, we were welcomed by a couple of young men. More and more people came to see our odd vessel. Unlike in PNG, people weren't hanging off the canoe, instead, they inspected it without touching. The most forthcoming of our observers were two teenage girls who went bonkers when they saw me. "Selfie, selfie," they sweetly demanded as one of them pulled out a smartphone. Soon the chance encounter was digitally eternalised.

As in in any typical PNG village, Masi Masi West Papua had a Chief, which in Indonesia is called the *Kepala Desa* (Village Head). I introduced the sailors and gave the *Kepala Desa* a postcard. His name was Nelson. He was a man of around 50 years of age with a flat white hat and grey sideburns. Again, as in most villages on the other side of the border, the people of Masi Masi were hospitable and loved our project, but there were also some obvious differences as I learned during a tour around the village. The houses were standing on the ground — not stilts — built in concrete and topped with metal roofs. Even more impressive were the electricity cables running from house to house via small posts, and the exposed iron piping delivering fresh water to the front of every house. The electricity was generated by a big communal generator, which also ran the water pump by the communal well. There was a school building and, of course, a church. The major religion in West Papua is Protestant Christianity — introduced by Dutch missionaries.

I was quite impressed by all this infrastructure, especially considering that Masi Masi was a remote island. If the villagers needed to buy provisions, they would sail to the mainland and then catch a bus to Jayapura or else go up the coast to the next big town of Sarmi. I learned that it was the government that had built the houses and provided funding for utilities. Although the islanders seemed to have the same limited income opportunities as their neighbours in PNG (and they had also had their gardens and the sea); I saw several people with smartphones and some of the houses had satellite parabolas — even the dogs looked well fed.

When we came back from the walk, Justin and Sanakoli were sitting at a table by the beach, shaded by a giant Sea Almond tree (*Terminalia Catappa*) and surrounded by curious villagers. Sanakoli was entertaining the eager bystanders with his phone by showing the 'Message in a Bottle' promotional video I had just made and afterwards his own recordings from our Jayapura leg. He even had some low-resolution photos from his old phone, of his wife, his kids and his village. Meanwhile, Justin was getting help from a young man who was transferring local music from his own phone to Justin's. Despite the language barrier, communication wasn't that big of a problem. We had been practising the most common *Bahasa* courtesy phrases in Jayapura and, during sailing, and I had also written a list of useful words on a short spare plank we had laying on the canoe. Our thesaurus plank contained words like: *ikan* (fish), *gelombang* (swell), *ombak* (wave), *angin* (wind) and *batu karang* (reef).

One thing that many of the Papuan men kept telling Justin and Sanakoli was that PNG and West Papua were '*sama sama*' (the same). They would lift their own fuzzy hair and then point to Justin and Sanakoli's hair and say, "*Sama sama.*" I was a bit paranoid about the political undertones behind these expressions of 'sameness,' but the sailors would nod and laugh in good faith and say, "*Bagus bagus*," (good, good) in return.

Before retiring for the night, we were invited to have tea and biscuits with the *Kepala Desa* and the village elders. The tea party was accompanied by Justin's newfound Papuan music. The next morning, we made ready for an early start. The *Kepala Desa* and the rest of the village came down to say goodbye. They loaded the canoe with bananas and coconuts and the *Kepala Desa* gave me a model of a traditional canoe cut in balsa wood, engraved with their traditional tribal design.

The next town on our map was Sarmi — only about 30 nautical miles along the coast. Nonetheless, it took us four days to get there. The waves were simply too big for sailing. Sarmi is located at the end of the coastal road that runs from Jayapura and it was our last safe harbour before the lowland marshes of the Mamberamo River Delta. The Mamberamo is the largest river in West Papua and flows into the ocean at D'Urville Point, at the northernmost 'shoulder of the dragon.' Passing the Mamberamo would be the first of many challenges from the 'shoulder' and the great Cenderawashi Bay that spans 220 nautical miles across to the 'back of the head of the dragon.'

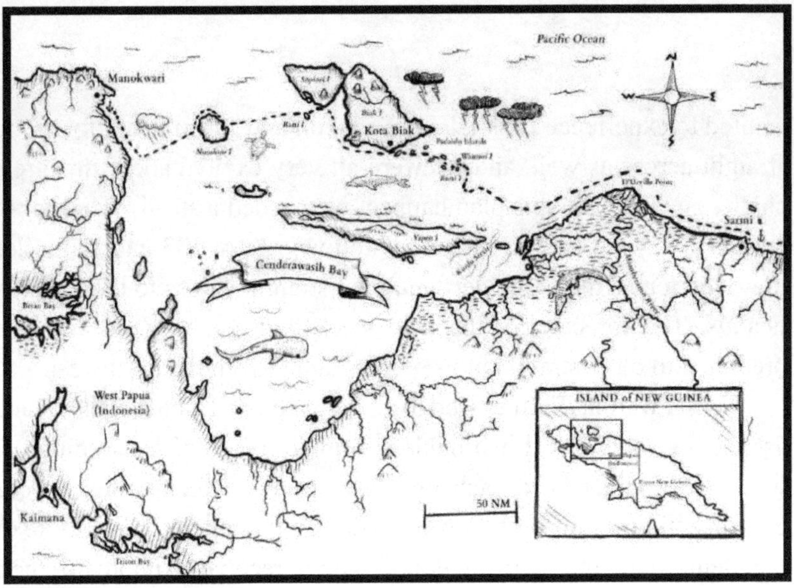

As we lay berthed in Sarmi, we discussed our sailing options. We would need at least 24 hours to reach the Mamberamo, from there, we had two options. The first was to follow the safer route of going into the bay, down to Yapen Island and then cross south of the elongated island to the other side of the bay. There were problems with this — we'd have to pass through the Kurdu Strait which we had been warned had very strong, surging currents. The south shore of the long island would protect us from the Pacific waves but the tall mountains running along the island would shield us from the wind — meaning a lot of paddling. When we had made it along the island, we could hop to another island and then tack upwards against the wind to reach the mainland and then follow the coast up to the town of Manokwari. Although the safest option, it could also turn into a very time-consuming detour.

The other bolder route was to go straight across the bay of Cenderawasih. From Mamberamo we could make an open water crossing to a group of islands and atolls called the Padaido Islands. From there we could island hop to the huge island of Biak, get fresh provisions, continue to the island of Numfoor and do the final full day crossing to the 'back head of the dragon' and the city of Manokwari. It was a tough call, but time wasn't on our side and I had always wanted to experience Biak Island. Sanakoli and Justin voted for going straight across as well, and we were all very excited about this great challenge. To make this plan happen, we needed a steady wind for at least two days to take us on a non-stop voyage of 133 nautical miles up to the top of the 'shoulder' and then straight across to the Padaido Islands. The forecast for the next week didn't look good and was predicted to blow straight at us — constantly from the northwest.

While waiting for the wind to change, I posted a Facebook update asking for donations. I had made a graphic image of a shopping list with prices attached to each item we needed. I then called on our growing 'fellowship' of followers to donate money for one or more of the items and, in return, a donor would receive a photo of their contribution to share on social media. Our followers loved this, and after a couple of days we went shopping. Afterwards, as promised, I returned photos of Justin posing with emergency flares, fishing lures, gifts for villagers and food items.

Expedition Log 1 February 2017

09:00 hrs. Tried to sail out, too much wind. Waste of time. Could have been working on FB posts or answering emails.

Expedition Log 4 February 2017

22:00 hrs. Departing Sarmi. YES! Cloudy and dark but not much wind from W-SW but the weather forecast is looking good for the next two days. A high-pressure weather cell to the north has made the wind turn to our advantage.

Expedition Log 5 February 2017

07:00 hrs. We have only covered 14 nautical miles in nine hours! Worrying. We need to cover more distance for this plan to work.

16:00 hrs. The wind is finally picking up but not enough to reach the Mamberamo before nightfall. I am worried about the river mouth. We don't know if there will be waves and, if we pass it in the night, there'll also be the risk of hitting logs or get entangled in debris.

19:00 hrs. We are nearing the river but the sea breeze has gone — and there is no mountain wind either. We're drifting into the sunset on a flapping sail.

Expedition Log 6 February 2017

01:28 hrs. Sanakoli just woke me up. We are surrounded by a silent, flat sea. It is truly like a sheet of glass, as the expression goes.

The thin cloud cover was reflecting on the surface of the water with a few patches of dark where the stars were shining through. The air was warm, but we were too far out to catch the distinctive herbaceous scent of the inland that was laying like a crouching black serpent to the southeast. On all other sides, I could see a panorama of infinite ocean — beautiful but daunting. Our entire existence was limited to this tiny speck — a two-metre wide canoe resting on a giant mirror — which threatened to shatter at any time.

Sanakoli suddenly spoke, "We take down the sail and sleep, no wind."

"Can you feel the current, the current from the river?" I asked nervously.

"Yes, it push us out," Sanakoli replied.

"Fast?" I continued.

"No, easy-easy," he retorted. I looked at my GPS. We were about six and a half nautical miles from the coast. I considered if we should put out the drift anchor (a type of underwater parachute that can slow a boat's movement and straighten it to face the wind) but I was too tired. Instead, I untied the knot holding the mast rope — a double line of two half hitches, then two turns off the *sowa sowa* and then I slowly slackend the last coil as Sanakoli pulled in the loose canvas before it fell into the water. When both yard and boom were resting on the *sowa sowa*, I tied it all off with a quick loop. Sanakoli made himself comfortable in the canoe. I laid my tired body on the rattan platform, tucked a lifejacket under my head and closed my eyes as the canoe quietly floated further out onto the great mirror.

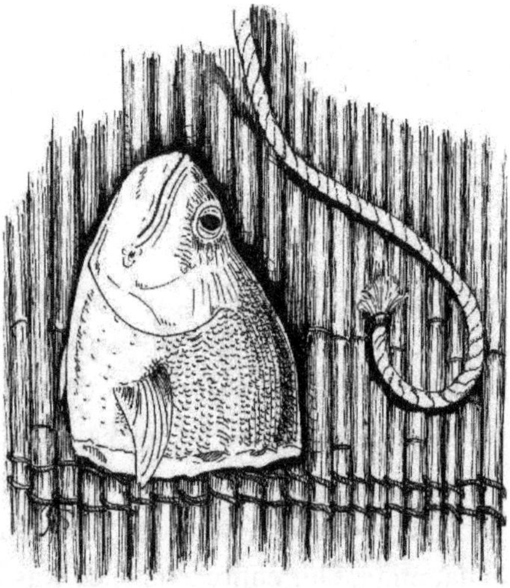

Expedition Log 6 February 2017

05:00 hrs. The sail is hoisted. The shore looks tiny. We have drifted five nautical miles straight out to sea during the night. Our lack of progress is worrying. We are still 98 nautical miles from our destination. The satellite weather report says we should finally get good wind today. Fingers crossed.

10:00 hrs. We are running a pleasant speed of three to four knots.

12:00 hrs. Our concerns about the waves produced by the river mouth were unfounded. There are some banks further in where the waves are breaking but no trouble out here.

12:13 hrs. "Kisooo!" Big fish. The line is jerking hard. Justin speaks to the sea. A good fight. He lands a beautiful queenfish almost a metre in length. Our first fish in West Papua! Justin is cutting the fish. I'll cleave firewood. FEAST time!

13:00 hrs. We are on the top of the 'shoulder' and now it is time to leave the land behind and start our open water crossing. Our destination is Runi Island, almost straight W, 71 nautical miles.

13:20 hrs. I keep telling Sanakoli to steer outwards but something happens to your psyche when you can't see land in front of you — you tend to steer towards what you can see. He has to trust our navigational instruments.

14:00 hrs. The wind is changing now. Back in to old N NW. We are being pushed downwards. Not good.

14:30 hrs. Looks like we have to change plans. We can't be *jig-jagging* all the way across to Runi. We must go south along the mangroves to Yapen Island. I don't like this. We can't land on the north coast of Yapen so we must go into the dangerous currents of the Kurdu Strait — and we'll probably have to pass through it during the night.

Of another world

Things never go as you expect on this voyage. Around 9 p.m. the wind turned back to the southeast. This was what we wanted, 'To hell with Yapen,' I thought aloud. I took a new bearing and we started running upwards in a north westerly direction towards Runi Island and its larger neighbour Wamsoi. The moon was increasing in shape and lit up the entire canoe; the wind was sweet and we covered good miles.

An hour later, Sanakoli had to 'throw his towel into the ring.' "We take down sail and sleep." I couldn't blame him. He had been steering almost all day and night, but we couldn't rest now. We were still 30 nautical miles from our goal.

I climbed out of the hull and up to the front of the canoe where Justin was laying. He was sleeping heavily. I woke him cautiously and asked if he could come and steer.

"We not there yet, hey?" he said, not trying to conceal his grumpy disposition.

"No, we still got four or five hours but the wind is good."

He rubbed his nose and looked around. "Ok, you give me one medicine bottle and I drink." I pulled out a *bilum,* clinking with small glass bottles of energy drinks. My head was humming from lack of sleep so I also downed one of the syrup-like caffeine pick-me-ups as well. The two brothers swapped places and *Tawali Pasana* bravely resumed her course.

I was standing in the hull, locking the sheet with my left hand, my right hand either bailing water or looking at the compass to guide Justin's course. There was supposed to be a lighthouse on a small island, Rasi, southwest of Runi but I couldn't see anything on the horizon except a few flashes of lightning in the distant sky. The wind was still generous and *Tawali Pasana's* bow chopped steadily through the black swell. The hours passed and there was still no sign of a lighthouse, instead the horizon had turned ink black, and the moon was smothered by ominous thick cloud. The flashes in front of us increased. It was now evident that we were sailing straight towards a vast thunder storm.

The next hours were of another world and the memory of that experience is still with me to this day. It was like being on the stage of a great theatre. The artillery barrage of lightning made everything contrast, changing from white to yellow to green. Huddled with the sailors in the hull, I was filled with fascination and wonder as well as dread and fear. The mast, with its metal point holding our flag and the wires running to the deck, was the only high point for 25 miles — this made *Tawali Pasana* a floating conductor, a lightning rod.

From the hull of the canoe, I could see it all unfolding — the clouds and the lightning made the sky almost seem tangible, as if we were sailing through a labyrinth of black caverns with testy giants throwing spears of electricity at each other. It was such an otherworldly spectacle. It struck me with a sense of immeasurable gratitude to witness — but, at the same time, mindful of a sense of impending doom. As mariners have done for millennia, I calmed myself by repeating a sort of mantra — a hopeful superstition of sorts. I said to myself that our course was true and our expedition noble. *Tawali Pasana* was running on good energy and, therefore, the giants at war above would leave us in peace.

We were in the middle of an enormous bay and there were no other boats to be seen in the night. If there had there been fishermen brave or foolish enough to venture out on this dire night, they would have observed the silhouette of a triangular sail tracking steadily through the swells, a speck on a vast drape toning from dark blue to graphite grey. In an instant, they would have seen the canoe lit up by a bright flash of white light, and in the next instance, disappear under a passing deluge of rain, only to reappear like a conjurer's magic trick. And surely these men would wonder how lucky this vessel was, gingerly plotting a course through the stratospheric havoc, avoiding the electrical supercharges. In the end, they might also doubt whether luck would follow this nimble vessel all the way to daybreak. With eyes that had spent a lifetime at sea, they would be able follow this vessel for a while but in the end, even they would lose sight of it as the triangle blurred into the abyss.

Suddenly, the lightning had stopped and everything was pitch black. I was so grateful that we were nearing the morning hours. I checked the GPS — only 8 nautical miles to Runi and safety. Then the sail flapped and the wind stopped. I turned my head north and saw another dark blue wall coming straight towards us. We had been momentarily in the eye of the storm. Instantly my face was hit by a cold humid blast of wind and the canoe started rocking. Justin yelled something in Basilaki and I turned to him. "Get sail down, get sail down," Sanakoli hollered as he jumped up from the front and ran to the mast.

The sail was let go and the spars hurriedly put on the canoe. "Secure the sail. Big wind!" Sanakoli yelled again. In the same instant, we were hit by an even more massive blow. Saltwater was spitting through the air as waves broke on the outrigger. It was now so black that I couldn't see my hand in front of my face. I turned on my headlamp and we wrestled the flapping sail into the hull. The canoe was rocking wildly from side to side. The outrigger was dangerously facing the breaking waves, being pulled down with every hit. Justin threw the rudder onto the platform and crawled into the canoe. Together we all held on to the spars and sail so they wouldn't be washed overboard. This was by far the most frightening conditions I had ever experienced at sea, made even more so because I had no idea of how much pounding the outrigger could take before it broke off. I turned to ask my comrades how dangerous this was, but words weren't necessary, one look at their faces and I knew we were in great peril.

The waves kept crashing onto the outrigger and flooding over our platform. I asked Justin if we should call for help. He didn't answer at first but then he said, "You call." I first thought of the SOS button on our satellite device. This would start a search and rescue operation, but in this part of the world such an operation could take a day to organise — or longer. Pressing that button would have meant the end of our expedition — and we were still afloat.

I then took out the VHF radio and called 'Pan Pan,' which is the international standard signal for assistance at sea. The canoe was jerking wildly. I kept on calling but there was no one on the radio. I then turned my attention to the immediate dangers ahead; we were being pushed towards the rocky shores of Yapen Island. Sanakoli was bailing water and I told him to throw out the drift anchor. I then looked at the GPS — the anchor didn't seem to do much for our speed or position. We were being pushed sideways with three knots of speed. This meant we would reach Yapen in under five hours. We still had time and the outrigger was still holding. There was nothing we could do but hang on and wait out the dark. As the light slowly revealed itself over the horizon, my heart filled with hope. The wind decreased in velocity and the waves stopped breaking on us.

At six in the morning, we wrapped the sail and booms in rope and cautiously manoeuvred the heavy items on to the platform. It was a difficult task in the high seas. We were tired and cold but focus was paramount. Then we lifted up the storm sail, pulled it into place on the *sowa sowa,* and hoisted it. It was such a revitalising experience hoisting that sheet; we were back in control. The sea was still rough and the wind against us but *Tawali Pasana* was sailing and that was the most important thing. As Justin and Sanakoli navigated us through the still treacherous swell, I made us all a breakfast of biscuits, jam and peanut butter that was handed to the sailors which they quickly devoured without taking their eyes off the sea. At this point, I would have wished that we'd reach the island and celebrated with a big lunch — but our perils were far from over.

The wrath of Zeus

My whole body was numb with fatigue. It was already afternoon. This was bullshit after such a night; we deserved to be on that island. It is right in front of us — so close but so far — white beach, coconut palms. There was no wind and, no matter how much we paddled, the current pushed us out. I checked the water container. We still had about six litres left so I mixed up a new bottle of *dirty watar*, gnawed on some coconut meat and resumed paddling with half effort.

The sky was now red and we still hadn't come any closer. On the contrary, the current had pushed us even further out. There were now 12 nautical miles to the nearest island. A pod of dolphins suddenly breached the smooth surface of the water with syncopated puffs from their blowholes. I turned off the music player and tried to catch them on camera but they disappeared. As the music was turned on again, they reappeared right next to the canoe. (Who would think that dolphins liked Johnny Cash). As the light dimmed and we entered the fourth night of the crossing, I saw something in front of us that made my hair stand on end and my heart sink.

With the new night, the wind returned. The fading darkness also revealed a more ominous weather in front of us, with lightning flashes that were becoming more and more dramatic. The good thing was that we finally had wind again and *Tawali Pasana* was shooting steadily through the sea. The down side was that we were going straight towards the next belt of heavy rain. I don't know what was running through the minds of my companions. I thought, 'Oh no, not another thunderstorm.' I asked Sanakoli, "Hey, can we tack up along the islands instead and then tack again in between them at the top?"

Sanakoli yelled back against the howling wind, "I don't know, maybe the current will push us out?"

So, I said, "Hey, let's give it a try." We turned the canoe and ran northward. After an hour it became evident that the current was still beating us. Dammit! We had lost an hour and had to turn back towards the storm again. It defied all my instinct to sail straight towards that menacing danger — but it was our only option — that or the full force of the Pacific Ocean.

As the hours passed, we slowly got closer to the islands — as did the thunderclouds. They were moving in from the other side now as well, as if they were growing out of Biak Island, which stood as a dark silhouette in the distance. It was as I imagined Mount Olympus — from where Zeus the King of the Greek gods would hurl his tridents of fire. As we passed below Rasi and its dead lighthouse, the waves fell and *Tawali Pasaña* picked up speed. The horizon in front of us had now turned into a massive brooding evil entity. I handed the last two 'medicine bottles' to Justin and Sanakoli, as they were the ones who were going to get us out of this alive. We tacked and aimed to hit

Runi. The moon was covered by clouds and everything had turned grey. We had tacked too early and missed Runi. Suddenly, white waves were breaking in front of us. Sanakoli slacked the sail just in time and we made a quick turn back. I was ordered into the front to look for reef.

On our second tack, we were on right course for Runi but as we closed in on the small dark island, we encountered the great reef again. Justin spotted a small gap where the breakers looked less aggressive. Either side of us were ramparts of surging water powerful enough to turn our brave craft into splinter wood. The sailors yelled at each other, took the chance and, in a moment of seafaring brilliance, crashed *Tawali Pasana* through the shallow reef wall hurling broken corals in our wake. The canoe was immediately lit up by a patch of luminous white sand lurking just below. We were inside the reef. There was some current flowing out between Runi to our right and Wamsoi to the left — but we were alive.

After half an hour of *jig-jagging* up through the channel, we finally reached dead calm water, paddling the last 50 metres to the sandy shores of Wamsoi Island. When *Tawali Pasana* had been secured with both a shore line and an anchor, it started to rain again — incessantly. We didn't care. We just coiled up in our tarpaulin and passed out.

Chapter Eighteen

An old turtle is spared

The long and dangerous sail to the Padaido Islands was well worth it. The islands were incredibly beautiful with lush low-lying jungle, white sandy beaches and living coral reefs. The villages were a mixture of traditional houses and concrete buildings with the larger islands having better infrastructure than the smaller ones. We spent nine days gently sailing through these picturesque islands and atolls before we reached the great island of Biak — still largely forested, and the largest in the bay, with a population of about 100,000 inhabitants concentrated in the main city Kota Biak.

Biak also holds historical significance as the first place, European explorers landed during their 'discovery' of New Guinea. In 1526-27, a Portuguese explorer named Jorge de Menezes landed his ship on Biak and named the island 'Papua.' Later the island was renamed after him, *Ihla du Jorges*. Decades later, it was renamed again after its native population the Biaks. The word 'Papua' stuck and has, through history, been widely used for the eastern part of the island of New Guinea. There is some argument about the origin of the name. Some say it is from the Malay word *pepuah* meaning 'frizzled hair.' Others say that it is named after the Biak phrase, *Sup i papwa* — meaning 'land below the sunset.' There's also a theory that the name 'Papua' was first used by the Sultanate of Tidora, whose merchants traded spices and Bird of Paradise feathers with this region long before Europeans arrived.

The name of the western part of New Guinea has also changed depending on stages of colonisation or the political status of the island. The Dutch, for example, named it Netherlands New Guinea. Later, when the Indonesian Republic took control, it was named Irian Jaya. Nowadays the Indonesian Government refers to Western New Guinea as Papua Barat (West Papua) and Papua, whereas the Melanesian population refer to the whole region as West Papua.

I had been excited about exploring the island, especially the interior, which promised green tree pythons and about thirteen endemic bird species including two species of Paradise Kingfisher. Sadly, I had to put my dreams of jungle adventure aside as we had already taken a month just to get here, and now we needed to get to Sorong as fast as possible so we could have the Northwest Monsoon at our backs, before the wind started to change again in April. We only spent one day in Kota Biak, buying provisions and getting our papers stamped by the authorities.

The task of having papers approved wasn't as easy as I had thought it was going to be. As I presented my documents at the Harbourmaster's office, the officer looked up at me with a surprised expression and said, "You don't have a sailing permit?" I immediately became very nervous and explained that *I most certainly had* and politely pointed out that our CAIT was still valid and in good time for renewal. The official shook his head in an educating manner. "That is the old system Mister. In Papua Barat we use the new system." I didn't know if I should laugh or burst into tears or just die but before I had time to do any of this the officer said, “Don’t worry Mister, you can use my computer and we register you now.” I sighed audibly and sat down next to him. After an hour we were registered. I thought now we must surely have all our papers in order.

After a night in the capital of Biak we set out, well stocked with rice, tinned mackerel and plenty of ‘medicine bottles,’ for the last leg of the giant Cenderawasih Bay crossing. The weather around Biak was wet and moody and we only made half a day’s travel up the coast before we had to seek shelter in the larger village of Somber, which had a smooth asphalt road leading to Kota Biak and a church that could be seen miles away. As we landed, I was surprised how few people were around. Luckily, we still got enough help pulling the canoe ashore.

Afterwards, I was shown around the village by a young man. As we came to the big ivory-coloured church, we met the whole congregation coming out from Sunday Catholic Mass — accompanied by all the important leaders of the village and their families all dressed in their ‘Sunday best.’ When the young girls saw me, again they all went crazy. “Selfie, selfie,” they screamed as they lined up next to me, taking turns posing with the white blond man. It was rather overwhelming and a very odd situation to be in. There I was, in worn flip-flops, standing in my damp sailor shorts and salt-encrusted T-shirt with an overgrown beard and greasy hair. I hadn’t been with a woman since I left Denmark and now all these lovely smelling girls in their late teens — and a couple of their mothers — were giggling and rubbing up against me. Meanwhile their pastor, parents and all the best citizens of the hamlet were watching me. I prayed hard that the hot blood rushing through my veins wouldn’t run to the nether regions of my shorts. Fortunately, I survived the spectacle without a scandal — relieved when my guide pulled me away to see the ruins of an old ice factory.

The next day, we continued up the coast and I reflected on the events at the church. During the entire voyage, I had avoided flirtations with locals, as I thought it would be an easy way to get into trouble. I asked Sanakoli what their custom was in regards to meeting women.

"When we sailors are home, we are married men, when we sail out, we are *young boys*, so if we meet a woman we like, we can go with her."

"What about your wives then, can they also be with other men?"

Sanakoli laughed, "No, no. When they are married, they must only be with their what, husband."

I continued, intrigued. "So, when you are a sailor, how do you pull a girl?" I wanted to know.

"You tell her that you like her and if she like you back, you maybe ask her if she want to go with you for a walk." It all sounded pretty simple to me.

The only flirt I had in PNG was back in 2015, during my reconnaissance at the canoe festival. This was with an Australian girl named Sophie who was working at the hospital in Alotau and would be returning to Milne Bay to do her PhD later that year. Sanakoli interrupted my thoughts, "You see your man Justin here." He made a snarky grin and pointed to his brother sitting in the front of the canoe. "He is what we call *man-sini.*"

"What is a *man-sini*?" I asked.

Sanakoli was only too happy to explain. "That is a man who got many girls." We both chuckled and I said, "Oh, Papua New Guinea."

We continued up the coast, sleeping in the village of Yendonker, before leaving the shores of Biak and sailing to a most beautiful elongated island called Rani. As I looked back at the giant green island, I felt a sting of disappointment. I had sacrificed my dreams of exploring Biak for covering mileage instead. This whole expedition had turned into a race against time, instead of the leisurely go-with-the-flow voyage I had envisioned in Denmark. There was an odd feeling of shame associated with this. Maybe because I hadn't done my homework properly with funding and papers and that was why we were now this situation.

I did have a highly interesting animal encounter though. It happened on the crossing from Rani to Numfoor. Suddenly, something heavy tightened the fishing line. We could see it trailing behind the canoe. It was a sea turtle hooked on our rapala lure. I thought it must have been caught by accident as sea turtles mostly feed on jellyfish and seaweed. Justin pulled it in and lifted the massive flapping creature onto the deck and turned it on its back so it couldn't escape. It was an Olive Ridley — the most common species of sea turtle in the world. Luckily, the jack hook had only pierced the fin and it was easy to unhook. Now I was worried that I had to argue the case about releasing the animal as sea turtle is a highly regarded delicacy amongst many a Milne Bay canoe sailor.

To my surprise, the sailors didn't seem interested in eating it — maybe because I had been talking to them about conservation and ecotourism. More likely, it was because we still had a good stock of provisions and it was a lot of work cutting up a turtle. Justin just said in an almost compassionate tone, "Oh look at the old turtle, he is swimming between islands, he must be tired. We bring him with us and let him go on a reef?" I suggested that it would be painful for the animal to lay on its back frying in the sun all day. The brothers agreed, and Justin pushed the reptile back into the sea and we watched him swim away.

After 12 hours of sailing, we landed on the west coast of Numfoor, and from here we had the last crossing to Manokwari. The next morning, I was eager to get going, the wind was good and the high tide would make it easy to pass through the reef. I started packing the canoe, taking down the tarpaulin covering the deck, putting the water bottles back into the canoe and clearing the platform. Sanakoli and Justin weren't there but I assumed that they were out saying goodbye to some new friends. The canoe was shipshape, although the sailors still hadn't shown themselves. My frustrations started to grow. Now the clock showed half past eight and the wind was fair. I went searching for them. I found Sanakoli under a tree with some locals, writing down Indonesian words in his notebook. "Hey Sanakoli, the canoe is ready, shouldn't we get going while the wind is good?" I asked in a restrained tone.

Sanakoli powdered his mustard stalk in lime and tried to look serious. "Me and Justin think it will be better to sail tomorrow." He made an apologetic laugh. "Too late now anyhow, wind is not good." I thought 'bullshit' but what could I do. Apparently the two brothers had already decided they didn't feel like going to sea today. I was so frustrated and cursed their lack of professionalism.

The whole day and afternoon a steady northerly wind was blowing — even Justin, who later showed up, remarked, "Oh good wind."

The next morning, on 24 February at 7.00 a.m., we sailed out. It was a hard crossing and the wind changed around against our favour and offered us a small squall and a couple of showers. As *Tawali Pasana* approached the middle of the wide body of water, the wind dropped and we had to start paddling. My GPS broke down so navigation became more challenging as night fell. Luckily, the entrance to the bay was well marked and, at midnight, we finally sailed into the protected waters of Manokwari. Our crossing of Cenderawasih Bay was finally over after 20 days and 235 nautical miles.

Sightseeing

Manokwari is the capital of the western region of Papua Barat. It is a charming place, located on a deep bay divided by a headland in the middle. The northernmost bay is the busiest, especially around some old shipping docks. The southern part looked to be rapidly expanding with new buildings on the low hillsides. Sandy had given me some good contacts, so the canoe was soon pulled ashore with the help of Mr Henry a Papuan man and Indonesian Naval Officer whose barrack office was located on a good stretch of local beach.

Now that the canoe was safe, we could focus on the usual tasks of buying provisions, submitting paperwork and attending to repairs. Our type of visa had to be renewed every month. It also required the support of a sponsor who had to be an Indonesian citizen. Our sponsor in Manokwari was Bram Darkim. He was of Chinese descent and came from Java (like many other businesspeople in West Papua). Bram spoke English very well, which was a great relief (my Indonesian vocabulary still only allowed me to engage in the most basic conversations, despite *Tawali Pasana's* thesaurus board now being full of inscriptions). He was about my age and had a friendly face. He was managing his family's iron business here in West Papua. On the side, he and his friend Adi had also started a small kayak rental company, called Kayak Wondama. This seemed like a good move as tourism was growing in the region, not least in the bottom of Cenderawasih bay where it was possible to swim with whale sharks. Despite this, however, Bram and Adi hadn't rented out a single kayak.

Bram offered me a car and a driver who took me around to the different government offices. After my visit to the Immigration office, it became clear that we would have to spend at least a week in town to get our visas renewed. This delay gave me an opportunity to follow up on some much delayed 'office work.' After Job's departure, I had become even more engaged in sailing and the daily chores, which was what I wanted. This extra responsibility also gave me less time for handling logistics. A thing that I hadn't accounted for was that Justin and Sanakoli's phones increased my workload, as I now had to manage their recordings as well, and regularly help them with installing apps or moving music files on to their devices. So this week of delay was actually a welcome break, and the outrigger also needed a proper drying.

The sailors and I spent most of the days apart, and I think we all enjoyed a break from each other. Henry and his friends took great care of Sanakoli and Justin, who were taken sightseeing and dining in all sorts of different places. On the other hand, I spent my free time with Bram and Adi and their friends, who were all businessmen. It was easy to bond with them. Bram collected knives just like me, he even helped me order a new knife and GPS. And Adi loved diving. One evening Bram, Adi and I went out to eat at a street restaurant that specialised in spicy Chinese seafood. We talked about their businesses and work. Adi had a smaller supermarket in a newly built house where he lived in an apartment on the top floor. The house and supermarket were funded by his family and now Adi was 'stationed' there with his wife to run that branch of the family business.

Bram told me that most Indonesian-Chinese parents wanted their children to become something prestigious, like a doctor. Instead, he chose to study architecture. His thesis project was to design a knife museum; he did graduate, even though he focused most of his attention on knives instead of the building. Bram's wife was actually a doctor but she didn't want to live in West Papua with their small son, instead Bram would commute between Manokwari and their house in the Indonesian capital of Jakarta. It was interesting to learn how Bram and Adi were in Papua to run their family enterprises. I suspected that their kayaking business was a side passion. Adi and Bram were curious to know more about PNG, so I told them about our voyage and when Adi asked about the supermarkets there, I said that they were much less elaborate but nonetheless, all run by ethnic Chinese. The two men laughed about this and Adi raised his glass of ice-tea in a toast — to the Chinese shopkeepers!

One thing that had become evident on our voyage around West Papua was that almost every shop, restaurant or government office was managed by Indonesians. The most visible exceptions I had noticed were in the police force and army, like Captain Henry. It is estimated that about one million Indonesians have migrated to West Papua through the government's *Transmigrasi* (transmigration) program, which only stopped in 2015. As well as a resettlement policy, it involved the detention of political prisoners, which was actually started by the Dutch.

Especially under President Sukarno and then President Suharto, poor villagers from the overpopulated islands of Java and Bali were shipped to West Papua where they were given a piece of land to farm or labouring work in the mining industry. This may sound like a sympathetic gesture from the government, but most of the new immigrants didn't have the skills or knowledge to make the earth prosper in this strange environment and their arrival created immediate conflict with local Papuan land owners. It was a cunning thing to do, especially if you wanted to expand your cultural and political dominance in a contested region.

Of course, the paperwork took longer than expected and, in the meantime, I developed a nasty slimy cough. After a visit to a local private hospital, I returned to my hotel room with a prescription of antibiotics, vitamins and painkillers. After a day of febrile haze and a lot of sleep in a real bed, I felt better and could resume work. During my sickness, I had looked through the film footage from our night of peril in Cenderawasih. It was mostly darkness and hissing wind but there were a few shots of Sanakoli and I looking justifiably distressed. The quality of the recordings could have been better but considering the circumstances it was pretty good. I had also posted about the incident on Facebook which had led to a phone call from my poor mother. To calm her down, I assured her that it wasn't, "As horrendous as it looked," and that Justin and Sanakoli were great sailors. The last part was at least true.

After 13 days, everything was finally in order and the wind was in our favour. Departing at 1 p.m., we said goodbye to Bram who gave me two knives as a going away present — a *golock* (an Indonesian bush knife that is also carried as a status symbol) and a folding knife especially made for sailing. Adi wasn't there as he had to meet up with Kayak Wondama's first two customers. We also shook hands with Tao Henry and his family who had been looking after the canoe. Before he helped push us out, he gave us some contacts in Sorong.

We rounded Cape Ampla at the end of the bay where we again encountered the full force of the now building Pacific swells. Ahead was our last leg along the exposed northern shores of the steep Bird's Head Peninsula — a leg that would take a lot of 'medicine bottles' and the goddess of caffeine to complete. In the opposite direction, I could see the shape of Biak on the horizon. I thought of the mysterious green island and decided to discard the regret I felt about not having the expedition properly planned out — this was nonsense. In reality, there was no right or wrong way to go about this adventure, since it had never been done before. We were covering good miles and I recorded some amazing film while having the adventure of a lifetime.

My grand philosophical contemplations were interrupted by the cliché ringtone of Sanakoli's phone. It was a local Papuan Christian Pastor who spoke *Tok Pisin* whom Sanakoli had befriended. Sanakoli took the phone off his ear and eagerly reported, "He's saying he'll be praying for us every day so we will have safe travels… he's on the point there waving at us now." We couldn't see anyone, nonetheless, we all waved back. We needed all the help we could get.

Chapter Nineteen

It's a long way to the top (if you wanna rock the Pacific)

It had been a hard night's sailing, with shifting winds and no moonlight. Now we were on the second day of our leg along the rugged north coast of the Bird's Head Peninsula. After making it through one squall in the morning, it was looking like more squalls were coming in from the open ocean. The grey sea was growing and we needed a rest. We had just passed a village but it was situated in a shallow bay. Although we hadn't seen a better landing place on this leg, the steep shoreline with its rolling breakers looked far from welcoming, so we passed.

Nasty clouds were now approaching from the ocean and the wind picked up even more. *Tawali Pasana* was being squeezed like a louse between two fingernails, steep coastline on one hand and incoming squalls on the other. The two sailors conferred.

"What are we doing guys?" I asked, whilst relieving the ever-filling hull from yet another helmet-full of water.

Sanakoli talked loudly over the top of the wind, "Justin says wind becoming too big. We turn and try our luck on that beach?"

The proposal made me uneasy, "Where do you want to land? Up in the corner there?" I pointed to the eastern end of the bay that was partially protected by a rocky piece of headland where the waves didn't look as big as those in front of us.

"We go easy easy, we can make it," he tried to reassure me.

We took down the sail and started paddling back towards the bay. Progress was fast because the big swell pushed us straight towards shore. As we lined up towards our landing site, it became evident that the beach wasn't as protected as first assumed and the waves started breaking more than 30 metres from the shore, pushing foaming water through a minefield of larger jagged rocks sticking up through the shallows. We were attempting a surf landing, on a beach littered with canoe smashing obstacles. I knew this was a very dangerous thing to do in a kayak, as you risked broadsiding and then rolling sideways with the waves. If this happened with our big heavy canoe, or if it pitched the bow into the shallows, it would get trashed and we would have to jump for our lives not to end up under it.

Sanakoli was paddling in the front while Justin was steering with the paddle in the back. They were yelling excitedly at each other. Sanakoli shouted to me, "You paddle full speed when I say so." The rumbling got closer as the waves grew in front of us. It was about catching the right set of waves. This whole scene looked to me like an accident waiting to happen and then it hit me — I needed to film this. I jumped to the mast and fastened my camera with PVC tape. In the same instant, Sanakoli yelled, "Paddle! Paddle!" Damn, the mast rope was swinging in front of the lens, 'should I secure it? — no, paddle.' I jumped down and started digging *Eneta* into the sea. The heavy canoe rose on the green swell, we accelerated, water was spraying from the bow and we paddled with all our might. The speed eased but there was no time to rest.

The final breaker was coming. The canoe started lifting from behind and the nose tilted into the sea. I could now see a tapestry of sharp black pinnacles lurking in front of us. Sanakoli again yelled, "Paddle, paddle!" Water sprayed from the bow, *Tawali Pasana* was surfing towards the shore. Several loud bumps, then foam. Sanakoli jumped into the waist deep whitewash to control the canoe in the back surge. We got a line around an exposed root and finally the canoe was secure. My whole body was shaking with adrenaline and we all laughed with relief.

The name of the village was Warmandi. It was a small place of about 20 houses with no road access. There was a steady downpour and I was shown around by a man wearing a taro leaf as an umbrella.

After the tour, I had gathered enough villagers to help us pull the canoe up into a small creek where it was safe from the swell. We learned that there was a gold mine in the mountains behind the village and sometimes the villagers would get work there but it was a half day's walk, through jungle. When I asked how the mining personnel got to the site, they explained that all transport was by helicopter. They offered to take me there. I declined.

We spent the following day resting and repairing the canoe. The rocks hadn't damaged the hull but the dove we had at the top of the mast had fallen down as we pulled the canoe ashore. It had been fastened with a long nail through the body, with a cola bottle cap as a washer — to make it spin freely in the wind. I repainted the dove white and also painted the letters 'PNG' on the red flag attached to it. I had used my *Eneta* paddle as a flat surface to paint on but the paint had gone through the flag and now there was also a big white 'PNG' on the paddle blade. I had unintentionally tagged my own paddle. I thought back to the New Year's graffiti battle in Copenhagen, this was the point I started to feel that I had achieved everything I wanted in my 'graffiti career' — I had reached my goals and from that point it would just be repetition. Also, graffiti is very self-centred. My paintings were only bringing pleasure to a very small group of other graffiti artists — the rest of society either didn't 'get it' or else loathed it and wanted to see me in prison. There was also a psychological aspect to it; the subtle but constant fear of being 'caught' was draining. I decided that it would be better to use my creative energy on something positive, like outdoor adventure and travel. That is how I ended up in Venezuela. There I could share my knowledge of the outdoors with tourists, give people great experiences and still get an occasional adrenalin kick.

My contemplations were set aside by a local man who we had called to come and carve the village design on our canoe. I shook his hand and gave him a pointy-ended knife and a hot plate of rice, and then showed him a blank spot next to a bird of paradise carving from the Padaido Islands.

In the afternoon we got ready to set out again. *Tawali Pasana* looked great, with clusters of green coconuts on the deck and a fresh carving of a leatherback turtle on the side. (The leatherback turtle is the world's largest turtle and a common sight on these shores). On top of this, we had a freshly painted dove on the mast. The mountain wind was growing and this would give us a good start on our last 100 nautical mile journey to Sorong. The problem now was how to get the canoe out of this treacherous bay. Most of the villagers had come down to see us off and, under Sanakoli's instructions, they helped push us out through the first set of breakers. From here we paddled behind the headland, hoisted the sail and shot out into the bay, while waving goodbye to our new friends ashore. Then a curious thing happened. As it had done many times before, the goodbye made the three of us very emotional. We had only spent about 30 hours with these people, nonetheless a bond had been formed — now the people of Warmandi had become part of the fellowship and their leatherback turtle would accompany us for the rest of the journey.

The mountain wind was sweet and that same night at exactly 11:23 p.m. we passed the top of the northernmost point of the island of New Guinea, just below the Equator. To me, this was a big deal but Sanakoli didn't really place any importance on this feat. He said, "Me, I will be happy when I get to Sorong because from then we will no longer be sailing away but be sailing back home." I was still fired up about this moment and scrolled through the music library on my phone to see if I had the AC/DC song, 'It's a long way to the top (if you wanna rock 'n roll)'. It's such a great track about the band in their younger days. They were having a tough time touring and being screwed by their manager, nonetheless they embraced the obstacles as all part of 'the long way to the top.' This was a metaphor I could definitely relate to. I didn't have the song on my device but that didn't matter, instead I hummed it to myself in the dark while controlling the sheet and occasionally bailing the hull.

At four in the morning, we passed two small islands. The plan was to rest there — it was hard to see a reef entrance in the dark. The wind was good, so we continued. Justin had finished our last 'medicine bottle' and taken over the rudder and Sanakoli was now sleeping. I had been by the sheet all night and felt the buzzing-irritated sensation of sleep deprivation. It was hard to stay awake when everything around you was black and you were crouched in the hull of a bopping canoe. My eyes closed, my chin fell to my chest and, in the same instance, I woke up again. There would be a section of offshore reef ahead. I crushed a hard toffee with my teeth and washed my face with sea water. Justin said, "You give me the sail and go look in the front. Maybe reef is coming?"

I handed over the sheet and almost kicked our stove over as I made my way to the bow. I grabbed the front of the sail and looked ahead. The sea was just one big graphite-black blurry mass. It was hard to distinguish anything. I was looking for white stripes that could indicate breaking waves or currents. My head soon started nodding in rhythm with the canoe. I looked down and saw one bioluminescent sea-jelly after another flying by. Ahh… so dreamy. I slapped myself and forced my eyes wide open again. It was too dangerous to be in the front, so I walked back to my position in the hull. I hadn't spent a long time there either before I dozed off again and woke as half my body was hanging overboard. I arched my back just in time and regained balance. This was too much. "Sorry Justin I can't stay awake any longer, should I wake up Sanakoli?"

"You give me the sail." I handed it over and huddled up on the deck.

Ghost mothers

In the early afternoon, we reached a most beautiful little island called Um, with a big flat reef in front and a clean sandy beach. What was spectacular about this place was that the trees were alive with flying foxes. I later learned that this was a popular picnic spot amongst the people of Sorong and that hunting was prohibited, which explained all the fruit bats. We spent the night there before sailing the last stretch to Sorong the next day. That evening I had a very odd experience.

I was laying in the canoe and I dreamt that an old Papuan lady was sitting on top of me, her upper body was naked and her breasts were long and pendulous. She had silver-grey hair and wore a shell necklace. I woke with the daybreak. Justin was already up smoking an Indonesian clove cigarette. I said good morning. He smoked a bit more and then he said, "I saw one of our mothers last night, she was standing right there, next to the canoe, looking at you."

"What do you mean? Where?" I replied quite surprised — not least because it was stated in such a matter-of-fact way. Instantly, goose bumps raised on my arms.

"Yeah! Right there," Justin pointed. "She was looking at you while you were sleeping."

"I dreamt about an old lady sitting on me."

"Yes, I saw her," Justin added.

"Have you seen her before?"

“Yes, many times,” he confirmed as he flicked his cigarette in to the sea.

Later when we were folding the tent canvas, I told Sanakoli about the old lady Justin had seen. Sanakoli answered in the same matter-of-fact way as Justin. “Yes, we have three mothers with us on the canoe. It is our, what, old *bubus* (grandmothers).”

“What do they do?” I asked curiously.

Sanakoli secured the canvas on the outrigger and again he answered in a nonchalant manner. “They look after us on the journey.”

I pressed him. “How often do you see them?”

He answered, “Me, I don’t see them, only Justin see them.” All I could think was that it was amazing that we had some of their ancestors with us — in spirit — and that they were looking after us.

Midday on 13 March, we finally arrived into Sorong. The wind was generous, the sun high, and there was a great mood onboard. I took out the map and made a measurement with my passer. “Guys, we have now travelled 2,700 kilometres. From here on, we are sailing towards home.”

Sanakoli spontaneously responded in a singing tone, “That’s the one!”

As we rounded the last point, we could see the low-lying city with its industrial harbour. There were several container and cargo ships anchored in front and I thought it wisest to avoid that traffic; it would be better to try our luck on one of the beaches before the urban settlements began. By following a satellite app on my phone, I guided us to a beach protected by a man-made seawall adjacent to the village of Suprau. To our great surprise, we saw a white man standing amongst the Papuans. As I got ashore and presented myself, I found out that he was an Italian lobster exporter named Kuki who had his operations right on the beach. Kuki, who had spent 17 years in Indonesia, helped translate our mooring request to his neighbours, and as the tide came in, we pulled the canoe up onto their beach.

We had hardly caught our breath before a police officer arrived. He was Indonesian, in his mid-40s, with shiny polished black shoes and overly tight trousers. He had a modest cluster of campaign ribbons on his chest, an authoritative black moustache on his upper lip, and a service revolver on his belt. He had heard that there was a white man with a canoe about. After presenting all our documents, he said in *Bahasa* (with Kuki translating) that I needed to report my arrival at the police headquarters in town. Although this wasn't unusual, I was surprised how fast the authorities in these parts were informed about something out of the ordinary.

The police visit was tiresome but successful, and with this began the usual chores of being in port. Sorong was a large and rapidly growing city, much larger than Manokwari. The reason for the massive expansion is that Sorong serves as a great transport hub between West Papua to the rest of Indonesia and the world, both through sea and air. There is also a growing industrial sector developed around mining, oil and gas, and a fast-growing tourism industry, not least because the Raja Ampat archipelago is only 55 kilometres off the coast. These islands are known for their hundreds of iconic round green mountains that rise like guardian monoliths out of a pristine sea.

The scuba diving there is some of the best in the world, mainly because the area is the centre of the so-called 'Coral Triangle,' a marine wonderland spanning the Seribu Islands of Indonesia in the west to the Solomons in the East and the Philippines in the north, featuring the greatest diversity of marine life in the world. To illustrate this, in the Caribbean you can find around 1,000 species of reef fish; in the Coral Triangle there's double that. Raja Ampat is also home to six of the seven species of sea turtle and an important migration route for whales. This melting pot of marine biodiversity is the consequence of the rich currents running like an aquatic superhighway linking the Pacific and the Indian Oceans, with an advantageous seabed geography that has allowed the marine life to adapt and survive changing sea levels across millions of years.

Raja Ampat was high on my to-experience-before-I-die list and Paul was also pushing for us to go there for a week or two, sailing and filming between the islands. I had a hard time selling the idea to Justin and Sanakoli, as it was not 'on the route,' and now that we finally had the wind in our favour, we needed to get the most of it before it changed again in April. Instead, I arranged with Paul that we would meet up in Triton Bay on the south coast of New Guinea, which was a small-scale Raja Ampat, and also an area that was lesser known.

A new deal

Now that we had reached the tip of the island, Justin and Sanakoli called for a meeting. It had been a while since we had a crew briefing and I was a bit nervous about what the two sailors wanted. We found a piece of beach to ourselves and planted our plastic chairs in the sand. I had made a list of practical things we could discuss but held back as I wanted to give Sanakoli some space to speak freely. Justin was sitting staring at the ground with his arms crossed, while Sanakoli was sitting, wearing a T-shirt he had been given in Numfoor, which sported a map of the island on the back. He was searching for his words and then he finally spoke.

"Me and Justin we think or we want to ask, what happened with the agreement you made with Job?" I asked which agreement he meant.

"You said that when we were on our way with the journey, you would pay us more."

I scoured my memory and recalled the conversation from the first day on East Cape and said, "Yes, that's true. I thought that we would be getting more money as we got more followers but as you know, we can barely keep the skin on our nose, we only get enough money from our Facebook donors to buy food and pay for all the permits and visa extensions." I then went on to explain how I was trying to get sponsorship from larger companies and there was also the possibility that we could get the promised funding from Vanimo, now that we were entering the month of March.

I said I would also try and contact the Minister for Tourism in PNG. I could see that this really didn't convince them and said, "I am really sorry. As you can see, there is no money now but look at it like this, what you earn now is almost double what a high-ranking office worker makes in a month, which of course is only fair, as you are out risking your lives every day. Also see it like this — what you are doing now is like making a garden, you are planting the seeds and, in a few months when we return to Tawali, you guys will be heroes. You will have done what no Milne Bay sailor has ever done before. You will have all sorts of opportunities if you wish to work in tourism or maybe even make commercials."

The two brothers were both looking at their feet without saying anything so I continued my speech. "What I will try to do is get you guys a good cash prize for when we reach our goal. Remember that that money will also run out one day but what you will never lose is the honour of having made Milne Bay sailing history; nobody can take this away from you."

The two brothers were still listening and then Justin said something to Sanakoli, who then nodded and spoke. "Me and my brother we have promised to help you sail around. When we went home to Milne Bay, Job said, 'We must stay there and not return to Vanimo.' That time on the canoe, when we sailed back from Jayapura, we saw you cry and we said, 'Oh we must help our brother here.' So now that Job is no longer our boss, we wanted to make new agreement with you."

I was very moved by Sanakoli's words but also surprised by Job's cunning subterfuge.

"So, Job said to you guys to leave me in Vanimo with the canoe?" I asked, feeling more than a little disturbed.

"Yes, he thought you were tricking him. He said that you were selling all your photos on Facebook and kept the money to yourself."

My immediate response was, "That's not how it works, you guys know that, right? You have just gotten your own profiles on Facebook and you have not received any money!"

Sanakoli said, "Yes we know," and shook his head at Job's misinformed suspicions.

Then he returned to the subject of our proposed new agreement. "So what Justin and I are thinking is that… we want a what, dinghy when we return."

"A dingy?" I said surprised.

"Yes, because then we can go fishing and use it for passenger transport. If we can get two, it would be the best but we can also share one." I was broadsided by this request, thinking it would be a very odd ending to our story if the brothers — the master canoe sailors of Milne Bay — were rewarded with a fibreglass dinghy for their achievement in championing traditional sail craft. On the other hand, it sort of made sense. 'Hadn't people always sought to improve their standard of living through technology?' I told them that I couldn't guarantee them a dinghy with an outboard engine as this was very costly, at least 28,000 kina, but I would do my best. That was good enough for the brothers. We ended the meeting by me asking how they wanted their monthly wages paid. They both said they only wanted me to send half to their wives this month as they would, "Just spend the money." The rest the two would use for shopping in Sorong.

"I am telling you this"

On one of the last days before departure, Kuki walked me through his lobster business. He was a tall pale man in his forties with big brown eyes and a thin grey mustachio. And although he had lived in Indonesia for nearly two decades and was married to an Indonesian woman, he still had the accent and gestures of an Italian. His house was always open to Papuans who wanted to sell lobsters. They came in from the outer islands in wooden dinghies with their live catch that they caught by hand free-diving. There were five different species of lobster, each type more beautiful than the other. Kuki would chain smoke while he and his helpers inspected the animals before dividing them into five shallow basins in a closed building. Here the animals would acclimatise for at least a day before being packed in eskies with frozen water bottles that would make the crustaceans hibernate on their flight to Jakarta. From there they would be shipped as live lobsters to the Asian market.

Kuki was quite the entrepreneur. He had also opened an ice-cream shop and a pizza/karaoke bar in Sorong. He explained that he would normally go to Italy for three to six months every year, while leaving his wife and kids in Sorong. He looked around and said, "Thor, I will share with you a secret." I nodded and stepped closer. He said, "Half a year apart from your wife is perfect. If you are together all the time, you get tired of each other but after half a year, you start missing each other and when you meet again you are both very happy — this is the secret to a successful marriage." He looked me straight in the eye. "I am telling you this." I laughed and agreed that it sounded like a very sensible thing. Kuki then took me to his shed where he pulled out a great gold coloured sheet of parachute silk. "This is my gift to you. I wanted to use it for a sail on my own boat but I never had time, so now you can make yourself a good sail. Yes? Just remember to think of your friend Kuki on your travels." This was a great gift and I couldn't wait to show it to my companions.

Expedition Log 18 March 2017

10:00 hrs. Departure. From here on it is 2,000 nautical miles of mangroves, crocodiles, tidal currents, big rivers, and nasty waves — before we reach the white shores of Milne Bay.

Chapter Twenty

Sharks, shrimps and national television

I spent our second day on the south coast on my sleeping mat with a fever. The sun was scorching and I felt nauseated. The only place I could find relief was under the little 'house' of sown palm fronds from Tufi and an umbrella to cover my feet. I hoped my illness was nothing but one of those 'shut-downs' I sometimes experience after a hard journey or big challenge. Conveniently enough, this down time always happens when there is room for it, like now, with the hassle of Sorong over and no longer having to battle the relentless waves of the north coast. What a relief it was to have a change of scenery. It was like we had been crawling along the thorny back scales of the dragon, and now we were running down towards its soft smooth underbelly. And like a great dragon, the sea was an amazing greenish-brown hue running out through the many estuaries that ran between the low shallow mangroves.

I wasn't the only one suffering under the sun. Sanakoli had just lost his new sunglasses and was complaining about his eyes. "You wait and see, they will get red and sore before the day ends; this is the pain of the sailor. If they sold eyeballs in the supermarket, I would be the first one to buy a pair." The coast was dotted with small islands. The first one we slept on was deserted. The second, Pulao Duo, had a tidal channel that divided the island in two at high tide. The beaches were black with silt and littered with plant matter from inland. The first inhabitant we met was a huge black water monitor casually inspecting the beach with its long-forked tongue. It was probably living off fish offal from the Indonesian and Papuan fishermen who were ensconced in small huts on tall thin stilts. We stayed with a group of them and they offered us sweet coffee and a shopping bag full of prawns, which we fried in oil.

The winds weren't much good in the mornings, so we just slowly bobbed along. I spent time cleaning our equipment boxes on deck. The boxes were actually 20 litre fuel containers that had the top part cut off. The white one was used for kitchen equipment like cups, plates, and utensils, and the green one held our spare cordage, fishing equipment, a spray can of oil, and some kerosene that had inconveniently leaked out over everything. "Hey, guys," I said, "maybe that's why we're catching no fish, there's kerosene all over our lines and hooks."

Sanakoli was quick to answer. "No, it's because you guys got no luck; when I hold the line, we always catch fish."

I laughed and came right back at him, "What are you talking about Sana, you haven't caught a single fish since PNG, think you are too *lapun* (an old man) to catch any."

Sanakoli replied "*Hohoo*, you are the *lapun*. I have seen how you sit close to the fire to get warm. Soon we must chew your food for you as well." We all laughed and I got back to scrubbing the greasy containers. In the bottom of the green container I found a palm-sized round rock under a plastic bag of rusty nails.

"Hey guys, what's up with this rock, should I throw it out?"

Sanakoli looked up. "That's Job's rock, we can use it as a what, hammer." I shrugged my shoulders, we already had a hammer under the deck but I kept it anyway.

That same evening, we crossed Berau Bay, a large stretch of water of about 21 nautical miles in width. The moon was absent and, at midnight, the rain came with strong winds. We quickly took the sail down and covered ourselves with it. The rain was hitting like bullets and soon I had water running down my neck; then the shivering started. It was the first time I had felt this cold on our voyage, so I put on a lifejacket to keep warm. After 15 minutes the squall passed and we crawled out of our plastic cover but now we were totally disorientated. Was that the back-mountain range we were aiming for or was it just clouds on the horizon? Justin grunted, "You check your compass." It was hard to believe the bearing. It seemed to point us out to sea, so I double checked with the GPS and then my spare compass and, sure enough, they were all pointing us in the same direction.

As morning came, we reached the opposite side of the bay and slowly continued up the coast with a perfect rainbow arching from one point of the horizon to the other. Then, as the midday sun started to burn, I found myself standing in the stern, steering with the rudder while holding the sheet. Justin and Sanakoli were both taking a nap on the deck. This was the first time they had let me sail without their close supervision. Although the conditions were the easiest imaginable, I couldn't help feeling an overwhelming sense of pride — Justin and Sanakoli actually trusted me to sail the canoe! Thinking back on the first days of the expedition, and my unrealistic ambitions, it was wonderful to see that I had reached the next step — from bailing to holding the sheet to now steering and sailing the canoe.

The next morning came with a light shower and then sunshine. We were anchored in a bay with mountains on all sides and jungle almost covering the yellow sandy beaches. Sanakoli came back to the canoe from his morning ablutions and said he had just seen two Crown Pigeons on the beach. Crowns are a fascinating grey, bluish fowl, the size of a chicken, with a tall mohawk of feathers on their heads. I jumped ashore with the camera and we followed the bird tracks up through the sand but they disappeared into the jungle. Instead, we got to study a juvenile Black Tip reef shark patrolling the shallows of the beach. Although I had done a fair amount of snorkelling on our voyage, it was the first reef shark I had seen up close.

We made a breakfast of porridge on the beach. We would have preferred rice but our rice bag had been spoiled by saltwater and we had no tinned fish left to complement it anyway. In PNG, we always tried to camp in a village but here in West Papua, the vibe felt different and we were enjoying the solitude. Still, we all became alert as a dinghy approached us at high speed. There was a young Papuan man in the front. As they came closer, we could see that there were a couple of older men and a woman and some kids. The sight made us feel easy and the family soon presented themselves. They were from a nearby village and they were on their way to the market in Fakfak, and they had stopped in to find out who we were. We offered them coffee and a postcard, however, only the two elder men accepted the coffee. After the group left, Sanakoli said, "Fakfak. How can you call a town Fakfak?" Justin just sniggered.

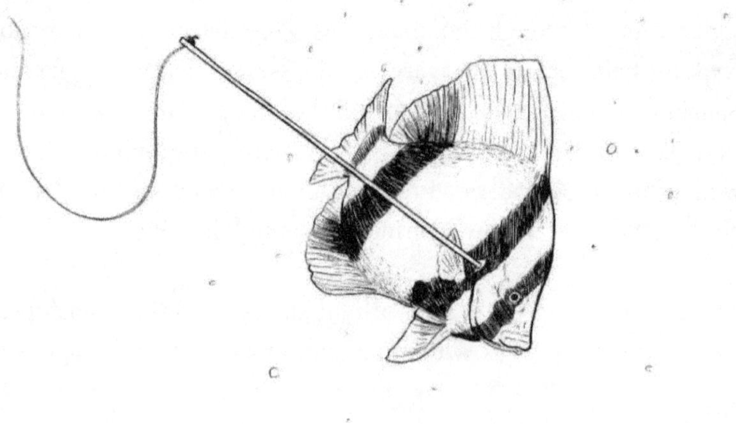

We had only sailed a couple of hours before we anchored the canoe 30 metres off the coast. It was a beautiful area with cliffs going into the sea. The bottom was white sand with clusters of colourful reef. Justin and I put on masks and snorkels. It was time to try the homemade spearguns I had bought in Manokwari. Justin was first in and he quickly surfaced, "Shark! You get camera and get in!" I turned the GoPro on and jumped overboard. As I got under the surface, I only saw the silhouette of the shark as it disappeared into the distance. Nonetheless, there were plenty of fish and some big ones too. It didn't take long before Justin speared a Batfish, which is a large triangular-shaped fish with black and white stripes and yellow pelvic fins. I wasn't having much success. I was struggling to get within shooting range of any fish. I dived down to see if I could find some lobsters under the rocks but as I stuck my head into a small coral cave, I got a shock as I found myself face-to-face with a one and a half metre tawny nurse shark. This species isn't dangerous to humans; they will usually spend the daytime resting in caves, and when night comes, they forage the reef for their main prey of octopus, as well as invertebrates and fish, which they can suck out of holes in the coral.

Justin surfaced with yet another Batfish and told me, "You go to the bottom and wait and the fish come to you. No chasing fish." I was pretty exhausted by then but still went back out. I found an area with several big fish. There was only three metres to the bottom, so I dove down and held onto a coral. And sure enough, slowly the fish that had been dispersing started to come closer, curious to see what was going on. There were a couple of larger types of Sea Bass that I had my eye on but they were cautious and stayed well out of reach. I am not a great free diver as I have trouble equalising the pressure in my ears. I had done a bit of scuba training and learned that it was very much about mentality, staying calm and keeping your heart rate down, not using up the oxygen in your blood too quickly.

I could feel my lungs screaming for air but I couldn't go up, I needed to get some spearfishing footage, and not least impress Justin and shut up Sanakoli. I could see a Batfish coming in from the right. I didn't want to turn towards it, instead I waited for it to swim past my view and the point of my speargun. My cheeks were pumping to move the last oxygen around my system. The striped triangular-shaped fish slowly swam into my aim. Wait for it... wait — now! I pulled the trigger. The barbed metal spear shot through the water. The aim was perfect, my lungs were pumping for air but the spear stopped with a jerk, just before it hit the target and the Batfish shot away. The string that was attached to the spear was too short. I hadn't been close enough. I burst through the surface to catch my breath. After a short break, I dived again. I really wanted a catch on film but I was too exhausted and returned to the canoe. Sanakoli was grumpy when I got on board, probably because we only had two masks and he missed out on a turn. He was offered the chance to go in but he didn't care and we already had two big fish anyway.

At mid-day, we arrived on the small island of Patu Buthi, about 17 nautical miles from Fakfak. We made a fire on the beach, and while Justin cooked the fish, Sanakoli and I went to collect sea snails. As we searched the shallows, Sanakoli told me about Justin's special powers, "Your man Justin, when he was born, our father put his what, umbilical cord, in to the stomach of a live fish and set it free. Since that day Justin belong to the sea, he is man of the sea, you don't see anyone dive how deep or spear how many fish than him." An hour later we feasted on ember-roasted batfish and snails complemented by dry coconut and *dirty watar*.

In the afternoon, the wind started to blow from inland and we launched the canoe towards Fakfak. Sanakoli said laughing, "I can't wait to tell my people back home where we were. I will say we went to Fakfak, and they will be saying, "Ey! Why is this man swearing?' and I will tell them, 'No that is the name — Fakfak!'" Both Justin and Sanakoli cracked with laughter.

The town with the curious name was actually rather charming built as it was along the hillside coast. The white and yellow sandstone, together with the colourful houses and the azure blue water, gave the whole place a Mediterranean atmosphere. The challenge now was to find a beach where we could get the canoe up and dried out. It soon became evident that there were no beaches but I spotted a big flat slab of cliff that could serve as a natural boat ramp.

As we got ashore, we were greeted by a middle-aged Papuan lady with strained grey curly hair and red teeth. She offered us a bottle of spring water and her daughter presented a bowl of *buai*, or *pinang* as it is called in Indonesian. After I had presented our intentions, she agreed to let us stay there — we would just have to wait for the tide and she would get her neighbours to help pull the canoe ashore. We thanked her very much and got up to return to the canoe. Sanakoli emptied her bowl of *pinang* in a greedy handful. As we climbed aboard, I asked him, "Hey wasn't it a bit much — you took all her *buai*?"

Sanakoli looked strangely at me and replied, "No, us people who chew, we do like this."

In the afternoon, the canoe was pulled ashore and we got to meet most of the community. They were very friendly people and the old lady (who we just called *Ibu* — an Indonesian courtesy phrase for an older woman) invited us for dinner in her concrete house. Now that we were ashore, I had to get on to raising some money. It was more important now than ever as we were practically bankrupt. I had tried to get hold of the Governor of Vanimo to see if we could get the promised funding released but although Imelda helped, things just stalled in the end. I had also tried to reach the PNG Minister of Tourism but didn't get a reply from him either. Rob Goodfellow suggested that I contact the PNG news media with the story, "To motivate the PNG government to help you." With Rob's help, I wrote a press release stating that we were stranded in Indonesia and calling on the government in Vanimo to release the funds promised so we could complete the circumnavigation.

I also contacted a journalist in Lae for EMTV. He came back almost immediately and asked me to send him some video from the voyage so he could do a news report. This was just what we needed. I gathered Justin and Sanakoli in front of the canoe and told them not to look 'too happy.' We made a short film of me stating the trouble we were in and that we were appealing for the help from PNG, then I uploaded it together with some dramatic clips from the journey and our Batfish dinner on the beach. The next day our report was aired on PNG national television, with the headline: 'Danish Adventurer and Papua New Guinean Companions Stranded in Indonesia Due to Lack of Funds.' The transcript read like this:

Speaker: *So far it has been an adventure of epic proportions, three men attempting to circumnavigate the island of New Guinea in a canoe complete with two master sailors from the Milne Bay Province, each step of the way filmed and photographed using cell phones, taking documentary filming to a whole new level. The conditions have been unforgiving, the men crossing into Indonesian waters in the middle of the monsoon season. The trio is led by Danish adventurer, Thor Jensen, his two Milne Bay companions, Milne Bay brothers Sanakoli and Justin John. They have already gone past the halfway-mark around the West Papuan coast into the town of Fakfak but they are facing serious funding challenges.*

Thor: *For two months, we have been fighting against the Northwest Monsoon, and the only reason we are still here today is because these two guys are such incredible sailors.*

Speaker: *Late yesterday Thor Jensen send this video appealing to their sponsor, the Sundaun Provincial Government to pay the funding promised to them when they were in Vanimo five months ago.*

Thor: *Our great problem now is that we have no more funding... we have been promised funding almost five months ago from the West Sepik Government. We haven't received this funding yet and now we are really struggling.*

Speaker: *The journey began in 2016 on a canoe built using traditional methods. Although the men are in high spirits, they would like to have the journey completed by August where they hope to reach Tawali where they started last year.*

Justin and Sanakoli watched the report over and over again on their phones and showed it to our new friends in Fakfak. The journalist also contacted the Minister of Tourism and the Governor's office in Vanimo for a comment. He didn't hear anything from Vanimo but the Minister of Tourism said that he would follow up on this, "As soon as possible." We didn't hear anything else from the PNG Government. However, the video did create an overwhelming response on Facebook. Our followers grew and the donations started ticking in. I spoke with Paul that same night. He was on an assignment in Japan but was planning to meet us in the next big town of Kaimana, in ten days' time.

Paul had seen the TV-report and I asked him what he thought. To my surprise he said that, "It might not be in our favour as Justin and Sanakoli looked really miserable — like they didn't really wanted to be there at all." I hadn't seen it like that. Perhaps a Papua New Guinean audience might have interpreted it as we were struggling, since we were far from home surviving just on fish and coconut, disappointed because we didn't get any help.

Although Sanakoli didn't say it on camera, his opinion on the matter was very clear. "The PNG Government, they think we are dogs, they don't care for us, we risk our lives and they just forget about us." Nonetheless, two days later we raised our biggest amount yet — more than $US1200. This allowed us to purchase a resupply of food and pay for a water truck to fill up the tanks of our hostess, not least so that we could have a shower.

On one of the last days in Fakfak, on the way back from the centre of town, I passed a type of 'outdoor shop.' They had all the usual stuff — backpacks, boots, tents and torches. This land of plenty put me in a position where I was again questioning my ideals. At the beginning of the journey, I had said that all the equipment we needed should be something a Papua New Guinean could find in a regular hardware store — so as to show that such a voyage could be done without fancy modern equipment. Now it felt silly not to get some good equipment while we had the chance. There had been some cold nights on this coast so I bought Justin and Sanakoli a sleeping bag each, together with two pairs of Oakley sunglasses — copies but good copies. I also bought two carabiners, which would make turning the sail much quicker. Justin and Sanakoli loved the sleeping bags, as they had never owned such a luxury item before. The carabiners were a hit as well and Justin said, "We must take them with us when we go on land or people steal them." In Sanakoli's view, the sunglasses were the best — almost as good as buying a new set of eyeballs.

Chapter Twenty-one

Different lenses

It was well past midnight and we had paddled for hours against a counter-current without much progress. We were on the third day of 'sailing' to Kaimana and I now found myself in one of those situations where I didn't know if I should opt out of paddling or stick with the effort. It was perpetually challenging to navigate my different roles: expedition leader, canoe sailor, problem solver, motivator, filmmaker, photographer, media manager, fundraiser and promoter. My first thought was that Justin and Sanokoli had it easy; they just had to be sailors. But on reflection this was not true. They were also documenting the trip, while negotiating complex relationships with the locals, doing repairs, guarding the canoe, being storytellers and keeping the *dim dim* safe.

My roles were to go from the canoe directly to government offices, draft and issue press releases, produce newsletters, back up recordings, post duplicate hard disks home, solicit donations, thank supporters, and provision. It was a full-time occupation, and this night my job was to paddle the canoe until the wind returned. But I had had enough and said, 'To hell with it.' I threw *Eneta* on the platform and gifted my aching body some sleep. I woke an hour later, looked up on the stars and the coast — we had barely moved. Justin and Sanakoli were still paddling.

Sailing into Kaimana was such a thrill. The town is situated in the corner of the headland where several rivers run into a shallow sea. As we approached this particular morning, a strong wind was blowing from inland. The outrigger rose out of the water and my companions got all fired up.

"You climb to the outrigger," Sanakoli yelled, and I positioned myself on the pontoon that was now shooting over the sea like a magic flying carpet — well… a magic log. I looked at the GPS around my neck; we were running 13 knots, which was an incredible speed!

"Hurry, you go bail," Justin ordered. I climbed into the hull that was almost sideways to the swell and emptied it of sea water with hectic motions. "Enough, you get back up," Justin yelled again as I climbed back into position.

Lifting the outrigger and sailing only on the hull is the hallmark of a master canoe sailor, a delicate coordination of the man steering and the man at the sail. It was like balancing on a knife's edge. If the sheet was pulled too hard or the blade turned out of rhythm, the canoe would flip upside down, as I had seen happen at the canoe festival in 2015. It took four men more than an hour to get the canoe right again. But Justin and Sanakoli were on top of their game and we all hooted with a combination of thrill and nervousness.

We came to a section with almost no waves and Justin yelled, "You come take the steer." But our speed was too great and I was afraid of crashing, so I declined. I was preoccupied enough just hanging on to the outrigger.

It was still early morning when we passed several shipwrecks that were laying stranded like the blackened rib cages of prehistoric creatures. We anchored the canoe on the sand-flats of Kaimana. Sanakoli was the first to jump into the shallow water. He had been agitated for days and couldn't get ashore quickly enough.

"You show me where the market is. No more play up," he said. I couldn't help laughing at him. He hadn't had betel nut for three days and was clearly craving his drug. I told him he could just go and find some but he replied, "Me I don't know this place, you show me."

"Hey, I've never been here before either." I laughed but then I found my flip-flops and jumped onto an emerging sandbank. As we got up onto the coastal road, we were met by the noise of traffic amplified by the still humid morning air. Scooters, cars and trucks flew by the shops on the roadside. We crossed a bridge over a river running into the ocean. It was choked with plastic bags and bottles and swollen disposable diapers.

"Oh, look at all the rubbish — like Jayapura," Sanakoli noted.

It was only 7:40 a.m. but the shops had already started opening. We quickly spotted a man with a foldable table selling Sanakoli's green 'gold nuggets.' "*Pinang, pinang*," Sanakoli laughed grabbing a pile of nuts and mustard. The vendor also had a dried version but Sana preferred his *buai* fresh. "The dry ones are good for travelling, they keep long but like lollies, too hard to chew." Sanakoli mumbled, while eagerly husking a nut with his canine teeth. We also bought three brown paper packages of Indonesian breakfast, or '*bungkus*,' which consisted of yellow fried rice and vegetables, decorated with pink prawn crackers and shredded dry coconut, topped with a curried boiled egg, some chilli and a piece of fried fish or chicken on the side.

The weather forecast looked great for the next week and, ideally, we would just have bought provisions, shown our documents and continued on but as we were having our breakfast on the canoe, I explained that we would have to stay in Kaimana. I had agreed to meet with Paul and it would be four to six days until he arrived. "So why will he be so late," Sanakoli wanted to know.

I explained, "He works as a photographer and guide for a company that creates special travels for some of the wealthiest people in the world, so he's busy flying around all the time." I removed some fishbone and continued. "We should wait for him because he's also the one who has sponsored our solar equipment and satellite communication kit and he'll be bringing me some spare camera gear as well. Also, he is going to take a lot of good pictures of us so we can get famous in magazines and stuff. You know, as I have told you before — one thing is to do this travel, another thing is to tell the rest of the world about it."

The two brothers nodded. Then Sanakoli asked, "How can he travel all the time, where is his what, family?"

"He doesn't have any kids," I chewed.

"So, he's a young boy!" Sanakoli remarked.

"Guess you can say that but I think he's about 47 years old," I explained.

"Hoo! Paul has no wife and kids and he travels — he's a young boy!" Sanakoli concluded to the obvious amusement of Justin. I laughed as well but I was also looking forward to seeing an old friend and having a different type of conversation.

We found a beach by a small Papuan community where the canoe was pulled safely on land. Then I checked into a cheap hotel so I could store our valuables and work on my laptop. I really enjoyed these days alone having space for myself. But despite being 'safe,' I would still be woken up by the smallest sound in the night and then get up to check if the door was locked and if there was anybody outside.

Three days later, I picked up Paul at the small but surprisingly elaborate glass airport outside of Kaimana, an indication of the growing number of passengers coming to the area. Paul looked like his old self — clean shaven with a brown short brimmed cap, blond hair tied up in a bun and a loose-fitting outdoor shirt. "Hey good to see you," he greeted me.

"You too," I replied.

Paul continued, "But by-crikey, it takes a lot of flights to get here."

"At least you didn't lose any of your luggage," I smiled, looking at his giant waterproof duffle-bag, camera-bag and Pelicase (a waterproof plastic box). Paul took this as a cue to excitedly tell me about the new drone he had in the Pelicase — a device I was pretty interested in as well, as this meant I could get some beautiful aerial shots for my documentary film. In the taxi on our way back to town Paul explained that he had been in touch with several magazines, but all of them wanted to see some images before paying for an article.

We got Paul lodged in the fancy part of my hotel — with a harbour-front view across the road. We spent three more days here before we were ready to sail out. I was restless by then and secretly calculated that we could have covered 300 nautical miles or so in the time we had been waiting in Kaimana. The plan was that Paul would accompany us for five days up through Triton Bay, which boasted some of the most spectacular coastline in West Papua, both due to its sheer karst cliffs (a topography formed when limestone is dissolved) and its abundance of marine life (which was only first comprehensively surveyed in 2006). The Kaimana Regency had been declared a Marine Protected Area in 2008 and is often described as the 'species factory of the Coral Triangle.' Here marine life has developed in an area isolated by estuarine coastlines to both the west and east of the bay. To an experienced dive master, such as Paul, this was like visiting 'Willy Wonka's fish factory,' so we planned to end his trip at Triton Bay Divers Resort, the only dive lodge in the area, from where the crew and I would continue onwards.

On our day of departure, everyone was helping pull the canoe into the water. I was worried though, as we hadn't seen any sign of Justin all morning. When *Tawali Pasana* was afloat, he finally turned up accompanied by a group of local friends. His nose was red and he had a funny smile on his face while holding a little gold statuette of an eagle between his hands. "They look like a happy bunch," Paul laughed. They were all reeking of alcohol. I cringed on Justin's behalf because, now that we had a guest onboard, I thought we ought to look our best. Nonetheless, we enjoyed a happy farewell to Kaimana and I steered us out while Justin climbed up the mast to wave at his drinking buddies. The favourable winds had turned against us and we made slow progress. But this weather wasn't all bad, as it gave our photographer room to move around with his camera and we needed all the space we could get. Paul was almost two heads taller than the rest of us, and with his big bags and the Pelicase on the deck, and Justin now sleeping in the front, *Tawali Pasana* seemed rather small.

Sanakoli was in a great mood though and kept cracking jokes, telling me that I was a *lapun* and Paul that he was a *young boy*. Paul bantered back at him, "So what about you Sanakoli, I hear you made many new wives on your journey?"

Sanakoli laughed and protested, "No, I'm a good married man but you, I know you got a wife in every country you go to — that's why you are a young boy."

In the early afternoon, we landed on a deserted beach behind the south point of Pulau, Namatota. Here the water was shallow and quiet and the beautiful island was framed by green mountains. There was a clearing from an old camp where we found sculpture of gigantic dirt-grey bones, which was likely from a Brydes whale, a 12–15 metre Baleen species that frequents these waters. Paul documented us as we went about the usual routines of setting up camp and cooking lunch. At first, it was a bit confusing to know what to do with oneself, now that there was suddenly a photographer following me around. But seeing Paul at work also gave me an outsider's perspective, which rekindled my own joy of documenting the voyage. Paul had been a mentor to me from when I first met him in Venezuela in 2010, where we both worked as guides for a company called Jakera Tours. Back then, he was already a veteran of the outdoor and travel industry and a well-known photographer. He also had a big expedition under his belt: paddling the entire coast of Mozambique by sea kayak, together with three other men, just as the country was recovering from 20 years of civil war. Since Venezuela, we had kept in touch and met up in different parts of the world. When I conceived the idea of this expedition, I asked Paul to join me but he was too busy. Nonetheless, he offered his support.

As the sky became red, we were walking up the narrow beach of Namatota, discussing subjects such as international politics, newly discovered fish species and the tourism potential in West Papua. We also came to talk about the rubbish along the shores that was more obvious in West Papua as there were simply more consumer goods available. I told Paul how it was a common practice amongst the people living along this coast to dump their trash directly into the ocean and, even on this remote beach, we saw plastic bottles and flip-flops and nylon rope amongst the natural debris.

Paul commented that he had seen Justin and Sanakoli throwing caramel wrappers into the sea as we were sailing. “Is this what they do every day?” Paul asked rather indignantly. I told him that I had encouraged them to use a bin-bag tied to the outrigger and even tried to explain the global problem of oceanic pollution but it was like they didn’t see how their tiny actions contributed to larger global problems. “Why don't you just tell them that they won’t get paid if they litter,” Paul said, becoming agitated.

“It doesn’t work like that.” I replied and continued, “They’re adults. I don't want to tell them what they can and can’t do — I want them to understand why they shouldn't litter themselves because that way they will return home and spread the message.”

“It doesn’t seem like it’s been working so far,” Paul noted with more than a hint of cynicism — and I had to agree with that.

"We better not tell this to anyone."

The next day was slow travelling, with a lot of photographing and filming along the inside of Namatota Island. In the afternoon, we tacked up through Koningin Sophia Strait and passed several *bagans,* or fishing platforms, with big surface nets set out to catch sardines in the night (a smaller version of the ones we had seen outside of Jayapura). Near one of the platforms, we suddenly saw the distinctive white dotted back of a whale shark inspecting the nets. But the wind and current were against us, so we couldn't stop to jump in and film. As we reached the east point of Pulau Namatota, we passed a village with a colourful mosque and steered towards the loveliest island called Pulau Tiga. It was late afternoon when we anchored in the turquoise lagoon surrounded by low cliffs and a palm fringed beach. There were some goats running freely around a small plantation of palm trees but, besides the goats, there were no other inhabitants.

We spent the evening exploring and filming. Justin had gone diving with his spear in a lagoon on the other side of the island. Suddenly, we heard him yelling. I was the first to arrive at the scene. Justin was standing on the beach still dripping wet and at his feet lay a sea turtle the size of a car tire — and it had a spear through its throat. I first shook my head in disbelief and thought, 'Poor creature.' Justin, who was obviously proud of his catch boasted, "I saw him on the reef and said, I must get him for photos."

"So, do you want to eat it?" I asked still looking worried.

"No, see, I just shot him through the skin, he will be all right." Justin pointed to where the spear had just pierced the loose skin under the throat of the creature. I was eager to get the spear out before Paul arrived at the scene but too late.

"Justin, you shot a turtle!" Paul exclaimed while trying to disguise his discomfort.

"Yes, now you get photo," Justin said proudly, obviously missing the subtlety of Paul's grimaced expression. I quickly explained what had happened while helping calm the flapping creature. Justin pulled the spear out.

Paul clicked some photos and then laughed nervously, "We better not tell this to anyone." I got a photo too and then set it free.

The next morning, we had a big breakfast of parrot fish, cuttlefish and lobster. The fish had been caught in the night while Paul and I were sleeping. The two brothers had been out with torches and bush knives in the shallows. After breakfast, the tide was getting low so I walked down to the canoe to anchor in deeper water so it wouldn't be stuck when we wanted to sail out. As I was managing the lines, I could hear the sailors talking to Paul about me on the beach. Sanakoli said, "Oh, he can't paddle."

"Ha ha, why can't he paddle?" Paul wanted to know.

"Every time we must paddle, our man always has to film." 'What the hell' I thought, 'As soon as they get the chance, they bad-mouth me,' but I didn't confront them, I guessed they just wanted to look cool in front of Paul. As I got back to the beach, the conversation changed.

I just said, "Are they telling you a lot of stories?" Paul looked a bit uneasy and the sailors shy. I later regretted that I hadn't spoken up.

After midday, we made our way out of the lagoon and sailed towards the entrance of Triton Bay. Justin and Sanakoli were even louder than usual in their joking, calling Paul 'a young boy' and me a '*lapun*.' Having to banter back all the time was putting me in a bad mood. The dynamics had certainly changed since we left Kaimana.

Triton Bay was an amazing sight. The white karst mountain walls started raising out of the sea with tones of green growing out of every crevice. We slowly navigated through this cathedral of geological wonder. Both Justin and Sanakoli were taken aback by the beauty of the place and documented it with their smartphones alongside Paul and I with our cameras. We came to a small white beach with a rock island in front and anchored the canoe. Paul's two cameras were shooting like automatic rifles as we tied the stern line off and explored the jungle between the beach and a cliff wall. Paul then said, "It would look amazing if we had the canoe up there on the other end of the beach, then I can get the sunset behind it." However, although it was in my interests to get the best photos possible, I was too exhausted to make it happen and instead helped set up our big batteries so he could charge his drone and laptop.

The morning was full of life. We saw fish hunting in the shallows and a couple of manta-rays off the beach. I tried to swim out to them but they were gone before I could see them. We then packed the canoe and, as I pulled up the anchor Sanakoli came out with yet another remark. "You hurry now, *Lapun*, no good we drift into the rock."

By then, I'd had enough and said loudly so Justin could hear it in the back, "Maybe we should take a break from the *lapun* jokes, they are becoming a bit tiresome." After that there was quiet and we all paddled the canoe into the bay.

The sun was already baking and there was no wind. Paul got the drone out and after several technical preparations it was ready to take off. It was a delicate manoeuvre to perform from a sailing canoe as there was the mast and rigging to avoid. So, I held it in my outstretched arms and then let it go when the propellers started humming. It flew upwards rapidly until it disappeared into the blue sky. With the aerial camera in position we could see ourselves but we had to hide Paul from the image so he covered himself with a *sarong,* which also gave his screen some shade. With everything set, we started to paddle in between two great cliffs that stood like guardian pillars on each side of the gates to paradise. As we all later saw, it was an amazing shot, with verdant green jungle and a baby-blue horizon framed by the massive karst pillars, with our little canoe slowly making its way across an azure blue sea.

After 13 minutes, it was time to land the drone. Paul hadn't had much time to practise flying but, nonetheless, he got it lowered down to my height. It was now hovering over the water, but he couldn't get it close enough to the canoe as the detectors on the drone picked up the rigging as a hazard. Meanwhile, the battery was running out, which was an even bigger problem. If the battery got lower than 15 percent charge, the drone would auto-land on the position where it had taken off, which was in the sea 300 metres behind us. After a lot of sweat and concerted attempts to retrieve it from different angles, Paul finally got the drone positioned so I could grip it by the landing frame. He changed the battery and the second landing went better. We spent an exciting morning like this, filming and paddling between great rock formations and imposing cliff walls.

By the early afternoon, we were back into open water and the wind gave our paddling arms a rest. As we were sailing along, we ate some lollies and Sanakoli thoughtlessly threw his paper in the water. Paul saw this and said in a sort of diplomatic but annoyed tone, "Sanakoli, in other parts of the world it would be considered selfish and stupid to throw garbage into the sea." Sanakoli tried to joke his way out of it but Paul said, "No it's not funny. It is a big problem in the world."

I took Sana's defence, "Paul, you can't expect people who come from a small island to see the scale of this issue — if you are used to almost everything coming from nature, and it all goes back in to nature, then the idea of rubbish is very different to them."

Paul then started to explain more broadly about the plastic in the oceans and Sanakoli agreed that there had been too much rubbish on the beaches in Indonesia. I felt bad that I hadn't made a bigger effort to educate my sailors but, seen in perspective, I would probably generate more non-biodegradable waste in one month than Sanakoli would in a lifetime. It was a relevant time, and place, to have this discussion though, as Indonesia is the second biggest marine polluter in the world after China. The Indonesian Government had just made headlines by announcing their ambitious goal of reducing their ocean waste by 70 percent by 2025 at the World Ocean Summit 2017 in Bali. There were fewer caramel wrappers floating in our wake after this.

In the afternoon, we sailed ashore at Triton Bay Divers Resort, which was situated in a protected bay on Aiduma, an elongated island about two nautical miles off the mainland. It was a beautiful little resort consisting of six stylish bungalows on the beach, a dive shop and an open communal area with a restaurant and bar. The resort manager, and part owner, was a very pleasant fair-haired lady in her 50s named Lisa English. She was expecting us, and Paul was set up in one of the cabins. I could probably also have made a good deal with her, but it felt weird to sleep in a fancy hut next to the sailors on the canoe. Paul was intrigued by the place and immediately saw the potential of using it as a future high-end travel destination. I asked him if it would be a problem that the beautifully styled bungalows only had ceiling fans and no air-condition. He said, "That's all right, to my clients this would be like going camping." It was impressive what Lisa and her business partner had built. It was like a secluded pearl, hard to find but when you were there, then you had some of the best diving in the world all to yourself.

Lisa had to leave us the next day as she was going to a meeting with the Indigenous family who owned the resort land. I asked if she encountered any trouble with the locals in such a remote area. She answered, "The 'liveaboards' still have some problems with the locals. They pop in and pop out, only staying maybe three days. The locals see these posh diving boats with lots of money and they feel they are not getting much back from them for being in their waters, so they aren't very keen on having them here." The resort was largely avoiding such problems, as Lisa had built up a good relationship with the landowners who had been made shareholders in the enterprise and re-sellers of fuel and building materials. "But then the other villages feel that they are left out." She continued, "And they all want money, so we try to employ different people from different villages." She added, "We also try and help them out too. We donated some cement to build their church. So we try to work with everyone in the area." It sounded similar to what I was trying to do, constantly nurturing relationships, negotiating challenges and solving problems in the pursuit of reaching my goal.

Although the area around the resort was a marine park, small scale fishing with lines and netting from the *bargans* was allowed. We met several of the line fishermen. They had small flat-bottomed dinghies, propelled by water pump engines, and they would come by the resort to sell fish and buy cigarettes and coffee. This way, Lisa could keep informed about what was happening in the area and if there was any illegal fishing going on. One of the fishermen we got to know was an Indonesian man called John. He came in one afternoon to sell us a coral trout. As Paul eagerly photographed the beautiful red fish with blue spots, he said, "This is one of the most expensive eating fish in Australia. I think they sell for near AUD$100 a kilo." We exchanged the fish for some coffee and a small bag of sugar.

John was a funny character with puffy eyes that seemed to hang over his moustache; he smoked *all* the time and told one story more fantastic than the other. First there was one about a giant octopus protecting a certain bay; another story featured a bay with resident mermaids; and one of his friends had even located a sunken Portuguese ship protected by a giant snake where he had found a gold mirror that he had sold for 15 million rupiah. But the visit to the sunken ship had also made his friend go half-mad. (We met the friend the next day and he did seem a bit off). John then went on to tell us about a dangerous area we would be passing through, where a missionary had reportedly been cooked by the locals in a big pot and then eaten. By the time the Indonesian military came to rescue him, it was too late; they only found his clothes and one boot. John then pointed to the area where these alleged 'cannibals' still roamed. He also marked some areas along the coast where separatist rebels were reportedly hiding and warned us to be careful not to be taken hostage by them. Justin and Sanakoli were fascinated by all these stories but, as Paul pointed out, "It's funny how his yarns resemble the usual stereotypes from colonial days: mermaids, people being cooked in big pots, and treasure."

Although I enjoyed these colourful fictions, they really were a lot of nonsense. Still, the next 350 nautical miles down to Timika would be through some of the most remote territory we had covered so far — and arguably the most inhospitable coastline in the world. Triton Bay was already pretty far from everything, with some very isolated tribes up in the mountains, and soon the swamps and mangroves would begin — and so would the saltwater crocodiles. We were delayed by bad winds and spent several days at the dive lodge sailing out to capture more drone photos. Paul was annoyed by the lack of good sunlight but I was keen to get some filming in rough conditions, as this would complement much of the footage I already had. Paul and I also went to film and photograph the 'underwater fish factory.' We only went snorkelling off the beach and it was beautiful — there was such an abundance of fish and I thought, 'Wow, is this how all coral reefs looked before humans arrived with their spears, hooks and nets?' What was particularly noticeable in this area was the abundance of soft corals, which were swaying with their feather-like braces, in black, green or red, contrasting with the blue underwater world.

Paul was straight to work with his camera. Just as above water, I was fascinated to see him at his trade below the water. He would work around a subject, photo after photo until he thought he had something special — like building up a painting by first sketching, laying down the base colours, and then adding shades and highlights, although you don't have to surface for air when working on a canvas. We didn't see the Triton Bay walking shark that is endemic to Triton Bay, instead I saw something just as curious — two large crocodile fish, a rugged-skinned bottom-dwelling fish species that has an incredible camouflage pattern and frills around its head. They just looked at me with their prehistoric eyes while I documented them with my camera.

As the wind finally turned in our favour, we prepared for departure. Sanakoli got Lisa's permission to fell new spare poles, or *towe* as he called them, for the canoe and I gave Paul a hard disk with all my recordings to be posted to Denmark. Lisa's staff had gathered on the beach to see us off. As a farewell gift, I gave her a hand-drawn map of Triton Bay, featuring a plethora of mythological creatures — as described by John the chain-smoking fisherman with the overly-active imagination. In return, she gave us all a Triton Bay Divers T-shirt — our first 'sponsor wear.' I said goodbye to Paul, thanked him and told him that his visit had rekindled the joy of documenting the expedition. We gave each other the same worried looks we did back at Tawali. There was danger ahead, and we both knew it. Paul wasn't the type who threw compliments around, but as he shook hands with Justin and Sanakoli, he said, "Good luck, what you are doing is very impressive."

The sea was dark like the coastal mountains as we hoisted the sail under a silver-grey sky. The magic colours of Triton Bay were fading and this new territory was beginning to look like the bleak tones of the north coast. Paul had captured vivid images of a magic adventure in splendorous surroundings — something we probably would have sailed right past if it we hadn't waited for him, and that would have been a great shame. I wondered in which colours my Papua New Guinean travel companions perceived this voyage? Despite our different palettes, the picture emerging in front of the splash boards of *Tawali Pasana* depicted a brown sea raised against us by the Southeast Trade Winds and a coast growing into a spider web of mangroves — all the way to the border of PNG.

Chapter Twenty-two

The Asmat

Bioluminescent plankton were shining like green stars in our dark hull. I was scooping them out but they kept flowing in. When I looked up, I could see them illuminating the surrounding darkness as they sprayed like welding sparks from our bow, hitting wave after wave. It was mesmerising but at the same time disconcerting, as it was the only light in the graphite-coloured mess of rain, fog and wind we were *jig-jagging* against. The only point of physical navigation was the black contour of Lakahia Island but that was all; we couldn't even see the mountains that were sending ripping gusts of wind towards us. It was a tough change from the placid conditions of Triton Bay. My hands and arms were already sore from bailing, but this was nothing compared to Justin by the *yabby yabby,* who was shivering violently from the cold. There was nothing we could do except continue — unless we wanted to be blown out to sea.

After two hours, the southernmost point of Lakahia seemed within reach. The waves changed and became flatter. Now we just needed to go up along the shore of the island and find the village. As we sailed closer, I noticed a most spectacular phenomenon. Under the canoe in the black deep below, green mushroom-shaped clouds were forming and bursting up towards us, sometimes almost reaching the surface. It looked amazing and I yelled, "Hey guys, check the green things below, it's like atomic bombs going off under us." Neither of the sailors replied, they seemed to be ignoring it, and me, and just concentrating on their work.

As soon as we neared the reef surrounding the island, Justin steered the canoe inside. In the same instance, a large thump was heard as *Tawali Pasana* bounced off a submerged coral head. I anxiously looked into the hull to see if the water level was raising — and if we were sinking — but nothing happened; the hull hadn't cracked. The island shielded the wind and the sail collapsed and was rolled down. "We cannot do more sailing, grab your *towe,* we push the canoe the rest of the way," Sanakoli said decisively. We had been warned about giant saltwater crocodiles in this bay, so we didn't want to take chances by camping in the mangroves that encircled the island. The next hour we pushed on with poles across the shallow reef while running the yellow circle of our torch along the coast, scanning for the characteristic red-eye reflection of the world's largest reptile. But all we saw were sea turtles floating in the shallows. At 10 p.m., we finally landed safely on the beach of Lakahia village.

The next morning, I was woken at 5 a.m. by an LED-torch shining in my face. "Mister, Mister," a guy was saying.

My whole body was aching as I turned and answered, feeling drowsy and annoyed, "*Tidak, tidak, terima kasih"* (No, no, thank you) But the man was persistent.

"*Makan mister, makan*" (food mister, food). I then realised it was the *Kepala Desa* who was inviting us for breakfast. After a hearty meal of sweet coffee, ripe bananas and fried buns, which were enjoyed with the whole village watching, I said that it was time to get going.

Sanakoli replied, trying me out, "We think the wind looks no good, maybe we wait till later?"

I showed them the weather forecast on my phone, "See, the whole week the wind will be with us. Wouldn't it be better if we covered as much of the new coast as possible while we can — it might be our last chance before the wind turns for good." They couldn't really argue against this and got their tired bodies up from the plastic chairs.

As we sailed out, the women of the village followed us along the shore singing with high-pitched nasal voices. With this song as a backdrop, I talked to Sanakoli about the wonderful green underwater clouds I had seen the night before but he quickly cut me off, looking very grave. "This is witchcraft. We know them from Milne Bay, it is what, floating rocks. They float in the water and hit you so you will sink." He shook his head and continued, "Oh, when we saw them, we knew, this is too dangerous, we must go in quick. But we didn't tell you, we didn't want to make you scared." I was about to suggest it might have been bioluminescent plankton being dredged up by underwater currents but then again, we had been hit by a rock, so I kept this to myself. *Tawali Pasana* turned past Lakahia's flat sand tail where the women were now standing in a long row singing and waving. Their colourful dresses and friendly features soon became undefined as the party shrunk to a mere row of sticks, their well-wishing voices dissolving in a generous wind that shot us up along the coast.

Expedition Log 21 April 2017

11:27 hrs. Running 7 knots. We have just passed a marine border. The contrast between crystal clear and murky sea water is so sharp that, for a few seconds, *Tawali Pasana* had both turquoise and brown currents under her hull. We have entered the Arafura Sea.

Expedition Log 22 April 2017

23:00 hrs. Sailing 6-7 knots on a steady mountain wind of the Surdiman Range. We clearly see the orange and magnesium white lights glow from a peak, it must be the Grasberg mine.

A controversial mine

It was midday as we reached the river delta by the Port of Amamapare and the great mouth of the Aikwa River that flows all the way from the town of Timika and the Grasberg mine above. We couldn't see the mine but instead I got a view of Punjak Jaya at 4,884 metres, the highest peak on the island and all of oceania. The summit is also known as Carstensz Pyramid, after the Dutch Captain Jan Carstensz who was the first European to 'discover' it on his reconnaissance of the New Guinea's south coast in 1623. When he came back, reporting that he had observed a mountain with snow on the top, no one believed him, as 'There couldn't be a snow-capped peak this close to the equator.' Nonetheless, he got his redemption by having the peak named after him.

The neighbouring Grasberg mine, which is run by the American company Freeport-McCormac, is the largest gold mine and second-largest copper mine in the world, and it is clouded in much controversy. The open pit mine has had a devastating impact, with people alienated from their land and waterways polluted. This has led to many armed clashes between the OPM rebels and the military. As it is a multi-billion-dollar business, it is well protected by the Indonesian Army, including the Special Forces — or KOPASUS. To avoid any suspicion or scrutiny by the authorities, my plan was to continue past the Port of Amamapare and Timika and the controversial mine.

The wind was blowing 18 knots from the sea and *Tawali Pasana* was flying along. I had been given the steer and was now battling with the heavy piece of wood to keep the canoe on course. The high-speed sailing was thrilling but it also meant that the fast-flowing water locked the rudder blade hard against the side of the hull. I could no longer push the blade with my foot, instead I had to jam my heel between the blade and the side of the canoe to make it angle. "Timika, Timika," Sanakoli yelled excitedly. The brothers were in great spirits, as they always were when *Tawali Pasana* was at speed on a steady sea. As the wind started to increase in velocity, steering became too demanding and I had to ask Sanakoli to take over.

It was at this time, after observing a debate between my two companions, that Sanakoli pointed to the sky and yelled, "Look, when the sky is dark like that — big wind is coming, we must go in." And he wasn't kidding. On the horizon, a thick blue haze was about to roll over us. Just in the nick of time, we ducked for shelter up a discreet tributary with a big sandbank, where some Papuan families had set up a fishing camp. We rested under our tarpaulins until 2 a.m. when a good mountain wind started blowing again and we took off into the darkness. In the afternoon we passed three fishermen in a dinghy. They had just emptied their gill nets that were suspended between poles along the shallow coast. We gave them three postcards. They gave us three fish and waved goodbye. We landed on a small island by a river mouth and collected firewood. We cooked the fish as we sailed onwards.

After a night of sailing, we reached the Aswet estuary leading to Agats. It was 10 a.m. Disintegrating black and white metal channel markers stood like deserted watch towers, indicating where logging ships and coasters could safely enter. Six days after leaving Triton Bay, we had sailed more than 350 nautical miles. We were all exhausted from the long haul and the outrigger was getting heavy again but our spirits were high. "Hey guys, let's get a photo of you two for Facebook," I said.

"Woohoo, Agats!" Sanakoli yelled enthusiastically as he let go of the sheet and gave a thumbs' up with a wide grin. Justin, who normally wouldn't pose for photos, stuck his leg into the air and smiled while holding on to the *yabby yabby*.

It took the best part of an hour to *jig-jag* up the wide river that ran flat and smooth like a six-lane highway through the jumble of mangroves. Finally, Agats came into view in a bend on the south-eastern bank. The town was laying like a long row of houses on stilts. The further down we looked, the more modern looking the houses became, although still on stilts. At the end was what appeared to be the commercial harbour.

I was very excited to visit Agats. The town is the administrative centre of the Asmat Regency (Asmat refers to both the area as well as being a broad term for the people living there). It is an expanse of remote coast and tidal mudflats within a World Heritage wilderness area of inland mangroves, winding rivers and lowland rainforest. This inhospitable natural environment combined with the Asmat's hostility to outsiders kept the region relatively unexplored until the 1950s. The Asmat were known as fierce warriors and cannibals but also skilled craftsmen who carved elaborate shields for war and wooden figures on tall poles (known as *bisj*) to hold the spirits of family members killed by enemies, which links with a common origin story from the area about the Asmat's ancestors being carved from wood. The region became known world-wide in the 1960s when the young Michael C. Rockefeller (the son of the Governor of New York State and a member of one of the wealthiest families in the world) disappeared on an expedition to collect tribal art. His cause of death was never confirmed, although many people went to look for him. Author Carl Hoffman recently published a book in which he presents evidence that Rockefeller was indeed killed and eaten by the Asmat.

As we approach the edge of town, Asmat became even more wondrous to look at. The chaos of the mangrove roots had given way to an odd Klondike-like menagerie of tide-blackened stilts supporting houses that mostly looked like rough wooden boxes with a metal roof. These less traditionally built dwellings were connected with each other by wonky wooden walkways — also on stilts. In front were several canoes lying in the low-tide mud. I was thrilled to see they still had the local style dugout canoes, which were very long and slender, without an outrigger — although the community seemed to own just as many Indonesian-style fibreglass dinghies.

We didn't have a contact in Agats but turned in all the same. We were looking for a piece of ground where the canoe could rest on dry land but the banks were too tall and steep (not least because of the outgoing tide). A small crowd was gathering above us on one of the walking paths. They looked like people of the swamp, dark-skinned and tall, with elongated facial features, which reminded me of the Sepik people from the other side of the island. Although they had seen most types of boats pass their village, a sailing canoe with two Papua New Guineans and a Dane must have been a first. The scrawny dogs barked chaotically and the kids screamed with excitement. We were guided up a small river bordering the community nestled against the wild mangroves and then pointed up a small muddy channel where we berthed next to an old dugout canoe.

I climbed up on the rough planks and started shaking hands. The sun was burning through my T-shirt, despite the garment being well impregnated with sweat and salt, so I felt relieved to be directed to a shaded deck with a small shop run by Indonesians. A Papuan man named Heru, who was at the halfway mark in his life, introduced himself. He spoke English fairly well. "Hello, what are you doing here?" he asked. I explained our purpose and our need of dry land. He didn't answer my request but instead sort of interrogated me. "Have you permit, police. Police permit?" I took out my papers and ensured him that we were going there straight away, as soon as we had a place to put the canoe. "We must go to police now and show papers," he pleasantly demanded. This eagerness to go to the authorities worried me, but I calmed myself with the fact there was nothing to hide (except my film kit and recordings). Heru organised two of the shopkeeper's boys and their scooters. It looked like the engines were missing but I then realised they were electric scooters running on batteries. I jumped on the back of one as our drivers set out on a bumpy run along wooden pathways elevated a metre above the mud and scrub, past small rivers drowning in garbage.

The police headquarters was an elongated bland-looking building — especially when compared to the army headquarters next door, which was painted in lavish camouflage colours and even had a statue of a giant rambo-knife and an equally enormous automatic rifle crossed about the entrance. After a bit of waiting I was shown to an office where I was interviewed by a detective. He was about my age and seemed to be impressed by our voyage. He didn't comment on our lack of stamps from Timika, which was a great relief. As we drove back an hour later, Heru seemed more welcoming now that our papers were in order.

It was already late afternoon and now we had to figure out what to do with the canoe. I suggested a piece of grassland next to their traditional longhouse. After the usual negotiations, we agreed that I would give the elders cigarettes and coffee as payment. As the sun sank into the mangroves, the tide rose and we manoeuvred the canoe as close to the longhouse as possible and, from there, we all began the long hard task of hauling it ashore. We were around 20 men, pushing and pulling the heavy log up the steep mudbank.

The mosquitoes were buzzing frenetically and the frogs were answering when *Tawali Pasana* finally came to rest on dry land. I thanked all the men and gave them a carton of cigarettes to share. The men stuck around as if they were waiting for something more to happen, then Heru came to me. He had just spoken with one of the chiefs in the longhouse. "You must pay 20.000 rupiah for each man who worked, it was very hard work." I looked around, the air was thick with sweat and tension. I said that we didn't have much money and it was the first time on our trip that we had been asked for payment to pull the canoe ashore. Heru then said that it was all right if we just paid 500.000 rupiah in total,

"But that is more than 20.000 rupiah per man," I argued showing a video on my phone that I had taken of the men pulling the canoe ashore. I counted with Heru, 15 Asmat men. "That's 300.000 rupiah,"

I said reminding them that I had already spent 300.000 rupiah on coffee and cigarettes for the Chief and elders in the longhouse.

Heru looked at the screen and continued, “Yes but there are also many children helping.”

I looked around. The men were still loitering and shuffling about following the conversation. The most important thing was for us to have a good night’s sleep and get the outrigger dried. There was no point arguing with our new hosts and, in the end, it was I who had come to them. I reluctantly counted out 500.000 rupiah and handed Heru the bills, which he kind of snatched from me like Gollum and the ring. Slowly the bystanders dispersed, some appeared happy whilst others made loud sounds that didn’t seem too approving. A few young men hung around with Heru to chew *pinang* with Justin and Sanakoli and to join us for dinner.

As it was time to go to bed, we secured all our valuables below deck and strung our mosquito nets under the tarpaulin. Finally, we could rest after six days of sailing. But we had barely turned off the light before there was a loud scream and something hit our tarpaulin. “What was that!” Sanakoli exclaimed and we all turned on our head torches and looked out. There was no one to be seen on the grass or the elevated walkway, except a couple of people who peaked through their windows to see what was going on. A long spear-like stick was laying in the grass next to our canoe. “We cannot trust these people,” Sanakoli whispered. Justin was just looking silently into the dark holding his bush knife.

Timika Timika

The next day Heru joined us for breakfast. Neither Justin, Sanakoli or I had slept very well, and I told Heru about the spear being thrown at us. He made a sound as if he already knew about it and said we shouldn’t worry, as it was, “Just some young boys playing up.” By talking further with him, I learned that the local Asmats were accustomed to having visitors. Several times a year a cruise ship would berth and tourists would flood their community, like a tsunami of wallets, to see them dress in traditional attire, perform a *sing sing* and make wood carvings. The cruise ship would pay the community a large sum of money that was then divided between the different families. It started to dawn on me that the tribe probably expected the same from us, although we obviously hadn't arrived in an elaborate cruise ship. So, I again explained our noble purpose, emphasised our lack of finances, and how our voyage would help promote Agats and thus bringing in more tourists. To make sure Heru was on our side, I gave him a 'fixer fee' for helping facilitate all of this. He was, after all, from the very beginning a consummate tout.

After a day of working in the centre of town, I returned to the canoe. I discovered, to my great annoyance, that Justin and Sanakoli hadn't elevated the outrigger from the wet grass as we had agreed upon — their only task for the day. But before I complained about the outrigger, I had to deliver some bad news. I had to go to Timika to renew our visas. I would fly out the next day. This meant that we would probably be delayed by three more days. Sanakoli said, "Why didn't you go fix our visas while we pass Timika?"

I wasn't in the mood for this clever-in-hindsight attitude, which was one of his lesser qualities, and answered, "I thought we could do it from here and I wanted the canoe to cover as much ground as possible while the wind was good."

He continued, not letting it go, "But now you have to go back anyhow."

"Yes," I shot back firmly, "But at least you didn't have to *jig-jag* to Agats." I was feeling dizzy from yet another foot infection and lack of rest and didn't need this.

By the early afternoon, I was flying in a nine-seater Cessna 208B over Timika town. The first thing you notice is that the Aikwa River runs directly from the mine above. It was once a river like any other, winding and carving through the jungle shaped by rocks and trees, but excessive amounts of tailings and acidic run-off have created a wide scar of channels and gravel islands all the way down the mountainside, before the contaminated water flows into the Arafura Sea (in the process, killing most aquatic life). We landed in one of the two big airports supporting the city. It took three days before our visas were processed but now they had a longer expiration date, which gave us a whole month to get to Merauke, the last city before the border with PNG. Being in Timika wasn't all bad. My infected wounds got a chance to heal and, from the comfort of a hotel room, I produced a beautiful promotional video with the help of a couple of friends. The soundtrack especially elevated the production, which was captioned rather than narrated to increase viewer engagement.

The video was finished on the day before my birthday on 1 May. To celebrate I had a cupcake for breakfast at a cafe. During my lonely celebration, I unexpectedly received a message from Sophie Pascoe who had returned to Milne Bay to do her PhD fieldwork on the remote Suau coast. Her message made me smile. I had originally reserved this as a day of no expedition work but the video generated a lot of positive feedback on Facebook and very timely donations again started coming in. So, my birthday was spent keeping the momentum rolling on social media and posting the clip to international news outlets. Paul Harris the manager from the Vanimo Surf Lodge donated a large sum that would take us all the way to Merauke. This was the best birthday present I could have wished for.

On the morning of departure, the flight was cancelled due to engine trouble. Now I was looking at three or four more days before I could fly back. This was too much. I called Heru to see what options were available and Heru had a solution, at a price, naturally. The next morning, I took a taxi through the jungle highway down to Amamapare harbour, which we had passed in *Tawali Pasana* a week earlier. It is a relatively busy port, where three pipelines transporting gold and copper concentrate from the Grasberg mine converge. The concentrate was treated there and then shipped out. But the harbour itself looked like a rough place, with rusty neglected-looking cargo ships being loaded and the shore littered with scrawny houses and run-down shops. I didn't go near the plant or the controversial mine.

At 1 p.m., Heru arrived with an obliging associate tout who was wearing a woollen hat. They were motoring a small red, yellow and green speedboat that looked more like an upscaled reggae toy than a seaworthy vessel. "Hi Heru, thanks for picking me up," I said cheerfully. It was right down to business for Heru who didn't beat around the bush.

"Hello mister, did you remember my gift?"

"Yeah don't worry," I said and pulled out a half litre bottle of whiskey.

"Don't show it here!" Heru bristled in a strained low voice. He looked around to make sure that none of the fishermen had seen the bottle.

In West Papua, alcohol is sold from officially-designated shops; it has a certain stigma associated with it as *apparently* Indonesian Muslims don't drink and many Papuans become very aggressive when they are intoxicated. For this reason, I had been hesitant when Heru asked for a bottle of strong liquor. I compromised by only buying half a litre. After a refuel, I climbed aboard the little boat that had a steering wheel and two seats in the front and a wide cushioned seat in the back. I was directed to the 'most comfortable' backseat, together with my shopping bags. The engine was turned on and, as soon as we were clear of the water hyacinths, Heru pulled the throttle, the pointy bow elevated and we shot out of the harbour like, 'A natural mystic blowing in the wind.'

The trip back was extremely unpleasant. The engine was loud and smoky and, although we were running inside the reef, the rasta craft bounced and banged in a syncopated motion from one small wave to the next. I was just praying that the engine didn't fail as we would have no means of getting ashore. Half way we changed fuel containers and Heru opened the whiskey. (I privately complimented myself on only buying half a bottle). Nonetheless, the ordeal was without accident and the little speed boat moored at Agats just as the light dimmed. The 91 nautical mile journey had taken us seven hours; *Tawali Pasana* took 37 hours of sailing over the same distance. When I returned to the canoe, Justin and Sanakoli were hanging out with some new friends and listening to Indonesian *Dandut* music from Justin's new white and orange boombox. (*Dandut* is a fusion of Arabic chanting, Bollywood cat-a-wailing and Malay melodies set to a thumping tabla drum beat.)

In the morning, I transferred the new promotional video to Justin and Sanakoli's phones. They loved it, not least because it presented both of them in a very complimentary fashion. I had also bought us some equipment to help survive the crocodile congested swamps — three Indonesian military bayonets that I had bought in an army disposal shop in Timika. Justin and Sanakoli loved them too. Justin first tried to see if one would sit on his lower leg and then on his hip. Sanakoli took out the long black blade and said, "That's the one. If crocodile take us, we..." he made a stabbing motion and said, "Hit it in the eye." We agreed to wear these knives in our belts at all the times. Our conversation then turned to the route ahead; I unfolded the map and measured with the dividers. "We are leaving tomorrow. From here on we have about 300 nautical miles to Merauke, which is the last town before the border with PNG."

"The weather how?" Justin asked.

"The weather seems to have turned against us already but let's see if we can make it to PNG before it gets too bad," I said. The sailors nodded.

Negotiations in the men's house

We didn't see any sign of Heru that morning. As I was doing the last of the shopping in the afternoon, I got a call from him. "Where are you now?" he asked slurring his words. "We must meet the elders in the longhouse and talk about money for stay here," he mumbled. I agreed, while reminding him that we had already paid but he didn't seem to be listening and hung up. This was the last thing we needed. I was so fed up with this place and couldn't wait to get out of there.

That evening I was introduced to Basil, a young Papuan man with an innocent-looking square face and eyebrows angled in a such a way as to give his eyes a look of perpetual worry, or wonder. It was easy to tell from his short physique that he wasn't from these parts, in fact, he was here as a student and originated from a village bordering PNG, hence his English was very good. "This is our new brother," Sanakoli explained, while pearls of sweat dripped from his forehead. Sanakoli's brown skin had almost toned to grey and I thought that the malaria had finally caught up with him.

"Hey, Sanakoli are you all right, you look sick," I asked in a worried tone.

"No, no." Sanakoli said, with a serious frown opening his red mouth, "We are chewing." I couldn't help but laugh, and then I looked at poor Basil who had pearls of sweat on his underdeveloped beard while his jaws were working double time to keep up with his new role models.

I asked if they had seen Heru and was told he hadn't been seen since the morning. I started to think this might be for the best. Then I asked Justin and Sanakoli if they thought we could push the canoe down ourselves. Sanakoli spat a thick red spelch of *pinang* saliva onto the ground and answered, "Hard work but we can do it. You don't pay them. We already pay them too much." 'That's for sure,' I thought and asked Basil to go into the longhouse with me as an interpreter.

"But I'm not from here," Basil tried to explain nervously.

"But you speak *Bahasa*, you'll do great," I said with exaggerated enthusiasm, patting him encouragingly on the shoulder.

The longhouse was an elongated hut about 30 metres in length on strong posts two metres above ground. It had no windows but several openings on both sides that let in air and light. The tall roof was thatched with sago leaves. This was a house for the men only; here they could socialise and live. If women entered, they would get sick, I was told. The night was dark and warm and we climbed up a wide ladder of old poles.

By the entrance sat a wood carver who had carved on our canoe earlier in the day. I told him that Heru had called us for a meeting with the Chief, now that we were to leave tomorrow. Basil translated the answer, "Heru is out drinking beer." We were then invited inside. There were several dim lanterns illuminating the large dark medieval-looking space that smelled of smoke and swamp. Groups of men were sitting around candle lights talking and working. I took off my muddy shoes and walked across the floor that was covered in palm mats. From the cross beams above us hung *bilums*, pieces of cloth and plant matter.

We were led to an audience with the Chief and three elders. The men told us to sit straight next to each other in front of them, and we obeyed like schoolchildren. The men were sitting in a straight line as well. Between us were a couple of candles that illuminated the men from below and made the folds in their skin and toned muscles look as rugged as the bark of an old mangrove. There was a pause of silence. Outside, the frogs were croaking. Somewhere down in the hut, a man coughed. Then one of the elders said some words and Basil translated. "You have a long way to go. If you give a donation to the gods, we will make sure they protect you all the way to Merauke." I thought, 'These men may not be head-hunters anymore but they sure know how to bleed me for cash.' I dug into my pocket and laid a 50,000 rupiah banknote in front of them. One of the elders studied the bill gravely and then nodded to confirm that it was an adequate amount. Then he tilted forward and started chanting in the Asmat language. The prayers floated in the stagnant air of the longhouse, rose the dust in the cross beams and rippled up through the canopy of spiderwebs and dead sago leaves. The town with its concrete roads, iron railings and electrical scooters were gone, as if it had never been.

When he finished, we all sat in silence until I took my cue to talk. "We thank you for your prayers and for protecting us, and for helping us on this journey." The men listened to Basil's translation with folds in their foreheads. I continued, "We wouldn't be able to travel around the whole island if it wasn't for the help of communities like yours. To show our appreciation, I have brought you these gifts." I then presented the Chief with a carton of cigarettes and a pouch of rough-cut tobacco together with a couple of bags of coffee and sugar. The men felt the presents, they looked pleased and I continued. "We apologise that we cannot give you a bigger present, but we have a long way to travel and no money left." The dark men in front of us seemed to digest my words and then the Chief smiled and Basil translated his words.

"They say they understand that you have travelled far and have long to go. They say thank you for coming all the way from Papua New Guinea to visit them — it is a very long way. They also say they will help put the canoe in the water." I was relieved to hear this. Then I had Basil tell the men that I was impressed by how strong the Asmat still were in their traditions, compared to many other villages we had visited. This seemed to please the old men who were now shifting their positions on the mats. They reached out smiling to shake hands. We were shown out and Basil looked grateful to be out of the house. As we climbed down the ladder he said, "I think it went well mister Thor."

I answered, "Thank you Basil, you are a much better translator than Heru." My heart was full of relief and I smiled too. It felt good to be leaving with a blessing from the Asmat instead of a bad spell or a spear in my back. And as we were soon to learn, there is something in the mud on this coast.

Chapter Twenty-three

Land of mud

The Dutch Captain Jan Carstensz, who explored this coast in 1623, had been ordered by the Dutch East Indian Company to investigate the reports of a 'Great South Land' (Australia) and whether it was connected to New Guinea. On his route from Ambon (Maluku Islands), he was to map the little-known southern coast of New Guinea and explore it, searching for anything of commercial value, including gold and spices. He was also ordered to bring back 'a couple of natives.' However, the tidal mudflats and treacherous shifting sandbanks made it hell to approach the coast in a sailing vessel. For a start, Carstensz risked running aground within a mile of the shore — at this point he would have a pinnace (small boat with sail and oars) launched.

When this small boat ran aground, his men would walk the remaining 100 metres through waist deep mud. When finally ashore, the party was attacked by hostile natives (all encounters along this coast were hostile). In the end, the sea became too shallow and Carstensz's two ships had to turn around and sail back out to open sea before they could continue southeast and explore the Cape York Peninsula. (He never did find out if the Great South Land was connected to New Guinea or not). Three hundred and ninety-four years later, *Tawali Pasana* was travelling the same expanse of estuaries, mud and mangrove but, with only 50 centimetres draft, she was perfect for this environment (and luckily, the inhabitants of the coast no longer greeted strangers with a hail of spears and arrows). Despite this, making landfall on this coast was still difficult, as we soon found upon arriving in the village of Bayun.

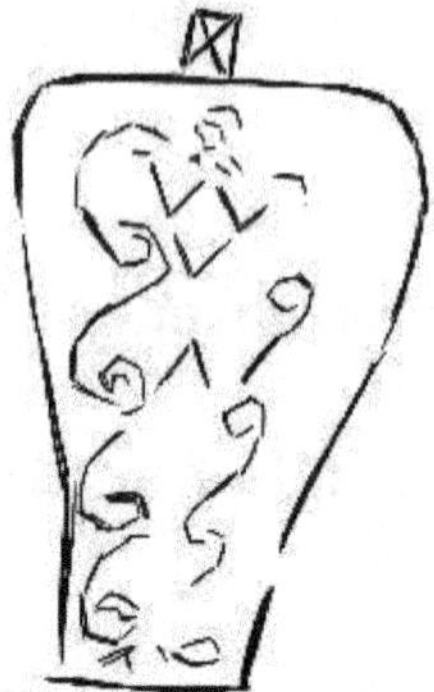

BAYUN

We approached at 9 a.m. as the tide was flowing out and continued towards the village until we ran aground. The distance to shore was still about 300 metres — of knee-deep vicious mire. The villagers didn't seem to mind and eagerly fought their way out to greet us with rolled-up trouser legs, pulling their feet out of the sludge with syncopated double sucking sounds. The first of them were invited on board. To clean themselves, they made a hole in the mud and allowed water to backfill, and then washed their feet and calves before jumping on deck. I gave them all cigarettes. Tobacco was introduced by Europeans and now almost everybody — well every man — in West Papua smokes, especially the Indonesians. I didn't smoke, but it was such an easy way to connect with people so I always had a carton on hand for that purpose.

As we were soon to learn, the tide plays a huge role in travel on the shores of the Arafura Sea. As the tide is produced by the gravitational pull of the moon, tidal patterns and water levels vary depending on location and seascape. In this part of New Guinea, tides rise and fall across six-hour intervals and each day the tide would come an hour later than the previous day, thus the whole cycle advanced an hour each day. This meant that we had two high tides every 24 hours. At 5 p.m., when the tide was at its highest, the canoe floated and we pushed it closer to shore. What we hadn't calculated on, was that next morning when we wanted to sail out on the tide, there wasn't enough water under the hull. This was because the night tide was higher than the morning tide. So, we then had to spend the whole day in Bayun waiting for the night tide at 6 p.m.

I took the opportunity to film the village, which was an eclectic jumble of traditional huts and wooden plank houses. The people were subsistence farmers and fishermen, as with most other remote communities in West Papua. Most of the women had their heads shaved (as I had also seen in old photos of the Asmat). The Chief was a sturdy man, also with a shaved head, and a big, full black beard. He was very friendly and invited us all to lunch. As we ate, blood-curdling screams were suddenly heard. A man was prowling up and down the main walking path with a bow and arrow ready to shoot. The Chief got his bow out with a handful of arrows and was standing by his house should the offender come too close. As I later learned, this yelling and threatening display was quite common when a man was angry or felt wronged.

As night fell and the fruit bats started to appear, we said goodbye and went back to the canoe ready to push off. But to our great surprise, the water had only risen by 10 centimetres, not nearly enough to raise *Tawali Pasana* out of the mud. What a bummer, we hadn't accounted for two factors when she was last afloat. The first was that there had been a powerful wind pushing water ashore and second, the moon was now waning, which meant less gravitational pull than the previous evening and, therefore, less tide. My heart sank at the thought of being stranded until the next full moon. We had to act quickly, so I ran back to the Chief's hut and he instructed his sons to alert the village. Soon we were all standing in the mud pushing the canoe. But the fine gooey silt was acting like a suction cup under the hull. The darkness was coming in just as fast as the water was running back out to sea. We started digging mud away from around the hull and then pushed with all our combined might. Nothing. One more time — the men yelled, "*Satu, dua, tiga*," (one, two, three). We all pushed so that the veins were protruding out of our necks but again, nothing.

It was like *Tawali Pasana* was cast in cement. We were hanging over the canoe huffing and puffing and people started to look back towards the shore. I cursed myself for not having foreseen this problem. Then a voice cut through; a short old man with a bucket hat and a green holed T-shirt was prying his shoulder onto the canoe. He yelled something inspirational. We wearily returned to our positions to for one final attempt. "S*atu, dua, tiga,*" we all hollered, and suddenly the canoe actually… moved. 'Go *Tawali Pasana*, go,' I thought and indeed she did. Gaining momentum, we all kept pushing in fear of her getting stuck again. Mud and water were spraying everywhere.

Finally, the canoe was afloat to the whoops and cheers of victory. We kept pushing outwards and jumped aboard when the sea was waist deep and we waved goodbye. Three teenage boys who were caught up in the spirit of things kept pushing as the villagers grew smaller in the twilight. The boys in the sea were hooting and laughing as if they couldn't imagine a better way to spend their Saturday night. After five minutes, the boys were chest deep in water. They bobbed up and had a cigarette while we hoisted the sail. I gave them all high fives, several packages of cigarettes and money to share with the community and left them laughing and grinning in the murky brown sea.

A strange coast

Expedition Log 7 May 2017

> 08:10 hrs. Wind changing, S to SE average 6-16 knots. The sky is as bland as the coastal vista. Here are few places to call in and the gill net poles are a constant hazard, especially at night.

At noon we passed a group of men standing ashore. They screamed and waved their long brown arms and shrieked at us, one started running out through the mud. I asked Sanakoli, "What's up with these people, do you think they need help?"

Sanakoli frowned, "These people are not good. You don't see other people act like this. They want trouble." He was probably right, good, there weren't enough water for their dinghy to reach us.

There hadn't been any 3G phone signal since Agats, but we could still keep our followers updated on Facebook. I spend a good hour every day on the satellite device sending text and low-resolution pictures to Sandy Robson by email. Sandy would then post them on my Facebook wall. It was a paradox, seeking to experience a far-flung corner of the globe and then spending so much energy on staying connected with the world. I really enjoyed being away from everything, soaking up the voyage but on the other hand, I felt a responsibility to share this wonderful adventure. Very few people would ever travel to such a coastline. It was long, flat, gritty and even hostile, but to the tribes living here it was home — a rich environment brimming with life, and not least mud, the ever so prevalent mud.

The silt washing out from inland was like a rich fondant full of all the jungle's best nutrients — a potent soup of bacteria, algae and other microbes — and the secret behind this evolutionary recipe was the change in tides. At low tide, UV-rays from the sun made the organisms in the mud multiply, rapidly. These tiny creatures then became food for worms, crustaceans and molluscs. The birds would be the first to dine on the invertebrates at low tide, and then as the tide rolled in and new nutrients were added, the 'rush hour' of fish dining on the critters of the mud began. Some of the big fish — catfish, barramundi, mulloway and shark, as well as the occasional crocodile — would be caught in gill nets and end up on the cooking fire. This environment was a true culinary treasure trove for those who could adapt to it, and it looked to have produced some very strong but also pretty wild people. My social media audience needed to see this fascinating place — indeed, what wasn't there to love about the mud.

As we came further south, the estuaries got bigger and wider. We were nearing the island of Yos Sudarso, which was actually a huge mangrove swamp and wetland area. The island is positioned under

New Guinea like the 'claws of the dragon' — and as we were soon to learn, those claws dig deep and won't let go. But now we had to choose what to do, either go around Yos Sudarso on the western ocean facing side, or else sail through the Muli Strait that divides the island from the mainland. We opted for the strait as we thought the open coast might give us too much trouble and the channel would be calmer with less headwind.

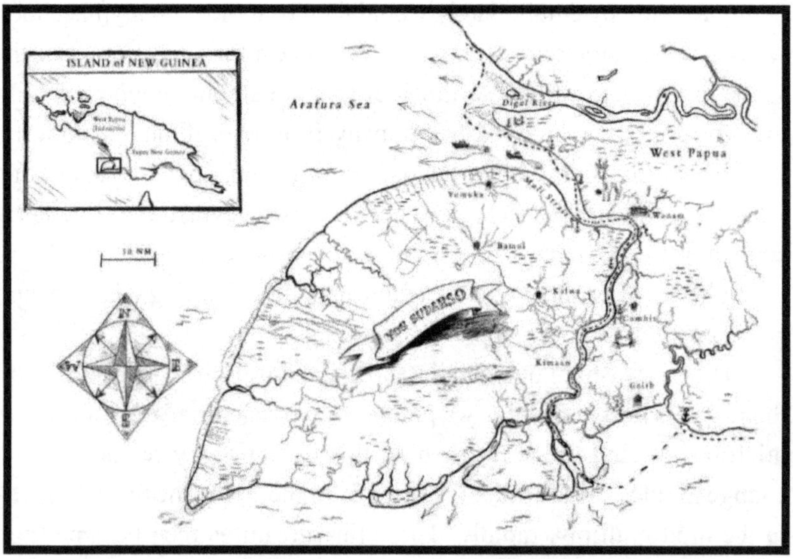

At the mouth of Digul River, we had to anchor. The tide was going down, which created a dangerously turbulent outflow. While waiting for the tide to turn, we cooked some rice and ate the last tin of fish. It was worrying that we were running out of protein, not that I hadn't bought plenty, it was just that we had been too generous when inviting people to dine with us. Our freshwater was also running low. We only had about seven litres of tank water from Bayun, and this had a fair number of wiggling mosquito larvae in it. After dinner, we studied the signal crabs on a mudbank, waving their claws to keep trespassers at bay, and the hermit crabs with their lustrous shells crawling around, oblivious to our presence. Sanakoli smiled and said, "In Basilaki, when we were small children, we would collect many of these crabs.

We would make small fences and play with them. We say they were our farm animals, cows, and chicken and pigs."

Four hours later, the tide was running in again and we sailed into the huge Digul River mouth. The crossing went well, although an accident that had been waiting to happen finally happened. During a *yaya-towa,* I accidentally kicked over our stove and one of the rusty spikes inflicted a painful gash on the side of my foot. I cursed the ridiculous piece of junk all the way to hell.

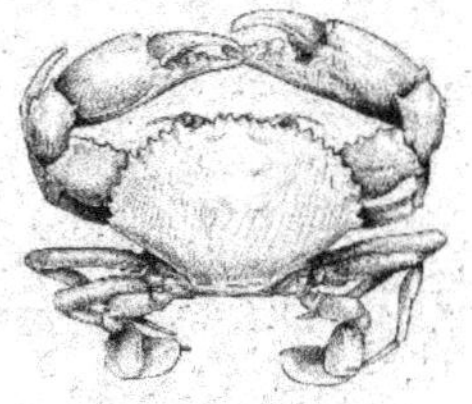

In the afternoon, we made landfall in a low hanging mangrove forest at the beginning of the Muli Strait. Some eight nautical miles across the water we could see Yos Sudarso, lying like a long olive slug. Past that, there was nothing but brown sea and a tall grey sky. The magnitude of this environment was daunting. "You tie off to that tree," Sanakoli instructed and I made a bowline knot around a young mangrove at the edge of the forest.

"Tide down, now time to look for protein." Justin said and we all jumped into the mud and immediately sank to our knees. Justin took his long harpoon, Sanakoli the saucepan, and I a camera. The first ten metres through the mud was difficult, and not least painful when stepping on submerged mangrove roots. As the forest closed in around us, the ground became denser and our bare feet only sank to the ankles. The hissing wind had died and the ambience of the forest engulfed us. It didn't take long before Sanakoli found a shallow pool and plunged both his hands in to it, and after a bit of fumbling pulled out a mud crab. "Ho, ho," he said in triumph. Bubbles came from the creature's mouthpieces as its pointy dark-green legs wiggled in mid-air. The claws looked thick and strong but Sanakoli expertly twisted the arms on the burger-sized crustacean and, with a crack, the crushing claws were pacified. Then it was put in the saucepan where it skated around on its eight legs. We foraged around for a while. I found a couple of mud crabs as well but just picked them up with the bayonet by stabbing them in the back shield.

The sun sunk under the clouds and coated the mud with a golden gloss. Justin was back on deck cleaning our catch — there was a whole pot full. "Hey Justin, what do you think of my catch?" I asked him.

He wrinkled his nose and pointed to the stabbing holes, "What is this, no good, you spoil them. Me, look, I get big ones." And he was right. A couple of his crabs were monsters, with claws as thick as my wrist. After a long boil, the feast was ready. It was divine; I could instantly feel the energy of the swamp pumping back into my shredded muscles. Justin and Sanakoli also slurped the yellow pulp of the organs. I had a go too but didn't like the bitter taste. The ones I had stabbed had their insides contaminated by mud and had to be discarded. Afterwards, we washed our hands with water from the hull, as that was the only clear water around. I used cold tea water to clean the wound on my foot the best I could and then disinfected it. It might sound daft to be running around in the mud for hours with a cut on your foot but the adventure was well worth the risk of an infection — not to mention the great film footage.

Expedition Log 10 May 2017

10:44 hrs. The Muli Strait is huge, much bigger than anticipated. With only 35 nautical miles to Wanam, we should be there in a day but progress is slow. The wind is straight at our nose and so is the current. When the tide is low, the current is too strong for travel; when the tide is high, the current subsides but the wind increases in velocity and we get waves. It doesn't bode well.

Expedition Log 11 May 2017

06:17 hrs. The canoe is resting on the flats. The tide will come in around noon.

We spotted a couple of wooden dinghies further up the coast and decided to investigate whether the owners had some water. The north shore of the strait was all grey sand and out in channel we could see several wooden fishing boats, anchored like ducks on a row, in the strong outgoing current. As we walked up along the beach, we noticed several dead fish had washed up, barramundi and another species I didn't recognise. "Huh, what is this?" Sanakoli exclaimed looking offended. "Good size fish, why so many on the beach?" As we walked, we saw more and more. We came by a camp with a couple of Papuan families. They had made elevated shelters behind the first tree line and the jungle. They immediately welcomed us and offered us all cigarettes. A young man with short dreadlocks and a clean Band-Aid over his dark forehead was the most outspoken. His name was Mickey, and he explained that they were collecting mud crabs and hunting deer. He took me to his wooden dinghy, in it were two deer, gutted and cut in half. In the bottom was also a net full of mud crabs. He explained that the deer would fetch 20.000 rupiah per kilo of meat. Individual mud crabs would range in price from 5.000 to 15.000 rupiah, depending on the size of the crab. They were going to sell their catch in Wanam. I asked him why they didn't fish and all the men got upset. Mickey explained they had been out-competed by the Javanese fishing vessels in the strait — the very ones I had seen in the current. I later learned the full story behind this.

There had once been a Chinese ice factory in Wanam, stocking and exporting fish from the rich waters around Yos Sudarso. But the factory was shut down by the Indonesian Government because of tax fraud. This meant that the local tribes could no longer sell their fish in Wanam, instead Javanese fishing vessels had moved in, undercutting the price. The problem was that there weren't any cooling systems on these boats. So, to get the most profit out of their time at sea, the Javanese would catch barramundi and mulloway, cut out the swim bladder called *gelumbung* and throw the fish overboard, as the *gelumbung* could fetch a much higher price when dried and sold as Chinese medicine. These vessels wouldn't fill their stockroom with anything but bladders until they decided to sail for a harbour where they could sell their fresh catch the same day. This explained why perfectly good fish were drifting ashore and why the locals had turned to hunting deer and crab.

Micky asked if we would like some fresh deer heart. The thought of red meat made me salivate. I nodded and said, "*Terima kasih banyak*," (Thank you very much). He then had his wife dice them up and cook a spicy stew. While the pot was boiling, he took me into the forest to explained how they hunted. It was very simple. They would go out in the night with flashlights, when they came across a deer, they would mesmerise it with the beam. A man with a bush knife would then run up and dispatch the animal. The hunters would mark the spot and continue the hunt. At the end of the night they would back track, collect the carcases and carry them back to camp.

We said goodbye to Micky and his family as the tide started to ripple in. I didn't ask them for water as they had very little themselves. As a goodwill gesture, I tried to give them a couple of packages of cigarettes but they laughed and explained that they got them for free from the Javanese fishermen. Justin was gifted two packages while I was handed our saucepan back with a steaming heart stew and a stack of boiled mud crabs. As soon as we got on board, the food was greedily devoured.

We didn't cover many miles though. The wind soon picked up and, after jig-*jagging* the headwind for a couple of hours, the sail was pulled down and we took refuge in a small bay of mud. The stew was long gone, so as soon as the tide dropped, we went out to find some more protein. It didn't take much poking around before I spotted a big mud crab under a root.

"Hey Sanakoli, there's one here. Please come and tell me how to catch it," I yelled with great enthusiasm.

Sanakoli came over, "You see the claws are resting by the what, belly, so you push down on the back and put your hands, so it cannot move the claws out."

I squatted and got ready, and then asked, "What happens if it bites you?"

"Oh," he said, "It destroy your fingers, I have seen many accidents, so dangerous."

'That was a pretty stupid thing to ask,' I thought to myself, as my hands neared the heavily weaponised animal. Nonetheless, now that I had decided to catch it, there were no room for hesitation. I stuck my hands in, pushed down and closed my fingers around the body and lifted it out of the water. Success! As I was about to revel in the triumph of man over crustacean, I felt a stinging pain — it wasn't the claws but the legs. They were as sharp as knives and were piercing the thick skin of my palms.

"Damn those legs hurt," I complained.

Sanakoli chuckled, "He he, now you take the arms and twist them." I complied and a cracking was heard as one of the arms broke off while the other was immobilised.

"That's all right," Sanakoli said patiently. I stuck the claw in my pocket and then he showed me how to fix the pointy legs by sticking them into the joints of the opposite leg until all legs were connected in pairs and the crab was hanging upside down like a basket.

Expedition Log 12 May 2017

13:00 hrs. Departure. Headwind.

16:00 hrs. Arrival Yos Sudarso. We have only covered eight nautical miles in three hours. Anchored in a narrow river, so good to be out of the relentless wind. Sanakoli has left with three fishermen on a dinghy to a nearby village somewhere in the swamp.

It was 7 p.m. and Sanakoli still hadn't returned, our throats were dry and hopefully he would return with fresh water. The night was calling from all sides but most dominant was the awful Euro dance music coming from Justin's boombox, "To scare the snipers away." To help further, he had tied a bright light onto the mast illuminating the whole canoe.

I started on a new course of antibiotics. My foot had begun to swell, the swamp was really thriving inside of me and I suspect our lack of food and clean drinking water hadn't helped. I should probably see a doctor soon. Finally, we saw the light of Sanakoli's dinghy.

As we awoke the next morning, we found ourselves at the 'V' bottom of the almost empty creek with mudbanks towering over us on both sides. Justin looked red-eyed. "Did the sand flies also keep you up?" I asked.

He rocked a bit and then said, “I don’t sleep, there is a lady who spoils me.” Is it one of the mothers?” I asked intrigued.

“No, she is here, she is a witch, I know her,” he replied with a frown of disgust.

“That doesn’t sound good but is she a live person?”

“Yes, but very strong. She is from Basilaki, she send spells for me.” He dusted some dried mud off his calf and said, “I can do magic too but sometimes she is stronger.” Apparently, the witch had been haunting Justin since we entered the river; he was looking exhausted — this strait had really taken a toll on him.

We fried some green bananas and boiled Sanakoli’s Yos Sudarso water that looked like tea and smelled of compost. It helped to mix sugar in the water, although it couldn’t really cover the awful taste. Both Justin and I jested about the doubtful water-finding skills of Sanakoli, who defended himself by saying, “You always ask for *dirty watar*, and now you complain when I bring you the real *dirty watar*!” Our tired bodies heaved with laugher.

At 10 a.m., the brown tide finally filled the creek and we sailed back out on a nautical race track of current and wind. It was a hard day of sailing but we could now see the harbour of Wanam in the bend and were determined to get there. “Oh, when will this river end,” Sanakoli said while balancing on the wet deck of the bouncing canoe.

“Yeah, surely the current must turn to our favour at some point,” I answered from the hull. I was bailing while awkwardly resting my infected foot on the deck. The wind rose to 22 knots and created some very difficult waves in the middle of the strait, nonetheless, we made it ashore. It had taken us three days to cover the 35 nautical miles from the entrance of Muli Strait to Wanam — and we weren’t even half way through.

Wanam was a wonderfully weird harbour. There were several tall wharves; the biggest had a fleet of rusty Chinese trawlers berthed. And in front were dozens of Javanese-style wooden fishing boats anchored. To the left there was a waterfront built on incredibly high stilts, with long narrow boardwalks in between. It looked like wild west town meets a kung fu movie — on stilts. Both Papuans and Indonesians had gathered to see us come in through the ripping waves. The first thing I did was to give a kid money to go fetch us some cold sodas. We must have looked thirsty because the bystanders yelled at him encouragingly as if his task were of the greatest importance. Soon the boy returned and we immediately emptied the cans. He then showed me up to the police station. The visit went well, but meeting the Indonesian Navy was a different story.

The Commander was a stern Indonesian man with an authoritarian moustache who didn't speak English — but one of his junior officers did. His name was Yanto. He was in his 20s, had a clean face and well-combed hair and seemed friendly enough — at first. While running through my papers, Yanto skimmed an outdoor magazine article about my journey, where I was described as, 'A Danish filmmaker.' His finger stopped abruptly on the filmmaker title. I thought, 'Dammit, why didn't I remove that article.'

"Mr Jensen, are you making a film? Do you have a permit?" Yanto interrogated me. An electric-shock of adrenaline surged through my body — but I stayed cool and laughed — nervously.

"No, no. I just make videos for Facebook."

"So, no permit?" Yanto continued, leaning his head to the side while looking me straight in the eye.

"Oh, you can't make a film here, it would be too dangerous," I replied, making an innocent grimace as if to indicate that it would be the most ludicrous thing in the world to do.

I then paused and pretended to look thoughtful. "But I might write a book about the expedition," I smiled, trying to keep up my cheerful countenance, suppressing my frayed nerves while feeling dizzy with fever. I took this as a chance to change the conversation. "Excuse me Sir but is there a hospital nearby? I have a bad infection in my foot." The two men discussed something in Indonesian.

Yanto then turned and smiled, "Mister Jensen, the hospital is old, but I will take you to a good doctor." I smiled back and thanked him but the next two things the officer said made me even more nervous than before. “It is not safe where you have your boat. You can anchor in front of the navy station. We also have a room where you can sleep.” I smiled, feigning the impression of being overwhelmed by the generosity of the Indonesian Navy. I thanked the Commander and Yanto heartily, while wishing I could go back into the mud.

Chapter Twenty-four

Naval Intelligence

I woke on a hard-wooden bench in time to catch the first morning light stream through a gap in the plank wall. My foot felt a lot better — the swelling was going down. I was in the navy base and I could hear army boots squeaking on the wooden floor. I crawled out of the mosquito net, put on my pants and staggered into the front room (it was so good to be wearing dry clean clothes). My movements woke one of the Special Forces guys nicknamed 'Sniper,' who had been snoozing on a camp bed in front of my door-less room. Next to him was a narrow table with a radio, binoculars and a rack of charging walkie-talkies. On the wall there was a poster that proclaimed: 'Indonesian Navy — The New Spirit.' It was written in both *Bahasa* and English. Underneath was a list of the Navy's core values, also in both languages. The room had a big open window and in front was a wide wooden deck on four-metre-high stilts (like the base). Beyond the elaborately painted main gate, the town folks of Wanam were walking past on the boardwalk overlooking the Muli Strait. I couldn't see the top of *Tawali Pasana's* mast, even though she was berthed out in front — the tide was too low.

We were guests of the Indonesian Navy, not that I felt I had much of a choice. And I still hadn't figured out if it was out of generosity or to keep an eye on us — it was probably both. I was paranoid that they suspected me of making a film without a permit and, thus, were going to have us deported — or worse. But so far, they hadn't gone through our belongings. If they did, they would find all my cameras and audio recorders and, even worse, my hard disks with all my precious recordings from Agats.

The safest way of securing my recordings was to post them to my friend in Denmark, as I had been doing since the start of the expedition. But Wanam was a very small place and, if there is one thing that spreads like wildfire in small places, it is word of mouth. I feared that the authorities would soon hear if I tried to send a hard disk out. Instead, I kept one on my person and another was hidden in a waterproof box in the bow of the canoe. I reckoned that the best course of action was to keep a low profile, be agreeable and get out of Wanam as quickly as possible. On a positive note, the Navy had the most guns and the most equipment and the most soldiers, so they were the highest authority in these parts, thus, being under their care meant that no one else would give us any trouble.

As I was studying the poster, the Commander walked in with his stiff posture, short cropped hair cut and clipped mustachio. He had a cup of coffee in his hand. I greeted him, "*Selamat pagi Bapak*," (Good morning Sir) and pointed excitedly to the poster and one of the core values — namely, *Dedikasi* (Dedication) — and said, "*Dedikasi, baik — penting*," (Dedication is good — important). The Commander nodded and pointed at me and then said the word '*Keberanian*,' (Courage).

"You… courage," he said in halting English. I objected with modest laughter and he smiled approvingly. Yanto then invited me to have breakfast in the mess hall, which was a small building (also on stilts) behind the main barracks. There wasn't room for more than eight people. We had rice and chicken with four Marines. They were all very friendly and interested in our journey but just as interested in how cold Denmark was, and if there were any polar bears. I answered the best my *Bahasa* allowed. (There aren't any polar bears in Denmark). In return, I learned that they all came from Java, where their wives or girlfriends remained. Yanto was a radio operator who dreamt of working for Naval Intelligence but he needed to improve his English first so he was more than happy to talk with me.

After breakfast, I checked on Justin and Sanakoli. They were with a group of new friends who brought them food and *pinang,* and a 12-

pack of plastic water bottles. When I had Sanakoli one-on-one, I repeated what I had told him and his brother the night before — "Don't show them any of our videos." With the crew in good hands, I got back under the mosquito net. I needed to find a way to get some cash because the only bank in Wanam wouldn't take my credit cards. But first I needed to rest my foot.

I had barely dozed off when Sniper came into my room. He wanted to show me some pictures on his phone. He was a bit awkward about it. I guess he was one of those people who didn't have a good understanding of personal boundaries. They were all pictures of men in camouflage kit, with guns on parade. Then there were videos of a sniper shooting even bigger guns. I have never really been into that training to kill other people stuff but of course I told him that his pictures were, "Cool." There was one photo though that made me smile. It was the picture of a three-metre crocodile basking in the mud under the stilts of our barracks. I asked Sniper if he shot the animal? He laughed and said, "*Tidak, tidak, buaya tidak makan orang — makan anjing*," (No, no, the crocodile doesn't eat people — it eats dogs). We both laughed. Apparently, the great beast would come in once in a while and snatch one of the scrawny dogs poking around in the trash at low tide. I reminded myself to warn my crew mates of this and soon slumbered off again.

In the afternoon, I had a disturbing experience that exposed the dynamics between Papuans and Indonesians. I was returning from an unsuccessful attempt to withdraw money, when a big Papuan man was pulled in on the deck in front of the navy base. The man was senselessly intoxicated. He was immediately thrown onto the crude planks while three soldiers yelled and pointed their rifles at him. People gathered on the walkway to witness the spectacle, most of them

Papuans. The Commander with the moustache came out and started scolding the man, pushing him around with his boots and slapping him with a sandal. The drunk was using his arms to protect his drooling face, all the time moaning. The Marines then lifted him up by the hair and threw a bucket of water at his face. I thought to myself, 'What is the purpose of beating up this poor man?' The only upside was that he was so completely wasted that he probably couldn't feel anything.

This whole scene — a crowd of dark-skinned people watching a few Indonesian soldiers rough up a big Papuan — was such a strong image. I thought about what it would take for the crowd to riot against the base. But I didn't detect any anger amongst the onlookers. Then one of the soldiers released the safety catch of his assault rifle as if he were getting ready to shoot. I heard the 'click.' He looked around. A wave of fright went through the crowd. Then it hit me; this was a display of power, a signal to the locals about who was in charge. That same night, I learned the whole story. The drunken Papuan had run amok. When his brother tried to stop him, the drunkard stabbed him in the arm and the Navy were called to sort it out. Later in the evening, the drunkard's mother, wife and sisters petitioned the Commander for his release. After the Commander had spoken some stern words to the women, they were allowed to see the prisoner and the next morning I saw the man stagger out of the base — sporting what looked like a bad hangover.

I was more than ready to get out of Wanam. I hadn't been able to buy many provisions as I couldn't get cash from the bank. I invited Yanto for an early lunch at a restaurant to thank him for taking me to the doctor on the day of my arrival. As we were having our rice and fish, Yanto looked as if he had something on his mind and then cautiously said, "Thor can I ask you something?"

I smiled and said, "Yes, of course."

He continued. "In Denmark, are you famous?"

I laughed (trying to disguise my discomfort) and said, "Not really."

"But are you in many documentary films?" He wanted to know. I started to feel very uneasy as I thought the interrogations were over — or maybe he was asking as a civilian? Or a friend? I had spent two days with this guy and he was a nice person. My graffiti exploits had put me in police custody more than a few times. This had taught me to deny everything — never give the interrogator anything to work with. Nonetheless, I was straight with him. I thought, in this instance, this would serve me better. I truthfully said that I had only made some kayak films that I had won a couple of prizes but only people who kayaked might know who I was. This information made him sit up straight. I thought he was about to dig deeper into my film work. Instead he kindly offered to lend me 300.000 rupiah so we could buy provisions. Phew!

Three hours later, the canoe was ready to launch. The wind was gusting at a blustery 24 knots, but I was eager to get moving. Most of the military personnel, as well as Justin and Sanakoli's new friends, came down to bid us farewell. The Commander gave me a long-sleeved green commando shirt as a present from the Force. I was really pleased with this, not only for his kind intentions but also because it might win the favour of Military Intelligence in Merauke — the shirt would be my 'social camouflage.' I put it on and we all took selfies and said goodbye.

Expedition Log 16 May 2017

12:00 hrs. Departing camp mud bank (high tide). Changing winds 6-15 knots.

14:47 hrs. The current has changed! We are running with the river at 6 knots of speed without a sail.

18:00 hrs. The wind came back 15-27 knots. Strong current against us.

19:00 hrs. Berthing on the mud by Cumbis lighthouse. Looks like a trade station.

Cumbis was indeed an odd place — and the dark night didn't make it look less so. The station consisted of a couple of ragged old buildings connected by rotten boardwalks, with several planks missing. A man from the island of Maluku was running a small trade store there, where Papuans from the inland and Yos Sudarso came to sell their mud crabs and buy commodities like rice, plastic buckets, fishnets and bush knives. We all went to bed exhausted but we didn't get much sleep though; a heavy thunderstorm broke, which pulled and ripped our tarpaulin so that the hailing rain even reached our sleeping bags. Soon we were cold and miserable. We finally fell asleep, although it wasn't for long. I woke with an odd sensation that I had felt on the north coast. I looked out from the tarp and saw the silhouette of the trade station floating by. No wait — we were the ones floating! We had forgotten to tie off the canoe before we went to bed, because it had been resting on the mud. I woke up my companions and we paddled the canoe back in and tied it to a pillar.

At dawn we paddled back out again. There was no wind and the current was slack, instead the river was covered in an odd dirty fog, like smoke rising from wet embers. When the current started to run against us, Justin jumped on land with a rope over his shoulder and began pulling the canoe along the clay-like shore, while Sanakoli and I were paddling. But soon the tide became too strong and we lashed the canoe to a tree trunk sticking out of the river. Justin walked into the bush. Meanwhile Sanakoli and I started cooking breakfast. I noticed that the tide was going down rapidly, so I pushed the canoe further from the bank, and then asked Sanakoli, "Hey Sana, shouldn't we put the canoe on the outside of this tree trunk, or else we will get stuck in the mud."

Sanakoli shook his shoulders and said in a matter of fact way, “You don't worry. It’s all right here.” I didn’t feel good about it but I went back to cooking.

As the rice was boiling, I noticed that the platform wasn’t rocking anymore. “Hey Sana. We’re stuck!” I yelled and jumped onto the bank and started pushing on the outrigger that was now standing in the clay.

Sanakoli answered with a tired indifference. “Maskim, it’s too late, nothing we can do.”

I was pushing desperately and raised my voice. “What are you talking about? We’ll be stuck here all day, come help.”

Sanakoli got up and made a half-baked attempt to push out with the *towe* but the canoe was stuck. “Nothing we can do,” Sanakoli repeated, shrugged his shoulders and got back into his seat. I climbed onto the canoe.

I had had enough of this channel and I was furious that Sanakoli now seemed to be working against me, “Man, I asked you if we should move the canoe — come on, you are the expert sailor.” I was boiling inside, but Sanakoli just ignored me so I continued, “You are supposed to know this stuff.”

“That is just an accident, now we sail in the afternoon,” he answered clearly annoyed himself. I was at my wits end. I desperately tried to control my frustrations over Sanakoli’s obvious indifference. I had to vent out somehow, so I put my head back and let out a long and loud “AAAAAAAARGH.” I was yelling at the mud, the jungle and the sailors who still didn't have a clue about why we were undertaking this journey.

After my lungs were empty and all nearby birds had left their branches, Justin came out of the bush with a cigarette in his mouth, looking curiously at us. “Hi Justin, we are stuck in the mud — again,” I said with a sour frown while squinting my eyes at Sanakoli.

“Stuck, hey?” Justin puffed. He looked around and picked up a three-metre-long log and carried the brutal piece of wood to the canoe and jerked it between the outrigger and the clay. He then leaned his shoulder onto the log and slowly pried the canoe free of the bank.

Seconds later, we were afloat. "Thank you, Justin," I said aloud. We then tied the canoe to a dead tree in deeper water and got back to our breakfast.

I offered Sanakoli a plate but he said he wasn't hungry, and we didn't' talk after this. I tried to reconcile with him but he just answered, "I don't like the way you treat us, in next town, what, Merauke, I go home."

That comment made me defensive and I burst out, "Treating you badly? I am giving you the adventure of a lifetime. You should be thanking me every day!" We didn't talk after this. That same evening, we anchored where the channel divided into two estuaries and ran into the sea. Sanakoli had been moody all day but as we were passed by an Indonesian fishing-boat with an abnormally banana shaped bow, we all started joking about it.

Sanakoli said, "Oh I feel sorry for the captain that has to steer such ugly boat."

I answered, "Yes it looks like a banana with a house on top."

Sanakoli laughed and said, "They must have eaten too many bananas when building it." We all shook our heads at the dreadful thing.

I was woken in the early morning hours by Justin and Sanakoli paddling the canoe; we were on our way out through one of the estuaries. Two hours later, we saw the sun rise over the ocean for the first time in eight days — that was how long it had it taken us to sail and paddle a mere 88 nautical miles through the Muli Strait. The strong light and the fresh air from the ocean felt liberating, and from here on, we only had 108 nautical miles to Merauke, the last town before the PNG border. Justin seemed happy to be out in the open too, but Sanakoli, who I thought had softened up, looked even more sour than the day before.

After an hour of spitefulness, I realised I had to do something about the bad mood onboard. I couldn't let it grow as it had done with Job. I decided to offer an apology. It was hard to build up the nerve to do so, especially because I didn't think he deserved it, but it was more important that our tree trunk continued sailing with good energy. I sat myself next to him and said, "Hey Sanakoli, I am really sorry that I got frustrated yesterday, you didn't deserve that." I started to choke up, like it had unlocked a hatch and now all sorts of built-up emotions were washing over me. "You have been working so hard, and you are such a good sailor. I am really proud to be on this adventure with you." Tears were rolling down my cheeks.

As Sanakoli heard these words his stern old mug melted like butter. "That's all right," he said clearly moved. And we didn't talk about that incident again.

With *Tawali Pasana* out of the Muli Strait mud, travelling went faster although at times the wind would be blowing straight against us. When there were such conditions, we would sail as close to the wind as possible. This led us far out from the coast where the waves became too big, then we came about or *yaya-towa* (as the sailors called it when turning the canoe) and sailed inwards until we neared the beach, and then we made a new *yaya-towa* and sailed back outwards. It was hard work. The coast had also changed. The mud had given way to grey flat sand beaches with an impressive tidal difference. When coming ashore, we found long grasses, broad-leaved paperbark trees and tall eucalyptuses — very much like the Australian bush. This wasn't that odd given we were nearing the Torres Strait that, 10,000 years ago, was a land bridge connecting New Guinea with the Australian continent.

After five days, we reached Merauke on 24 May at 11 a.m. Merauke is a large city of nearly 90,000 people. It is long and flat and situated on the south side of the entrance to the Maro River. We sailed up the river, which had several channel markers; one of them was a half-sunken rusty wreck, which now had a red lantern positioned on top. We desperately needed a break, as we were all puffy-eyed from lack of sleep and the waterlogged outrigger was gasping to come ashore and dry out. I was also rather nervous; this was the last potential ordeal we could face before we were out of the grip of the Indonesian bureaucracy.

We had been warned that Merauke had a lot of military personnel protecting the Indonesian southern border, not least against weapon smugglers coming from Australia or PNG to supply the OPM. I was worried they would search us, so I divided my camera gear into different boxes and places. I had also departed with a defective audio-recorder, a corroded microphone and some other equipment I never really used. But this wasn't all I had to consider. Our visas were due for renewal and our cruising permit would expire within six days. And finally, there was the weather. Paul had sent me an email the day before, warning that it looked like the south-easterlies were finally manifesting themselves. This meant three months of 15-24 knot winds straight against us — much worse than the Northwest Monsoon that almost knocked us out of the game. Everything told me that we had to get across the border as quickly as possible.

In the same instance, I heard Justin fumble with the rudder behind me and then grab at my shoulder. I turned around and saw him fall into the sea. I reached out but his hand slipped and he disappeared in our wake. I instantly slacked the sail, nonetheless the canoe started turning to the wind which would tip us over. Sanakoli yelled, "Quickly get the rudder" but he had already picked it up. Seconds later, he dug it in and got us stable. I threw out a line and Justin swam up to it. I pulled both he and the rudder onboard.

"What happened?" I asked. Justin checked if he still had his precious *bagi* necklace around the neck, then he giggled with embarrassment and wiped his face.

"I don't tie the *yabby yabby* to the outrigger, so when I lose balance I say, eh, nothing to hold me and I fall."

"Bugger! We'll have a rest soon," I reassured him.

As the big fishing harbour came into view, we noticed a dinghy approaching us at high speed. It was an Indonesian Navy dinghy in camouflage. When the soldiers saw me they started making hectic gestures and yelling commands at us. The dinghy came up on our side and they ordered us to come with them — immediately. I explained, "*Tidak ada Johnson*!" (We do not have an outboard engine). One soldier turned around for a second, obviously thinking about what to do, and then he threw us a rope. We were pulled upstream until we reached the harbour. Here they berthed on the side of a big trawler. Then began the questions.

Chapter Twenty-five

Run for the border

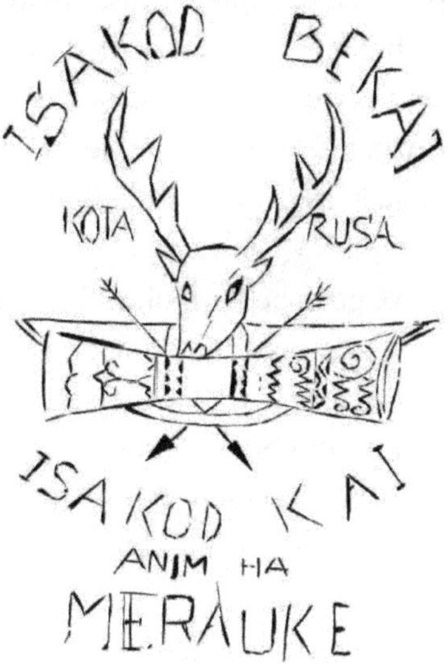

In Merauke, there are a large number of authorities serving to protect the border: the land, the sea, the town, the people and the fisheries — I know because I was questioned by all of them. There were the regular Police, the Property Police, the Sea Police, the Fisheries Police, the Military Police, the Navy, Customs, Immigration and the Harbour Master. In the beginning, the whole thing was pretty farcical because the two naval personnel who had taken us on tow clearly didn't know what to do with us. So, we were just berthed on the side of a local boat that was moored by the side of three giant Chinese trawlers that had been apprehended for illegal fishing and had been slowly disintegrating there for three years. This meant that all the eager officials wanting to investigate us had to climb across four ramshackled ships to get to *Tawali Pasana* which was minding her own business amongst the nets and fish offal. After a couple of hours, the humour of it all started to wear a bit thin and it became harder to keep up my positive façade. Nonetheless, I held out until sunset when the last group of bureaucrats dispatched their duties. Our well-presented papers and my army shirt must have done the job because none of them, not even the customs people, wanted to see what was in our canoe. It was just as Rob Goodfellow had said: 'Form over substance.'

Next morning, we got a better look at the place where we had been instructed to berth. It was on a mud bank on the inside of a massive concrete pier, and now that it was low tide, we could see that it was about ten metres tall. Although the whole area was protected by the fisheries, and we had been offered to use their toilet and shower, it wasn't ideal as the outrigger would get wet on every high tide — where the water rose a whopping five metres! There had also been rats on the canoe during the night — the place seemed to be teaming with the industrious rodents. I thought, 'To hell with this, let's just get stamped out and sail straight for the border with a heavy outrigger.' Our salvation came in form of a honking scooter. It was none other than Justin and Sanakoli's chewing protégé from Agats, Basil. He had come to Merauke a couple of days ahead of us (on one of the small ferries that connects the major towns along the coast) and was staying with his sister. This was perfect. With an interpreter, I would be able to get out of here in no time. So I hired him to take me on a run to the government offices.

The town was wide and flat with very few houses over two stories in height. But as we went from one closed office to the next, I realised it was some kind of a holiday and thus almost everything was closed. It looked like Merauke was going to be yet another delay — and so, we needed to take care of our outrigger there and then. One of the authorities who had interrogated us was the Property Police. The Captain was a very friendly man. One of his subordinates was a loudly spoken Papua New Guinean with red teeth, who had moved to Merauke in his youth. The Captain had given me his number in case we needed any assistance. I duly called them and they helped negotiate a relocation of the canoe with the Navy. They allowed us to move *Tawali Pasana* to a seaward beach where the outrigger would dry properly (and the rats wouldn't keep us awake at night).

A perpetually worried frown

Two days later, *Tawali Pasana* was resting by a naval beach post. But the canoe had barely been pulled ashore before two Indonesians in sharp looking shirts and sunglasses pulled up. It was the Naval Intelligence people, and now they started to look through our papers and ask all sorts of difficult questions. They hadn't heard that we had been allowed to move the canoe and found it suspicious. I had long ago burned all of my documents containing any words resembling 'film,' and was now complimenting myself on this. Then one of the officers, a handsome fellow with crocodile-skin shoes, crocodile-skin belt and a crocodile-skin case for his phone, asked me, "You have camera?" I had three, plus our phones — but of course I didn't tell him that.

Instead I said I had, "This," and showed him one of my GoPros.

"You show me," he ordered. I played one video after another of us monotonously sailing through waves, while excitedly telling about every minute detail of our technique. He soon completely lost interest and then pointed at Justin and Sanakoli "You two show me your phones."

This re-triggered my heart rate but my friends had been smart enough not to photograph any Free West Papua symbols or other suspicious things. The agents then both turned their attention to Basil — and they really put the squeeze on him. They took turns yelling questions at his face so he almost bent backwards while attempting to reply. After a five-minute screaming session, they eased up and left, with instructions that we weren't to leave and that they would check up on me and come back. I clapped poor Basil on the shoulder and said, "I'm really sorry you had to go through that my friend."

Basil looked at me with his big eyes and perpetually worried frown and answered, "Don't worry Mister Thor, they always do to me like this."

We had barely caught our breath before an even more unusual party arrived. It was the General himself — the most powerful military authority in West Papua. He was out on a jogging stroll with his personal staff of high-ranking officers. They were all in regulation track suits and were followed by a slow rolling convoy of black cars. The General was a fit man with ivory white teeth and the same mannerisms as the surf-obsessed character Lieutenant-Colonel Kilgore from the film *Apocalypse Now* — the one who said, 'I love the smell of napalm in the morning' — only an Indonesian version with a moustache. Of course, I tried to look my unshaved-ragged-barefooted best and greeted him politely. He inspected the canoe and then asked me some questions about the voyage. He laughed loud and hard at my answers and clapped me on the chin and told me that I was a, "*Remaja nakal" (*naughty boy)," but that I was also, "*Berani sekali"* (very brave). Afterwards, the other officers shook my hand. One of them even promised he would send a man by with some army rations for us, then they all got in their cars and drove off.

As things had finally quieted down, the commanding officer at the naval station laid out the rules in his broken English. "General say: You sleep in room in navy post. The canoe you cannot move. If you go for shopping, we drive you — you never go alone." So we were practically under observation, or protection, depending on how you looked at it. It felt like I had gone from the ashes in Wanam to the embers in Merauke. We were so close to being out of Indonesia — and now this.

I calmed my paranoia by rationalising that the Navy might think we were a good example to the troops, even an inspiration, as they were all about honour and bravery and that sort of thing. Now that we had practically made it all the way around West Papua, it would also make them look pretty bad if they stood in the way of our record attempt. They probably just wanted to get us out of Merauke without an accident or worse — an 'incident.' Nonetheless, the soldiers at the beach post did keep an eye on us — all the time. For that same reason, I kept my cameras, hard drives and laptop hidden, which stalled a lot of my work.

Reciprocity and touch phones

In the meantime, the southeasterlies started to blow and they blew hard. The sea was very shallow so the waves didn't grow tall, instead they grew sharp with short nasty intervals. I was standing on the beach with Sanakoli, looking at the rows of whitecaps rolling in. He said, "Oh this wind we call *Caluabu-bolime.* When it begin it will never rest, it will never give stop. It blow all the way to October." I agreed that it didn't look good but told him that we had to exit Indonesian territory. "We have a break when in PNG?" Sanakoli asked.

"Yes, just get us over the border. Then we can have a good rest and make a plan," I reassured him. I wasn't much for this whole 'break' thing. I knew that Sanakoli wanted to go home and see his wife. I had spoken with Justin, who had told me,

"Your man Sanakoli, he thinks too much on his missus. I tell him 'you go find a girl.'" Justin made a gesture in towards town with a great grin and continued, "Me, you don't see on the phone, calling my missus all the time." I couldn't help laughing at Justin's wonderfully pragmatic approach to things. "Me, when I sail, I sail. When home with my missus, I think of my missus," he concluded.

Despite the two brothers' different relationship philosophies, consumerism was definitely on their mind — they both wanted to shop for cheap Indonesian electronics to bring home to PNG. They had promised their wives a smartphone each and Sanakoli's Rachel also wanted a laptop. The brothers had also been given cash to buy some of their relative's cheap smartphones but those amounts weren't enough. This put my friends in a predicament, as relationships in their culture are very much based on reciprocity or rather reciprocity works to maintain relationships. Sanakoli was especially in an awkward quandary because a pastor from home had asked him to 'sponsor a touch-phone — only if he could afford it.' So Sanakoli had both traditional reciprocal obligations and the weight of the church on his shoulders. I advised them to give the cash back and give a small gift instead of sponsoring phones for the community.

Our efforts to bring this journey to the attention of the international media finally succeeded. An Australian journalist wanted to interview me live via Skype for ABC Australia. Finally, we were getting some international exposure. More exposure would mean more followers, more donations and, not least, bring our adventure to a wider audience. But as I stood in the navy post that morning, looking at one of the officers raising the Indonesian flag, I had second thoughts. Maybe international exposure of this scale would compromise us. We had been doing a good job of flying under the radar and avoiding any Indonesian press. What if this story blew up and my filmmaker title should appear in the news? Maybe I was just paranoid because I didn't trust the authorities. It was a hard call, but I concluded that it wasn't worth the risk. Getting the tree trunk back to Tawali was our first priority. I cancelled and apologised, saying I would be happy to do an interview on the other side of the border.

> *Expedition Log 6 June 2017*
>
> 11:00 hrs. Finally departing Merauke. Wind 'only' 18 knots (normal 22-26 knots). Still, the local fishermen warn us not to sail out but we have already checked out of the country. Distance to the border is approximately 60 nautical miles. With the wind

against us, we can do it in three days... or more. Canoe packed with consumer electronics and donated army rations.

Basil was there on the day of our departure. Luckily, the two Navy Intelligence guys hadn't returned as they had warned. To make up for all the hardship, I had made Basil a goodbye present — it was a certificate of appreciation. I had it framed and made an additional copy that he could use if he applied for a job or tried to get into medical school as he hoped. "But Mister Thor, how do I use the certificate," he wanted to know.

"You put it as part of your application. Remember there will be many people applying, some of them with better credentials than you, but you will stand out from all the rest as you helped make a world record. It says so right here on the certificate." Basil's perpetual frown eased and his face lit up.

"Thank you very much Mister Thor." I shook his hand.

"We are the ones thanking you Basil. Hopefully we'll meet again."

The sea was rough, the sailing tough and *Tawali Pasana* was carving hard into the wind. As afternoon closed in, the tide rose and the wind increased to a dangerous 26 knots in velocity. This was extreme sailing and we each had a role that matched our expertise. Justin was at the *yabby yabby*, Sanakoli worked the sail and I was bailing. We would tack outwards until the waves became too big, then Justin would yell, *'yaya-towa'* — then began a rapid secession of choreographed motions. Sanakoli handed me the sheet, he then ran to the bow and untied the flapping sail where he'd give me a look when ready. I'd throw the excess sheet into the sea and run towards his end as he walked the boom to the opposite end by pushing his feet against the strake, thus turning the whole sail.

This was the most dangerous time, as the sail and spars would be thrusting to and fro in the aggressively gusting wind. Justin would run after me with the big rudder under his arm and angle the outrigger windward, and then slacken the rigging if need be. I then pulled the sheet with all my might, groping for a carabiner on the sheet running freely between the boom and a shackle. I'd connect the carabiner to the canoe and then pull the sheet that ran through the shackle. The sail would expand and the canoe resumed its speed, again heading towards land. Sanakoli then ran to us and took over the sheet and I'd be back to bailing the hull. It was hard work that made your hands burn and arms ache. On one of these *yaya-towas,* we heard a loud bang from the yard and the sail ripped. We all looked at the mast as if waiting for something to break apart, but nothing happened and we resumed our wild ride for an hour or more before taking shelter in the shallows.

After we secured the canoe in the mud with the anchor and a couple of *towes,* Sanakoli called a meeting. The light was rapidly dimming. We were dressed in the yellow raincoats I bought from a hardware store in Manokwari. Sanakoli spoke, "Justin and I are concerned to the safety of this expedition, because we coming home safe is the most important. We cannot travel in wind like this. If we continue, we are gonna bump. You saw what happened today. It is too much." I agreed that the wind had been too strong. Then Sanakoli suggested that we'd go back to Merauke and fly home for two months until the worst of the winds had subsided. 'No chance in hell,' I thought, but instead explained that we had already stamped out of Indonesia. If we were to return to Merauke it would give us a lot of trouble — our visas and permits had expired — in fact, we would be arrested and then deported and then we would have to pay for flights. Sanakoli seemed to understand some of this. I then suggested that we sleep on it, go ashore in the morning and sew the sail, and then go back if the weather didn't allow us to travel.

That night I hardly slept. Sanakoli was right, this weather was insane. On one hand, I was responsible for the two sailors and I couldn't just insist on pushing on and ignoring their expert advice. On the other hand, it's also the job of a leader to inspire and push his men to achieve the extraordinary. My friends had already proven themselves beyond what any other known Milne Bay sailor had ever accomplished; they had mastered seas and situations they would never have encountered — or imagined — in their islands. Wasn't this one of those threshold moments that would make these sailors legends? Or was it the final blow that would sink *Tawali Pasana* and my dreams? It was a very difficult decision but, in the end, lying on the hard plank in the rocking canoe, I could envision us crossing that border. I decided we should push on, take it day-by-day and, if worse came to worst, we could always turn around and run back with the wind to Merauke with the snap of a finger.

The next morning, the sail was repaired and the yard inspected, with no sign of cracks. In the evening, the wind came down — a little — and we continued through the night. By morning, we had covered 14 nautical miles and anchored about half a mile off the coast. We were all exhausted and rolled up in our tarpaulins like burritos but the sea rose and the waves splashed into our shelters so we only got an hours' kip and had to continue.

The following day, we encountered such strong winds that the sail had to be lowered; there was no lee, so we pushed the canoe up along a mangrove coast littered with fallen trees, and walked about a mile in yeast coloured water with the bayonets swinging in our belts. The progress was made even slower by the mud on the bottom. Sanakoli, who was pulling in the front, yelled, "You watch your feet, sharp rocks here." At that very moment, I cut my toe on a rock — another infection was surely now due. This was prime crocodile habitat and I wondered if the animals could sniff out my blood but I reasoned that the reptiles probably wouldn't go out in these waves. We finally found shelter in a natural harbour of mangroves where a group of friendly Javanese fishermen had their camp, fishing for *gelumbung*.

We covered the tarpaulin over the canoe and got a break from the hissing wind. Justin had strong back pain and ate some paracetamol and went straight to sleep. I asked Sanakoli what he thought of the conditions and he answered grimly, "We are facing the wind and the current is coming with the wind, so all my blood and my system is not happy travelling anymore… so what I am aiming for is we get on to the border and stop… rest." He paused, his eyes were yellow and had a distant glare, then he continued, "No other sailor would sail this wind. If you go to Milne Bay, all the sailors are pulling their canoes up. No sailing around now."

The following afternoon we arrived at a sandflat next to a small creek where our presence disturbed a large flock of pelicans. The wind was whipping up clouds of sand that were itching our skin and stinging our eyes. Sanakoli used our last spare piece of plastic to repair a new rip in the sail, while Justin went up the creek to hunt mud crabs. I cooked one of the foul-smelling salted barramundis we had been given by the Javanese fishermen. Justin came back soon after and said, "Eey, crocodile in the river back here."

"Wow, how big was it?" I jumped up with excitement.

"Big enough to kill you," Justin answered in his typical matter of fact style. Apparently, the animal had slid into the creek as soon as it saw Justin, and he reckoned he better abandon his mud crab adventure. After dinner, we went out with torches and a camera to find the reptile but we didn't see it. It was another uneasy sleep on the canoe.

On 11 June, just as the sun sunk into the ocean, we saw the last Indonesian border post located on the western shore of the Bensbach River mouth — the physical border between Indonesia and PNG. There was a tall lighthouse with a big rotating light that became sharper as night fell. Its beam swept over the dark sea like the Eye of Sauron scouting for a small band of hobbits nearing the climax of a mighty quest. There was no activity to be detected around the buildings. I knew that the locals who travelled across the border would check in with the post on every crossing. I hadn't been told to do so and, since we had already completed all our papers, I saw no reason to call in — not least because I had no desire to go through yet another interrogation, this time explaining why it had taken us five days to sail the 60 nautical miles from Merauke.

We needed to cross the border as quickly as possible and the moonless night gave us good cover. We reached the Bensbach River at 7:30 p.m. The current was strong but I was more worried that we would suddenly hear the motor of an overly conscientious Indonesian army dinghy. Suddenly, I saw something in front of us that wasn't supposed to be there. It took a couple of seconds to realise that it was a channel marker — a giant metal pole right at our bow. "Left, left, turn left," I yelled. Justin angled the rudder and the outrigger passed the dead channel marker within half a metre. I looked at the map, there was supposed to be three and they were supposed to have a light on them. In the same instant, Sanakoli spotted another one that we again barely avoided. My nerves were shredded. It was as if Indonesia wouldn't let us go.

The current eased and the canoe took up speed. I looked at my GPS, we had finally passed the entrance and thus had crossed the border. "Guys we made it! We made it back to Papua New Guinea! We are in Papua New Guinea now!" I yelled at the silhouettes in the dark. But oddly enough my friends didn't answer. When we were about a quarter of a mile from the river, we anchored. I was anxious to make greater distance but the wind was too strong. Instead, I untied the Indonesian flag from the flagpole, leaving the smaller Milne Bay sail beneath flapping in the wind. I was blabbering loudly; rejoicing that we were finally back home. How incredible it was that we had made it around all of West Papua, a region that was known for its notoriously complex bureaucracy — and we had done it at the worst time of year. It had taken us five months and I was able to film most of the journey, undetected. Now we only had 740 nautical miles to Tawali. Then, I went on to apologise that I hadn't bought any beers for this celebration but complimented my companions on their great achievement. But the brothers didn't really share this enthusiasm, they didn't seem to understand that we had crossed an invisible line and were in PNG.

At 2 a.m., we continued onwards. As the sun rose, it illuminated a coastline that looked the same as the day before, although now that we were heading east the sailing became easier. At 8 a.m., we saw an odd vessel sailing towards us. It was an old aluminium barge with two motors on the back and a small skipper house in the middle. On board were a handful of PNG soldiers. We all waved at them and they waved back, while Sanakoli yelled, "Samarai, we are from Samarai." We then gestured that we were continuing in their opposite direction and the soldiers gave us a thumbs-up and continued without even slowing down. "Ho ho, you see that," Sanakoli yelled excitedly, "That is Papua New Guinea Navy, not like Indonesia, 'passport, passport,' they see we are Papua New Guinea, they let us sail right through."

The two brothers cracked with laughter and Justin said, "Oh Papua New Guinea."

An hour and a half later, we anchored on a mudflat in Health Bay in front of the Morehead River. I rummaged through my barrel and pulled out the Papua New Guinean flag which Justin attached to our flagpole under the excited guidance of Sanakoli. As we made breakfast, the brothers started talking about how good it was to be back on home territory, and how the local Papuans didn't have any work in West Papua, "You just see Indonesian fishermen, never local people," Sanakoli said. Then he went on to talk about the Papuan resistance and how in every village we had visited, except Biak, people had told them that they were, 'Ready to fight against the Indonesian occupation.'

Now that we were back in PNG, it was time to consider what our next move should be. It was evident that the wind was extreme but we were still in the middle of nowhere, and if we were to have a break, it would be prudent to rest close to the town of Daru, where there was at least some infrastructure and a 3G network. Sanakoli enquired, full of confidence, "You find out how far the distance to Daru."

I knew already and told him, "It's about 115 nautical miles. But now we are sailing mostly east, we can go fast on those days, the wind comes straight from the south. We can probably do it in four to five days." Then I promised the sailors that we could have a proper break and that they might even be able to fly home. Secretly, I hoped that I could convince the brothers to continue up across the Fly River and even all the way to Kerema in the Gulf of Papua.

In the afternoon, the tide came up and we sailed up the river to the village of Bula, a long row of grey stilted huts with ragged paper-bark roofs, situated in the first bend of the river. We went up there to spend the night and re-provision with water and coconuts — or so I thought.

The villagers were very respectful and welcoming but after a couple of hours, the Chief who was also a Pastor, a man named Mark Bizesu, suggested that this was a good village to leave the canoe while we rested and that they would look after it. This offer surprised me and then I learned that it was Sanakoli who had announced that we had come to deposit the canoe there while we waited for the winds to subside.

I told the Chief that this was a misunderstanding and then ran out to get hold of Sanakoli. I found him chewing *buai* with some locals and pulled him aside, "Hey Sana, what are you doing telling people that we are going to leave the canoe here?"

Sanakoli looked a bit shy. Then he answered, "Me and Justin, we say it is too much. Too dangerous, we must wait for July or August, then the wind will calm down and we can sail."

I cut in, "But we just agreed to go to Daru, before we had a break, and remember you guys told me that you would go all the way around the island when you came back to Vanimo!" I was melting with frustration but cooled my voice and asked, "And Justin agrees to this?"

"Yes, he wants to go back too," Sanakoli replied.

I tried to argue that Bula was too far away from Daru but Sanakoli had already spoken to a guy who would take us by dinghy for the cost of fuel only. The two brothers had seemingly already made up their minds, and the whole village were more than happy to look after our gear. But even if I wanted to, I had little energy left to fight them — I was defeated. The next day, the canoe was pulled ashore on a good piece of land; we removed the bilge pump and stored the sails under a long hut where we also stocked our equipment.

As we were carrying the dry bags and boxes, I asked Justin about how we could strengthen the canoe when we came back for the final leg. He then said something that confused me, "If we go home, I don't come back for next round." I stopped with the kitchen box in my arms.

"What do you mean Justin? Sanakoli said you wanted to go home."

Justin puffed on his cigarette, “No, I always say let’s continue. No sense making break before finish. But if we go home now, I don’t come back.” I couldn’t believe what I was hearing — Justin had wanted to continue, like me, but now he was going to opt out of the final leg of the expedition if we went back to Milne Bay.

I found Sanakoli by the canoe and confronted him. “What is this I hear from Justin. It is only you who wants to go home! Justin says he wants to continue sailing.”

Sanakoli’s face became red and it was like he was rummaging through the recesses of his mind for an answer but all he came up with was, “The wind is too much, no good sailing anyhow.” ‘Dammit’ I thought, Sanakoli had played his cards well. As soon as he got the chance, he pulled the emergency break, and now he was going home to his wife to watch movies with her and their kids on their new laptop. I accepted my defeat.

The day after, we motored to Daru where I bought three flights to Milne Bay. I could only hope that Sanakoli would get tired of watching movies and Justin would change his mind about not wanting to come back.

Chapter Twenty-six

Lords of the Fly River

It had been almost two months since we had seen Bula and now we were approaching the village in a noisy fibreglass dinghy that divided the brown water into two wide wakes, stirring the water plants along the banks and frightening a three-metre long beast of a Saltwater crocodile. The boat was packed with fresh provisions as well as nylon string, wood sealant, a roll of black plastic and a new 30 metre x 30 metre tarpaulin. Both crew members were on board. Sanakoli had been down with malaria but was now eager to finish the voyage. I had been more worried about Justin but he came through in the end.

A week earlier, Justin had called me from Dawson Island and announced, "Me, I come back and sail." I was relieved to hear this and had told him so.

"That is such good news Justin. I know that you are the best sailor, we couldn't have done it without you." Justin didn't explain what had changed his mind but I suspected that it was his wife, Nailoilo, who had encouraged him to return; and he was probably getting bored in the village anyway. I had spent the last two months doing the usual stuff, searching for funding and putting my filming in order. The struggle for sponsorship had actually proved fruitful. The shipping company Consort, together with Pacific Maritime Training College in Port Moresby, had both committed to support the voyage. The break had also allowed me some time for reflection about how to finish the journey.

Rob Goodfellow had reminded me that, "It is not how you start a journey but how you end it that people will remember." And he was right. What better way to complete our epic than at the 2017 National

Kenu and Kundu Festival, which was scheduled to start on 4 November. This was do-able. It would mean a lot of media coverage, new sponsors and, not least, a proper celebration of our achievement with the people of Milne Bay. Personally, it would also be fitting to end the journey where my education in traditional canoe sailing had all started. These plans had already been discussed with Justin and Sanakoli, who loved the idea of arriving home to the salutations of family, friends and fellow sailors. I had also suggested that we'd bring Job to Bula to join us for the rest of the way but the brothers didn't like this idea. "He is bad luck," Justin said and then explained. "You see, when Job on board, we bump first day sailing, and in Bobongara too, you see him fall off and we almost sink." I could, of course, try to argue against their reasoning but deemed it wiser to just let it go and keep our three-man band together.

The first thing we did after greeting the good villagers of Bula was to see *Tawali Pasana*. She was looking exactly as we had left her and all our stocked equipment was untouched. The next day we went to work. We refitted a broken *kialo* and changed some of the thinner ones as well. The cracked sealant between the hull and the side boards was replaced with window putty. (The old sealant was tar — cooked from World War Two Japanese oil drums that Justin and Sanakoli's *small father* had salvaged from the bottom of the ocean). Finally, much of the nylon string was renewed.

In the afternoon, a familiar boat approached our work area. It was the barge we had seen on our first morning back in PNG. The captain came along side and said a friendly, "Hello." He was a big dark man in overalls. He told us that he was sometimes hired to sail soldiers on patrol along the coast, mostly looking for illegal Indonesian fishermen but usually these rogues would outrun his small barge with little effort. He then told us that he also owned two dinghies but that one of them had just been held up. "My boys were sailing from the Fly River when a dingy with *raskals* start harassing. They have guns and bush knives and scare my boys to jump in and swim for land."

"So, they took your dinghy?" I asked.

"Yes, I will never see my dinghy again," he replied with a sigh.

"What about your boys?" I continued.

"Ohh, the *puk puk* (crocodiles) didn't get them. They were found next day on a beach."

After four days of work, *Tawali Pasana* was shipshape. There was still a strong wind shaking the tops of the sago palms but, nonetheless, it was time to get moving and I announced that our departure would be the next day. As the morning sun lit the grey clouds, Justin stalled the launch, declaring that there was some last-minute replacement needed of the *patoto* sticks connecting the outrigger to the *kialos*. "We make them properly, if one break, all soon break. And we sink." Then he disappeared.

I asked Sanakoli what was going on with his brother and he answered, "That man think he is too important, he get his own mind now, he is not listening to me anymore." I thought, 'Hmmm, maybe I was too generous with my compliments.' In the evening, the canoe was finally in the water and we could sail out but now it was no longer an outgoing tide. Justin and Sanakoli also both seemed very hesitant to leave.

I found out that the two brothers had been pumping the barge captain and villagers for all sorts of pirate stories and warnings of 'tricky people' and dangerous conditions ahead and now they were worried. I tried to reason with my crew. "Hey guys, I understand that you are concerned but remember people love telling stories and the best stories are the scary ones. You never hear someone saying, 'Oh, we had the most delightful dinghy ride today.'" The brothers smiled and I continued. "This is how it has been since we started the journey. In the village they say, 'Oh we are good people but those people up the coast, you can't trust them, they are *raskols.*' And what happens when we go to the *raskol* village? They are friendly… but then they warn us about the next village ahead, saying they are *raskol* people."

The brothers laughed and looked more at ease and Sanakoli said, "Yes that is true, we have always met good people." To be honest, I was worried myself. It was a very rough coastline and, despite the numerous offshore oil and gas drilling platforms and inland mining and logging, this was the poorest and most neglected area we had experienced so far.

Expedition Log 17 August 2017

11:00 hrs. Departure Bula and Morehead estuary. Sea still rough but wind less aggressive.

17:00 hrs. Arrival in Jari fishing camp. Total distance covered 10 nautical miles in six hours. Slow start.

A day later, we got stuck on low tide in Mari Village. However, what made this place memorable was that it had a giant telephone tower that had recently collapsed. Luckily, the metal construction had fallen in the opposite direction of the village so no houses or people had been hit. The other curiosity was a traditional sailing canoe, named *Mari Karakia*. Justin and Sanakoli got very excited when they saw it and we immediately inspected the craft.

Mari Karakia was a lot bigger than *Tawali Pasana* and had two small outriggers, a big hull, two masts and a bowsprit (a spar projecting from the bow of the vessel). It seemed to have been inspired in part by 19th Century European sail craft design. We were hosted by the canoe builder himself, who served us some tough boiled dugong meat. Our host told me that he was the only person left who knew how to build a traditional Mari canoe and he would still use it for sailing crops to market in Daru. My fellow sailors seemed to like the place and, as we were gnawing through a greasy dugong steak, the brothers announced that we would probably have to stay a couple of days waiting for the right wind. I slapped my forehead.

The next morning, I gave my friends a motivational speech to get them into gear. First, I explained, "We have two and a half months to finish this voyage, and there is 800 nautical miles until we reach Tawali — this means that we have to cover at least 11 nautical miles a day to make it in time for the festival." Then I drew a map in the hard-packed sand and continued. "And the reason we want to make it in time for the festival is so we can get as much media exposure as possible because what our sponsors want is for us to show their logo. If we can guarantee our sponsors that we will be showing their logo when we are being celebrated for making a world record, the sponsors will be saying, 'Oh we want to help these guys and give them our money.'" The sailors laughed at this optimistic prospect.

Then I drew the three different sponsor packages I had been offering in the sand, adding numbers on how many sold and how many more we needed to sell to get the sailors a good portion of cash, or even a dinghy. It was paramount that we made it in time. The brothers studied the plan and asked a few questions, and then we all agreed to proceed. I encouraged them to take photos of the sand plan so they could look at it later. Now that we had a common goal and were all motivated, we got ready to face the spring tide that was running in fast, like a long line of boiling white froth.

The windiest two months of the Southeast Trade Winds had passed, although gusts were still ripping our storm sail and the seas were pounding our canoe. There were other challenges ahead too. After Daru, we would have to pass the mouth of the massive Fly River, then cross the Gulf of Papua that is notorious for its high swells, and then there was the National Capital District, the region with the highest crime rate in the country, and possibly the greatest concentration of pirates. The physical coastline from Port Moresby was said to be relatively calm thanks to the offshore reefs that skirted the mainland. These reefs would then dissolve and the final hurdle was to make it past the rugged Suau coast, where waves came straight in from the Coral Sea and slammed against the cliffs all the way to Milne Bay.

First, we had to navigate the Torres Strait, which is a shallow body of water dotted with islands and shoals spanning 43 nautical miles between New Guinea and Australia. There is a lot of current running through this strait which connects the South Pacific and Indian oceans.

Expedition Log 20 August 2017

12:00 hrs. *Jig-jagging* against both the current and the wind up through a small channel between the PNG mainland and two Australian islands — Kawa and Mata Kawa.

18:00 hrs. Rest in mangroves. I have been pulling the sheet all day and my hands are so sore from chaffing that the crude rope feels like glass cutting in to my palms.

19:30 hrs. Arrival Buzi village. Hands burn. Can't hold the pen.

Daru

After five days and about 118 nautical miles since we departed Bula, *Tawali Pasana* arrived at the dirty harbour of Daru Island. It had been a long haul but Daru wasn't a very flattering place, so we didn't plan to stay there long. The small island was overpopulated with people coming from the mainland looking for financial opportunities, which they seldom found. The town itself was connected by a grid of holed roads and the centre of town consisted of ragged sheet metal buildings surrounded by fences and topped with rusty barbed wire. You wouldn't have to walk far before you found one lovely garden after another encircling old box shaped houses built with modern materials, which gave the place its own rugged charm. And, as with any small town in PNG, most people were friendly, welcoming and helpful. We had some good contacts in Daru too, including a now retired local legend, Mr Jowi Gauga, a former radio host at NBC, who stood on the pier ready to greet us, together with his son, offering help with any logistics and inviting us for dinner.

The first night Justin had stayed on land but just as Sanakoli and I had gone to bed, we could hear him calling out. Sanakoli said from his mosquito net, "We just ignore him, he can go stay in our friend's house." But I felt bad about leaving him to walk all the way back to the house so I crawled out and slagged our anchor in the bow so I could pull us ashore. As I was struggling with our line in the strong surge, my foot suddenly slipped and I fell into the putrid water that was full of rotting garbage and what other human waste the neighbouring canoes would relieve themselves of.

I could hear Justin and his friend on the shore saying, "Oh, sorry," as I crawled back on board the boat. I was so furious that I forgot to feel embarrassed; I had had enough. They yelled that I should come in and go to the house and have a shower but I was done with people and sailing and just wanted to rest. Sanakoli came out and helped me anchor the canoe again and I fell asleep, cursing the island.

The next morning, I went straight up to the only hotel in town and got a room for the night. I needed to work and needed a break even more so. Justin and Sanakoli took turns looking after the canoe and using the shower in my room. I knew that I wouldn't have any chance of getting online for the next many hundred miles so I worked until well past midnight. I had barely fallen asleep when I was awoken by someone knocking on my door. It was Justin. His eyes were glazed over from drinking and he said that he needed to borrow 100 kina. I asked what he needed the money for and he explained that he had been with a girl and now her brothers had come after him, demanding 100 kina. I asked him, “If you pay this money, are you out of trouble then?” He confirmed this and I gave him a bill, then I told him it would come from his wages and shut the door.

I was awoken early the next morning by another knock on the door. This time it was Sanakoli and he looked very distressed. “What’s going on Sana?” I asked, half worried and half annoyed. Sanakoli started to give me a long explanation where he cursed and apologised for his brother at the same time. Apparently, Justin had brought some drinking buddies on board who had stolen our bag of *ox and palm* (tinned meat). They had even nicked one of our water containers — however they managed to do that.

I then told Sanakoli about Justin’s late-night visit and Sanakoli became even more red in the face. “This is what happens when you let that man out of sight.” Sanokali almost yelled. I told him not to worry and pointed out that Justin was a good sailor and we should just keep his focus on that. We all felt we were more than done with Daru and, after our local friends helped us find a new water container, we said goodbye and sailed off.

In the afternoon, I steered the canoe ashore on Param Island where we were welcomed by a group of families in a fishing camp of small shelters covered in ragged plastic sheets. They were accustomed to visitors, as the island served as a ‘bus stop’ for dinghies crossing the Fly River delta. We were all worried about this next leg as the Fly River is the greatest river in the country, if measured by outflow, and its mouth spans some 50 nautical miles. We were advised that, at this time of year, dinghies never went straight across but instead, navigated up river between several islands to avoid the waves that accumulated when huge masses of river water collided with the pounding swells of the Gulf of Papua.

The locals also told stories of a giant stingray that would become angry and suck down whole dinghies that dared to cross the mouth of the river. It was no doubt a dangerous place and the river had taken many lives but as Sanakoli said that night during our meeting, “We mastermind it good and we can do it.” We also had an ace in our *bilum* — the moon above was full, which always meant calmer winds and, sure enough, the weather forecast was favourable for the following day. The decision was made to sail straight across and take our chance with the giant stingray.

Expedition Log 25 August 2017

> 08:10 hrs. Start crossing of the Fly River. Slack tide and 15 knots of wind from SE, conditions are perfect. This crossing demands good timing.

As we entered the river, we realised that it was greater than we could had ever imagined. It looked like a giant brown ocean that only ran in one direction and our worry was that, if we capsized or lost control of the canoe, we would be swept into the huge Gulf of Papua — and be lost. There were several low-lying islands in the river we could use for navigational points and our first safe landing was Kiriwa Island, 19 nautical miles northeast. However, we soon experienced how easy it would be to get into trouble as we passed sections where sandbanks suddenly appeared and created large crashing ‘A-frame’ waves.

“No play up, you keep bailing.” Sanakoli yelled confidently. The brothers were in top form though, and we made it past one ‘minefield’ after another of great surges of brown water obstructing our brave little canoe. It was a race against time as we had to get the most out of the incoming tide before it turned and enhanced the speed of the river and the size of the waves. We made it across the first section of giant outflow and then got caught in some shallows in front of Kiriwa Island at 11:50 a.m. After some 40 minutes of *jig-jagging,* we were back on course towards the next island of Ulmuda. After three hours of fighting the current, we made it into a channel as the tide was running out and we found a camp for the night at 5:20 p.m. The next morning came with grey weather and the wind had picked up. We continued passing one big Malaysian ship after another, carrying timber from the inland. A hard shower came in and we wrapped ourselves up in our yellow raincoats. Red paint had leaked on Justin's coat and now he looked like a mass murderer with a club as he stood by the *yabby yabby*.

Expedition Log 26 August 2017

15:00 hrs. Passing Bell Point on the northern shore of the river. We have crossed the mighty Fly River.

We were all high on this achievement and continued up the delta coast to the village of Gori. As we arrived at this small cluster of traditional huts on black sand, we noticed several of the women scream and grab their nearest children before running into the jungle. We soon got in contact with one of the village elders and convinced him that we came with good intentions. Later, the women came out of hiding to say hello. One of the women laughed and said, "Ha ha, when I saw that strange ship, I said to myself, I don't want to die. I take to the bush."

The onward sailing became more and more challenging. Deception Bay lived up to its name as we were almost capsized by giant waves rolling over a particularly nasty section of sandbank. The bay guarding the Kikori territory is a delta area of complex channels and swamp. People there live off fish caught in gill nets and sago, or *sak sak*, as it is called in these parts. Many different tribes inhabit this great wetland, but the main language is Motu. I noticed their canoes were beautifully painted in round patterns and sailed without an outrigger like in Agats, West Papua.

Expedition Log 30 August 2017

15:00 hrs. Miri point. Expedition anniversary. We left Tawali one year ago, nonetheless, we still have 450 nautical miles to the finish line. I am celebrating the event by eating *ukaru karu* (green tree grubs) with three bush knife wielding kids, all about eight to ten years of age.

That evening, I sat alone reflecting on the fact that I had been away from home for almost 13 months. Although I loved every single day of this adventure, I started to feel it would be nice to see some family or old friends. I opened a folder on my laptop. It was a selection of clips from my farewell party in Copenhagen. I plugged in my earphones and clicked on the first file. There they were, all my friends. They looked so pale, although it was high summer in Scandinavia. Their clothes were so neat. Some of them were with spouses and babies and they were all smiling and talking with drinks in their hands.

I caught myself touching the screen and laughing at their jokes and well wishes. It was my friend Katrine who had suggested that I have a party, as she said, "We don't know if we will ever see you again." But she was right — there was a good chance of me not returning. One could ask, why go on such dangerous adventure? And my answer always was, 'Why not challenge yourself by escaping the safety net of Scandinavian society and push yourself to the limit?' To be honest, I had a growing sense of anxiety watching my friends settle down and start their families. I was not ready to commit to this — I needed (at least) one momentous adventure. And I wanted to share this adventure with the world. Anyway, Denmark would still be there, even if the voyage took us another year — should I return. Seeing all my friends in Copenhagen did make me feel lonely however.

The overcast morning brought us a new problem — the sea along the shore was far too rough. We tried to sail out from the point but it was like sailing in a washing machine; unpredictable waves of brown water came from all sides and, when they became too big, we turned and ran back to the calms behind the point. A local fisherman recommended that we sail in through a channel behind the beach and try to enter the sea by the estuary next to Mariki village. Four hours later, the inshore channel brought us to our destination. The rain was pouring down, which could have been to our favour as heavy rain usually takes the top off the waves but the torrent was so extreme that it was hard to distinguish the sea from the sky, and the waves were still roaring. We would just have to wait and see how the sea looked in the morning.

As we were cooking under our tarpaulins that now doubled as a freshwater catchment, a mixed soccer team of teenage boys and girls from Mariki came to check us out. Some of them started to become a bit cheeky, picking up our things and wrestling with each other.

Sanakoli stood up and addressed them like an orator, "Why you see us risking our lives making a world record is that we want to show the world the what, good picture of Papua New Guinea. In Europe and America, they still think we eating people and wear grass skirts. But we want to tell that we are good Christian people with good traditions." The speech had caught the attention of the crowd. All the kids were standing in the rain listening. Sanakoli finished by reinforcing, "If we show the what, white man, that we are good people, more tourist will come." After the kids had dispersed, I complimented Sanakoli on his speech and suggested he could tour the country speaking and inspiring school children. Sanakoli liked this idea.

The morning revealed a sea in great unrest and it became evident that there was no chance we could make it out from this place any time soon. 'What to do now, we are losing precious miles every day,' I thought and cursed the prospect of having to sail back to Mari point to try and exit from there again. As I looked over my maps, I noticed the matrix of rivers and channels running like a huge delta behind the shore. This reminded me of something I had seen before — then I remembered a document Sandy Robson had sent me. It was a PDF with her directions and notes for the route from Port Moresby to Daru. I had totally forgot about it because of sheer mental exhaustion. I found the document on my phone.

Sandy had plotted a route that she had taken through jungle channels to avoid the waves of the gulf; maybe we could do the same, although it would be a lot of paddling, about 28 nautical miles, crossing several big rivers. Justin and Sanakoli liked the idea and we conferred with the people in Mariki. They said it was possible with our canoe but also warned us not to sit too close to the bank at night as there were huge crocodiles in those rivers. Soon after, we had said goodbye and entered the first jungle channel — thus began a long hard day of paddling. Despite this, the slow travel was a welcome break from the hissing winds and constant drenching. Now colourful lorikeets were flying above and the earthy aromas of the damp jungle engulfed us.

The innocent bliss of 'paddling in paradise' soon came to a halt when we saw the splash of a crocodile diving from the bank in front of us. Sanakoli reminded me, "Crocodile scared of us as we are scared of it," which was true, at least as long as we were moving. Two hours later, we were stopped by a low hanging tree growing over the river — too low for our mast. We roped the canoe off to the tree, then we cooked breakfast. During this stop, we all avoided getting too close to the water. As the rice was ready, it started pouring down. We ate like the old man in Mambututu. Afterwards, the riggings were untied and we carefully lowered the mast and placed it on the deck. Now we could move under the tree and continue the tiresome paddling against the current. That night, we berthed the canoe on a river bank with giant bamboos and swarms of mosquitoes. There was no moonlight and the river was dark and slow running — and we were all worried about, 'snipers.' Justin, who always slept on the platform, was the most exposed so we positioned the outrigger towards shore and Justin barricaded each end of the platform with a *yabby yabby* — in case a crocodile should try and crawl aboard. That night, I woke several times to turn on the torch and sweep the river for red eyes but I didn't see any.

The next afternoon, we finally reached the endpoint of our river travels, the village of Apiope by the mouth of the Purari River, which branches out into two river mouths the Aeivi and the Alele passage (little did we know that this would make our exit out to sea even more dangerous). My shoulders were sore and my hands burning from the rough paddle handle; I had had enough of paddling. As we approached the village, it looked like it was empty of people but there were still smoke and pigs and dogs scuffling around in the mud. We then spotted a young man on a sandbank and landed next to him. He was carrying a bamboo bow with a handful of arrows. Justin whispered, "You look at him, scared of us, that is why village ran away." Justin was right. He did look nervous and there was an arrow ready on his string.

I smiled at him and greeted him by showing him both my hands in a disarming gesture and quickly said, "We are from Samarai, Milne Bay, we are making world record." The young man lowered his bow and presented himself as Elias. He soon eased up and said he would show us the village. Now as I looked over, I could see faces peeking out through the windows of the stilted huts.

The following morning, we inspected the sea. It was too rough to sail out. I looked at the weather forecasts but they were all bad — 17-23 knots from the southeast with 1.8 metres waves. Nevertheless, I stayed optimistic and said to the sailors that we should study the sea and be ready to depart out as soon as a possibility presented itself. I also asked the villagers for their advice but there was little encouragement to gain. On the contrary, they told me about a dinghy that had capsized at the Aievi Passage the week before. Luckily, the passengers who had been floating about in the waves for half a day were rescued by another dinghy that just happened to be passing. All this resistance from the sea and the villagers made me even more determined. We had a canoe festival to reach and, of more pressing concern, I had to get to Port Moresby to renew my visa.

That afternoon, I went to a point where there should be phone reception and dialled Sophie's number. She was in Silosilo. I knew it was her birthday. I was answered by a recorded voice telling that there was no network. After a few tries, I sent her a text message instead.

The next morning, Justin and I scouted the beach for possible launching sites but it was still too rough. Sanakoli didn't join us. Later that day, when I told them, "We should try and have a look tomorrow," Sanakoli called for a meeting. The sailors' agenda was soon clear.

Sanakoli said, "We must wait for the right weather. If we go too fast, we are gonna bump. The villagers here tell me, they cannot let us sail out because it will be on their hands if we sink. They say, 'Too many lost lives in these waves.'"

The brothers had been told that sailing out was impossible and now they believed it too. We had made really good progress, 350 nautical miles in thirteen days and now, after a mere four days of modest struggle and some frightening stories, the sailors had lost their spark. To make things worse Sanakoli asked, “Maybe it is not so important we make the festival on time, maybe people will still give us presents if we come what, later.” That was the last straw. I was about to explode but somehow managed to answer him in a polite although still sarcastic tone, “I don’t think changing our date is a good idea, because now we have told our sponsors that we will be coming and they’ll get upset if we don’t turn up.” It was clear that we all wanted the same thing — to get back to Tawali safe — but I was blinded by frustration. The crew’s lack of an against-all-the-odds vision was wearing me down.

The next day, I arranged for the canoe to be pulled ashore and then I jumped on a dinghy to Kerema. My rationale was, ‘Better risk my life in the waves on a dinghy and get my visa renewed than hang around listening to ghost stories.’

Chapter Twenty-seven

Rise to fame

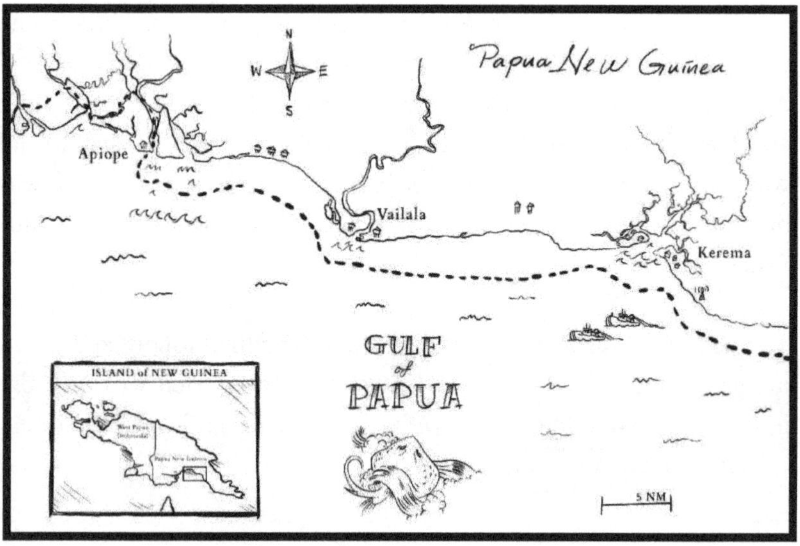

The Gulf of Papua was a frightful sight, and even more daunting was that people actually ran dinghies through this maritime Mordor of two-metre-high brown barrelling destruction. Now I was on one of those vulnerable fibreglass crafts, speeding between long rows of breakers. The driver would see the forming pattern ahead and steer out of one churning boil after another. Every time we made a last-minute escape from a collapsing brown wall, the dinghy driver would widen his eyes and exclaim, "*Zazazazahhhh*!" There was no doubt that we had a skilled captain and that he was in that perfect 'sweet spot' — that place where your skills are challenged to the extreme but you prevail, although I didn't know how long this would last because he and his mates were hitting the *JJ* (Jungle Juice — home brew) pretty hard.

I was sitting in the bottom of the dinghy next to a middle-aged man, a couple of older ladies and a mother with two children. The man was the only one wearing a life jacket. He said to me, “Those children, they are so innocent.” Maybe he noticed that I looked strangely at him after he explained, “I always get worried when running with children, last year, same time, we were running to K-town (Kerema). On board was a woman with two small children. We were hit by a big wave, by Vailala entrance. The dinghy sank and we all struggled to find something floating to keep us up. The mother lost both her children in the sea.” I got a lump in my throat. The man sat with a distant stare and concluded, “So innocent those children, they had never done any wrong.”

This was my second dreadful run with a dinghy through the Gulf of Papua. I was on my way back to meet my crew in Apiope after spending five days renewing my visa. Unfortunately, I wasn’t bringing back much food. I hadn’t been able to withdraw money in Kerema, so the last of my cash had been spent on essentials such as coffee, lollies, cordial and tinned fish.

When I arrived in Apiope, I was greeted by the sailors and our host Frank, who was a fifty-year-old health worker, although he didn’t have much to do as he rarely received new supplies of medicine from the National Department of Health. I was worried about how the crew were feeling about taking our chances in the Gulf, so I was glad that I could at least deliver a positive weather report. This promised fair winds and lower waves for the next couple of days. Then I unfolded the map and explained, “We have about 430 nautical miles to Tawali and about seven weeks to make it to the festival — I believe we can do it.” The sailors looked interested and I pointed to the route ahead. “There are some difficult sections by the river mouths but if the wind is down and we take the route in safe steps, first Vailala, next day check the weather, then go to Kerema, then we should be all right.”

I paused in anticipation. Would the sailors agree to sail or dig their heels into the sand and insist on staying until the sea calmed down and the skin grew back in our palms? Sanakoli just replied, “Good, we have been here for too long." He had been calling his wife Rachel. The twins were all right but she had some bad news from home. Sanakoli looked grave. He explained, "You remember the *lapun* with the bucket hat. He cut your paddle what, *Eneta*." I said I remembered and he continued, "That old man is dead — from asthma." Sanakoli and his brother looked down.

"Oh, I'm sorry… he was a nice guy, at least we have his paddle to remind us of him," I reasoned and my friends agreed. The next day, I had a small pig killed and we had a feast with the villagers of Apiope. This was both the proper way of thanking our hosts and also a timely opportunity to raise the spirits of my friends and mend our differences. It also seemed appropriate as the family in Nuakata would be having a mortuary feast for the old man.

Facing the giant stingray

Early the following morning, we tied everything down on the canoe and pushed out. The wind and sea looked promising but we were vigilant all the same — we were about to sail the most dangerous stretch of coast in the entire Gulf of Papua. The first difficulty was to get out from the beach. Then we had to sail east, passing the two conjoining river mouths by Apiope (where a dinghy had capsized two weeks previous to our arrival). Unlike a dinghy, *Tawali Pasana* couldn't turn on a plate, we had to use the wind and y*aya-towa* every time we needed to change direction. The sailors would have to calculate our course with reference to the lines of breaking waves ahead and thus avoid dangerous sections of canoe-floundering waves. But if anyone could pull this off, it would be Justin and Sanakoli John. Soon one geyser after another exploded off our bow. *Tawali Pasana* resolutely dug through the growing breakers.

The sheet was tightened then slackened by Sanakoli as Justin, with stoic alertness and short clear commands, cautiously navigated us out through the maze of chaotic swells. I was fully occupied emptying our ever-filling hull and recording the excitement with a

GoPro camera. As we could no longer distinguish the worried faces of our friends ashore, the canoe turned east and sailed through the unruly swells of the river mouth. This was a most dangerous and delicate manoeuvre. If we went too close to land, then the brown estuarine turmoil would devour us. If we went too far out, the incoming ocean swell would break over us. It was intense sailing and several surprise waves just appeared out of nowhere and crashed over our outrigger. After what was the longest half hour of my life, we were past the river mouths and steering towards Vailala.

Our risky exit was celebrated with *sak sak* and *dirty watar*. I warmly complimented my companions for their skill. The plan now was to sleep in Vailala, which was a village inside a river where the brothers had family. However, when we reached the estuary at 1:30 p.m., it became evident that going inside the sandbank leading to the river would be too difficult — we needed protected waters to land the canoe. "How far to K-town?" Sanakoli asked.

I looked at my notes and said hopefully, "I think we can make it before dark."

Five hours later, we approached Kerema, the capital of the Gulf Province, which is a large bay almost entirely encircled by mountains. We could see the lights of the town being turned on as we approached the long white rows of in shore breakers that were reflecting the rapidly receding rays of the day. As we neared the entrance, the waves grew — as did our anxieties. "Where do we go in?" Sanakoli asked, looking concerned.

"It's hard to tell. I think we can come in by the beach — over there — and cut past that reef and then double back in," I tried to explain while making my way across the rocking platform. My explanation didn't sound very convincing and I didn't actually believe it was possible myself. Trying to navigate those breakers in the dimming light at this time of year would be virtual suicide. There was little we could do except go back out to sea and take our chances overnight in the Gulf, hoping that the wind wouldn't pick up — and that we wouldn't disturb the mythical giant stingray.

This was the beginning of a mysterious night. It was a new moon so there was little light; instead, the mountains began to spit winds at us in strange guests. We came dangerously close to two fishing trawlers that didn't seem to notice our lantern or heed my calls on the VHF radio as they hummed past us like glowing bugs. The wind then became steady and *Tawali Pasana* shot up along the undefined coast, dodging a breaking reef — again, at the last minute. A strange cold rain began to fall in sheets and, as it passed, clouds of hypnotic marine bioluminescence shimmered in our wake, lighting up the hull. Then the wind suddenly subsided and Justin handed me the sheet and passed out in the front.

It was well past midnight but still several hours until dawn. Sanakoli was sitting by the rudder — nodding off. Then I noticed someone cooking on the platform. It was an old lady. She seemed familiar — it was the same old woman I had seen when we were sailing off Um Island, West Papua. I felt that having a good meal was just what we needed. I could feel the warm fire. Then I snapped out of it — as if waking from a dream. I turned my head light onto the platform. There was no one there. As morning came, we were bobbing through a clear turquoise sea and the land looked different. The Fellowship of the *Tawali Pasana* had made it through the mighty Gulf of Papua — and during the treacherous southeasterlies. Perhaps the spirit mothers really were looking after us. Of that, the brothers had no doubt.

Fancy living

Our travels down the coast went well, especially after we crossed the border into the Central Province and entered the clear waters of the Coral Sea. It was still hard work although the conditions had become more agreeable, but that didn't mean we had any luck catching fish. When we were trolling a line, the recurring topic onboard was who could claim to have caught the fish (should we even catch one).

Sanakoli would banter, "I catch the fish, you always see me casting the line — you people got no luck."

I would make an expression as if my friend was talking rubbish and feigned protest, "No it's the man who pulls in the fish. Anyone can cast a line," I argued. Justin would then set about educating the two of us.

"Both of you got no luck. Me, I tie the hook and put nylon on the spool — all the fish are mine." These differing points of views would, of course, change depending on who had thrown the line last, or who tied the bait.

On 19 September, we approached the capital of PNG, Port Moresby. Central Province is dry most of the year and this morning was no exception. The red, barren hills and high-rise buildings reflected the growing sun, as the crowded morning traffic came into view. We were all full of excitement. A lot of preparation had gone into our arrival. I had been writing press releases as well producing short videos acknowledging our sponsors. I had also been busy on the phone (whenever there was reception) coordinating both the media and our sponsors for our arrival into Moresby. As we didn't want to have sponsor stickers on our canoe, I had instead got a banner printed with all our sponsor logos. Berthing *Tawali Pasana* in Moresby was taken care of as the Royal Papua Yacht Club and the local canoe club, Konedobu Kanu Klab, who enthusiastically invited us pull the canoe ashore in their protected marina. Our sleeping arrangements were sorted too, complements of the biggest and newest hotel in Port Moresby, The Stanley. Our days in the big city were looking promising.

We had scheduled our arrival for 12:00 p.m. but we were already there by 9:30 a.m. The wind had been good and as Sanakoli said, "Less chance of *raskols* if we make it in quickly." We were welcomed by the club staff who helped berth the canoe. Afterwards, we were offered a divine meal of beef burger, coke (sprite for Sanakoli) and fries. As we shovelled the fat and protein in, journalists started to arrive along with my photographer friend Robert Weber, who was to document our time in the city. We were all interviewed and then we walked to the canoe and met the staff from Consort Shipping and the Maritime Training College. After a lot of posing and selfies, we sailed the canoe out to give the media a display of *Tawali Pasana* in action. When it all was over, we were picked up by the Operations Manager from The Stanley, Russell Madre Deus. Suddenly we were sitting on leather seats in an air-conditioned luxury car looking at buildings, traffic and people pass by. It felt surreal. Nonetheless, I enjoyed being in Port Moresby, even though it has a reputation of being one of the most dangerous cities in the world.

The Stanley stood like a giant shining sentential in the centre of the city and soon we were rocketing upwards in a brand-new glamorous elevator. Our suite on the 14th floor had a spectacular balcony view overlooking the city. After unpacking and a shower, Justin and Sanakoli had their first introduction to a washing machine, which they loved, but they were even more impressed by the dishwasher. I explained that not all people in Denmark had such conveniences (I didn't) and that this apartment was extravagant compared to what the common *dim dim* lived in. I don't think they believed me.

We sat on the big sofa with our bare feet on the table and a cold beer in our hands as the evening television news bulletin came on. Suddenly we were presented on the giant screen — "Thirty-six-year-old Dane, Thor Jensen and two of Milne Bay's finest sailors — Justin and Sanakoli John." The news report showed *Tawali Pasana* sailing into the harbour surrounded by enormous white fibreglass yachts. Damn that canoe looked good, but my friends and I looked absolutely wasted. I was shocked at how dishevelled we appeared. Then I was interviewed about the voyage. I should have insisted on Sanakoli saying a few words, as it was as much his journey as mine, but at least I credited the two sailors for their extraordinary sailing skills. They were more than happy with the broadcasts. We celebrated with more beers and a dinner before an early retirement to our giant, clean beds.

Progressing PNG

After breakfast, someone knocked on the door. It was Russell, who handed us the morning newspapers — *The National* and the *Post Courier*. We were featured in both. One headline read: 'Epic Journey Around Island of Papua.' The other read: 'Sailing into History.' We spread the papers on the table and read the flattering stories out loud. The articles also mentioned our sponsors. I made sure to point this out to Justin and Sanakoli. "Now all the other companies can see, 'Oh when we sponsor these heroes, we will be mentioned in the media.'"

This was the start of three very hectic days in Port Moresby. We did another EMTV interview, went shopping, got recognised by strangers on the street, and had all our drinks bought when we went out at night. Justin and Sanakoli (well, mostly Sanakoli) gave an inspirational talk to a class of school children. The Pacific Maritime Training College invited us to a graduation ceremony where Sanakoli imparted words of wisdom to the new cadets and the three of us were awarded our own honorary diplomas. The newspapers loved us and kept reporting on everything we were doing.

Despite the rush of the city, Justin and Sanakoli found time to socialise with their sister who worked in a downtown bank. I met up with a local friend, Kevin Alo, who had been helping me from the start. He was a property lawyer in his mid-20s who, together with a friend, ran the only model casting agency in the country, as well as writing a popular fashion blog. Both of Kevin's parents had grown up barefoot in a remote bush village. From these humble origins, his mother had established herself in hospitality and his father advanced to become a police detective. The couple had worked hard to give Kevin and his three siblings a safe home and a good education, while maintaining the connection with their village. This was an example of the rapid social change PNG has experienced over just two generations. For me, Kevin was an example of how young entrepreneurs were progressing PNG, while maintaining their connections to their origins and traditions.

Expedition Log 25 September 2017

10:00 hrs. Departing Port Moresby. Wind southeast 17 knots. The outrigger is dry as a cork. There's an uneasy mood on board, we are all worried about pirates and keep the VHF radio on and the phone ready to call for assistance. But for now the headwind is a bigger nuisance. The only thing we haven't had in excess during the last five days of city living is rest, but we still have 500 kilometres to our 'homecoming' as I posted on Facebook.

During our stay in Moresby I had got in contact with Sophie who said that her village was expecting us. The brothers were pleased about this as well. "The Suau coast, they are sailors too, that's where Milne Bay Province begin," Sanakoli confirmed. Our ambitions of reaching Tawali before the canoe festival still seemed within reach and both the sailors were happy about this. "At the Kenu and Kundu Festival we are really excited because we sail with plenty sailors," Sanakoli said and continued, "Plus we play all our skills and tell stories of sailing. In our dreams we used to mark the month so if we miss out, we feel no good, if we take part, we feel really good, because we sail every day, every year all our life."

The following evening, we landed in the village of Gaba Gaba. Our host was a sturdy man by the name of Thao. He had a house on the beach which was very unusual, as most other houses in the village were standing on stilts along the shore of the shallow bay. That same evening, I heard Sanakoli and Justin talking with Thao about building a sailing canoe. The Central Province was known for their *Hiri* trade, where *Lakatoi* sailing canoes travelled from the dry Central Province to trade clay pots for sago and other garden produce with the tribes in the Gulf of Papua. Now, only a few of these canoes still existed and no one in the area knew how to build one. "My *bubu* (grandfather) build *Lakatoi* but I don't know." Thao said.

Sanakoli then replied, "That is our problem, we don't know. Where are we? We are not like white people and don't know our *bubu's* traditions either." The three men got stirred up by this lack of traditional knowledge and then Thao said that his father might still know how to build a *Lakatoi*. Sanakoli said, "You build it, we come and help you sail." And then they started to talk about how this it could kickstart tourism in the village. Sanakoli exclaimed, "At the canoe festival, we get 20 kina for sailing one *dim dim* on our canoe. Good money! On your *Lakatoi,* you can bring how many tourists?"

Travelling the coast of Central Province was encouraging because now everybody knew who we were. When we arrived in a village people would show us our newspaper articles which they had saved. Some even had pictures of us hanging on the walls of their huts. Justin and Sanakoli clearly enjoyed the attention, everyone wanted to hear their stories and the *buai* was plentiful.

The closer we came to Milne Bay the more tangible our success became — but for every nautical mile, it also felt like we had more to lose if something went wrong. It was as if I were climbing a tree and suddenly realised how far down there was to fall. Then doubt started to sneak in. 'Would I reach all my objectives with the trip? Would I learn to sail the canoe properly? I hadn't even tried to fly the outrigger. Another concern was if I had captured the right film recordings to create a good story. This gnawing doubt didn't do me any good, so I concluded it was best to just keep 'climbing the tree' and focus on the next branch at hand. My companions seemed to be getting the scent of home waters and several times a day they would ask, "You check your GPS," or "How many miles?" One morning Sanakoli even became grumpy because I was packing too slowly.

He said, "No more play up, we sail, want to finish."

Expedition Log 2 October 2017

> 11:27 hrs. Progress slow and strenuous. Some days we only cover 14 nautical miles, on good days 30 nautical miles. The wind is steadily blowing the strength off our bones. We pass two yellow sea snakes, coiled together like a knot.

That evening on the deserted Grange beach, I was tending to a more… well… personal infirmity — my perpetually wet shorts were chafing my groin and now I was trying to ease the burning sensation by secretly washing the 'Danish crown jewels' in fresh, cool water. Meanwhile, Sanakoli was rinsing his sore eyes, also with our drinking water, while saying, "When I come home, I ask one of the mothers for *susu* milk. That is the best for eye pain."

I looked up from my delicate ablutions and said, "You mean *susu*, like in breasts? You wash your eyes in breast milk?"

"Yes, it is the best," Sanakoli said with an air of considerable authority.

Justin, who was laying, stunned with painkillers, like a crucifix on his back in the sand, spoke into the air. “How we make tea tomorrow… now you two spoil our last water!”

On 4 October, we arrived at Inuoro Island. As we approached the beach, the wind disappeared as we were in lee of the island. We almost touched the coral beach. I was standing ready to jump ashore when a strong current suddenly took our bow and started sweeping us off the beach toward a section of breakers. ‘Damn,’ I thought. A kid spearfishing had seen it all and he reached his hands out. I threw the line and he quickly tied us off to a coral head. Yet another close call.

We were completely spent as we staggered ashore and greedily drank the green coconuts that were offered to us. Inuoro was the first island in the Milne Bay Province, which made my friends very happy. I was excited too because, from here, it was only a days’ sail to Silosilo where Sophie was waiting but alas, we got up late the following morning and the tide was down. This meant we couldn’t drag the canoe over the coral. The following day, the wind was too violent and we had no wish to take our chances in Orangerie Bay, which was 23 nautical miles of exposed water lined by crocodile-ridden mangroves.

We were accommodated by a Pastor from the mainland. He had a big house and offered me a room to sleep in. This was just what I needed — a space of my own away from the ever-curious villagers. I had barely laid down when there was a knock on the door. It was Justin and he was shaking with fever. I tested him for malaria but he proved negative. The Pastor organised a bed so he could get some rest. Soon after my phone rang. It was Sophie calling from Silosilo on her satellite phone. She wanted to check if we were safe and see how far away we were. I could hear she was tired. I thought, ‘Being a young woman in a remote PNG village must be very challenging.’ We both talked about the stress and dangers of the island. “We are all looking forward to your arrival, the whole village is expecting you," she said. As I hung up, I smiled. She sounded sweet.

The next morning, Justin was back on his feet, so we sailed out. The weather forecast didn't look good, but we thought we could manage. Leaving Inouro Island went well. A reef protected our launch from the incoming waves but as soon as we were free the waves grew, yet they were still manageable. "*Kisoo*," Justin suddenly yelled. The nylon line tightened. I untied the string from the mast just in time for the fish to make a violent jerk that burned my hands. I almost lost the reel. "Ha ha, that is the pain of the fisherman," Justin mused. After a lot of struggle, a silky shark came into view but, instead of a bush knife, Sanakoli used a paddle to bump the rapala lure out of the shark's mouth and the creature disappeared into the deep water. We immediately eased the line out again. Before long, the nylon again started making aggressive jerks. I got to work while balancing on the deck of the bouncing canoe. After some painful minutes and an explosion of adrenaline, I heaved in a one-metre-long mackerel.

"You watch the teeth, they are like razors," Sanakoli warned.

The big fish was thrashing violently. As the spear-like head came out of the hull, I dispatched it with two sharp blows using a piece of firewood. "Ho hoo," Sanakoli yelled, "Now we are home. That's how we fish in Milne Bay Province."

Justin joined in, "Gulf nothing. Central small fish. Milne Bay we catch big fish." We were all excited — the sailors for being in home waters and I was on my way to see Sophie, with a beautiful fish, it was going to be a feast. The joyous hype soon evaporated. As I scooped the blood out of the bilge, the wind started to gust, so we made a *yaya-towa* and went inwards, but here a sandbank created a nasty chop so we went outwards again. Out there, the waves had now grown even bigger. There was nothing to do but diligently *jig-jag* while trying to stay between the two extremes.

We suddenly found ourselves in a very bad situation. The chop was tall and angry. The two brothers did their best, but the waves were breaking on the outrigger with a force that rattled the whole canoe. A flapping noise was suddenly heard. The black plastic had given in and a two-metre-long slit appeared in the sail. There was no time to dwell on this, as swells broke on the bow and our water containers started to float in the hull. I dumped the bailer and got to our bilge pump. I started to get that same dire feeling as when the waves were breaking on us in Cenderawasih Bay and I started to think, 'How much pounding can our *Tawali Pasana* take?' The dreadful answer came soon enough. Justin yelled in Bwana Bwana. Sanakoli turned his head and looked shocked. I followed his red eyes. Disaster! Two *patoto* poles had already broken off from the outrigger. I looked around. We were surrounded by high seas, six nautical miles from land and the same distance to Bona Bona Island. My heart sank as I instantly recalled Bula where we refitted the outrigger... and Justin's cautionary words — "We make them properly, if one break, all soon break. And we sink."

Chapter Twenty-eight

Tree trunks of glory

Justin and Sanakoli acted quickly and so did I — by turning on the camera. Sanakoli took over the *yabby-yabby* while controlling the sheet with his free hand and teeth. Justin got our bush knife and crawled to the rising and falling outrigger. Salt water was surging over him as he sharpened the broken *patotos* like spear tips.

"Hammer, hammer," Justin yelled. I ran to the front boards to search below deck. I turned to the green box, fumbled between the rope and fishing lines and hit the jackpot. I pulled out Job's round rock. Justin threw the knife aside, grabbed the rock and started hammering the first pole in like he was slaying Count Dracula. Then the second spear tip was firmly banged into the soft wood. The knots were checked and we resumed our wild ride. Half an hour later, another *patoto* broke and it was repaired with the same desperate resolve.

After some anxious hours, we reached the calmer waters between Bona Bona and Delami Islands. As we made our way in over the coral, I looked for *Eneta*, but the paddle was nowhere to be found; it must have been taken by a swell. From Delami it was only nine nautical miles to Silosilo but we had enough of sailing. As soon as we were on safe ground, I excavated an old chocolate bar from the bottom of my barrel, which we ate in silence.

The next day, we entered the village of Silosilo. It lay hidden in one of the many deep bays on the rugged Suau coast. As we neared the natural harbour, we could see a group of people standing on the shore in front of the most charming little village. However, what made this scene different from so many other village landings was the sight of a 25-year-old girl with fair skin, red hair and sunglasses — wearing a long black dress. We ran aground and I walked ashore to meet the welcoming party. As Sophie approached there was an awkward moment. Should I shake her hand or give her a hug? The situation was saved by Sophie presenting me to her 'sister' Rosa and to her 'adopted' local family. Rosa said, "Come to the shade. In Silosilo, we welcome visitors with *buai* and coconut… that is tradition." My companions were of course thrilled about this, not least because they knew the local councillor, who was a renowned canoe sailor. I tried to engage in the conversations but was constantly distracted by Sophie. She had the most wonderful big brown eyes. Afterwards, we were invited for a meal in the hut where Sophie had lived for the last ten months of her doctoral fieldwork.

Sophie's hut still smelled of fresh bush materials. On the walls were maps and hand drawn family trees. She had two small camping chairs, a table and a kitchen with a gas stove. It was extravagant by village standards. During dinner, Sophie explained that she was researching climate change, conservation and local livelihoods in Suau. Most people in Suau depended on subsistence agriculture so there are complex intersections between land use and environmental change.

After the meal, people began to disperse and finally we were alone. Sophie and I shared our frustrations and joys as we connected over our mutual fascination with the island. The conversation flowed and we discussed how our future would look after PNG. We chatted until well past sunset; it was like talking to a long-lost friend.

Expedition Log 10 October 2017

08:30 hrs. Departing Silosilo. Wind speed 12-15 knots. The sea is rough but *Tawali Pasana* feels as light as a feather or maybe it is just me.

It was early morning on 13 October when we arrived at Samarai Island, the old Australian colonial headquarters of Milne Bay, or as Sanakoli happily sounded, "Now we are back home." The island was slowly disintegrating from its glory days of colonial administration but there was still a concrete wharf and the ubiquitous Chinese general store that supplied the most basic necessities (as well as solar chargers and sports equipment). Justin and Sanakoli were busy greeting friends and family, so I went to the shop.

On the way back, I found Justin chewing *buai*. He said, "Me, I say hello to my son."

"What do you mean? Is your son here?" I asked rather surprised.

"Yes, he came on that *sailau*," Justin replied, pointing to a sailing canoe anchored off the wharf.

"Can I meet him?" I asked with great anticipation. Justin led me to a group of men smoking *bruce* in the shade. It was easy to recognise which of them was Justin's offspring. Mala Justin was in his early 20s and had Justin's square frame. His light-skinned face was also similar. The pronounced cheekbones around and his clear eyes gave him a look of innocence, and in his sleeveless shirt, he looked like a Melanesian boy model with the arms of an 80s action hero. Like his father, he didn't say much. I shook his hand and told him that his dad was a great sailor.

From Samarai Island we could reach Tawali and the finish line within a day. A part of me just wanted to touch that Tawali pier as quickly as possible before something went wrong — but before we could complete the voyage, the canoe needed one last carving. We had to sail to Basilaki Island — the birthplace of not only my fellow sailors but also the canoe. As Sanakoli pointed out several times, "We have design from all villages on the island but no Basilaki design."

At 11 a.m., I was more than ready to take off but, unlike me, the two brothers were in a whole different headspace now that they were practically home. After a lot of struggle, I pulled them from their friends and brought them to the canoe. Sanakoli was clearly annoyed. "Why this rush?"

I tried to suppress my frustration. "Why is it always me who has to push this project forward?"

Sanakoli snapped back, "We are already there!"

I snapped back in return. "No… we are not. This is the most dangerous part of the journey."

"What you mean?" he questioned me clearly confused.

"Because when you think you are safe that's when you let down your guard — that's when accidents happen!" Sanakoli thought about this for a moment and I continued. "When we reach Tawali, then we can relax, because then we have made the full journey, not before."

Then, just like a self-fulfilling prophecy, something happened. Justin and Sanakoli's friends were standing onshore as we pushed off.

As we hoisted the sail, a piece of it got stuck on the outrigger. In the same instant, the wind started to blow us towards the wharf. I quickly gave Justin my folding knife. He cut the sail free. I resumed hoisting the sail single-handedly. It was heavy but I couldn't give up — we were about to crash and the whole beach was watching us — our sailor's honour was at stake. In a last second thrust with the *yabby yabby* Sanakoli steered *Tawali Pasana* free of the rocks. I finally got the sail up — I tied it off and we safely waved goodbye to the crowd as we struggled to disguise our shock from the near capsize.

As the setting sun turned the sand pink, *Tawli Pasana* landed in the lagoon of Lumo Lumo. Lea, Justin and Sanakoli's mother, was standing on the shore together with one of her sisters. I wondered if their mother would start wailing as she had done the day we left. Instead she just walked into the water to pull the canoe ashore. The emotional outburst came from another direction. As I greeted her sister, she hugged me tightly and started wailing loud and hard. I could feel the tears wet my shoulder. After a good three minutes, she finally stopped and dried her eyes. Sanakoli said in a low voice, "We lost her son, our brother cousin two weeks ago. Young man like you but he got strong cancer."

Despite the sad news, it was good to be back and soon sisters, brothers, cousins, aunties and uncles all started dropping by — even Sebastian the dancing man who had sold us the canoe was there. On Sunday, Justin, Sanakoli and I were invited to the church service in Bedauna village. The church was a small mint green wooden building on top of a hill overlooking the blue ocean. As we walked up, we were met by the community choir. We sat next to each other as guests of honour as the elders greeted us back from the sea by placing a flower in our hair or shirts while all the time singing. The Pastor then delivered a short sermon. I learned that the entire community had been praying for us every Sunday. It was very touching. Then it was my turn to speak. "Thank you so much for the beautiful welcome. You can all be proud of your two sons, my friends Justin and Sanakoli. They have been exemplary Papua New Guineans, working hard, honest and always making new friends." The community nodded in approval.

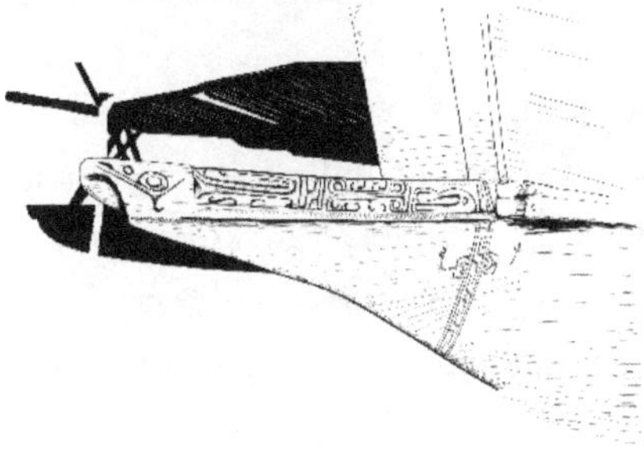

After four days on Basilaki, we were ready to sail off to claim our prize. Through the satellite receiver, I had been emailing Paul who suggested that we'd hold off for a week so he could document us sailing into Tawali. Paul deserved to be part of the celebration, however there could be no more delays. I was paranoid that a freak disaster could ruin everything we had fought for. (Little did we know that our troubles weren't over). Instead, we agreed that he could cover us at the festival. Our brave vessel must have looked marvellous as she glided out of the lagoon. Both *kabaéiaese* (head of the canoe) had been carved after Basilaki custom and we had sown a new, even larger, main sail that was decorated with creases made of Kuki's golden parachute silk. Across the blue sail were the black letters: *Tawali Pasana.*

Expedition Log 18 October 2017

16:30 hrs. Depart Lumo Lumo. We are racing against another sailing canoe. The big new sail makes *Tawali Pasana* feel light and alive. This is going to be a good run to Nuakata. We'll be in Sanakoli's village by nightfall. And then Tawali tomorrow. Can't wait to touch that pier and claim our victory.

17:00 hrs. We have outrun our friends and made ready to turn Mwanamwanalai point. It looks like we are barely going to avoid the rocks off the point, they are submerging and protruding with the swell.

As we passed the point, a swell suddenly pushed us towards rocks. The sea ran back out over our hull and we got stuck on a lava head. The outrigger began to flounder. Sanakoli jumped onto the rock and started pushing us as the canoe slowly moved on. When *Tawali Pasana* was free, he jumped back on and we continued with pumping hearts.

"Wow close call," I said rather shocked.

"Sharp clamshells, I cut my foot." Sanakoli said, while inspecting his bleeding soles.

We made good progress over the dark sea because now we had the southeasterlies from the side, pushing our now massive sail. The horizon grew to a dark blue and the wind picked up.

"You sit on the outrigger, big wind coming," Sanakoli said. The outrigger rose out of the water and we started running with a crazy speed. There was no hooting or exhilarated shouts, instead, we struggled to keep the big sail from tipping the canoe over. I was hanging with half my body out from the outrigger, wishing myself heavier. 'This was what happens when you lower your guard,' I kept saying to myself. After a harrowing hour, we made it ashore behind Rat Island. My nerves were shaken.

We sailed out at dawn. The winds were beautiful and Sanakoli said, "Soon we come to my reef, then you see me catch fish."

Of course, I couldn't let that comment fly. "Let's see Sana, so far I have never seen you catch a single fish on that reef."

My friend got all worked up and yelled, "Now I throw the line and you don't touch it, you got no luck." We all cracked with laughter. The wind was steady and I was given the rudder.

Justin sat with the sheet on the platform and said, "You keep sailing like this." It was hard work, the high swell made standing by the *yabby yabby* like balancing on a seesaw. Justin then pulled the sheet, the sail tightened and the outrigger rose out of the water. The speed increased and I could feel the pressure on the *yabby yabby*. Every muscle in my body was tense as I bounced up and down with the rising swell. The sea was spraying from our bow — I was flying the outrigger. The sailors hooted and I joined in.

An hour later, we approached the lagoon in front of Awatowtowa. We had two beautiful fish in the hull — a long mackerel and a blue torpedo of a tuna — and yes, Sanakoli had caught both on 'his' reef. Rachel and the twins were waiting at the beach, together with her father and the rest of the community. Rachel, who wore one big smile, hugged her husband briefly and the two twins crawled into their father's arms.

I asked if she was happy to have him back.

"Yes very," she smiled shyly.

"You don't want us to go on another journey soon?" I joked. She protested loudly and flung her arms around Sanakoli who made a coy laugh as he went red in the face.

After the practicalities were sorted, we sat on a mat under a big mango tree while waiting for breakfast. We decided to sail out the next morning and pick up Madiu Jaymes, the reporter from NBC Milne Bay, who had been covering our voyage from the start. I still hadn't met him in person but had agreed that he could sail with us to Tawali and make a program about the finale. As we sat on the mat, I wanted to say a few words to Justin and Sanakoli.

I thought that we had had too many close calls in these last days so I said, "Guys, I will tell you a story about a great sailor. His name was Odysseus. He was on his way home after being at war for ten years." The sailors were all ears.

"Odysseus's ships approached their home island of Ithaca. They were so close that they could see smoke from their family's fires ashore. Odysseus thought he had made it home safe and sound, so he took a snooze. While he slept, Odysseus's men were curious to see what he had in his leather bag. Little did they know that it contained all the winds of the world, so when they cut it open, a great storm broke loose and pushed the whole fleet back out to sea."

The men obviously enjoyed the story but as I was coming to the point, Sanakoli interrupted. "Hey, who's that *lapun* coming here?" A pair of bare feet made their way over the mango roots and a familiar smiling bald head came in to view.

"Yeh, hello," Job said as he stopped in front of us with his nylon *basket* over the shoulder. We all got up and hugged our old friend.

"Hey that's our man," Justin said.

I had called Job from Samarai and asked if he wanted to sail with us to the finish line. After all, Job had helped prepare this expedition and he had sailed the canoe a quarter of the voyage. Our friend from Normanby looked well. He told us that he'd been busy in his garden and was supplying the local hospital with food. He also had a great surprise — an eight-month-old daughter. He never did tell us that his wife was pregnant, which may explain why he wanted to leave the circumnavigation.

The first and the last

The next morning, on 20 October 2017, *Tawali Pasana* sailed from Nuakata to complete 'The World's First Circumnavigation of the Island of New Guinea in a Traditional Sailing Canoe.' We had a *sailau* escort with three young locals on board. The big sail was pulling well and our escort was soon left in our wake. There was a buzz of excitement on board. This was the day we all had been waiting for and now it was finally about to happen. After a while, we reached Obstruction Island. We got close to shore and did a *yaya-towa*. Job wasn't used to the new carabiner system and fumbled with it long enough for wind spilling down the island to catch our giant sail. The outrigger started sinking and the hull rapidly rose out of the water. "Sail down," Sanakoli yelled but Justin was already there and the sheet fell into the sea and the canoe bounced back up, which restarted my heart after it stopped for a few seconds. "Guys we can't keep doing this!" I trembled. The sail was hoisted and soon saltwater was pulsing from our bow.

We landed at East Cape where I saluted several of the dinghy drivers, not least the captain of *Home Alone Two*. As we were waiting for the radio host, a white Land Cruiser arrived and out jumped a sturdy man in black clothes with red lips and a dark face. He looked familiar, then I realised that he was the suspicious guy who had been pumping me for information outside the tourism office in Alotau back in 2016. "Mr. Jensen," he said and walked towards me. Then I noticed the NBC logo on his shirt — it was our radio host. He laughed and presented himself as, "Madiu Jaymes, NBC Radio." I thanked him for sharing our journey with the whole Province and he said, "Of course bro, everybody loves what you are doing." With our passenger on-board, we could finally resume travel and the last leg of our journey around the world's second largest island.

Tawali Pasana was running a pleasant pace and Madiu Jaymes turned on his recorder and did a live interview that was broadcasted nationwide. This really cemented the significance of this day for my friends and elevated the mood even more. *Pidgin*-rock was playing from our waterproof loudspeaker and everyone was cracking jokes about taking another trip around the island.

Then Sanakoli boasted gravely, "No one will copy this travel, it is too hard. That's why I tell people, 'It is the first and the last.'" As the outcrop of Tawali and the white charter boats came into view, we made ready for our arrival. Our routine of securing everything below deck and not leaving any tempting objects out wasn't necessary this time. Sanakoli began cleaning his teeth with a *buai* husk using his phone as a mirror.

I turned my camera towards him and asked how it felt to be finishing.

He answered, "Now that I see Tawali resort, I think woohoo, I'm already to the end. Because, on the journey, I was all the time dreaming of Tawali Resort, now, when I see it, I'm really happy." Job got the same question. He was sitting in his yellow shirt handling the sheet. "I am feeling happy now, because… we are gonna close the trip. We have planned the trip and now finish the what… events." He smiled.

I then turned to Justin. "How do you feel about being one of the only three people in the world to sail around the island in a traditional sailing canoe."

Justin didn't answer at first, he was just sitting by the *yabby yabby* with a blissful smile, then he grinned and just said, "Proud."

On the first day of the expedition, *Tawali Pasana,* our reef flower, had a clean strake, old outrigger and a platform of green rattan. The platform was now grey, the outrigger felled in Bucava and the strake decorated with carvings from villages we had visited. Along the outrigger, flags from all the provinces we had travelled were fluttering in the wind. From our flag post hung a small Indonesian flag, and of course the Danish flag, and atop waved the now weather beaten and ragged flag of Papua New Guinea — all now a memory heirloom of encounters, dangers and ghost mothers.

Like Justin, I was proud. I was proud that I had prevailed, despite all the difficulties. I had been privileged to be able to focus on one single project for almost 14 months. I had learned to sail the canoe 'like a local.' I also learned to catch mud crabs, charm Indonesian authorities, ask sponsors for help and communicate with the press. I had honed my skills in writing and filmmaking too and, not least, I fell in love.

We could now hear the drums and see the movement of people on the pier of Tawali Resort. The mountain wind dropped and we had to support the sail with our paddles. I crawled into the bow and began digging towards the pier. As the end of our great adventure approached, I felt a profound sense of sadness. Soon it would all be over, the good times at sea with my friends, the beautiful mornings, the animal encounters, the arrival at strange places and the welcoming people, and that certain magic that was so prevalent on this great island. The rhythm of the drums grew louder and the dancing, spear-waving warriors screamed. It was surreal. I had once felt like the little boy who had taken too big a mouthful but, now that I had emptied my plate, I couldn't be more satisfied.

I reached out and slapped the crude planks. We had made a world record — sailed, paddled and pushed. We all climbed ashore to the racket of drums and snapping cameras. Young women gave each of us a flower lei of frangipanis. We stood there a bit befuddled smiling, then I remembered that we needed a photo to capture the moment and I handed Matt my camera. I raised my arms into the air and loudly announced, "The expedition around the Island of New Guinea has been completed on this day, after 13 months and 21 days." I then added, "And we have covered 6,300 kilometres!" The spectators clapped and I turned to shake hands with Sanakoli, Justin and Job. The new resort manager, Armando, congratulated us and said that they had prepared a welcome and certificates for us on the top deck.

After a beautiful dinner, we retreated to our luxury apartments. We were high on the experience, although we didn't celebrate much. Now it was time to tell the rest of the world of our achievement — email our sponsors and supporters and send press releases and video clips to news outlets. I spoke with the sailors. It was like there was something missing. There was no one to celebrate with except the staff and a few locals. We spoke of the canoe festival that was 14 days from now. I said, "Tomorrow, I'll got to Alotau with Armando and work from there, promote our achievement and find you some sponsor prizes for the festival."

Sanakoli said, "And you must buy us a new sheet for the race, so we can pull the sail quick."

"What do you mean, you want us to participate in the canoe race?" I said, surprised by his suggestion — and his enthusiasm.

Sanakoli nodded with a serious expression. I continued, "We have just sailed around the entire island, what is there left to prove? Can't we just let the other canoes race?"

Sanakoli shook his head, "No, now all the sailors want to race *Tawali Pasana*. If we don't show up, they will say we are afraid of them — they say we are *girly girly*." I laughed. Of course, it was important for Justin and Sanakoli to prove their master sailing skills to their fellow sailors. In my mind, crossing the finish line at Tawali had been the symbol of our achievement, but for the sailors this had to be validated in the eyes of their friends and peers.

The great circumnavigators

On 4 November 2017, *Tawali Pasana* sailed in as guests of honour at the National Kenu and Kundu Festival, followed by an armada of sailing canoes with proudly bulging colourful sails. We aimed our bow towards the shore that was packed with people, and as our old tree trunk hit the sand, we were greeted by a dance group of screaming spear-wielding warriors with thumping *kundu* drums. Lea was standing in her finest dress dancing and honouring her sons. Justin, Sanakoli and Job threw one handful of *buai* after another to the crowd. Paul was there with his cameras, weaving through the crowd to immortalise the moment. Sophie was there as well, with her Suau family, ready to celebrate.

The sails were up and we got ready to push out. On both sides were *sailaus* with men just as eager to win as we were. The course was straight across the bay, where we were required to pick up a green branch on land and then be the first to touch shore at the starting point. The race was sounded and we worked like clockwork — the big sail that had almost sunk us twice now shot us well ahead of the armada. Dinghies were racing along besides us hooting as I was hanging off the outside of the flying outrigger documenting the event live for our Facebook followers.

We touched land on the other side. People ran from shore to throw green branches onto our platform. We made a quick *yaya-towa*. Running towards Alotau and her mountains. I have never seen my friends so fired up. We were flying high and *Tawali Pasana* won the race leagues ahead of her nearest competitor. The crowd became nearly hysterical as we were led up through the throng to the grand stage. The loudspeakers boasted, "We present to you the great circumnavigators!" Sir Chris Abel, who was a descendant of one of the first Christian missionaries in Milne Bay and the father of the Deputy Prime Minister, awarded us all medals in recognition of our achievement, then we were bestowed with sponsor prizes and cash for winning the race. My three friends all had big nervous smiles. I tried to get Sanakoli to say a few words but he declined. Then I was asked to speak about our journey.

As is custom in PNG, I recognised the important people in the crowd and thanked everyone who had helped with the festival. Then I acknowledged my three fellow sailors. "These are the bravest men I have ever met. They risked their lives to show the world your seafaring heritage. These men are national heroes!" There was a thunderous applause. I was out of breath but continued. "One thing I will bring back to Denmark is the Melanesian hospitality. We have encountered this everywhere we travelled around this great island of New Guinea. It is something unique and precious. Our big dream in making this world record was to promote this beautiful island and to inspire the youth of New Guinea to have pride in their traditional culture. The *Tawali Pasana* is a great symbol of this. It is a traditional vessel but also constructed of modern materials too — just like Papua New Guinea. *Tawali Pasana* is like all the other beautiful things you have inherited from your ancestors — their knowledge of sailing, of fishing and making gardens — and today *Tawali Pasana* has made a world record."

The crowd went mental and we all bowed.

In the afternoon, we dropped Job off at his church and I took Justin and Sanakoli to the Driftwood Resort where I was staying with Sophie. I had arranged to temporarily keep the canoe there. The sponsor prizes had been generous but, nonetheless, I had a more long-sighted proposition for my friends. The manager had offered the two brothers jobs. He was keen on selling canoe sailing tours to his guests. As we stood on the pier looking at the white bungalows along the beach, I presented those future prospects to the brothers. Sanakoli politely humoured the idea. Justin just smoked his *bruce*, while studying the fish under the planks. The more we talked about the practicalities, the more difficult it seemed. Justin was the one to tell me straight, "Me, I don't want to work here, I go back to my island." I understood. These men were sailors and that was what they knew and that was what they loved.

Five days later, Sophie and I stood in the small departure hall in Gurney Airport just outside Alotau. As I was typing the concluding post for our online followers, a taxi pulled up. It was Justin and Sanakoli, who had come to say goodbye. I looked at my friends. It was like we had known each other forever. Justin took his *bagi* from around his neck and gave it to me. "Now you remember us," he said with a serious frown.

"That is a great honour," I replied.

"You are our, what, brother," Sanakoli smiled.

I looked up and clapped his shoulder and said to my brothers, "And you are the great circumnavigators!"

Soon, I was sitting in a cramped aeroplane cabin 30,000 feet above the azure blue sea. My tired face caught its reflection in the double plexiglass window. Sophie squeezed my hand as I took a last look at the dragon-shaped island where sailing canoes ornament the reef like flowers.

THE END

Epilogue

I woke with a jolt as the phone rang. I was jetlagged and had no concept of time. Outside the window there was nothing but the winter darkness. It was December and I had just returned to Denmark from Australia where I had stayed with Sophie at her grandparent's property in the country. Now I was looking at spending three months at home before she would join me.

Recovering from the expedition was taking time. Earlier in the day I had been out seeing my brother performing jazz guitar at a Christmas event. Although I enjoyed the music, I felt estranged from the holiday crowd.

The nights were the worst. When I finally did sleep, I would wake at the slightest sound and then get up to check that there was no one in the room.

The touchscreen read: Justin John. I picked up. "Thor, Thor, you there hey?" Justin said excitedly. "Your man Sanakoli, he took your canoe."

I sat up in bed and exclaimed, "What, why? We were supposed to sell it together and have it displayed?"

Justin continued in a rapid voice, "Yes, he went to Driftwood and got it. And now he is sailing and fishing and telling people that it is his canoe."

I rubbed my forehead and said, "At least he should have shared with you!"

"Yes, that's the one," Justin continued in an indignant tone. I assured Justin that I would get hold of Sanakoli and sort it out.

At first, the news actually made me angry. Then, after some reflection, I understood Sanokoli — *Tawali Pasana* was now a national symbol and he had a special connection with the craft but at the same time, it was like he had taken the keys to my Maserati to cruise around the islands and show off.

Clearly this great expedition was not over yet. As I laid down on my comfortable bed, I couldn't help laughing. The phone call just reaffirmed my philosophy for the trip — that every challenge was good for the story — and so, a missing canoe seemed like the perfect way to end this book.

Glossary

Asmat — Lowland region in the South West of Papua, also a broad term for the original inhabitants of this area

Bagi — Red shell-money necklace used for trading in Milne Bay

Baik — Good (*Bahasa Indonesia*)

Bruce — Cigarette made from local tobacco and rolled in newspaper (*Tok Pisin*)

Bigman — Leader or man of wealth and importance (*Tok Pisin*)

Bilum — Hand woven bag (*Tok Pisin*)

Bolibolimai — South wind (*Bwana Bwana*)

Buai — Betel nut (*Tok Pisin*)

Bubu — Grandparent or grandchild (*Tok Pisin*)

Bwana Bwana — The language spoken in eastern Basilaki and nearby islands, literal meaning: island

Dirty watar — Cordial, primarily cola-flavour but later other flavours as well

Dim dim — White person, European

Dugong — Sea cow, an herbivorous marine mammal

Eneta — 'That's the one,' an expression in the Nuakata language

Gelumbung — Dry swim bladder from either a Mulloway or a Barramundi (*Bahasa Indonesia*)

Gunwale — Edge of upper plank on a ship or a boat

Jig jag — To tack

Johnson — Slang for outboard motor (*Bahasa Indonesia*)

Kabaéiaese — Canoe head (*Bwana Bwana*)

Kenu — Canoe (*Tok Pisin*)

Kepala Desa — Village Head (*Bahasa Indonesia*)

Kialo — A pole connecting the outrigger to the hull on a sailing canoe (*Bwana Bwana*)

Kina — The currency of Papua New Guinea, named after traditional shell money

Kula Exchange Ring — A system of relationships of reciprocity amongst islands of Milne Bay

Kundu — Traditional hourglass shaped drum (*Tok Pisin*)

Lakatoi — Double hulled canoe from Central Province PNG (*Motu*)

Lapun — Old man or woman (*Tok Pisin*)

Longhouse — Elongated traditional hut, often with a customary purpose

Lime — Powder of baked and crushed shells that, when mixed with betel nut, creates a euphoric sensation.

Mansini — A philanderer *(Bwana Bwana)*

Maski — 'Never mind/ it doesn't matter' (*Tok Pisin*)

Motu — The people of Central Province, also a language spoken in the Central Province and in certain areas of the Gulf Province

Mustard — The seed pod of a vine chewed with betel nut and lime

Nautical Mile — Unit used in measuring distance at sea, equal to 1,852 metres

OPM — *Organisasi Papua Merdeka*, the Free West Papua movement *(Bahasa Indonesia)*

Patoto — A wooden stick connecting the outrigger to the platform (*Bwana Bwana*)

Pinang — Betel nut (*Bahasa Indonesia)*

PMV — Public motor vehicle

Puk puk — Crocodile (*Tok Pisin*)

Pulau — Island (*Bahasa Indonesia)*

Rapala — A fishing lure in plastic or wood that dives due to a spoon on its front (invented in Sweden)

Raskol — A criminal or thug (*Tok Pisin*)

Sago — An edible starch extract from the sago palm

Sailau — A Milne Bay sailing canoe with a dipping lug rig

Sak sak — Sago

Salimé — Outrigger (*Bwana Bwana*)

Samarai — An island in Milne Bay that was once the headquarters of the province and now a nickname of Milne Bay people

Shunting — To tack a boat with reverse ends

Sing sing — Traditional dance or festivity (*Tok Pisin*)

Sowa sowa — Arching pole supporting the mast

Size 28 — Nickname for Milne Bay people, refering to their waist size as they are generally small in stature

Sniper — Saltwater crocodile (Normanby slang)

Splash board — Board covering the top of each end of the canoe to reduce incoming splash from waves

Susu — Breast (*Tok Pisin/ Bahasa Indonesia slang*)

Strake — Side plank running from bow to stern on a boat or canoe

Tapa — Bark cloth decorated with red and black patterns

Tapioca — Edible root crop

Tawali — Coral reef (Tawala language)

Tawali Pasana — Reef flower or beauty of the reef, or something that enhances the beauty of the reef, the meaning varies depending on the language

Terima Kasih — Thank you (*Bahasa Indonesia)*

Tidak — No (*Bahasa Indonesia)*

Towe — Pole used for polling the canoe, also used for anchoring in sand or mud

Tok Pisin — Pidgin English, one of the national languages of Papua New Guinea

Yabby yabby — Steer paddle used as rudder (*Bwana Bwana*)

Yams — Root crop

Yard — Spar suspended from the mast from where the sail hangs

Yaya-towa — Tack or turn the sail (*Bwana Bwana*)

Yayauve — Tree sort used for outrigger

Young boy — Unmarried man, also the status of a sailor during travels (*Tok Pisin* slang)

Yellowfin — A species of tuna

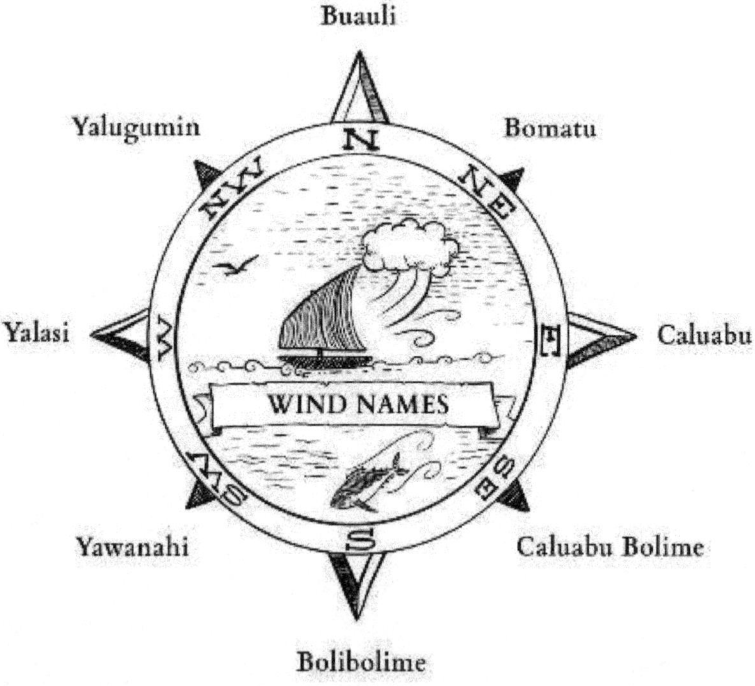
Buauli
Yalugumin
Bomatu
N
NW
NE
Yalasi
W
E
Caluabu
WIND NAMES
SW
SE
S
Yawanahi
Caluabu Bolime
Bolibolime

Tawali Pasana

Names of canoe parts (Bwana Bwana language)

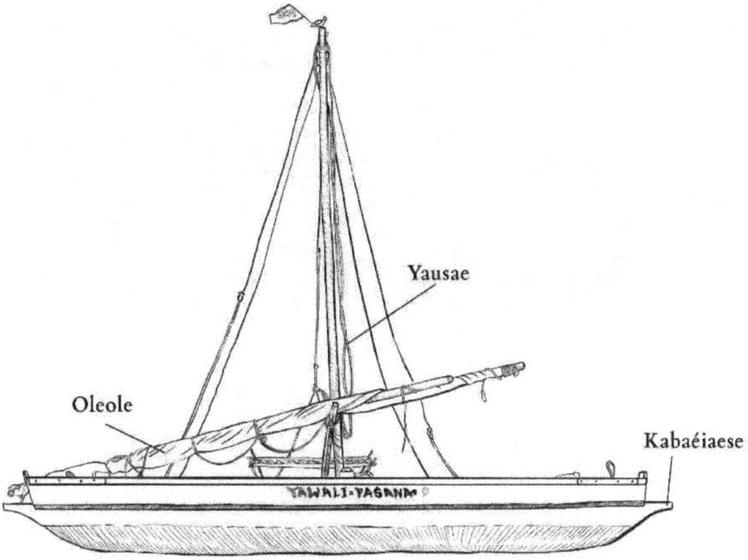

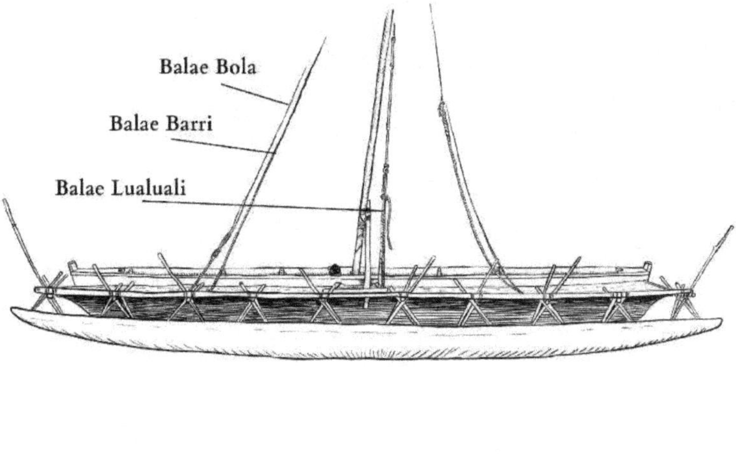

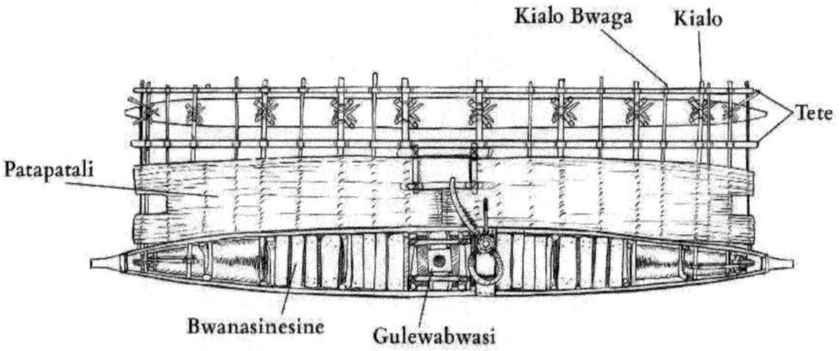
Kialo Bwaga
Kialo
Tete
Patapatali
Bwanasinesine
Gulewabwasi

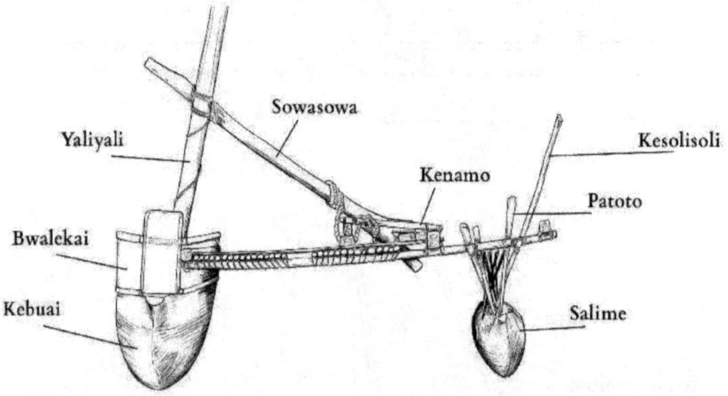
Sowasowa
Yaliyali
Kesolisoli
Kenamo
Patoto
Bwalekai
Kebuai
Salime

From left: Sanakoli John, Thor F. Jensen,
Justin John and Job Siyae
Tawali Resort, 20th October 2017.

CPSIA information can be obtained
at www.ICGtesting.com
Printed in the USA
LVHW091934150120
643732LV00002B/219

9 781784 656850